The Twelve Jays
of Christmas

ALSO BY DONNA ANDREWS

The Twelve Jays of Christmas

A Meg Langslow Mystery

Donna Andrews

MINOTAUR BOOKS
— NEW YORK —

First published in the United States by Minotaur Books, an imprint of St. Martin's Publishing Group

THE TWELVE JAYS OF CHRISTMAS. Copyright © 2021 by Donna Andrews. All rights reserved. Printed in the United States of America. For information, address St. Martin's Publishing Group, 120 Broadway, New York, NY 10271.

www.minotaurbooks.com

Library of Congress Cataloging-in-Publication Data

Names: Andrews, Donna, author.
Title: The Twelve Jays of Christmas : a Meg Langslow mystery / Donna Andrews.
Description: First Edition. | New York : Minotaur Books, 2021. | Series: Meg Langslow mysteries ; 30
Identifiers: LCCN 2021026562 | ISBN 9781250760180 (hardcover) | ISBN 9781250836571 (Canadian) | ISBN 9781250760197 (ebook)
Subjects: GSAFD: Mystery fiction.
Classification: LCC PS3551.N4165 T84 2021 | DDC 813/.54—dc23
LC record available at https://lccn.loc.gov/2021026562

Our books may be purchased in bulk for promotional, educational, or business use. Please contact your local bookseller or the Macmillan Corporate and Premium Sales Department at 1-800-221-7945, extension 5442, or by email at MacmillanSpecialMarkets@macmillan.com.

First U.S. Edition: 2021
First Canadian Edition: 2021

10 9 8 7 6 5 4 3 2 1

The Twelve Jays of Christmas

Chapter 1

December 21

"Look out! The wombats are loose again!"

I'd almost dozed off, even though I was sitting upright in a hard kitchen chair, but that woke me up in a hurry. Had someone actually shouted something about wombats? Or had I only imagined it?

The kitchen was—well, quiet didn't apply. The Christmas carols playing over the little hidden loudspeakers were a trifle louder than optimal. I should find the remote and fix that. But it was peaceful here. Just me, sipping a cup of hot spiced cider left over from last night's holiday party and enjoying a few moments of relaxation before I opened my notebook-that-tells-me-when-to-breathe to start what I knew would be a busy day.

I heard scuffling noises coming from somewhere. Hard to tell where over the dramatic trumpet introduction to "Joy to the World." I got up and limped over to the kitchen window, still favoring the ankle I'd sprained a week ago. No random wombats running amok outside. No marsupials of any kind in the backyard, and given how loudly heaven 'n' nature were singing over the little loudspeakers, a herd of elephants could have been stampeding in the front yard without my noticing.

I picked up the remote and dialed down the volume so the carols were almost subliminal.

Now I could hear the scuffling sounds again. They were coming from the basement.

I limped over, opened the door to the basement, and—

"Shut the door!" a ragged chorus of voices shrieked. "Shut the door! Quick!"

I slammed the door shut, but not before I spotted the furry object lumbering up the stairs. A large and rather bearlike furry object. More the size of a cub than a full-grown bear but still—large.

Something hit the other side of the door with a thud that shook the house. I spared a brief moment to feel grateful that we'd coughed up the money to restore our house's original heavy, solid-wood doors rather than replacing them with cheap, hollow modern doors.

Human footsteps thundered up the stairs, from at least two pairs of feet. Maybe three.

In the scuffle, the wide-brimmed straw hat I was wearing had fallen off. I grabbed it and jammed it back on my head.

"You get him back into the pen." I recognized my brother Rob's voice. "I'll explain it to Meg."

"Can do." The other voice belonged to Kevin, the tech-savvy nephew who had set up housekeeping in our basement.

I crossed my arms, frowned, and stared at the basement door. The scuffling sounds grew more distant, and after thirty seconds or so the basement door opened and Rob slipped out, looking so tanned and relaxed that I felt a brief pang of envy.

"When did you get back?" I asked. "I thought you and Delaney were going to stay in Florida for another few weeks."

"And miss Christmas in Caerphilly? With the family?" He gave me a quick hug. "We decided to hop back and surprise everyone. Maybe get in some cross-country skiing with all that snow they're predicting. We didn't get here till three a.m., so I figured we could save the glad cries of welcome and the fatted calf–slaying till morning."

"Consider yourself welcomed." I grabbed a hat from the rack by the back door and handed it to him. "We're fresh out of fatted calves, although I might be able to arrange a plate of bacon and eggs. But first I want to know why there are wombats in our basement."

"It's a long story." He frowned slightly and stared at the hat—a well-worn wide-brimmed gray fedora. "What's this for?"

"Protection from birds," I said. "Put it on, or you'll be sorry. Let's get back to the wombats."

"Birds? In the house?"

"Birds in the house." I took a deep, calming breath and sat down to spare my ankle. "Three northern mockingbirds. *Mimus polyglottos,* if you care about the Latin name."

"You sound like Grandfather." He snickered at the idea. Yes, being the granddaughter of Dr. J. Montgomery Blake, the eminent naturalist and environmentalist, was having an effect on me. Probably a good idea if I avoided mimicking his legendary curmudgeon's temper. I took another deep breath.

"They're loose in the house," I went on. "If you startle them or invade some part of the house they've decided is their territory, they will swoop down to attack. They also seem to enjoy pooping on humans' heads. So wear the hat. Especially since any day now I expect they'll be joined by up to twelve blue jays. If Grandfather were here, he'd probably inform you that jays and mockingbirds are two of the birds that most commonly display aggression toward humans."

"Then why do you have them in the house?" Rob looked understandably puzzled.

"You first," I said. "You explain the wombats, and I'll fill you in on the mockingbirds. I'll even help you out—it has something to do with Grandfather, right?"

"Naturally." He popped the fedora onto his head and tilted it to a jaunty angle. "It's one of his new projects."

"Promoting the wombat as a domestic pet?" I suggested. "Aren't they a little large? Not to mention being an endangered species."

"No, these are actually just on temporary loan from the zoo," Rob explained. "Kevin volunteered to help Grandfather with his observations."

"Observations of what?" My resolution to remain calm was wearing thin. "Why is Kevin babysitting wombats in our basement?"

"They glow in the dark!"

"Wombats?"

"Yes." Rob nodded vigorously. "Isn't that cool?"

"Reasonably cool," I said. "Can't you find a dark place for them to glow in that isn't our basement?"

"It's more convenient for Kevin to have them here." Rob almost made this sound like a reasonable explanation. "Grandfather wants to learn more about their bio- . . . um, bio—"

"Biofluorescence?" I suggested. I knew the term because I'd almost memorized the sign beside the tank of jellyfish at the zoo, thanks to my twin sons' fascination with them when they were little.

"Yeah, that's it," Rob said. "Grandfather wants to see if it's constant or if it varies depending on stuff like the time of day and whether the wombat is hungry or full. And whether it changes during their mating season."

"I do not want wombats mating in our basement," I said. "I know Grandfather feels very strongly about all those programs to breed endangered species in captivity so they can be reintroduced to the wild, but I draw the line at him taking over our basement for it."

"They won't be breeding in the basement," Rob protested. "They're named Ian and Bruce, so I'm pretty sure they must both be boy wombats. So no matter what they get up to, there won't be any baby wombats."

"Let me amend my previous statement." I realized I

sounded a bit testy and tried to rein it in. "I do not want any wombats in my basement. Not even celibate wombats. I am declaring the basement a wombat-free zone. If Kevin wants to help Grandfather with his experiments, he can go out to the zoo. And furthermore—"

Just then the doorbell rang.

"Damn." I closed my eyes and shook my head. "It's starting again."

Chapter 2

The doorbell rang a second time. Someone was impatient.

"What's starting again?" Rob asked.

"People showing up to harass Castlemayne." I headed for the front door, grabbing my makeshift cane along the way. It was actually a shepherd's crook left over from the recent church Christmas pageant. My ankle was sufficiently healed that most of the time I no longer really needed it for support, but in the last few days I'd found it useful for intimidating some of our unwanted callers.

"Castlemayne? What's that?" Rob trailed along behind me. "Or is it a who?"

I reminded myself that he had been away for the past two weeks and probably hadn't paid all that much attention to what was going on here in town even before he'd left.

"Roderick Castlemayne the wildlife artist," I said. "You know, the one Grandfather hired to do a series of bird paintings to go with his new book."

"Oh, him." Rob almost bumped into me when I stopped just inside the front door. "But why are they showing up here to harass him? Isn't he working out at the zoo?"

"Not anymore. He's working in our library. And all his enemies are showing up here to harass him." I looked through the peephole and saw nothing. But the doorbell rang again, so clearly someone was still there.

Either our caller was deliberately standing aside to avoid being spotted through the peephole—and some of

the harassers were sneaky enough that they'd started doing that—or it was someone very short. Could it be—

I flung the door open and was delighted to see the short,
plump form of our friend Caroline Willner standing in
the doorway, almost hidden behind a stack of presents.

"Welcome," I said. "You have no idea how glad I am to
see you. Rob, help her with the presents."

"More in the car, but don't call Josh and Jamie to help."
She handed her present stack to Rob and enveloped me
in a quick hug. "I've got something for them that's too big
to wrap."

"Don't worry." I helped her out of her coat. "Michael
took them skiing for a couple of days. They won't be back
till tomorrow, so there's plenty of time to hide their presents."

"You don't ski?"

I lifted my right foot and pulled up my pants leg so she
could see the elastic bandage.

"Ouch." She winced in sympathy. "What happened?"

"Roderick Castlemayne."

"Oh, dear." She shook her head. "What's he done now?"

"He's the reason for your sprained ankle?" Rob reappeared from taking the presents into the living room.
"What happened? And why is he here instead of out at the
zoo?"

"He's here at your house?" Caroline looked alarmed.
"Why?"

"He doesn't like working at the zoo," I said. "Says the
environment in the aviary isn't conducive to creativity.
Grandfather talked us into letting him use our library."

"But he's supposed to be painting the birds from life,
isn't he?" she asked. "Which is why Monty set him up to
work in the aviary—they can just fill a habitat with whatever birds he's trying to paint and turn him loose. How
can he possibly paint in your library?"

"Grandfather had his staff haul cages full of birds into our library," I said. "Enormous cages," I added, to avert any concern she might have about the birds' well-being. "Unfortunately, shortly after they arrived, Castlemayne claimed that the bars of the cages interfered too much with his ability to paint them. And it never occurred to him that the mockingbirds would do anything other than sit quietly on the table for him to paint them."

"So he let them loose?" Rob hooted with laughter. "What a maroon!"

"The poor birds!" Caroline exclaimed. "What happened to them?"

I didn't resent the fact that she worried about the birds first, without a single thought to what happened to our library when the fourteen overwrought mockingbirds had made their break for freedom. She was a birdwatcher. She ran an animal sanctuary. And it wasn't her library.

"We caught most of them—in humane traps that Grandfather set up." I didn't want her imagining us leaping around the house with giant butterfly nets. "And a few of them are known to have escaped through open doors. But there are still at least two loose in the house. Possibly three. You might want to wear this."

I grabbed a hat from the collection on the hall hat-and-coat stand and handed it to her. It was a particularly nice hat in deep red velvet with a little sprig of holly and a tiny fir cone frosted with fake snow—and it had a reasonably wide brim.

"Perhaps I could also help recapture the birds," she suggested.

"I would love it if you did," I said. "Rob, can you bring in the rest of Caroline's bags? I'd help—"

"But I bet Dad has ordered you not to overdo it until your ankle is all better. No problem." He held out his hands. Caroline tossed him her keys, and he hurried out.

"Nice, having a doctor in the family," she said. "Especially one like your dad. Must save on trips to the hospital."

"Not this time," I said. "Dad insisted on having my ankle X-rayed. But at least I know with certainty that it's only a sprain, and rapidly improving. And—"

"Um . . . Ms. Langslow?" came a timid, quavering voice from behind me.

I turned to see a slight figure standing in the hallway. Actually, cringing was more like it, and he had the usual anxious expression on his face.

"Morning," I said. "Caroline, this is Harris, Mr. Castlemayne's assistant. Harris, this is Caroline Willner, the owner of the Willner Wildlife Sanctuary. She's an old friend of the family and often spends the holidays with us."

"Especially since that daughter of mine got into the habit of going on holiday cruises," Caroline said. "Ever since that disastrous cruise your grandfather got us into, I prefer caroling on dry land."

Harris nodded his head, mumbled something that might be "how do you do," and clutched more tightly with both hands at the stack of dirty dishes he was holding, as if terrified that Caroline might be expecting a handshake.

"Lovely to meet you." Caroline, observant as always, had detected his obvious reluctance to shake hands and pulled hers back. "It must be fascinating to work for such a distinguished artist."

Harris looked more anxious than usual, as if he interpreted this question as an attempt to trick him into saying something that would get him in trouble. I took pity on him.

"Why don't you take those dishes back to the kitchen," I said. "And I'll come help you put together Mr. Castlemayne's breakfast tray."

"I think he just wants coffee right now." From Harris's agitated tone, you'd think the appearance of an unexpected hot breakfast would enrage his boss. Actually, from what I'd seen, it probably would.

"Then I'll get you the coffee." After a week, Harris probably knew where to find it. But given his incredible klutziness, I was just as happy to have him keep his hands off our coffee maker.

"Wouldn't mind a cup myself," Caroline said. "If you're making it anyway."

"It's already made." I headed down the hallway. "Rose Noire already started it before I got up. And she will be very grateful if Harris takes Castlemayne his cup so she doesn't have to."

When we arrived in the kitchen, Caroline seated herself at the kitchen table and I got busy with the coffee mugs. Harris delivered the dirty dishes to the sink, then darted back to stand awkwardly in the doorway, fiddling with the brim of the Irish tweed cap he was wearing as if it really bothered him, wearing a hat indoors—and in front of women to boot.

"Probably just as well to have me take it in rather than Rose Noire," he said finally. "He can be very rude with staff, unfortunately."

"And he doesn't seem to have noticed that Rose Noire isn't staff," I said as I poured the coffee. "She's family. My second cousin once removed."

"Oh, dear!" Harris was so perturbed by this news that he almost dropped the mug of coffee I was handing him. "I'm so sorry. I didn't know. And I'm sure he had no idea—"

"And wouldn't treat her any better if he did know," I said.

"I should apologize to her," Harris said. "I've been giving her orders as if she were a servant."

"Your orders probably sounded like polite and deferential requests," I said. "Don't worry about it. Or if you feel guilty, help me organize it so she never has to deal with your boss again."

"I'll try," he said. "Really. I understand. The creative temperament is so difficult to deal with. I'm doing my best to keep him in a positive, productive frame of mind." With that he ducked out of the kitchen and I could hear him almost running down the hall that led to the library.

"Creative temperament, my eye!" Caroline exclaimed. "Castlemayne's a menace!"

Chapter 3

I started slightly at Caroline's vehement tone. I hadn't even known she was acquainted with our visiting artist, much less that she shared my low opinion of him.

"Well, arguably, he's creative," I pointed out.

"So what?" She snorted slightly at the thought. "I have any number of highly creative friends—painters, sculptors, musicians, writers, craftspeople, actors—and not one of them behaves like that."

"Same here," I said. "So yeah—for 'creative temperament' substitute 'a self-centered, narcissistic, misogynistic jerk' and you'll be nearer the mark. I gather you know him."

"Oh, yes," she said. "And to know him is to loathe him. Didn't I tell you about the horrible way he treated Millard Fillmore last year?"

I was initially puzzled. I happened to know more about Millard Fillmore than the average American, thanks to the fact that one of Michael's former protégés in the Drama Department had written a legendarily awful musical about the thirteenth U.S. president. Fillmore had been dead at least a century and a half, which made it hard to fathom how Castlemayne could possibly have mistreated him last year. Then I remembered Caroline's naming system for the injured birds of prey she rehabilitated at her wildlife refuge. She named owls after scientists, hawks after European royalty, and bald eagles after U.S. presidents. Evidently Millard Fillmore had been the thirteenth bald eagle to arrive at the Willner Wildlife Sanctuary.

"I didn't even know you had a Millard Fillmore," I said. "The last time you were here you'd only just acquired James K. Polk. So what happened?"

"Polk turned out to be a she," she said. "And quite the hussy—Andrew Jackson and Martin Van Buren have come to blows over her several times. And—"

"I meant fill me in on what Castlemayne did to Millard Fillmore," I said.

"Oh, right." Her face took on a thunderous look. "Some crazy politician hired the jerk to paint his portrait with a bald eagle perched on his shoulder. Castlemayne talked me into letting him come down to the sanctuary to paint the eagle from life. He inspected all of them and decided Millard Fillmore was the most presentable of the bunch—he can't fly, but he's got both of his wings and looks pretty impressive. Andrew Jackson and William Henry Harrison both have only one wing, and John Quincy Adams was going through a really bad molt right about then. Anyway, I set up Millard with a comfortable perch and left them to it—but I wasn't sure how much to trust Castlemayne, so I planned to drop by regularly to keep an eye on things. And a good thing I did. First time I checked on them I found him trying to make the poor bird fly by throwing stones at him. And all Millard could do was shuffle back and forth on his perch."

"Horrible," I muttered. "And just the sort of thing I'd expect."

"You'd think he'd have the common sense to realize that if a bird had healed enough to fly, we'd have released him back into the wild," she said. "Anyway, I kicked him out and told him never to come back. And I could have sworn I told your grandfather about it when it happened, so you can imagine how I felt when I heard he'd hired Castlemayne for his book."

"I wish you'd talked him out of it," I said.

"Don't think I didn't try," she said. "Unfortunately, by

the time I'd heard your grandfather was considering it, the old goat had gone and sealed the deal. Well, he'll know better next time."

From the look on her face, I suspected she'd already given Grandfather an earful. She was a good influence on him. She was one of the few people whose wildlife expertise he respected enough that she could usually talk him out of his crazier ideas. And even when she failed to head off disaster, she was fun to have around, since she was also one of the few humans on the planet who would come right out and say "I told you so!" to his face.

"Castlemayne's rude to everyone," I said. "Beyond rude. He bullies poor Rose Noire. He tried to bully Josh and Jamie, but I set him straight on that. And being bullied seems to be part of poor Harris's job description."

"I wouldn't put up with that," Caroline lifted her chin as if to declare her defiance. "But I suppose Harris needs the job."

"Yes," I said. "So I try not to upset him. His life's hard enough as it is. Castlemayne's way behind schedule on the project, he and Grandfather have been having shouting matches over it, and Harris is caught in the middle. And he doesn't handle stress well—seems as if every time I see him, he's taking more aspirin."

"Harris." Caroline looked thoughtful. "Is that his first name or his last?"

"Last." I joined her at the kitchen table. "It's what he wants us to call him. He only uses his initials when he has to divulge more than just Harris. I've deduced that he loathes both his first and middle names."

"I wonder why," she mused.

"Because—" I glanced around to make sure no one else was within earshot. "Because they're Abelard and Hezekiah."

"Gracious—what were his parents thinking?" She shook her head. "We should find him a nickname."

"You're welcome to try," I said. "So far I haven't thought of anything that seems to fit. We just call him Harris. Like Sting. Or Madonna."

"But a great deal less charismatic." She shook her head. "And I can't imagine him being the slightest use helping you keep his boss in line. Why do you have him here, anyway? Castlemayne, I mean. He has a studio, doesn't he? Wouldn't it be more efficient for him—and a lot more pleasant for you—just to deliver the birds to his studio instead of having him here underfoot? And during the holidays, too. I can't imagine he contributes much to the Christmas cheer."

"Apparently his landlord padlocked his studio for nonpayment of rent," I said. "Which, he was careful to explain, he was deliberately withholding until the landlord did some kind of repairs that they've been arguing over."

"He could be telling the truth," she said. "He's a quarrelsome wretch, and I certainly wouldn't want him as a tenant."

"And from something Harris said, I gather he was living in an apartment over his studio," I added. "Which would mean he's locked out of that as well."

"You're almost making me feel sorry for him," Caroline said. "And I wouldn't have thought that possible."

"So regardless of the reason, he doesn't have access to his studio at the moment," I went on.

"Which is why your grandfather went to the trouble of setting aside a room at the zoo he could use as his studio."

"Yes," I said. "But he doesn't like it. And frankly, Grandfather doesn't really trust him to get the work done on his own—Castlemayne's suing and being sued by one of his previous clients over some paintings—they claim he didn't deliver them and he claims they must have lost them."

"I remember hearing about that," Caroline said. "The Audubon Society, wasn't it? Or was it the American Birdwatcher's Association?"

"You'd have to ask Grandfather," I said. "I'm not sure I want to know. Lord knows why Grandfather hired the man after hearing how much trouble other clients had with him."

"He's a brilliant wildlife artist," she said. "I'm sure whatever he produces will be outstanding. And your grandfather probably thinks he can cope with keeping a temperamental artist on track."

"No, I think he assumes that *I* can keep Castlemayne on track," I said. "With a little help from him, and a lot more practical help from Mother."

"And from me." She assumed a look of fierce determination. "I'll make him one of my projects while I'm here."

"Lovely," I said. "And if you can also tackle helping me evict Grandfather's wombats from our basement, my joy will be complete."

"In your basement? Good heavens. Why in the world do you have wombats in your basement? They're not exactly suitable house pets. In fact, when full grown they're rather vicious. Do—"

"My bellhop duties are complete." Rob ambled in and handed Caroline her car keys. "Do you have any idea what time Mother is coming over?"

"I told her I'd give her a call when I got in," she said.

"Can you wait till I make my escape?" Rob asked.

"Is there some reason you're trying to avoid Mother?" I asked.

"Kind of." He sighed. We sat in silence, until Rob finally went on. "Delaney and I called her and Dad yesterday while we were laid over in Atlanta and broke the news to them. We've decided to get married."

"Congratulations," I said.

"Wonderful," Caroline exclaimed. "What's the date?"

"Well, that's the sticky part," Rob said. "We don't really want a big, fancy wedding."

"Uh-oh," I muttered.

"We thought we'd just have a big bash for New Year's Eve, invite all our family and friends, and get married at the stroke of midnight." He beamed for a few seconds as if delighted with the idea. Then his face fell. "For some reason neither of the moms took it that well."

"Of course not," I said.

"Remember, Meg and Michael eloped and cheated your mother out of the big, fancy wedding she and Michael's mother were hoping for," Caroline pointed out. "And I seem to recall that your older sister Pam did much the same thing."

Yes, she had—and for much the same reason: because she wanted a small, quiet ceremony and knew if she tried to plan it, Mother would seize control and inflate it to proportions that would rival a royal wedding.

"Yeah," Rob said. "And Delaney's an only child, so you can probably imagine how her mother took it. We're going to sit down and talk to the mothers about it, but we'd rather wait till Delaney's mother gets here and we can talk to both of them at once."

"How soon is she arriving?" Caroline asked.

"She's flying down on Christmas Eve," Rob said.

"Today's only the twenty-first," I said. "If you seriously think you can avoid talking to Mother about this for three days—"

"Yeah, I know," he said. "But maybe if I can avoid her today and you tell her we want to sit down with her and Delaney's mother and discuss the whole thing, she'll calm down a bit. Because we have a lot to catch up on at work over the next day or so."

I nodded, although I knew that probably only meant that Delaney had a lot to catch up on, since she was head of the game development department at Mutant Wizards. Rob, as the company's founder and titular CEO, had few responsibilities other than periodically exercising his peculiar talent for coming up with ideas his staff could turn

into best-selling computer games. But nice that he was trying to be helpful.

"I'll do what I can to appease Mother," I said. "But she
could show up at any moment so—"

"Laters!" He turned, and ran out the door. Then he
stuck his head back in the kitchen. "Oh, by the way, I bet
I know how all Castlemayne's enemies figured out he was
here. Have you seen that new website someone started—
Caerphilly Confidential?"

"Yes," I said. "And to know it is to loathe it. You think
they published his whereabouts?"

"I know they did." He held up his phone. "I just checked
and saw it. Where the devil do you think they get their
information?" He shook his head as if in grudging admi-
ration for the ingenuity of the website's unknown owners
and then pulled his head back. We heard his footsteps
half-running down the hall and then the front door opening and slamming closed.

"Bother," I said. "I should have interrogated him a little
more about the wombats before he left. And asked him to
do something about them."

"You let me worry about the wombats." Caroline's voice
sounded firm and confident. "You just get on with whatever you need to be doing."

She stood up, squared her shoulders, and marched
down into the basement.

I decided that what I needed to be doing at the moment
was pulling out my phone to check the Caerphilly Confidential website. If I ever figured out who ran the site, I'd
recommend a design makeover. The current look, with its
tiny white type on a black background and garish red and
yellow accents, was hard enough to read on a computer
screen—almost impossible on a phone. But maybe that
was intentional—to annoy the readers as well as the subjects of its posts. And I had to admit, it certainly looked like
a sleazy gossip rag from the forties or fifties. They'd even

stolen their masthead slogan from *L.A. Confidential*—"Off the record, on the QT, and very hush-hush." Although I'd have said that only applied to the identity of the person or persons running it. Anything else that happened, whether around town or on the Caerphilly College campus, eventually showed up here. Forget the design makeover—if the site's owner were ever identified, they'd probably need to leave town before the irate citizens showed up with tar and feathers.

I was still studying the website when Caroline reappeared from the basement.

"Rob's right," I said, looking up from my phone. "Here it is. 'Attention autograph hunters and bill collectors! Roderick Castlemayne, whose reputation as a wildlife artist greatly exceeds his talent, found working conditions at the zoo uncongenial—so now he's snugly ensconced in the comfortable Victorian home of Caerphilly College drama professor Michael Waterston and his wife, blacksmith Meg Langslow. Any bets on how long they'll put up with his tantrums?' Posted yesterday at eight thirty-five a.m.—which is why all the people who want to bother him started showing up here as early as ten o'clock."

"You've got to give them top marks for timeliness and accuracy," Caroline said.

"No marks for respecting anyone's privacy, though," I said. "I'd love to give whoever runs that site a piece of my mind. At least now I know how all of his enemies found him so fast. I'd better take him his tray." I glanced out the kitchen window and spotted a well-muffled figure in the yard. "Rose Noire's outside feeding the menagerie. When she comes back in, tell her I've done the breakfast run." In fact, from what I could see, she'd finished feeding the chickens and the llamas and was throwing balls and sticks for the resident puppies in a valiant attempt to bleed off a little of their excess energy before bringing them back in the house. A noble but ultimately futile effort. It was amazing how fast a pack of eight-month-old Pomeranians could recharge.

"Good news about the wombats, by the way," Caroline said.

"They're gone already?"

"Alas, no," she said. "But at least they're juveniles."

"And that's a good thing?" For some reason, when it heard the word "juvenile," my mind tacked on "delinquent," and conjured up a picture of two furry forms slouching in a corner of our basement with cigarettes dangling from the corner of their mouths and a litter of beer cans at their feet.

"Juveniles tend to be much less ferocious," she said. "Sometimes downright friendly if they're zoo-raised. Because once they grow up, even the ones raised in captivity all too often fit the stereotype of Australian animals as out for blood. And in addition to claws and teeth, wombats have been known to crush predators' skulls with their tough cartilaginous posteriors."

"Lovely," I said. "I want them out of our basement."

"On it," she said, as she took out her phone.

I put the finishing touches on Castlemayne's breakfast tray. I made sure that the bacon, scrambled eggs, and toast weren't actually touching each other, that the butter had been out of the refrigerator long enough to be pliable, and that the jam was strawberry rather than one of the flavors he loathed so much that he'd pour them out onto the floor. Then I nodded to Caroline and headed for the library. Time for the day's first confrontation.

Chapter 4

I took my time walking down the long hallway to the library, letting the Christmas music drifting down from all the little speakers hidden among the evergreens work on my mood. They were playing a particularly nice selection, a hammer dulcimer rendition of "The Wexford Carol," and when I reached the library door, I paused to hear the end. Then I knocked on the door, opened it, and took a look inside. Whatever good mood the music had created evaporated instantly.

The blue jays were jeering raucously, as usual, but I didn't see any of them flying around, so with luck they were all still in their cages. Normally the library would have been beautifully decorated for Christmas, but once Castlemayne set the mockingbirds loose Mother had had the decorations taken down so they wouldn't be damaged. The temporary plastic covers she'd had installed instead did a good job of protecting the books from bird droppings, but they were industrial rather than festive. And the room reeked of cigarette smoke.

I closed my eyes and started counting to ten. Losing my temper at Castlemayne wasn't going to help.

"Either come in or close the door and go away, dammit!" Castlemayne's hoarse voice broke off into what I suspected was a smoker's cough.

I walked in and slammed the door behind me. Harris, standing nearby, jumped and uttered a slight yelp. Castlemayne hastily stuck his hand behind his back and glared at me. With his round face and belly, his long and badly combed white hair, and his unruly white beard he looked rather like Santa Claus's dissolute black-sheep brother.

"You've been smoking in here again," I said. "I told you yesterday that if you can't work without a cigarette in your hand, you can take your easel out in the yard."

"It's below freezing out there," Castlemayne said. "And it looks as if it's going to snow."

"I don't care," I said. "You can also go back to the zoo if you like. We don't want our books and upholstery to stink of tobacco. We don't want our kids to inhale secondhand smoke. And if Grandfather finds out you've been exposing his jays to nicotine poisoning, he'll throttle you."

I was improvising with that last bit. I had no idea if cigarette smoke was all that harmful to blue jays, but I knew Grandfather loathed the smell of tobacco even more than I did.

"There's no risk to the birds," Castlemayne said. "I haven't been smoking inside. You're just smelling the tobacco odor from my clothes."

I set the breakfast tray down on the nearest library table and glanced around until I spotted the ashtray he'd shoved behind one of the sofas. It was overflowing with ash and cigarette butts. I picked it up and slammed it on the library table nearest him. Some of the ash spilled out onto the table.

And then I stared at him. He still had his right hand behind his back, and I could see a thin plume of smoke drifting up over his left shoulder. He couldn't hold a lit cigarette indefinitely. Sooner or later—

He swore, whipped his hand out from behind his back, and crushed the cigarette butt out in the ashtray, knocking even more ash onto the table.

"Try again," I said. "I mean it. Final warning. You smoke one more cigarette in here, and you're out on your ear."

He uttered a sound more like a growl than any kind of

human speech. Harris, who had been looking anxiously back and forth between us, spoke up.

"Sudden nicotine withdrawal could have a very detrimental effect on Mr. Castlemayne's creative process."

"Then get him some nicotine patches," I suggested. "Or gum. I'll find someone to give you a ride to the drugstore if your car suddenly isn't working. I mean it. He lights up in here one more time and he's history."

Castlemayne mumbled something. I didn't quite catch all the words, but I didn't really have to.

"And if you call me that again, maybe the next time your ex-wife shows up I'll escort her back here instead of trying to chase her away," I said.

"Ex-wife?" Harris sounded anxious. More than usually anxious.

"Which one?" Castlemayne didn't sound particularly worried.

"You have more than one?"

"There are two," Harris said. "I don't suppose she told you her name."

"No." I shook my head. "She just said she was his exwife. And that he was months behind on his alimony."

"Could be either, then," Harris murmured. "When did this happen?"

"Yesterday afternoon," I said. "I told your boss at the time."

"You should have warned me!" Harris yelped.

"I was focused on my work," Castlemayne said. "Was it a bottle blonde or a blowsy redhead?" he asked, turning to me.

"She was blond," I said.

"That would be Madeleine," Harris said, with a lugubrious nod.

Castlemayne grunted and rolled his eyes.

"If you don't stop smoking in here, I'll send you back to the zoo and tell her where you are," I said. "And maybe even give her an all-access zoo pass so she can get to you. And then I'll email the editor of Caerphilly Confidential. They're the ones who spilled the beans about you being here."

"Who cares?" Castlemayne said.

"If that's the way you feel, I'll just send all your callers back here instead of fending them off," I said. "Better yet, I'll put up a sign saying that anyone looking for you can come around the back of the house and knock on the sunroom door."

"I'll do what I can to help with this situation." Harris sounded contrite and earnest, but I already knew he had no influence over his boss.

So I didn't say anything. I strolled over to the nearest of the enormous cages. It contained the expected four blue jays. I rattled the cage door to confirm that it was securely fastened. I stood there for a minute or so, studying them. They seemed fine. A little annoyed at being in the cage, but perfectly healthy.

Castlemayne uttered an impatient snort.

"What are you waiting for?" he snarled at Harris. "I haven't got all day."

"Sorry!" Harris hurried over to the easel. Beside it was a card table covered with paint, brushes, palette knives, tins of turpentine, and the entire cluttered collection of tools and supplies that seemed to be a necessary part of the painter's profession. Harris began squirting dabs of paint out of tubes onto a palette and mixing them up with a brush. I wondered if this was typical of famous painters, or if Castlemayne was unusually lazy, getting his assistant to do all the mundane chores for him.

At least Harris was a neat freak—so much so that I'd stopped worrying about having turpentine and oil paints in the library. If anything ever spilled—and it would be Castlemayne who did the spilling, in all probability— Harris would take care of it. Following Castlemayne around with trash bag and a clean white rag seemed to be a major part of his job.

Castlemayne himself strode out of the French doors at the end of the library. I could hear him stomping across the tile floor of the sunroom beyond, and then the noise of the sunroom's outside door slamming as he went out into the backyard.

Harris scurried to close the French doors and shuddered slightly at the cold draft they'd let in. Then he returned to mixing his boss's paint.

I moved on to examine the other two cages. Each contained the requisite four jays and each was securely closed. I turned back to Harris.

"I mean it," I said. "He stops smoking in here or he goes back to the zoo. And if he wants to sleep here at the house, I can put him in one of the bedrooms upstairs. I'd rather not have him drooling on our sofa all night."

"I think he's just been taking the occasional catnap," Harris said, looking nervously at the sofa, which had been made up with a pillow, an embroidered sheet, and a blue blanket. Pilfered, I suspected, from the Caerphilly Inn.

"Yeah, right," I said. "He has a cushy room at the Inn— why would he want to sleep here?"

"They're pretty strict at the Inn." He was dabbing at the nearest table with a white rag, mopping up a speck of paint so tiny as to be invisible to me. "About the smoking, that is. And they banned him from the dining room."

"Do I want to know why?" I asked.

Harris hunched his shoulders, rather like a turtle pulling in his head. He didn't offer any explanations.

He didn't have to. I could ask Ekaterina, my good friend who managed the Inn. She'd probably welcome the chance to vent about a guest like Castlemayne.

"The jays stay in the cages, remember," I said. "If he has to see them with no obstacles in the way he can crawl in with them—the cages are big enough. And incidentally, the longer you leave the dirty dishes lying around, the harder they are to wash and the more likely they are to attract insects. So bring them back when he's finished. Or if he's got you too busy to do that, text me and I'll pick them up."

"He doesn't want to be interrupted when he's painting." Harris flinched slightly at the thought. "And I'm already trying so hard to keep him on track. On schedule."

"I appreciate that. Just shove the dishes outside the door and text me," I said.

Harris nodded glumly. Which meant he'd try, but the odds were his boss would distract him, barking orders and insults, and I'd have to unlock the library door and fetch the dishes myself. Castlemayne would be annoyed.

Well, let him be annoyed.

"Sorry," I said. "I don't mean to take it out on you. I know you're doing your best."

He smiled as if touched by my sympathy. He meant well—what a pity his best efforts were totally inadequate.

I decided to leave him in peace. Or as much peace as he could find while he was at Castlemayne's beck and call. But before I left, I looked around for any signs of the fugitive mockingbirds. Our library was two stories high, with an inside balcony running around three of its four walls, giving access to the upper shelves. The mockingbirds seemed to favor perching on the highest shelves or on the light fixtures that hung from the ceiling. I took a long, slow look to see if any of them were perched there now. Then I nodded to Harris and left the library. I was pulling out my keys to lock the door behind me when I heard footsteps inside the library.

"What the hell is this?" Castlemayne bellowed. "This food's stone cold!"

I opened the door again.

"The food was piping hot when it got here," I said. "If you don't like it, you can go hungry."

He growled.

"And don't send poor Harris over to my kitchen to microwave it and then complain that it's dried out, or I'll kick you out in the cold and lock the door behind you."

I slammed the door closed, stuck in the key, and turned it as hard as I could.

Then I took one of the deep, calming breaths Rose Noire was always recommending.

It didn't help much.

I pulled out my phone and composed an email to Grandfather.

"Castlemayne has worn out his welcome here," it said. "Please make arrangements to send him back to the zoo."

I studied the text for a minute or so. Then I added another sentence.

"Surely the tigers could use some fresh meat."

I pressed the send button and felt ever so slightly better. And while we were talking about returning unwanted visitors to the zoo . . . should I have mentioned the wombats in my email?

No, better to leave that to Caroline. Or talk to Grandfather in person—once I'd finished dealing with our unwanted human guest. And I had a few ideas about how to do that.

I moved to the far end of the hall. Far enough away from the library door that no one inside could hear me—but still with a good view of the library door, so they couldn't sneak up on me. Then I called Kevin.

Chapter 5

Kevin picked up just as the fourth ring was about to send me to voicemail.

"What's up?" he asked. I could hear the high-pitched barking of Widget, his Pomeranian, in the background.

"How are the wombats?" I kept my tone light. Even sweet. So sweet that I was sure he'd easily figure out how I really felt about our uninvited guests.

"They're fine. Pretty calm now that Rob isn't here riling them up."

I decided not to ask what Rob had been doing to rile up the wombats.

"Glowing nicely?" I asked instead.

"Yeah. Kind of pretty, actually."

Okay, I was getting a little curious about the wombats. But still—

"Don't let them get too comfortable," I said. "I'll be talking to Grandfather about expediting their return to the zoo. Meanwhile, I'd appreciate it if you could do a little something for me." I was hoping to make use of any guilt he felt about his part in installing the wombats in our basement.

"Um . . . sure. What?" Definite signs of guilt.

"Remember those cameras you set up to keep an eye on what was happening in the library back when all the actors in Michael's show were using it as their lounge?"

"The cameras you had me take down because you didn't want anyone spying on friends and family here in the house?"

"Yes, those cameras," I said. "Can you put them up again? Because these days it's mostly Castlemayne in the library. He's certainly no friend and thank God he's not family, and I'm worried that he'll either set loose more birds or burn down the library with his wretched cigarettes. I've told Grandfather he needs to send the jerk back to the zoo, but that could take a few days to arrange, and in the meanwhile I want to keep an eye on him."

"He won't like it, having cameras installed in his lair."

"If he gives you any trouble, let me know and I'll deal with him. Or better yet, I'll get Mother and Caroline to deal with him."

"That'd be worth seeing." Kevin sounded amused.

"And can we also set up cameras that let me see who's coming to the door without having to trot there every time the bell rings?"

"Easy," he said. "And maybe a sound system so you can tell them to get lost without opening the door?"

"You've read my mind," I said. "How soon can you get them up?"

"I'll see if I can find where I put the cameras I was using in the library," he said. "If I do, I can put those back this morning. If I can't find them, I'll pick up some new ones when I get the hardware to cover the doors. Might take till tomorrow. I'll keep you posted."

If he could find them. Well, considering how very much random computer equipment had taken up residence in the basement with him, maybe finding the cameras wouldn't be all that easy, even without whatever complications the wombats added.

"Okay," I said. "While you're at it, why don't you set up some cameras for the wombats?"

A brief silence.

"You mean like the panda cam they have at the National Zoo?" he said. "That might be pretty cool. We'd need some special low-light cameras, of course, but setting up the web interface wouldn't be all that hard, and then people all over the world could observe the biofluorescence and—"

"I was actually just thinking you could set up some cameras so *you* could observe the biofluorescence. At a distance. Then the wombats could stay in their nice, comfortable habitats out at the zoo, without Rob riling them up, and you could still observe them as much as you wanted from your nice, comfortable habitat here in our basement."

Another brief silence.

"Yeah, I guess we could do that. Not as much fun as having them here."

"But less stressful for the wombats," I pointed out. "Remember, we'll have at least a dozen relatives staying here for the holidays, not to mention the ones staying at Mother and Dad's and spending most of their time over here. Do you really want them all trooping down to the basement to rile up the wombats?"

Actually, he was probably looking forward to that.

"And they'll be tripping over your computer cables," I went on. "Punching random keys on your machines. Knocking things over. Unplugging things at the most inconvenient moment. Asking—"

"We've got the wombats in a pen," he said. "They can't get anywhere near my hardware."

"I was talking about the relatives."

Another pause.

"Okay, good point," he said. "I'll take care of the library cameras as soon as I can. Although I should probably wait to do that until after I get the wombats ready to travel."

I pictured the two wombats sitting up on their stubby hind legs and clutching battered, old-fashioned suitcases in their front paws. For some reason my imagination chose to dress them in floppy red hats and bright-blue coats, like a pair of oversized Paddington bears, and they were staring at me with expressions of regret and disappointment in their beady black eyes. I resolutely banished the image.

"Thanks," I said. "Keep me posted."

I hung up and continued into the front hall. Just as I got there the doorbell rang, so instead of turning left for the kitchen I turned right and approached the front door. I peered through the peephole. Again, no one there, but since I wasn't expecting any more visitors quite as short as Caroline, I continued to peer out. I caught a glimpse of a car at the far end of the front walk. Not a familiar car.

Then a form came into view as our visitor rang the door-bell again. A woman. Not anyone I knew. But, on the bright side, she wasn't the belligerent ex-wife who'd come calling yesterday. Or the aggressive reporter. Or the bill collector. She was a redhead, although probably not a natural one. Her skin was tanned to the kind of golden brown few red-heads could achieve. And I could detect the barest shadow of dark roots at her hairline.

She showed no signs of going away, so I arranged my face into an expression that was polite but not exactly wel-coming and opened the door a foot or so.

"Yes?" I asked.

"Merry Christmas!" she said with an unconvincing show of cheerfulness. "Mind if I come in?" She reached to push the door open, but I had my foot against it.

"Yes, I do mind," I said. "You want to tell me who you are and why you're here?"

"I'm looking for Roderick Castlemayne." Did she think I couldn't feel the pressure she was still putting on the door? "I'd like to talk to him."

Realizing I wasn't going to let her push her way in she took a step back and assumed what she probably thought was a friendly look.

I studied her, not even caring if she saw that I was doing it. She was only about five foot four, so I had a good six inches of height on her. And while neither of us was skinny,

I was pretty sure my blacksmithing work meant I was in better shape—she had the plump, round-shouldered look of someone who spent their time behind a desk. Curious, then, that my first reaction was to assess her as a threat. Something about her manner.

And she was a redhead. How had Castlemayne described his other ex-wife? "A blowsy redhead." I wouldn't have called our latest visitor blowsy, though he probably would. She looked pretty normal for someone in her forties—maybe even well-preserved if she was in her fifties. And she had a kind of capable, no-nonsense air that might have made a good impression on me if she hadn't started out by trying to shove her way into our house.

"It's pretty cold out here," she said, with what she probably intended to be an ingratiating smile. "Why don't you—"

"Last I heard, Mr. Castlemayne had a room at the Caerphilly Inn," I said. "You might try reaching him there. Although he's supposed to be working at the zoo, so if he's not at the Inn you could leave a message for him there." None of that was actually a lie.

"The Inn's pretty snooty," she said. "They claim they're giving him my messages, but I'm not sure I believe them. And I wouldn't know where to look at the zoo."

Her smile was probably intended to be disarming.

"Sorry," I said. "I have no idea what to tell you. But if I run into him in either place, I could tell him you were looking for him—what was the name again?"

"I'll just keep looking, thanks."

She turned and slowly made her way across the porch, down the steps, and up the path to her car—a nondescript dull-gray compact sedan of some sort. She glanced back at me before getting into the car, and I couldn't help suspecting that if I hadn't been watching she wouldn't have gotten in. I pictured her sneaking across the lawn and peering into our windows, the way the blond ex-wife had yesterday. I raised my phone and quite openly snapped a picture of her. Seeing that, she waved and favored me with one last insincere smile before getting in and driving off.

"The other ex-wife," I said, nodding. I could confirm that later by showing the photo to Castlemayne or Harris. I was about to close the door when I spotted a car approaching in the distance.

"Prepare to repel boarders," I muttered.

Chapter 6

But just as I was putting on the stern face I used for unwanted visitors I recognized Mother's blue sedan and relaxed. A little. There was still the likelihood that she'd be
on the warpath about Rob and Delaney's plans, but with
any luck I could enlist her help in chasing away intruders.

"Meg, dear," she called as she trotted up the walk. "Is
Holly here yet?"

"Holly who?" I asked. "Or is that a Christmas knock-
knock joke?"

"Holly McKenna." Mother sounded ever-so-slightly impatient. "Delaney's mother."

"She's not coming until Christmas Eve," I said.

"Change of plans." Mother gave a quick peck that almost
landed on my cheek as she dashed past me. "She's coming
down early to help us solve the new problem."

"I assume you mean Rob and Delaney's announcement
that they plan to tie the knot in the middle of their New
Year's Eve party instead of having a formal wedding." I
glanced up and down the road to make sure the redhead
had disappeared before following Mother inside. "I don't
suppose I could convince you to be happy they didn't just
decide to stay engaged for the next few decades?"

"Was that Caroline's car I saw in the driveway?" Mother
handed me her coat and studied the available selection of
hats on the hat-and-coat stand.

"She's in the kitchen."

"Good." Mother picked out a hat—a faded but still elegant pink straw hat that boasted a wide brim and a spray

of silk flowers—and adjusted it carefully on her impeccably coiffed head, using the mirror at the center of the hat-and-coat stand. "I'm sure she'll take a sensible view of this. Holly's flight was delayed and wasn't going to get into Richmond until four a.m., but she was going to drive up here, check into her room at the Inn, put her feet up for a little while, and then head over here so we can start strategizing. She could be here any time now." She set off down the hall toward the kitchen with a businesslike stride.

"Don't open the basement door," I called after her as I hung up her coat. "Long story."

I didn't feel like explaining about the wombats just yet. I wasn't sure how Mother felt about wombats, but I suspected finding out wouldn't improve how my day was going.

My phone dinged to signal an arriving message. I braced myself before looking down at my phone. And then my ill humor melted away. Michael had texted a selfie with Josh and Jamie peering over his shoulders. Then a picture of the boys with their friend Adam Burke, toasting marshmallows over a fire pit. And an action shot of two figures in familiar-looking ski clothes sailing down a mountainside with what looked like great form.

"I see you're having a wonderful time!" I texted back.

"Wish you were here!" he replied. "Literally. And see you tomorrow." Followed by a bunch of heart emojis.

I felt much better. I missed Michael and the boys, but I was glad I'd insisted that they go forward with the planned ski trip. Just because I couldn't ski for the time being didn't mean they couldn't.

I forwarded the picture with Adam to his grandparents and was about to head back to the kitchen when I heard a hammering noise outside.

I opened the door and peered out. At the far end of our front walk, my cousin Horace, wearing a bulky down jacket over his Caerphilly County deputy's uniform, was using a hammer to pound on a stake holding a sign. His boss, Chief Burke, was hovering over his shoulder, looking at his phone. The chief looked up, saw me, and waved.

"Merry Christmas, Meg," he called. "And thanks for the picture."

I strolled down to the road to see what kind of sign Horace was installing. And when I saw it, I approved—a No Trespassing sign.

"I saw the item on Caerphilly Confidential," the chief explained. "The one about Mr. Castlemayne being here at your house instead of the zoo. And I figured you'd be overwhelmed. If I ever find out who's behind that blasted website—!" He left the sentence unfinished, but his scowl left me in no doubt how he felt about the unknown gossip-monger.

"This should help fend off your unwanted visitors." Horace straightened up and tested the signpost to make sure it was firmly fixed.

"Or if it doesn't, it will give us solid grounds for arresting them," the chief said. "Horace, can you put the last one down at the far end of their yard?"

Horace nodded and trotted off with another sign in hand.

"You had any unwanted callers so far today?" the chief asked, turning to me.

"Only one," I said. "Probably one of Castlemayne's ex-wives."

"How many does he have?" The chief frowned slightly.

"Only two that I know of," I said. "And only two according to Harris, who probably knows. This one was reasonably well-behaved."

"Still, keep your eye on them," he said. "And if the other one comes back and tries to sneak into the house or peer in your windows—"

"Kevin's going to install some surveillance cameras," I said. "Today, if possible."

"Good idea." He glanced up at the sky. "Snow's supposed to start in a few hours."

"Yes, with the first of those two back-to-back storms
they're forecasting," I said. "And don't tell me how many
inches they're currently predicting. It would only depress
me."

"And whatever we get will be staying around for a while,
too." He shivered slightly. "The temperature's not supposed to get above freezing until after New Year's. I hate
to be a Scrooge, but I think having a white Christmas is
overrated. I wish the blasted snow would stay out there
in the Blue Ridge instead of complicating our lives down
here."

"Amen," I said. "But don't say that in front of the kids.
I just hope it doesn't interfere with Michael and the boys
getting home tomorrow."

Actually, I also hoped that the snow wouldn't make the
roads bad, since Mother and Dad would need to travel
back and forth from their farm to our house regularly
over the next few days for various holiday celebrations—
Mother and Dad and the dozen or so relatives staying with
them. And that it wouldn't interfere with our going to
see the chief's wife, Minerva, leading the New Life Baptist Choir's annual Christmas concert for non-Baptists on
Thursday night. And most of all that we didn't lose power
right in the middle of the orgy of cooking that would be
taking place over the next few days.

The chief's phone rang. He glanced down, smiled at the
picture of Josh, Jamie, and Adam—evidently he'd set it as
his new screen saver—and pressed the button to answer it.

I took a step or two away, both to give him a little privacy and to check on how Horace was doing. I nodded
with satisfaction when I saw the neat row of No Trespassing signs—five of them lined up very precisely along the
entire front of our yard.

Caroline strolled out the front door, waved to the chief, and joined me.

"Well, that should help with the unwanted visitors," she said. "Do you—"

"Blast!"

Caroline and I both started, and turned to see the chief frowning down at his phone. "Sorry," he said, seeing our surprise. "Merry Christmas, Caroline."

"Merry Christmas," she replied. "Something wrong?"

"Could be." He frowned and began texting something on his phone. "We arrested Curly this morning."

"Curly?" she echoed.

"Most of the time, Curly is the entirety of our local homeless problem," I explained.

"Ah," she said. "The one your mother and the rest of the Ladies Interfaith Council are always worrying about."

"Yes," I said. "They now officially have a Curly Committee. He always turns up his nose when they try to find him a job or a place to live—says he's a free spirit and doesn't want to be beholden to anyone. But he doesn't seem to mind the chief arresting him for being a public nuisance whenever there's bad weather coming."

"Or at Thanksgiving and Christmas," the chief said. "We picked him up a little earlier than usual this year on account of the weather forecast. Got him bathed and deloused and tucked up all comfy in his favorite cell, and even took his order for what kind of pie he wants with his Christmas dinner—we have it catered by Muriel down at the diner, you know. But I got a call just now—some well-meaning but clueless young lawyer just showed up trying to force us to let him out again. With the temperature already dropping below the freezing mark and up to half a foot of snow predicted. I need to go deal with that. Call me if any of your trespassers show up again."

He strode over to get into his car and drove off at a slightly higher speed than usual.

Horace had finished pounding in the last sign and strolled over.

"I thought I'd take a quick break," he said when he and Caroline had exchanged Christmas greetings. "See how Watson is doing."

"Watson?" Caroline looked puzzled.

"Horace's puppy," I explained as I led the way back inside. "One of the Pomeranians. Horace drops him off here when he's on duty. They're probably in the kitchen with Rose Noire."

"I don't want him to be lonely," Horace said. "Dogs are pack animals, you know—it would be cruel to leave one alone all day."

"Very sound." Caroline nodded with approval.

If you asked me, Watson and his six brothers and sisters led the life of Riley. The various people who'd adopted them seemed to think that the puppies would pine away if separated from each other for very long, so it was a rare day when we didn't have two or three visiting Pomeranians on top of the ones Rose Noire and Kevin had adopted. I'm sure the fact that their visits to us gave people an occasional break from dealing with the Poms' unbelievably high energy levels had nothing to do with it. And when here the pups had Tinkerbell, Rob's Irish wolfhound, as their surrogate mother, and Spike, our eight-and-a-half pound furball, to tease and torment. Although I tried to keep him and the Pom Bunch apart as much as possible. I wasn't sure if it was for their protection or his. Spike had more than earned his reputation as the Small Evil One, but the puppies were definitely giving him a run for his money.

Today there were only four puppies in the kitchen, all clustered at Rose Noire's feet whining with impatience as they waited for her to set down the bowls of organic, nutritionally balanced homemade dog food she was preparing for them. Not, I had been relieved to learn, vegetarian dog food—Rose Noire might not accept humans as carnivores, but she didn't quarrel with canines' preferences. One puppy broke away from the pack and ran yipping to jump into Horace's arms and lick his face.

"This is Watson," Horace announced as he held up the gleeful, wriggling fur ball. "I'm training him for scent work."

"Really," Caroline said with genuine interest. "Are you going for drug detection, or search and rescue, or what?"

"We haven't decided yet," Horace admitted. "I'm still figuring out where his talents lie."

I had already figured out where Watson's talents lay—in spite of his small size, he had all the makings of a guard dog. All the puppies were hypervigilant, but Watson was almost always the first to start barking at the mere suspicion of an intruder. And while his tiny little sharp teeth probably couldn't inflict enough damage to deter a burglar, his yap was so high-pitched and penetrating that only a hearing-impaired housebreaker could possibly endure it for more than a few seconds.

Probably not a good idea to mention this to Horace, though.

"What happened to Mother?" I asked instead.

"She went upstairs to lie down with a cold compress on her forehead," Caroline said.

"I told her she could use our room," Rose Noire added.

Our room? I wondered for a moment if Rose Noire had taken to using the royal we, then remembered that Caroline was bunking with her, to make room for more out-of-town relatives. I hoped Caroline was forewarned about the Pomeranians that slept with Rose Noire.

"Does Mother know about the wombats?" I asked.

Caroline and Rose Noire exchanged a glance.

"Well, no," Rose Noire said.

"The news about Rob and Delaney rather did her in,"

Caroline said. "We didn't think this was exactly the right time to tell her anything else distressing."

"I'm not sure there will ever be a right time to tell her that our basement is infested with wombats," I said. "So let's keep her in the dark for now. With any luck we can get them returned to the zoo before she ever finds out."

They nodded. I could tell they didn't think much of our chances of fooling Mother. Neither did I, dammit.

"I'll be back," I said.

Chapter 7

I needed a break from wombats, visiting relatives, and the doorbell. Especially the doorbell. I picked up my notebook-that-tells-me-when-to-breathe, which had been lying neglected on the kitchen table, grabbed the old coat I kept by the back door, and stepped outside. I took a deep breath. The air was clean and bitter cold. The sky was that luminous gray that always heralds a coming storm. The chickens were scratching restlessly at the ground. I'd help Rose Noire round them up when the snow started. And make sure there was plenty of hay in the llamas' shed. They, at least, could be trusted to round themselves up well in advance of the storm. Was that natural instinct or had we conditioned them to do this by stocking the shed with such a plentiful supply of apples, oranges, and other favorite llama treats whenever it started snowing?

But all that could come later. I headed for the barn. I cast a longing look at the tall iron security fence that walled my blacksmith shop off from the rest of the barn. Maybe I could find an excuse to come out and do a little work later. I could always pretend to be making a last-minute commission that someone needed for Christmas, and hammering on iron even for a few minutes was bound to improve my mood.

Later. For now, I went to the other end of the barn and opened up the room that used to serve as the tack room and was now my office.

I sat down at my desk and pulled up the hay bale I'd had the boys drag in so I'd have a way to elevate my ankle.

I leaned back and sighed with contentment. Peace and quiet and some uninterrupted time with my notebook. Life was good. And—

I heard the sound of a car pulling up in front of the house.

"Somebody else can get that," I muttered.

But curiosity got the better of me. I limped out to the barn door and peered toward the road. The familiar white van belonging to the Caerphilly Animal Hospital was parked in front of our house, with Clarence Rutledge, the local vet, at the wheel. He was leaning out of the driver's window, talking with my grandfather.

"Gotta see a man about a wombat," I muttered as I headed their way.

Grandfather spotted me when I drew near and stood waiting for me.

Clarence called out a Christmas greeting and then turned back to Grandfather.

"Just give me a heads-up if you need a ride back," he said. "Unless you want me to wait."

"I appreciate it, but I have no idea how long this will take," Grandfather said, his voice half a growl. "Got to see what that blasted man is up to. I don't suppose he's finished doing the blue jays yet."

"He's hardly made any progress in two days," I said. "I think you should take him back to the zoo, where you and your staff can keep a closer eye on him. And speaking of keeping an eye on things, we need to talk about the wombats."

"Aren't they fascinating?" Grandfather beamed as if glow-in-the-dark wombats were his own invention.

"Fascinating," I echoed.

"And how amazing that it took us two centuries to discover their biofluorescence!" Clarence added.

"Well, I've had my suspicions for a long time," Grandfather said.

"Actually, I'm not the least bit surprised it took so long for us to notice that they glowed in the dark," I said. "In fact, when I heard about it, the first questions that popped into my mind were whatever possessed some scientist to aim a black light at a bunch of wombats, and what was he smoking at the time."

Grandfather frowned slightly, but pretended not to hear. Clarence smothered a chuckle.

"Unfortunately, however fascinating they might be, they don't belong in our basement," I added. "One of them almost escaped this morning. And unless Kevin is better at cleaning up after them than he is with his puppy, by now there are probably wombat droppings all over the basement."

"Yes," Grandfather said. "They're cubic, you know. Their droppings. Scat's a better term, actually."

"I don't care if they're covered with gold dust and diamonds," I said. "I don't want then in our basement."

Grandfather's expression showed that he was deeply disappointed by my shortsighted failure to appreciate the geometric perfection of wombat scat.

"It's only temporary," he said. "And they need to be there so Kevin can conduct his observations."

"He can conduct them out at the zoo," I said.

"You can't expect him to uproot his whole life to spend two or three months out at the zoo."

"Two or three months!" I exclaimed. "No. No way."

"But—"

"My definition of 'temporary' in this case would be a couple of days at most," I said. "And even that's too long to have wombats as our uninvited guests. It wouldn't disrupt Kevin's whole life to spend some time out at the zoo. As long as he's got wi-fi and a source of caffeine, he could control the world from there if he wanted to. Or if he doesn't want to go there, I bet if you gave him a day or so, he could set up some kind of remote system that would let him monitor the wombats in their habitat without even leaving the basement."

"Well, yes, but—"

"And quite apart from my not wanting to put up with a menagerie in our basement for the next two to three months, have you thought of the serious potential danger to the wombats?" I said. "The stress they're probably already feeling at being away from their familiar surroundings? The unsettling effect of having a constant stream of relatives trooping downstairs to see them?"

"Well, you'd have to warn the relatives to—"

"Who knows what strange things the visitors will feed them?" I went on, relentlessly. "And worst of all, what happens if we have a power outage? You have generators out at the zoo, but we don't. I'm not going to stand by and let you risk having those poor wombats freeze to death!"

I'd actually rendered him speechless. He stood there with his mouth open, clearly searching for the right rejoinder and coming up empty.

"So I'll call the zoo right now and arrange to have them relocate the wombats to safety back in the zoo—immediately," I said. "Before the snowstorm starts."

"You have a good point," he said. "But we're short-staffed at the zoo today. I'm not sure—"

"I'll call Manoj," I said. "I'm sure he can organize something. And if he can't—well, I'm sure Seth Early can lend me the truck he uses to haul his sheep around. He doesn't clean it very often, so they'll probably be a little smelly when they get home, but better smelly than frozen solid."

"But you don't have any experience with wombats," Grandfather protested.

"Neither has Kevin as far as I know," I said. "No time like the present to learn. And I'll borrow Seth's sheepdog. I haven't seen an animal yet that a border collie couldn't handle."

"I think it would be preferable to have trained zookeepers transporting the wombats," Grandfather said, in his most dignified tone. "Please tell Manoj that I've authorized the move, and ask him to give it top priority, in light of the meteorological forecast. I will go and supervise the preparations for their return."

With that he strode off, head high.

"By this time tomorrow, he'll have convinced himself that returning the wombats to the zoo was all his idea," Clarence said, with a chuckle.

"And that bringing them here in the first place was my crazy notion," I said. "I know. Just as long as they're gone."

"If Manoj needs any help, have him call me," Clarence said. "I've had some experience wrangling wombats. Just be glad I nixed the first plan Kevin and your grandfather came up with."

"Do I even want to know?"

"Tasmanian devils," he said. "Kevin thought they'd be a lot more fun than wombats—in spite of the fact that they're louder than a hyena and almost as smelly as a skunk. I think he's still sulking a bit, but he gave up on that idea after I pointed out how impossible it would be to keep them penned up in the basement. For their size, they have one of the most powerful bites of any animal on earth. Powerful enough to bite through thick metal wire—they'd have gone through the chicken wire Kevin was going to use like damp tissue. Ah well. See you later!"

"You're coming to tonight's dinner, I hope?" I asked.

"Wouldn't miss it," he said. "Rose Noire says she's arranged some special winter solstice treats. Which reminds me—what should I bring?"

"Your appetite," I said. "And whatever over-the-counter medicine you want to have if you overeat."

"You mean when I overeat," he said. "Hard not to at your bashes. See you then!"

Still chuckling, he put his van into gear and drove off.

Probably just as well, because I was having a hard time stopping myself from asking him why he hadn't vetoed the wombats along with the Tasmanian devils.

I limped back to the barn, settled down again at my desk with my ankle elevated, and called Manoj, the long-suffering zookeeper who served as Grandfather's right-hand man out at the zoo.

"Meg!" He sounded happy—no, make that relieved to hear my voice. "Exactly who I needed to talk to. There is a person staking out the zoo. What should I do?"

Chapter 8

"Someone staking out the zoo?" I echoed. "Who? And what is he doing?"

"It is a lady," he said. "She came and asked to see Mr. Castlemayne, and I kept telling her he was unavailable—because I was under the strictest orders not to reveal his actual whereabouts, as you know. And she kept insisting he was here and she had a right to see him and that she would report me to the cops if I didn't take her to him—"

"Which is nonsense," I said.

"Well, I knew that," Manoj said. "But nothing I said would satisfy her, and I think I would still be there arguing if Dr. Blake hadn't come out of the gate just then."

"I bet Grandfather straightened her out."

"Well, he was frightfully rude to her. But at least she stopped trying to force her way in."

"Good," I said. "If she comes back and Grandfather's not available, give me a call. If I can't come out myself, I'll draft Mother to help."

"That would indeed be awesome to see," he said. "And it might be necessary, because she is still here. Sitting in her car in the parking lot, a couple of rows away from the staff entrance. Every time someone comes in or goes out, she stares at them through her binoculars. The staff are becoming agitated."

"A woman," I said. "A redhead in her forties, about five foot four? Hang on—let me send you a picture."

I texted him the picture I'd taken of the redheaded woman I'd chased away earlier.

"Yes!" he exclaimed. "That is her! So you know who she is?"

"Not for certain," I said. "But I suspect she is one of Castlemayne's ex-wives."

"One of his ex-wives? How many does he have?"

"Only two that I've heard about," I said.

"But this could be dangerous!" Manoj exclaimed. "It could escalate into an incident of domestic violence. I am getting a very bad vibe from this."

I was about to tell him not to be silly, but then I stopped myself. I hadn't exactly gotten a reassuring vibe from the redhead myself.

"Call the police," I said. "Explain the situation. Have them drop by to check her out."

"They will only think I am overreacting."

"Tell them it was my idea to call them and that I thought she was hinky, too."

"Hinky?"

"Creepy and suspicious. But tell them I said hinky. And once you've done that, can you come and fetch the wombats? I talked Grandfather into letting them go home before the snow starts, since you guys have a generator and we don't."

"Oh, thank goodness! I have been so concerned about them! I will gather up a few other staff members and come right over. But what if that woman follows us to your house and spots Mr. Castlemayne?"

"I'll warn him to lie low. Get here as soon as you can, before Grandfather changes his mind. In fact, you worry about the wombats—I'll call the cops on the redhead."

"It's a deal."

When we hung up, I pondered for a moment, and then called 911. Debbie Ann, the dispatcher, answered in the middle of the second ring.

"Nine-one-one, what's your emergency, Meg?"

"Not sure it's an emergency," I said. "More a concerning

situation, so if you get another call, just dump me and have someone call me back."

I explained about the redhead, first showing up here and then staking out the zoo. "Manoj wasn't sure he should call, because she hasn't actually done anything except be persistent—"

"If he and the other zoo employees feel threatened, we should check her out. Because he's right about domestic situations. You mentioned that you had a photograph of her—can you text it to me?"

"Absolutely," I said. "And thanks."

We hung up, and I texted the redhead's photo to her. Then I sat back and focused on my ankle. It was throbbing a little. Not surprising. I'd been running around a lot. More than I'd planned on. I felt a brief pang of nostalgia for the two days I'd spent in bed right after spraining my ankle. It had been nice the first day, with Dad dropping off stacks of mysteries while Michael and the boys brought up elegant trays for every meal. Of course, since they seemed to have adopted the meal plan used by hobbits—breakfast, second breakfast, elevenses, luncheon, afternoon tea, dinner, and supper—I'd probably gained several pounds a day under their care. And by the second afternoon, to my great surprise, I was actually getting tired of doing nothing but eating and reading.

And evidently Kevin and Grandfather had used the time when I was laid up in bed to sneak the wombats into the house. Probably a good thing I was back on my feet.

Just not a good thing to spend quite so much time on them. Someone had jacked up the volume on the speakers while I'd been out of the room, so I found the volume control and turned the carols down a bit. Then I opened my neglected notebook and began the calming, satisfying process of checking off completed tasks and adding in new ones. Of course, it was always the most satisfying when I got to check off more than I added, but fat chance of that happening this close to the holidays. This time of year, it was a great day when I added less than a page of new items. But even when the items were multiplying like rabbits in springtime, I could achieve some peace of mind, knowing everything I had to do was captured in my notebook.

I was happily crossing off and scribbling when I heard a familiar noise—the door to the sunroom flapping in the breeze. The lock had become tricky, so unless we closed it just right, it came loose at the slightest puff of wind. Clearly my last attempt to fix it had failed.

I was about to add "get sunroom door fixed" to my notebook, and paused. Instead, I texted Randall Shiffley to say "Merry Christmas! And even though it's so close to the holiday, any chance you can you send someone out soon to fix the lock on our sunroom door?" Maybe it was overkill to text the owner of a construction company about something that really wasn't any more than an odd job, but I knew if I went straight to Randall, he'd get it done.

I hadn't even picked up my pen again when I heard the ding of a reply.

"No problem. Can definitely get someone out there tomorrow. Maybe today if we finish up the snow prep in time."

"Tomorrow's fine," I texted back.

Now that I knew the repair was scheduled, the occasional rattling of the door was merely another background noise, no more annoying than the clucking of the chickens or the humming of the llamas.

Although it wouldn't hurt to close it again. And remind Harris about the need to close it properly whenever Castlemayne left it hanging open. After all, given the fuss he made whenever anyone made the slightest noise in the hallway outside the library, surely the banging noise was interfering with his concentration.

I shoved my notebook in my tote and reluctantly heaved my foot off the hay bale. Dad had ordered me to elevate it a minimum of two hours a day. Yesterday I hadn't come close, and I wasn't optimistic about today.

As I was about to pull the barn door closed, I spotted another car coming down the road from town. I ducked back into the barn and peered out. Maybe it was someone going to visit one of the four farms that were farther along the road. Or someone heading for their storage unit at the Spare Attic, which was right by the creek where the road dead-ended.

No such luck. The car slowed down and stopped. A few seconds later I heard a car door slamming and footsteps tapping up our front walk.

So instead of dealing with Castlemayne and the unfastened sunroom door I went in through the kitchen. Better to tackle the latest visitor with a solid wood door between us, just in case.

As I stepped into the kitchen, I heard voices coming from the dining room.

"Oh, no, I can get it." Rose Noire said.

"No, let me do it," Mother replied. "I know you've dealt with way too many unwanted visitors lately.

Actually, Rose Noire hadn't, because everyone else in the house knew how softhearted she was and always tried to keep her from answering the door. She'd not only let in the persistent reporter yesterday—she'd served him tea and cookies and was in the middle of giving him a tarot reading when I found them. Luckily I managed to kick him out before he'd managed to sneak off and badger Castlemayne.

"Don't worry," I called as I limped past. "I'll get it."

I reached the front door and peered through the peephole. A redheaded woman stood on our doorstep, fingering the fresh holly garlands that were wound around the porch columns. Not the woman who'd started staking out the zoo after I chased her away—yet another redhead. About the same age or a little older—forties or fifties. A

natural redhead this time, to judge from her pale, freck-
led skin. She wasn't wearing a hat—foolish in this weather.
Her hair was pulled back in a low, loose ponytail. So was
this the ex-wife? In which case, who was the woman I'd
fended off earlier—another bill collector? Another reporter?

No use waiting around to find out. I took a deep breath
and opened the door a foot or so.

Chapter 9

The latest visitor greeted me with a slight smile.

"Yes?" I kept my tone—well, friendly would be an exaggeration. Carefully neutral. After all, there was always the possibility that she was a cousin I hadn't seen in years, dropping by for a little holiday visit.

She looked at me for a couple of seconds. Then her smile widened.

"It's Meg, isn't it?" she said. "I'd know you anywhere. And, of course, Delaney's told me so much about you."

I suddenly realized that this must be Delaney's mother and was overwhelmed with guilt—I'd been treating her as if she were just another stalker.

"You must be Mrs. McKenna," I said. "Come in. So sorry if I seemed unwelcoming, but we've had some persistent annoying callers lately."

I stepped aside and motioned for her to enter.

"Oh, that's all right." She stepped in and gave me a quick birdlike hug. "I don't expect anyone told you I was coming. And it's just Holly. No need to stand on formality when we're about to become family."

"A little sooner than you and Mother expected," I said. "She'll be delighted that you're here—she's in the dining room. Let me take you back there."

Mother and Rose Noire were there, holding up napkins against the various Christmas decorations—apparently they were deciding which of three almost indistinguishable shades of green looked best with the rest of the holiday decor. They looked up when we walked in and from the look of delight that spread across Mother's face after a few seconds I realized she had either recognized Delaney's mother or deduced her identity.

"You must be Holly!" Mother exclaimed. "I'd know you anywhere!"

Hugs. Air kisses. Exclamations of delight. I could tell Mother and Holly were well on their way to becoming brand-new best friends. Rose Noire allowed herself to be introduced and then slipped away, bearing the napkin candidates with her.

I wondered if I should warn Rob and Delaney that the mothers had joined forces and would be plotting against them. As if reading my mind, they turned in unison and fixed me with stern looks.

"You mustn't tell Delaney and Rob that I'm here," Holly said. "Please! Promise me that."

"I'm sure Meg understands how disappointing we would find that," Mother added.

"I promise I won't tell them," I said. "But if they figure it out, I won't lie to them, either."

They appeared to study me for a few seconds. Then their tense faces relaxed, and they exchanged a smile.

"We should probably make sure you keep a low profile," Mother said, turning to Holly. "Ordinarily, I'm sure Meg could find a bedroom for you—"

"But it would be too difficult, trying to dodge Rob and Delaney if I were staying here," she said. "Rob still lives here, doesn't he? Don't worry—I've got a room at the Caerphilly Inn."

"And besides, we've got at least three dozen family members either staying here or coming and going regularly for meals," Mother said. "Most of them are perfectly reliable, of course, but in any crowd there are bound to be a few people who can't resist the urge to gossip."

"Dad, for example," I suggested. "He always means to keep secrets, but he's very bad at remembering who he's supposed to be keeping them from. And, of course, Roderick Castlemayne's not to be trusted an inch. If he knew we wanted something kept secret, he'd probably tell the world, just to spite us."

"Roderick Castlemayne?" Holly sounded puzzled. "The name sounds vaguely familiar—is he part of the family?"

"No, an unwanted houseguest at the moment," I said. "A painter who's staying for the time being while he does some wildlife paintings for Grandfather."

"I have an idea," Mother said. "Let's go have tea in Rose Noire's greenhouse."

Mother bustled into the kitchen. We followed her. Holly sat at the kitchen table, gazing around with undisguised curiosity. I limped over to the window and peered out. The sunroom door was still loose and banging. Probably rude to run out right after Holly had arrived. As soon as she and Mother headed out to the greenhouse, I'd go and deal with the door.

"Where is this artist person that I should be avoiding?" Holly asked.

"In the library, which is at the other end of the house." I pointed in the general direction of the library. "Don't worry—he doesn't come out much—at least not when Mother and I are here. I annoy him, and she scares him."

"Don't be silly, Meg," Mother scoffed.

"Speak of the devil." I was still peering out of the back window and had spotted something. "My latest no-smoking-in-the-house ultimatum seems to have had an effect. He's actually gone outside to have his cigarette."

Mother and Holly dashed over to peer over my shoulder. They watched in silence as Castlemayne pulled a new cigarette from his pack, lit up from the stub in his hand, and tossed aside the butt.

"There's a perfectly good outdoor ashtray not two feet away from him," Mother said. "I set it up myself. I have half a mind to go out there and make him police the flower bed."

"What a dissolute-looking man," Holly exclaimed. "I suppose you have to make allowances for the creative temperament, but still. I shall definitely do my best to avoid him."

"We'll wait till he goes back inside," Mother said. "Such a rude, nasty man."

So I stood at the window where I could let them know when Castlemayne finished his second cigarette, tossed the butt into the flower bed, and stomped back inside. Leaving the sunroom door still banging freely. I sighed in exasperation.

But I had to laugh when Mother and Holly set out across the backyard, both glancing over their shoulders at the sunroom door before half-running across the open space and disappearing behind the barn. A few minutes later they reappeared in the distance as they slipped into Rose Noire's combination herb drying shed and greenhouse.

The basement door opened and Kevin stuck his head out.

"Another relative arriving?" he asked.

Kevin wasn't a gossip. But he worked for Mutant Wizards, Rob's company. He was close to Rob and Delaney and probably shared their jaundiced view of big weddings.

"Friend of Mother's," I said. "They've gone off to plan some big project. You might want to give both of them a wide berth—any time now they could get to the stage where they start recruiting volunteers to do the heavy lifting."

"Gotcha." He pulled the door closed, and I could hear his footsteps hurrying down the stairs.

I opened the door to call after him.

"By the way, Manoj will be over any time now to collect the wombats."

Widget, his Pomeranian, barked twice as if to acknowledge what I'd said. Kevin remained silent. Probably still sulking over the impending loss of the wombats.

I decided to venture into the basement.

I found Kevin in his lair, a combination bedroom and computer workroom at one end of the main basement. I didn't see any sign of the wombats, so I assumed he was keeping them in what we called the basement annex—the part of the basement that was under the library and had only dirt floors.

"I heard you," he said. "Wombats returning to the zoo—check."

"Good," I said. "And I'm probably going to regret asking, but are you taking the wombats outside to poop and pee?"

"It's too cold for that," Kevin said. "And it's not as if they're leash-trained or anything."

"So you're turning our basement into a wombat litterbox." I repressed several pungent comments that I knew would have no effect on him.

"We clean it up once a day or so," Kevin said. "And their droppings are cubic, you know." He made it sound as if their unusual shape made it okay to have them deposited in our basement. "Take a look. I saved a couple of particularly good ones."

He pointed to a shoebox on the floor. In it were half a dozen brown objects. They were, indeed, cubic, with surprisingly flat sides and rounded corners.

"Nifty," I said. "They look like dice. Maybe you can preserve them and use them in your Dungeons and Dragons games."

For a moment Kevin looked thoughtful, as if he were taking my sarcastic suggestion quite seriously.

"Yeah, but they only come in six-sided," he said. "You need a lot of other kinds of dice for a D and D game. Four-sided, eight-sided, ten-sided—"

"I'm sure the wombats can be trained," I said. "Or would it require selective breeding? Grandfather can probably figure it out. Meanwhile, I want them gone. They're going home for the holidays. Have them ready to travel."

I went back upstairs, closed the basement door, and made sure it was latched. Then I set out to deal with the sunroom door. And Castlemayne. My ankle was starting to ache a little, so on my way through the front hall I grabbed the shepherd's crook, in case I needed it.

I was six feet away from the library door when the screaming started.

Chapter 10

It was a woman screaming. She appeared to be alternating primal screams with shrieks of "Bastard! Bastard!"—with or without the F-bomb as a modifier. And Castlemayne was roaring back at her.

"Get the hell out of here!" he bellowed. "Stupid cow! You're trespassing!" And more of the same, increasingly laced with obscenities.

I recognized the woman's voice—it was the ex-wife. The blond one I'd had to chase away several times yesterday. I stopped a few feet from the doorway and pulled out my cell phone.

"Nine-one-one—what's your emergency, Meg?" Debbie Ann asked.

"We have a trespasser," I said. "The blond woman who had to be escorted off the premises yesterday. She's back. I think she got into the house through the library door, and now she and Castlemayne are going at it hammer and tongs."

Just then I heard a sound of glass shattering. Or possibly china.

"And she's breaking things," I said. "Or Castlemayne is."

"Horace is a few minutes away," she said. "And Vern might actually beat him there. Stand by."

"Roger."

"Stand by" probably meant that I should keep the library door closed and wait for the cavalry. But just then I heard something else shatter, and I couldn't stand it. I pulled out my keys, unlocked the library door, and opened it a foot or so, just enough that I could peek in.

Castlemayne was up on the balcony, leaning over the railing and shouting imprecations and obscenities down at the woman. She was standing directly below him, shaking her fist. On the floor around her were the shattered remains of the dishes in which I'd served breakfast. Harris was nowhere to be seen.

She made a sudden rush for the spiral wrought-iron staircase that led up to the balcony. He ran to the top of the staircase and began lobbing heavy books down at her. She began kicking the staircase in frustration.

"Stop it! Both of you! Stop this minute!" I shouted.

The woman turned, uttered another primal scream, and threw a coffee mug at me. I dodged and heard it shatter against the door behind me. Then she began lumbering toward me, hands outstretched as if she intended to throttle me. She was plump, sedentary-looking, and almost half a foot shorter than me, but her eyes glittered with a look of near-insane anger, and I knew better than to let her any closer. I held up the crook and aimed the bottom of it at her stomach. She ran right into it, knocking her own breath out—mercifully that put an end to the shrieking, at least for the moment. Before she could get her breath back, I used the crook to shove her backward until I had her pinned against the wall beside the staircase.

"Take that, bitch," Castlemayne said.

"Not another word from you," I snapped. "Or when the cops get here, I'll have them haul you away, too. I'm sure they can find something amusing to charge you with."

He shrugged but at least he shut up. He leaned against the railing and looked down at us. He was still doing that, and his ex-wife was starting to spit out the occasional breathless insult as she scrabbled uselessly at the crook, when Horace and Vern ran in—Horace through the French doors from the sunroom and Vern from the hallway behind me. Horace had his hand on his service weapon. Vern actually had his out.

"You can let her go now, Meg." Vern holstered his revolver and stepped up beside me. "If she's smart, she'll behave herself. And if she doesn't—well, assaulting a police officer is a class-six felony. Six-month mandatory minimum sentence."

I wasn't sure which was more impressive—the fact that Vern appeared to have memorized the entire criminal code of Virginia or the clever way he used it to help defuse situations like this. The ex-wife gave him a look that ought to have qualified as simple assault, but she pulled herself together and stopped fighting against the crook. I cautiously tugged it away.

"Did you invite her in?" Vern asked.

"No," I said.

"He did," the ex-wife said, jerking her head in Castlemayne's direction.

"Did not," Castlemayne said.

"Trespassing," Vern said. "Which one of them broke all your nice crockery?"

"He did," the ex-wife snapped.

"She did," Castlemayne said, almost at the same time.

"I have no idea," I said. "She threw a coffee mug at me."

"Did it hit you?" Vern asked.

"No, it just broke against the door." I pointed to where the remnants of the mug lay, surrounded by a wide area where the coffee had splashed.

"Still simple assault." Vern smiled with visible satisfaction.

"She hit me with that . . . that . . . thing," the ex-wife snarled. "And he hit me."

"Not until Maddie hit me first," Castlemayne said.

"Horace, why don't you take some pictures of the damage here," Vern said. "Maybe take possession of that broken crockery as evidence. I'll take Ms. Castlemayne down to the station for booking, and we'll get another deputy out here to haul in the gent."

Vern led the ex-wife away. She didn't struggle, but she told him exactly what she thought of the situation, of him, and of his ancestors—at the top of her lungs, all the way down the long hallway to the front door.

I decided not to leave Horace alone with Castlemayne. I limped over to the nearest comfy chair and sat down. My ankle hurt again—if that wretched woman made me aggravate my sprain—

"Everything quiet here?"

I looked up to see Chief Burke standing in the doorway.

"Vern took in the trespasser," Horace said. "I expect she'll want to file charges against Castlemayne."

"Baseless charges." Castlemayne assumed an air of great dignity. "I, of course, wish to file assault charges against her."

"Why don't you come down to the station with me, then?" the chief said. "And we can sort out all of that."

Castlemayne sighed as if to imply that this was a horrible imposition, but he didn't protest. He stomped a little on his way down the spiral staircase, but picked up his winter coat and left the library without a word.

"Grandfather wouldn't like it if you kept him in jail," I said as the chief turned to go. "Since he's already way behind on his schedule. But everyone else around here would celebrate. Having him here for the holidays is like playing host to the Grinch and Ebenezer Scrooge."

"I'll keep that in mind." He smiled briefly, then turned to go.

"If you're finished taking photos, I'd like to start cleaning up in here," I said to Horace. "And take a few photos of my own so I can explain to Grandfather why I'm kicking his artist out."

"Almost finished—start with the books."

I picked up the books that had landed downstairs—twenty-three of them. Luckily, only two of them seemed damaged, and I wasn't sure I could prove it was new damage. I hauled them all up to the second story and put them back in their proper spaces on the shelves.

"Finished," Horace said. "I'll see you later when I pick up Watson." He strolled out, carrying several brown evidence bags that contained the bulk of the broken objects.

"Laters." I began cleaning up the spilled food. And grabbed a couple of clean white rags from Harris's supply to deal with the stains. The coffee from the smashed mug had only splashed on the wood of the door and the nearby floor, so it was easy to clean up, but the greasy stains on the carpet defied my efforts, as did the bits of ground-in egg and jam. I texted a picture to Mother, who knew a stain-removal wizard—and more important, could talk said wizard into making an emergency house call if needed.

I was doing a spot inspection for places where the egg or jam might have gotten on books when the door opened and Harris scurried in.

"I had to go to two places before I found—oh!" He looked startled. "What are you doing here? Where's Mr. Castlemayne? He didn't go looking for me, did he?"

Harris looked terrified at the prospect.

"He's down at the police station," I said. "Filing assault charges against his ex-wife—the blond one. And possibly having her file assault charges against him."

"Oh, my God." He turned pale. "What happened?"

So I gave him a blow-by-blow account of the battle. Probably a good thing he hadn't been around to see it happen—just hearing about it seemed to stress him to the limit.

"Oh, dear. Oh, dear." He sat on the edge of one of the

sofas, shoulders hunched, hands clasped. "She's dangerous. They'll see that, won't they? And keep her in jail?"

"Probably not." I sat down on the facing sofa and elevated my ankle. "The chief tends to be softhearted about
letting people spend the holidays with their families. Unless she hauls off and punches the arresting officer, and
she doesn't look quite that stupid. Still, we can hope."

"He'll be expecting me to protect him," Harris said.

"Surely not," I said. Which probably wasn't the most
tactful thing to say. Castlemayne, who was in his sixties,
might be past his prime, but he still seemed like someone
who could take care of himself in a fight. Harris, on the
other hand, though half his employer's age, looked as if
he'd keel over in a stiff breeze, and I wouldn't bet on him
in a fight—not even if his opponent were one of the Pomeranians. But men, even feckless, weedy ones like poor
Harris, always took it so badly if you called their fighting
prowess into question, so I hastened to clarify. "She's *his*
ex-wife. Why in the world would he expect *you* to fight that
battle for him?"

"He expects me to do everything else." Harris's tone was
sharper than I'd have expected. Maybe he had some back-
bone after all. "I'm sorry. That sounded ungrateful, didn't
it? And I don't really feel that way. After all, it's a privilege
to work for someone as brilliant as Mr. Castlemayne. And
I'm learning so much from him."

"Like what?" Probably not a tactful question, but it just
slipped out.

"About technique," he said. "And staying true to your
artistic vision. And I'm making so many contacts in the
art world."

"Technique," I echoed. "You paint yourself, then?"

"Yes." His face lit up. "Of course, my own work's nothing like that." He gestured dismissively toward the easel
where the half-finished blue jay picture stood. "I mean,
representational art is so . . . obvious, you know? My work

tries to bring out the inner reality of the world instead of copying its mundane outward appearances—we have photography for that. But there doesn't seem to be much of a market for my kind of work these days, so I'm very grateful to Mr. Castlemayne for hiring me. At least I'm still in touch with the art world. And he's demanding, but he pays reasonably well."

"That's good," I said. "Because I'm sure you have that inconvenient habit of having to eat every so often."

It took a couple of seconds, but he chuckled at my admittedly feeble joke.

"Oh, yes," said. "Eating, and paying the rent, and then there are the student loans. I went to the Rhode Island School of Design, you know."

I hadn't known, but I was impressed. "Excellent school," I said.

"But not cheap." He sighed. "My student loan debt is bigger than many people's mortgages. And if I lost this job, I'd have a hard time finding another that paid as well. So maybe I should go down to the police station and see what he wants me to do."

"Let me give you the names of a couple of good defense attorneys." I took out my notebook, pulled out a blank page, and jotted down a few names and numbers. "Just in case he needs one."

"Thanks." He took the paper, read it carefully—was he checking to see if he could decipher my handwriting?—then folded it and tucked it into his wallet. "I'll see you later."

"By the way," I said. "My nephew Kevin is going to set up some surveillance equipment. A security camera or two. I'll see if he can do it while you're both out to minimize the interruption."

"In case Madeleine comes back." Harris nodded.

"Well, that too," I said. "But mostly so I can keep an eye on your boss and make sure he stops stinking up our library with his cigarettes. Cameras, and maybe a smoke alarm." I'd only just thought of the smoke alarm, but I was pretty sure Kevin could manage it.

Harris froze.

"Oh, dear," he said. "I assumed you meant cameras to guard the doors. Cameras inside here? He wouldn't like that."

"I don't imagine he will," I said. "But I'm tired of telling him not to smoke in our house. He either takes it outside or I'll kick him out immediately."

"But—" Harris cut himself off and looked at me for a long moment, with an expression of sad reproach. "I'll tell him. When he's calm again. Meanwhile, the sooner I get down to the police station the better. It's going to be hard to get him back on track after all this. Please make sure your grandfather knows that it's not really Mr. Castlemayne's fault about today."

He put on his oversized and antiquated coat, which reeked strongly of mothballs and transformed him into a reasonable facsimile of those well-muffled and shapeless Edwardian gentlemen who frequently appear in Edward Gorey's cartoons. He replaced his wide-brimmed indoor hat with a plaid wool cap that featured generous ear flaps. Then he plodded grimly out of the library.

Chapter 11

The library was quiet and peaceful again. A pity it wouldn't stay that way for long. I leaned back and focused on my ankle. Which was throbbing. I had probably reinjured it doing battle with Maddie—was it Maddie Castlemayne? Or had she given up his name? Assuming she'd ever taken it in the first place. I didn't actually know. And I wasn't sure I cared. Though it might be useful to know in case I had to phone in any more police reports on her.

I glanced up at the library clock. It was nearly one. I'd been awake for six hours, and on my feet for way too much of that time.

"I've been overdoing it," I said—to no one in particular. It wasn't as if the jays were listening. Someone had recently replenished their seed bowls and they were loudly squabbling over the goodies. "I'm taking to my bed."

I eased myself carefully upright. The stab of pain I felt in my ankle when I put weight on it assured me that I was making a wise decision. I snagged the shepherd's crook and used that for support as I limped over to make sure both the sunroom door and the French doors were closed and locked. Then I locked up the library and made my way slowly and carefully down the hall.

When I reached the hall, I heard a soft knock on the door. Call me paranoid, but it was exactly the kind of knock I might try to get away with if I were inclined to be sneaky and wanted to justify saying "But I knocked and no one answered." I limped over and peered through the peephole.

I recognized the person slinking off the front porch—Justin Vreeland, the reporter from the *Washington Star-Tribune* who'd badgered me half a dozen times yesterday. I threw the door open so violently that he uttered a startled yelp and whirled to face me.

"You're trespassing, Justin," I said. "And don't tell me you didn't know it. Your car is parked right in front of one of our nice new No Trespassing signs."

"You're interfering with the freedom of the press." He thrust out his chin truculently. Combined with his stoop-shouldered posture and scrawny frame, this gesture made him look like an underfed buzzard.

"Freedom of the press means you have the right to circulate news and express opinions without government censorship." I'd consulted my lawyer cousin Festus on how to respond to this claim of Justin's. "It doesn't mean anyone has to talk to you if they don't want to, and it sure as hell doesn't give you the right to harass me repeatedly, much less sneak into our house like you did yesterday."

"Aw, come on." He'd changed his approach, and was favoring me with what he clearly intended to be an ingratiating smile. Maybe even a flirtatious one. I decided I preferred him truculent. Did he really think he was going to get anywhere by batting his eyes at me? I wasn't particularly susceptible to tactics like that from attractive men. From someone who'd have been perfect in the role of the white rat Cinderella's fairy godmother turned into a coachman? Forget it.

"I just need a comment from Castlemayne about the newest lawsuit filed against him," Justin said.

Okay, I admit that roused my curiosity. I had deduced from accusations Maddie had made yesterday that their lawyers were dueling over his failure to pay alimony, and from what Castlemayne and Harris had said I suspected the same thing was happening to the other ex-wife. Had one of them gotten fed up and filed a lawsuit? Or was this another round in the legal battle between him and the folks at whichever wildlife organization was suing him? For all I knew he could have other legal entanglements I hadn't even heard of yet.

But in spite of my curiosity, I kept my face neutral and my mouth shut. If someone really had filed another lawsuit, I could read about it when the *Star-Tribune* printed Justin's article. Better yet, the Caerphilly Confidential website probably already had the scoop. The last thing I wanted was to be misquoted in either. And however tempting it might be to reveal that Castlemayne wasn't even on the premises at the moment—bad idea. With luck, Justin would leave before the police brought Castlemayne back.

"I'm serious, Justin," I said. "You're trespassing. I have nothing to say to you. I want you to stop harassing us. Don't even think of trying to sneak in the back door again—if you don't get off our property, I'm calling the police."

I deliberately turned my back on him, shut the door, and twisted the knob to engage the deadbolt. But I immediately put my eye to the peephole to see what he did.

He frowned at our front steps for a while and glanced up, as if considering whether to knock again. He aimed a disgruntled but halfhearted kick at the steps. Then he glanced to his left and seemed to hesitate. Probably trying to decide if I was serious about calling the police. I had my cell phone at the ready. I wasn't sure whether I was relieved or disappointed when he grimaced, turned, and strode back to his car. I was a little surprised when he actually got in and drove off. But his car had been headed away from town, and he drove off in that direction. The road deadended at the creek a few miles farther along, but maybe he hadn't figured that out yet. I waited a minute or so, to give him time to make a U-turn. When I didn't see him drive by on his way back to town, I went into the living room and peered out of the window there. He had made a U-turn all right, but instead of heading back to town he had parked on the other side of the road, just beyond the farthest No Trespassing sign. And he was staring with his binoculars along the left side of the house—the side where the library was.

Damn. Justin the Weasel was at it again. Someone should keep an eye on the creep.

I texted Rose Noire.

"Can you keep an eye out for unwanted callers?" I said. "My ankle's bothering me. Going upstairs to rest."

"Okay," she said. "Do you need anything?"

"No thanks," I texted back. I was in no mood to fend off her attempts to get me to drink whatever herbal tea was good for sprained ankles, since her herbal teas invariably tasted ghastly. I wouldn't have minded some of her all-natural organic salve, the one with a penetrating but not unpleasant odor of wintergreen, peppermint, camphor, menthol, and eucalyptus. But I was too tired to risk a battle over the tea.

I shoved my phone back in my pocket and limped on, leaning heavily on the bannister when I was going upstairs.

Any other year I'd have been stressed to the max at retreating to bed for the afternoon so close to Christmas— and so soon after spending two full days in bed. But when we made our plans to take the boys for their skiing trip— which served as their Really Big Present for this year—I knew I couldn't possibly enjoy it unless I cleared my schedule. I'd finished most of my holiday preparations early. What I couldn't do in advance I'd either delegated or postponed. I'd been all set to take off for the mountains of West Virginia with my notebook-that-tells-me-when-to-breathe as close to empty as I'd seen it in a decade.

And then came the sprained ankle. Which wouldn't have happened if Castlemayne hadn't set the mockingbirds free, and then slammed into the ladder I was climbing up to retrieve one of them, sending me and the ladder flying. I sent a few venomous thoughts his way and then tried to clear my mind. Rose Noire's latest mind-cleansing technique was to imagine all your cares and fears and negative thoughts appearing on a giant movie screen and then rolling away to disappear in the distance, like the opening crawl in a Star Wars movie. I began imagining them all sailing off into the starfield—Castlemayne, both of his ex-wives, Justin Vreeland, yesterday's bill collector—even poor ineffectual Harris. I wasn't sure how effective this was at clearing my mind, but it was curiously satisfying to see all of them sailing off into the distance and eventually disappearing.

Upstairs I took some ibuprofen to fight the pain and inflammation. With luck all the ankle needed was a little rest. If it wasn't better by evening—no, make that morning—I'd have Dad take a look at it. But right now the last thing I wanted was another trip to the ER. I slipped between the sheets and sighed as I wriggled into a comfortable position. I glanced at the book on my bedside table. I'd do a little reading later. Right now I just wanted to relax.

My phone rang.

It was Mother.

"Meg, dear," she said. "Could you come out to Rose Noire's greenhouse? We'd like to run something by you."

"No," I said. "I think I reinjured my ankle while keeping Castlemayne's ex-wife from killing him just now. I plan to stay in bed—can't you tell me over the phone?"

"Oh, dear." Mother sounded genuinely worried—did I sound that bad? "Have you had lunch?"

"Not really hungry," I said.

"You can't not eat—we'll bring you a little something," she said. "Something light. You'll feel better. You just relax and we'll take care of it."

I attached my phone to the charger cable and burrowed in under the covers. I wasn't the least bit hungry. And I had no desire to hear whatever plan they wanted to rope me into. Maybe I could manage to be fast asleep by the time they got up here.

But to my relief, when she and Holly McKenna arrived, they seemed to have postponed any plans they had for enlisting me in their schemes.

"Chicken soup," Mother announced, setting a large mug on my bedside table. "And French bread."

"And hot chocolate." Holly set another, smaller mug down.

Then they both sat down and chatted. Just chatted—not a word about the crusade to foil Delaney and Rob's plans. Mother did most of the talking—Holly mostly sat, laughed with delight when Mother said something amusing, and studied her surroundings discreetly and unobtrusively. I rather approved—after all, she was meeting her only child's future in-laws in person for the first time. In her shoes, I'd be doing the same thing.

To my surprise, I found I had an appetite after all. And once I'd polished off the meal, Mother held her hand to my forehead for a moment, nodded her approval of my normal temperature, kissed me on the check, and tiptoed out with Holly in her wake.

I turned over and snuggled down in the covers. Maybe I'd manage a nap. Maybe—

"Woof."

I turned over and peered over the side of the bed. Spike stood there, looking cross, as if annoyed that I hadn't already provided whatever it was he wanted.

We stared at each other for few seconds. Then he barked again and touched the side of the bed lightly with one paw.

If it were any other dog, I'd assume he wanted to join me. Spike wasn't prone to this sort of togetherness. Not with me, anyway.

"You want to come up?"

He touched the side of the bed again.

Okay, I can take a hint. I sat up and reached over to lift him, bracing to jerk my hands away if he changed his mind and tried to bite. But he allowed me to pick him up and put him down on the bed. He shook himself, then walked to the opposite side of the bed, curled into a ball, and went to sleep.

He probably missed the boys. I could understand how he felt. Or maybe he just was getting much sneakier about lulling me into complacency.

I was in no mood to worry about it. I was in no mood to worry about anything. Mother and Caroline and Rose Noire would have to guard the fort for a while. I turned over and surrendered to the unfamiliar luxury of a long, lazy afternoon nap.

Chapter 12

The shadows were long when I woke up. Of course, since tonight was literally the shortest day of the year, it wasn't that late. Not quite four o'clock.

But tonight's big potluck dinner would be happening soon—earlier than usual, so the visiting relatives who weren't staying with us could get back to their beds before the snow started, or at least before the roads got bad.

I slipped out of bed and went over to the window. The snow had begun to fall—only lightly, but so much for getting everyone back before it started.

I could see cars parking on both sides of the road, and people making their way down the middle of the road and up the walk to our front door. Everyone was muffled up with only their eyes showing, and most carried foil-wrapped plates or covered casseroles for the potluck supper.

I didn't recall inviting quite this many people. But then, once she found out about my ankle, Mother insisted on organizing the dinners this week. If she'd invited more people than originally planned, she'd have made sure there would be enough food for them. Maybe I should work on spraining an ankle every December.

I could just stay in bed. Eventually someone would start worrying about me and bring up a tray.

But it occurred me that if I were one of Castlemayne's stalkers, I might be thinking this evening's festivities gave me a golden opportunity to sneak into the house under cover of the crowd. And I was the one who'd had to fend them off for the past couple of days. I was probably the only one who'd recognize them.

Suddenly I felt a lot more energetic.

Back on the bed, Spike gave one brisk bark. No doubt he was afraid of being marooned on the bed, which was slightly higher than he felt comfortable jumping down from.

"You want to get down?" I asked. He just stared back. I repeated the question several times, hoping to get across the point that when I picked him up, I'd be doing so at his own request and not for any nefarious purpose like taking him to the vet. Eventually he growled slightly and pawed at the edge of the bed, so I picked him up and put him down on the floor. He scurried off without a backward glance, and I could hear him going down the stairs. Probably hoping to find the boys had returned.

"Sorry," I said to his departing tail. "Not till tomorrow."

I grabbed my straw hat and my shepherd's crook and made my way downstairs more slowly.

The hall was filled with visiting friends and relatives. The hat-and-coat stand overflowed with wraps, and someone had brought out the portable rack we used for large parties. We'd run out of hats for the new arrivals, but Rob and Delaney and several teenage cousins were sitting on a floor in one corner of the hall, repurposing our stack of old newspapers by folding them into hats for the new arrivals. There was a line going into the dining room, and a stream of people exiting with plates and glasses in hand. The Pomeranians always reacted with enthusiasm to visitors—tonight's crowd had inspired them to truly manic excitement. And someone had tied big red bows to all their collars—we'd see how long that lasted.

I tried to take my place at the end of the buffet line, but as soon as the assembled guests spotted me limping up, they insisted on waving me past. In a few minutes, I found myself sitting in a chair near one corner of the dining room, with a glass of red wine at my elbow and a plate in my lap. I was relieved to see that all the elaborate food-themed holiday decorations Mother had set up on every horizontal surface had been cleared away to make room for real food in epic quantities: ham, turkey, roast beef, dressing, fried catfish, mashed potatoes, candied yams, macaroni and cheese, green bean casserole, tomato aspic, cranberry sauce, plum pudding, half a dozen different salads, and an uncountable variety of desserts. A steady stream of aunts and cousins dashed up to offer me servings of the various dishes, to the great satisfaction of my nephew Kevin, who was sitting on the floor to the right of my chair. He took large helpings of almost everything— especially the meat and cheese dishes that were suitable for consumption by the Pomeranians, who regularly raced up to beg for tidbits.

"How many of those things do you have, anyway?"

I glanced up to see Harris standing to my left. He had a plate in one hand and his back against the wall. He looked a little wild-eyed. Unlike the Pomeranians, he seemed to dislike crowds.

"How many of what things?" I asked.

"The n—noisy little dogs," he said.

I had the definite impression that he'd been about to say "nasty" and stopped himself. Curious—I wouldn't have taken him for an animal hater. Maybe he just didn't like small, yappy dogs. There were days when I could understand that feeling.

"Only two in residence," I said. "My cousin Rose Noire and my nephew Kevin both adopted puppies from a litter of seven the local vet rescued from a kill shelter. My cousin Horace and my friend Aida each adopted one—they're both Caerphilly County deputies, and when they're on duty, they like to drop off their puppies so they won't get lonely. And at the moment we're dog-sitting for the one that was adopted by Chief Burke's grandson, who's off skiing with my sons. The other two belong to the local librarian and the rector of Grace Episcopal, both good friends, so we sometimes have all seven back together."

"They're all here tonight," Kevin said, through a mouthful of potato salad.

Harris shuddered slightly.

"But they won't be for long," said a new voice. I looked up to see Aida Butler, still dressed in her deputy's uniform, holding a plate and waiting for the buffet line to move. "I'm finally off duty. Taking my fur baby home as soon as I finish dinner."

"Just make sure you take the right one this time," Kevin said.

"I didn't take your silly pup by mistake," Aida protested. "He smelled my bacon cheeseburger and jumped into my patrol car on his own."

"Do you have that much trouble telling them apart?" Harris asked.

"The owners don't," I said. "But the rest of us do. And it doesn't help that the people who adopted them all gave them names beginning with *W*. Horace has Watson, for example, and Kevin has Widget."

"I thought the one that lives here was Solstice," Harris said. "That's not spelled with a *W*."

"Yes, Rose Noire's dog," I said. "It's short for Winter Solstice. And Ms. Ellie had already named hers Teddy, but she made his official name Teddy Who. Robyn has Whatsit— named after the character from Madeleine L'Engle's *A Wrinkle in Time*. Adam Burke named his Willie Mays. And Aida's is Whatever."

"Whatever?" Harris looked puzzled.

"I was still trying to find a name," Aida said. "Which would have been hard enough even if I hadn't had all of them pressuring me to pick something that began with *W*. About the hundredth time they made a bunch of suggestions and told me I should hurry up and pick a name or the poor puppy would never learn to answer to it, I shrugged and said 'Whatever.' It stuck."

"I think it's a cool name," Kevin said.

"It's been useful." Aida chuckled. "Used to drive me crazy how Kayla, my daughter, was always saying 'whatever.' Now if she says it, the dog comes running up expecting a treat. I don't hear 'whatever' nearly as much as I used to."

"Good result," I said.

"Yeah." She sighed. "But I might need to adopt another puppy—one I can call 'As if.' I hear that a lot more than I like these days. Oops—line's moving."

She focused back on the table and began adding slices of country ham to her plate.

Just then Spike strolled up and stopped in front of me. He uttered a short, peremptory bark and stood, looking up at me and waiting, with an impatient air.

"That one looks different." Harris frowned at Spike, who glanced at him and curled his lip in a perfunctory growl before returning his stare to me.

"Completely different breed." Kevin managed to refrain from his habitual eye roll, but you could almost hear it in his tone.

"He's an adult dog who finds the puppies annoying," I added. And some days, I could see his point of view. I braced myself, bent down, picked up Spike, and set him in a vacant dining room chair on the other side of Kevin. Spike turned around the requisite three times and curled up for a nap. This was a new routine and still rather unsettling—not the turning around or the napping, but Spike expecting me to pick him up. Normally he was quite ready to bite even hands that were feeding him—with the exception of Jamie and Josh, who had somehow won his evil little heart. When they were small, we'd had a hard time keeping him from lunging at anyone who came anywhere near the boys. But these days whenever the twins were absent, he considered me the human responsible for feeding him, letting him in and out, and rescuing him from the annoying attentions of the Pom Bunch. And I knew better than to say "you're safe now" and give him a reassuring pat on the head—the minute he was out of the puppies' reach, I reverted to just another human who needed biting. I had the scars to prove it.

"So, do you prefer cats, then?" I asked Harris as I sat down again.

"No." Harris wrinkled his nose slightly. "Nasty things. I'm allergic to them."

"But not to dogs?"

"Not that I know of." From the way he was looking at Spike, I suspected he'd probably claim a fictitious allergy and use that as an excuse to move elsewhere if there were anyplace else in town to go. I knew for a fact that he'd called at least two bed-and-breakfasts in town to see if they had any vacancies. "Probably just as well I didn't have any," one of the B&B owners had confided to me. "He sounded a little faint when I told him our room rate."

"If it makes you feel any better, we keep them out of the library," I said to Harris. "Since they're still at the age when they think everything's a chew toy."

"Good to know," he said. "I should be going. You think anyone would mind if I cut in line to fill a plate for Mr. Castlemayne? The line's gotten so much longer—I'm afraid if I have to wait on it he'll get impatient and come barging out yelling that he's starving. He likes his dinner promptly at seven, and it's almost that now."

"I gather he's back from his visit to the police station, then," I said.

"We got back an hour ago," Harris said.

"And I bet it didn't improve his temper."

"No." Harris shuddered slightly.

"That'll be fine, then," I said. "Not that he wouldn't be welcome to come out and join the party if he wants to." I hoped Harris would recognize this as a polite fiction.

"Probably better if he doesn't." Harris winced, as if recalling past disasters that had occurred when his boss had been turned loose on unsuspecting dinner parties.

"By the way," I said. "Having him work here in our library was an interesting experiment, but it's not working out. He needs to go back to the zoo. Break it to him if you like, or you can wait till tomorrow and I'll tell him. But he's got to go."

"Oh, dear." Harris turned pale. "I can't say I'm surprised, but—um, do you want me to leave as well?"

"Goodness, no," I said. "You haven't caused any problems. You're welcome to stay. Probably be a nice change, having him a few miles away instead of within shouting distance."

"I suppose so." Harris grimaced. "He won't like it, though. If it's all the same to you, I'll let you break the news tomorrow. I should go fill his plate."

Evidently he'd spotted the gap in the line, caused by Aunt Esme's close scrutiny of the ingredients of several casseroles near the beginning of the buffet. He hurried off.

"What a weirdo," Kevin muttered. "He actually ran away this afternoon."

Chapter 13

"Ran away?" That didn't sound like Harris. "Why?"

"He kind of freaked out when he saw us loading up the wombats."

Not evidence that Harris was a weirdo, if you asked me. More like proof of his sanity.

"So the wombats are back at the zoo?" I made a mental note to thank Mother and Caroline.

"Mmph na gromaph," he said. At least that's what it sounded like, thanks to the large mouthful of roast beef he'd just taken. But since he also nodded, I assumed his undecipherable words were some kind of affirmative.

"Great," I said. "And did you find the time to install those cameras we talked about?"

"Cameras?" He looked blank for a few seconds. "Oh, right. Cameras. For the library and the doors."

"That's right."

"I sort of ran out of time to work on that," he said. "What with all the logistics of moving the wombats back to the zoo. And then I used the equipment I had to set up the Wombat Cam."

"Ah, so we have a Wombat Cam now." Not a surprise.

"Yeah—wait till you see." He pulled out his phone and began tapping on it. "Here—I'll send you the link."

My phone dinged. I pulled it out and clicked on the link he'd texted me. I could see two furry mounds, illuminated by a shaft of light.

"Sleeping wombats, I assume."

"They're nocturnal, you know." Kevin was staring

fixedly at his own phone. "Almost sunset, so they'll be up and around soon. And watch this."

He did something with his phone. Suddenly the two furry mounds were glowing a faint, icy blue.

"Great told me he didn't want the UV light on all the time," he explained, using the nickname his cousins Josh and Jamie had invented for their great-grandfather. "Could interfere with their metabolisms or something. So I set up a web-based on-off switch."

"Cool!" Rob had appeared and was looking over my shoulder. "Bioluminescence!"

"Bio*fluor*escence," Kevin corrected.

"There's a difference?" Rob asked.

"Bioluminescence is when something actually emits light because of a chemical reaction," Kevin said. "Like a firefly. With biofluorescence the organism absorbs low-level light and then sends it back out again as a glow. Kind of built in and automatic, like in the wombat's fur."

Clearly Kevin had been paying a reasonable amount of attention to Grandfather's lectures on marsupials.

"Still pretty cool, whatever you call it." Rob tried to take possession of my phone and I slapped his hand away.

"I need that," I said. "Indulge your marsupial voyeurism on your own phone—Kevin would be happy to text you the link."

"Sure thing." Kevin tapped on his phone, and soon he and Rob were both glued to their screens.

I glanced down at my own phone. The two furry lumps were still motionless. The soft glow of their fur was appealing, but apart from that I couldn't quite see the fascination.

Maybe wombat watching was a guy thing. Or at least a guy-in-my-family thing. When I looked up, Horace and Grandfather were peering over Rob's and Kevin's shoulders.

It occurred to me that Josh and Jamie might feel deprived if they found out that they'd missed the wombats' brief stay with us. Perhaps the Wombat Cam would help ease their disappointment.

I texted the link to Michael, adding "Wombat Cam—in case the boys need some kind of amusement when it gets too dark to ski."

"Awesome!" he texted back. And then my phone rang.

"I decided I'm too tired to text more than a word or two," he said. "So how was your day?"

I filled him in. Caroline's arrival. Holly McKenna's arrival—after a quick glance to make sure Rob was out of earshot. Castlemayne's various visitors, including the combative ex-wife.

"We need to get rid of him," Michael said. "Don't you worry about it—when I get back tomorrow, I'll deal with it."

"Actually, with luck I can guilt-trip Mother and Caroline into dealing with it tomorrow morning," I said. "They managed to evict the wombats this afternoon while I was napping. I think they're ready for bigger game."

"He won't know what hit him. I should go—all three boys have informed me that they are on the very brink of starvation. Love you!"

I took a final glance at the Wombat Cam before shoving my phone back into my pocket. Rob was helping Grandfather by carrying his plate as he went around the buffet table. Horace was filling his own plate, somewhat hampered by the fact that he was carrying Watson on one shoulder, like a baby.

I glanced down and saw five more Pomeranians sitting in a circle around Kevin, waiting their turns as he handed out small chunks of chicken.

"When you've finished eating, why don't you gather up the Pomeranians and take them downstairs to play," I suggested.

"People like seeing them," he said.

"I'm sure they do," I said. "But the house is getting pretty crowded. What happens if some elderly aunt trips over them?"

"People should watch where they're going." He didn't seem overly upset over this possibility.

"Or worse, what if someone steps on one of them?" I added. "Someone big enough to injure them—or one of the cousins wearing spike heels?"

"Good point." He heaved himself off the floor, picked up two of the Pomeranians, and began threading his way through the crowd with the other three Poms at his heels.

I glanced over at Spike's chair. He was watching the puppies' departure with a puzzled expression, as if unsure whether to be glad they were gone or upset that they might be heading off to receive some treat denied to him.

I felt so sorry for him that I cut off a small piece of roast beef, set it on a napkin, and slid the napkin onto the chair seat beside him. He gazed down at it in astonishment for a few seconds, then inhaled the whole piece.

"Trying to tame the savage beast?" Aida reappeared, dragging a chair with her, and took a seat at my side.

"He leads a hard life these days," I said. "The Poms outnumber him. So what happened with Castlemayne and his ex down at the station?"

"They both filed charges, and we got them both lawyers, and now they've both got court dates on the twenty-third," she said. "I gather this isn't the first time they've done this particular dance."

"Not surprising," I said.

"By the way, what was the deal about the stalker at the zoo?" she asked. "They sent me down to check on her, but by the time I got there she'd disappeared."

"Bother," I said. "Then again, maybe she saw your cruiser and decided to make herself scarce. If she comes back, I'll call nine-one-one again. I don't know for sure, but I think she might be Castlemayne's other ex-wife, and I don't want another pitched battle in our library."

"Please," Aida said. "His other ex-wife? There can't possibly be two women on the planet crazy enough to marry that old goat."

"There must have been. We don't just have his word for it—Harris confirms it," I said. "At least they both saw the light and dumped him."

"There is that. I gather Harris is the long-suffering assistant who showed up to bail out his boss?"

I nodded.

"The ex-wife give you any reason to think she might get physical?" she asked.

"Apart from literally trying to push her way into the house, no," I said. "And she's not going to win that game— I've got half a foot on her, and I don't think she does anything nearly as physical as blacksmithing."

"Good deal." She studied her plate, her fork hovering between a bit of ham and the mac and cheese. "By the way, what about—"

"Mockingbird! Mockingbird!"

I wasn't sure who started the cry, but soon at least a dozen people were shrieking the same thing. The few new arrivals looked around in confusion while the family and any visitors who had been around a day or two hastily covered their plates. In a well-practiced routine, Mother and Rose Noire protected the food on the dining room table with a couple of old but clean tablecloths from a stash we'd begun keeping nearby. Which would have been dangerous to do to the sideboard, given all the little fires burning under the chafing dishes, so we'd been strict about having only covered dishes there. And within seconds at least half the guests were holding napkins or sweaters at the ready and looking around for a chance to pounce on the intruder.

"He won't come down if you're all staring at him," Rob said.

"Try to look nonchalant, everyone," Kevin added.

Everyone immediately began ostentatiously pretending not to be staring up into the overhead Christmas decorations. I decided to do something more practical. I reached under the napkin that covered my plate and began tossing bits of my fruit salad on top of the gingham-shrouded table.

A grape. A bit of strawberry. According to Grandfather, mockingbirds were very fond of fruit. Another bit of strawberry.

The mockingbird swooped down. At least half a dozen people whooped and pounced. Caroline emerged victorious.

"Got him!" she crowed.

"Dammit, don't kill the poor thing," Grandfather shouted.

"Remember, it's a sin to kill a mockingbird," Kevin intoned, in a fair imitation of Gregory Peck as Atticus Finch in what had long been one of our family's favorite movies.

Caroline and Grandfather hurried off with the prisoner, and the rest of us pitched in to restore the dining room to order. Within a few minutes the party was back on track, and I probably wasn't the only person feeling more cheerful at the thought that the mockingbird infestation was down to a single wily bird. When we caught him, we should name him Houdini.

"Meg, dear."

Mother bent over to put her hand on my forehead. She nodded, apparently to indicate that my temperature was satisfactory, and sat down on the very edge of Spike's chair. Spike gave her a baleful look, but wisely refrained from nipping her. "You look better."

"I feel better," I said. "A little better—you know what would make me feel a whole lot better? A kind of early Christmas present?"

"Getting rid of Castlemayne?" Aida guessed.

"Bingo," I said. "Michael wants to kick him out when he and the boys get back tomorrow, but I told him not to worry—we could take care of it before then. Assuming you're willing to help me deal with him."

"Help you? Good heavens, no!" Mother lifted her chin and assumed her Joan-of-Arc pose. "Caroline and I will take care of it tomorrow. You've already spent far too much time dealing with his nonsense—to say nothing of reinjuring your ankle. Which was his fault in the first place. You just leave it to us. We'll simply pack up his things and get a few burly young cousins to carry them to the car. And him, too, if he doesn't cooperate."

"You have any trouble, just give me a call," Aida said. "I'm off duty tomorrow, thank goodness, but it wouldn't take me any time at all to throw on the uniform and come over to help intimidate him."

"Thank you, dear." She beamed at Aida, then frowned slightly. "By the way, has anyone found Curly? I heard that annoying young lawyer kept interfering with your efforts to get him safely back in jail and we're all really worried about him."

"No, ma'am," Aida said. "But the lawyer finally took off—wanted to get home before the snow got bad, I expect—so the chief's put out a BOLO on Curly, and he should turn up pretty soon."

"The temperature's still dropping." Mother glanced at the nearest window, which showed the snow still falling. "The Ladies Interfaith Council was wondering if we should get together some volunteers to drive around and look for him."

"Better to stay off the roads and let us do the looking," Aida said. "Vern's on the case, and he's pretty familiar with all Curly's usual haunts. We'll find him."

"I hope so." Mother looked troubled for a moment, then nodded. She turned back to me.

"Don't stay up too late," she said. "You've had a tiring day."

I wasn't planning to stay up. But strangely, now that I

was downstairs and in the midst of family and friends, I felt energized rather than drained. I still wished Michael and the boys were home, but at least for the time being the assembled family members seemed like a reasonable substitute. I sat in the dining room and chatted with everyone as they went past, filling their plates for the first or second or even third time, like so many hobbits. I finally had to leave the dining room, because everyone kept trying to refill my plate and my glass, even after I couldn't hold another bite or sip. I settled in the living room, between the tree and the fireplace, with my feet tucked under Tinkerbell's warm, furry side. I joined in the Christmas carols. The storytelling. The charades. For a while, the snow remained light—I don't think we got more than an inch in the first three or four hours. Even so, the younger set had a great time, scraping together enough snow to throw a few snowballs and make modest snowmen. But by around eight the snow started to come down a little faster. Everyone who had someplace to go packed up and went, and nearly everyone else said good night and headed upstairs to curl up in nice warm beds.

Including poor Harris, who looked rather despondent. He was probably fretting about the fuss his boss would make when we evicted him. I hadn't noticed Castlemayne leaving, which meant he was probably sacked out on one of our sofas. Well, let him, this one more time, I thought, as I peered out the kitchen window toward the sunroom. By tomorrow, we'd be rid of him. The sunroom door was closed, and there was one faint light coming from the library. As I watched, it went out.

I'd delegated the job of checking all the doors and windows to Caroline and Rose Noire, but since I was there anyway, I made sure the back door was locked. Then I picked up the glass of milk I'd come to fetch and went out into the front hallway. I glanced into the living room. The fire was still burning, with Spike and Tinkerbell curled up beside it. A couple of young cousins were sacked out in sleeping bags on the sofas or on the floor nearby. Not a creature stirring. Even Spike, stuffed to the gills with the bits of chicken and beef I'd been feeding him, was out for the count. None of them even noticed when I went over to turn off the Christmas tree lights.

I limped upstairs and into the master bedroom as quietly as possible.

I sat down on the bed and sighed with relief. It had been a long day. Way too long, way too busy, and in spite of resting for most of the afternoon my ankle was aching slightly.

I was trying to decide if I had enough energy to take a long, hot, soaking bath with my favorite rose-scented bath oil or if I should just throw on my nightgown and crawl into bed. Then someone knocked on the door and opened it almost immediately. It was Rose Noire.

"I brought you company!" she trilled.

She was holding a Pomeranian. I still had a hard time telling them all apart, but I deduced from the plain, utilitarian khaki collar that it was probably Watson, Horace's pup.

"Thanks," I said. "But I'm good. And dogs are pack animals, remember? He'll probably be happier staying with you and Solstice."

"Ah, but Watson's used to sleeping with humans now," she said. "He likes playing with his siblings, but I think at bedtime he prefers being the only canine in the pack."

That probably meant she needed to separate him and Solstice to get them to stop playing and go to sleep.

She deposited Watson on the bed with a satisfied smile. Watson lifted one hind leg and began scratching behind his ear. Something the Pomeranians were prone to doing when bored or stressed, I had noticed. I stilled the busy leg and replaced his sharp little claws with a gentle finger. Watson eagerly leaned in to enjoy being rubbed.

"See! You'll be just fine."

She hurried out, no doubt suspecting that if she stayed much longer, I'd force her to take the dog with her.

I was settling down in bed again when I heard a scratching at the door. I got up and limped over to open it.

Spike.

He gazed up at me with the vaguely peeved look that signaled I was already overdue to perform some vital service for him. Or maybe he was just in a bad mood after several days of being without the boys. His invariable routine was to start the night with Josh, who tended to go to sleep slightly earlier than his twin. Then at some point in the wee hours Spike would trot next door to finish the night with Jamie, who was a little more likely to sleep late. And heaven help the entire household if either boy forgot to leave his bedroom door open the requisite few inches.

Normally Spike just sulked when the boys spent a night away from home. And followed his usual schedule, sleeping about half the night in each empty bed. Was he mellowing enough that he'd settle for my company in their absence?

"You want to join me?" I asked, opening the door a little wider.

I could have sworn Spike was about to step in when Watson spotted him and began barking enthusiastically.

Spike looked up at me and curled his lip slightly. Then he turned and trotted away. I watched him slip into Josh's room.

He'd done perfectly fine by himself dozens of previous nights when the boys were away. Why did I feel so guilty?

I eyed Watson glumly.

"Gee, thanks," I muttered.

He wagged his tail as if I'd paid him a compliment. Or perhaps as if he'd done something brilliant.

I shut the door and returned to bed.

Okay, I wouldn't necessarily be stuck with Watson all night. The minute he proved a nuisance, I could take him somewhere else. The basement. I could wait until Rose Noire had gone to bed, then smuggle Watson downstairs and let him into the basement with Kevin and Widget. He'd like that, and Rose Noire probably wouldn't even notice—or if she did, I could claim that Watson was restless and I thought he'd be happier with his brother.

But it would be wiser to wait until she was asleep. I'd give it an hour. I could read for a while.

I left Watson on the bed while I went to the bathroom to brush my teeth. When I got back, he was lying in the exact middle of the bed, sprawled out as if doing his best to claim the whole thing as his own. And he was fast asleep.

I gently edged him out of dead center and slipped under the covers carefully, because having the Pomeranians around had given new meaning to the wisdom of letting sleeping dogs lie. I picked up the book I'd been reading and opened it up.

Watson suddenly stood up and shook himself. I braced myself. If he was in a playful mood—

He padded toward me, burrowed under the covers, and curled up in a tiny ball against my side. Then he uttered a small contented sigh.

Why did the little devils have to be so darned cute?

I focused back on my book. Which wasn't easy—my eyes were heavy, and it wasn't making sense. I should probably get a running start on this, I decided. I flipped back to the beginning of the chapter and propped the book up on my chest.

I woke with a start when the book fell over and hit me on the nose. Watson barely stirred.

"This is ridiculous," I said to no one in particular. It was two minutes past midnight. I needed my sleep. I reached up, put out the light, carefully turned over onto my side, and settled under the covers.

Maybe Watson would sleep through the night. If he didn't, I'd worry about him when I had to.

Chapter 14

December 22

I drifted up from sleep with the vague awareness that something wasn't quite normal. I couldn't blame Watson—he was still plastered against the small of my back, a little furry ball of warmth. The house was quiet—uncannily quiet. I lifted my head to look at the clock and see what time it was.

There was only darkness where I'd normally have seen the soft glow of squared-off numbers on the digital clockface. The power must be out. I fumbled on the bedside table and picked up my phone. Two forty-four. I remembered that it had been just after midnight when I went to bed, so the power had been out less than three hours. And probably a great deal less. I suspected what had awakened me was the gradual realization, even as I slept, that the normal noises of a modern house had shut down altogether.

Just then I heard something—the sound of a plow blade scraping against ice and pavement. I got up, limped over to one of the front windows, and pulled up the blind. It was a lot brighter outside—the light of a nearly full moon glowed behind the clouds and reflected off the expanse of snow that covered everything in sight—except for the road in front of the house, where a snowplow was slowly making its way. Since the entire plow was bedecked with twinkling Christmas lights, I could identify it as Beau Shiffley's plow. Osgood Shiffley, who drove the county's other plow, had limited his seasonal decorations to a fiberglass reindeer mounted atop the cab, with a solitary red light twinkling on the tip of its nose. I waved to Beau—not that he could see me. I reached to pull the blind back down, to make sure I was getting the full benefit of the insulating properties its maker had advertised, then changed my mind. The eerie glow of moonlight on snow would keep me from needing a flashlight if I had to make a trip to the bathroom later, so I left the blind up a foot or so.

I limped across the room to peer out into the backyard. Everything was covered with a soft blanket of snow. Only about five inches, but it was still coming down. Coming down lightly at the moment, but the flakes were small— what I thought of as businesslike little snowflakes, as opposed to the big, sloppy, wet flakes you got when the temperature wasn't really low enough for the snow to stick around.

Behind me Watson whimpered softly. I turned to find him standing on the edge of the bed, looking forlorn and abandoned. As soon as I took a step toward him, he wagged his feathery little tail furiously and began dancing up and down on the edge of the bed.

"I just hope you're not telling me you need to go out," I muttered.

No, he only seemed to want my company. When I slipped back into the warmth of the bed, he squirmed up to lick my face a couple of times before worming back under the covers and settling down again.

Well, this could have its advantages. If anyone tried to wake me up early to perform some necessary but unappealing chore, I could beg off. "Sorry—you'll have to ask someone else. I'm a doggy security blanket at the moment. Watson's happiness depends on me."

A little while later—fifteen minutes? Half an hour? I didn't bother to check—he growled softly, fought his way out of the blanket cocoon, and began barking hysterically.

"Shush," I muttered. "This is why I tried so hard to get you guys adopted by relatives from out of town."

He wasn't listening. He was running up and down Michael's side of the bed, yipping nonstop.

Outside I heard a car engine and a crunching noise that was probably the car's tires on the icy margins of the road. And then a squeal of brakes and several quick thuds.

I leaped out of bed, grabbed Watson, and ran over to the window that overlooked the front of the house.

"See?" I told Watson. "Just a car. They drive by all the time."

Of course, most of them didn't drive hell-for-leather in the middle of a snowstorm and skid off the road onto our lawn. I could see the whole front half of the car poking through our front hedge. One of the NO TRESPASSING signs was stuck to its front bumper.

At least Watson had stopped barking, thank goodness, but he was still uttering the occasional surprisingly low-pitched growl.

I walked back to put him down on the bed and grabbed my phone from the bedside table. I'd call 911 to report the accident. Then I'd throw on some clothes and go down to see if the driver was okay and—

I heard an engine revving. Watson began barking again. I grabbed him and ran back to the window. The car appeared to be trying to back up and was having a hard time untangling itself from the hedge. The noise increased— the driver must have floored it. The car popped out of the hedge and skidded backward across the road, taking out a section of the fence enclosing Seth Early's sheep pasture. Then it jerked forward, lurched back onto the pavement, and set off down the road, skidding from side to side, shedding bits of hedge as it went. And dragging something behind it. Could it be—yes, a chunk of the fence.

I called 911.

"What's your emergency, Meg?" Debbie Ann, the dispatcher, must have been pulling a double shift today. Although come to think of it, I wasn't sure I remembered ever calling 911 and getting anyone other than Debbie Ann. I stifled a yawn and focused back on the call.

"I'd like to report a dangerous driver careening down the road between our house and town," I said.

"What's the make and model of the vehicle?" she asked.

"I have no idea," I said. "But it shouldn't be hard to spot. It might still be towing one of Seth's fence posts and a tangle of barbed wire, and it's definitely going to have quite a lot of boxwood stuck to the front bumper. Along with one of those nice new No TRESPASSING signs Horace and the chief were kind enough to install today."

A brief silence. Although I thought I could detect the rattling of her computer keys.

"Oh, dear," she said finally. "And they were driving erratically?"

"Very erratically," I said "Neither our hedge nor Seth's fence was blocking the roadway at the time. Does wrecking them count as a hit-and-run?"

"I have no idea," she said. "Certainly makes for an interesting night. But not in a good way. I'm sending out a BOLO to everyone. Let's see if you can remember anything else that could help."

I tried, but Debbie Ann soon figured out that I'd exhausted what little I'd seen.

"And we should notify Seth," I said finally. "He's probably got his sheep in the barns in this weather, but we don't want him turning them loose before the fence is fixed."

"Already in progress," Debbie Ann said. "Randall's going to drop by and see to it. He might even be able to fix the fence."

"You haven't seen the fence," I said. "Thanks."

With that we hung up.

I took a final look out the window. The car had torn out

a big chunk of our front hedge. I knew from bitter experience how expensive it was going to be to buy new boxwoods large enough to repair the hedge. I hoped if they caught the driver—no, I resolved to think positively: *when* they caught the driver—it would turn out to be someone with either deep pockets or good insurance.

I limped back to bed. Watson had fallen asleep on my shoulder during my conversation with Debbie Ann. I put him down carefully on the bed, pulled the covers up over him, and then slipped in beside him. Tomorrow would be a busy day. All the busier thanks to the hit-and-run on our hedge. And technically it was already tomorrow. I needed my sleep. I closed my eyes and tried to let go of all the stress.

That's when I noticed the tapping noise. Or maybe it was more of a thumping noise. Not a steady noise—it seemed to correspond with gusts of wind outside.

Then I recognized it. The sunroom door—the one leading out to the backyard. Someone had left it open again, and it was being blown back and forth with the wind, banging now against its frame and now against the outside of the sunroom. If it had been any other door, the wind would probably have slammed it closed by now, but the sunroom's latch was tricky. It would rattle and bang all night if no one went down to close it.

"It's all Castlemayne's fault," I muttered. He might have left it open if he went outside to smoke. Although knowing him, I thought it was a lot more likely that he'd gone outside, realized how cold it was, and retreated back inside to smoke in the library. And if it wasn't him, it would be one of the people who'd been harassing him. If he chased them out of the library, bellowing at the top of his lungs, they might not wait to close the sunroom door properly.

I got up and looked around for my clothes. After all, he could be sacked out on one of the couches, and I'd much rather be fully dressed when dealing with him.

I threw on jeans, T-shirt, and slippers. I grabbed my phone, my keys, and the flashlight I kept in my bedside drawer. All the while Watson was whining softly, making it clear that he wanted to go with me, so I scooped him up and headed downstairs.

Not a creature stirring other than Watson and me, and he appeared to be falling asleep on my shoulder again. The house was starting to feel a little cool. It would get downright chilly if the power outage persisted—there's only so much you can do to insulate a house that's over a hundred years old. But since power outages were common in our very rural part of the county, Michael and I had amassed an impressive collection of useful gear for dealing with them. When morning came, I'd be doling out blankets, sweaters, earmuffs, battery-operated heaters, flashlights, camping lanterns, LED headlamps, and whatever else the visiting relatives needed to keep them safe. And if the power was still out by breakfast time, we'd break out the grills and camping stoves.

Problems for later. All I needed to worry about now was securing the sunroom door so it wouldn't keep banging and waking people. And make sure Castlemayne hadn't left the door between the sunroom and the library open—not that I cared about his comfort, but the less cold air we let into the house the happier everyone would be. Our half-dozen kerosene heaters could only do so much, and I foresaw a battle royal for places around the fireplace. Maybe we'd have to send people to places with generators.

On the bright side, maybe, if the library got cold enough, the power outage would make it easier to evict Castlemayne and send him back to the greater comfort of the Inn and the zoo, both of which would have heat, thanks to their emergency generators.

The door between the library and the rest of the house was locked, of course. With luck, Castlemayne had gone back to his room at the Inn. But in case he hadn't, I rapped briskly on the door half a dozen times before unlocking it.

I swung the door open and shivered. The library was freezing. I flicked the flashlight beam to the right. Both of the French doors were wide open.

Something flew up with a squawk, bounced off the side of my head, and flew off again.

Blast the man—he'd set the jays loose.

I shut the library door behind me before any could escape.

Okay, the first thing to do was to shut the French doors, to shut out the cold and keep in any jays that hadn't already escaped. Figuring out how many were still here and how many had escaped would have to wait till daylight. At least they were sturdy native birds. They might not be thrilled about returning to the wild in the middle of a snowstorm, but any that escaped would be okay. We'd probably find them sheltering in the shrubbery near the house.

And at least I didn't see Castlemayne sacked out on any of the sofas. I began carefully picking my way across the room, scanning the floor in front of me with the flashlight beam so I could dodge any obstacles. Like dirty dishes. Nearly empty beer bottles. Offerings from the birds.

My flashlight beam revealed a shoe sticking out from behind one of the sofas. A shoe that was standing up on end in a way that suggested it enclosed a foot and was attached to an ankle.

I took two careful steps forward, keeping my eyes—and my flashlight beam—on the shoe. Yes, there were definitely a foot and an ankle. And a body. Roderick Castlemayne's body. His eyes were open and staring. His hands were clutching his throat. No, clutching at something that had been stuck into his throat.

A Swiss Army knife. The kind with half a million special-purpose attachments. The corkscrew stuck out to the right, between his fingers, and I could see the top of the fondue fork peeking out from beneath his fingers on the left.

I heard the door bang again and walked out into the sunroom. Someone had tracked in snow from outside, and the sunroom was cold enough that the clumps hadn't melted all that much. I gave them a wide berth as I limped over to pull the sunroom door closed and flip the switch to lock it. I minimized the chance that I'd mess up any fingerprints by reaching up high to grab it in a spot no one was likely to have touched and using the hem of my shirt on the switch. I went back inside and did the same thing with the French doors between the library and the sunroom. Then I retreated back to the spot where I'd first noticed the shoe and called 911.

Chapter 15

"Nine-one-one—what's your emergency, Meg? We haven't found that reckless driver yet if that's why you're calling."

"I hope you find him," I said. "Him or her. Because I think there's a good chance whoever was running away in such a rush might be the same person who killed Roderick Castlemayne. I just found his body."

"Oh, dear." I heard the rattling noise of keys. "Are you sure he's dead?"

"I didn't try for a pulse." I inched forward again. "I can if you like, but I was pretty sure I wouldn't find one. His eyes are wide and staring. And there's a Swiss Army knife stuck in his throat."

"Oh, my."

"And there's blood," I added. "Not sure how much—it's kind of hard to tell with just the flashlight. Our power's out."

"Power's out most everywhere in the county," she said. "As usual with a snowstorm. Either Vern or Horace should be there soon. And I'm going to put in calls to the chief and your dad."

"I'll go wait for them by the front door," I said. "The body's in the library."

"Goodness," Debbie Ann said. "That sounds like something out of an Agatha Christie novel. Or the game of Clue."

I nodded. I'd been keeping my flashlight trained on the foot, except once or twice when I heard a soft rustling noise coming from someplace else in the room. Then I'd flick my flashlight in the direction of the sound, only to find a sleepy-looking blue jay perched someplace. Watson was still asleep on my shoulder, a tiny ball of surprisingly comforting warmth.

"I should go and meet Horace or Vern or whoever," I said. "Tell them to knock instead of ringing the doorbell when they get here—no sense waking the whole house."

"Good idea," she said. "Not that your doorbell will be working, of course."

"Duh," I said. "Clearly I'm still half asleep."

After we hung up, I picked my way back to the library door. I looked around to make sure there were no jays poised to make their escape when I opened it. Then I slipped quickly out of the library and locked the door behind me.

No one had started knocking by the time I reached the front hallway, so I headed for the kitchen and opened the door to the basement. I heard a soft, peremptory bark coming from the bottom of the stairs. I aimed the beam downward and saw Widget, Kevin's Pomeranian, standing at the bottom of the stairs. I put Watson down. He began scurrying down the stairs, and Widget scrambled up to meet him halfway. They touched noses briefly, then scampered down and disappeared into the darkness.

I shut the door behind them, feeling curiously alone without the soft, warm weight of Watson on my shoulder.

Any minute now I'd have plenty of company, I reminded myself. I returned to the front hallway and sat down on the bottom step of the stairs, since all the chairs in the room were piled high with presents—presents people had moved there last night to make more space for caroling in the living room and hadn't bothered putting back under the tree where they belonged.

I was still convincing myself that I had more important things to worry about than putting presents back under the tree when I heard a soft knock on the door. I peered out the peephole to see both Horace and Vern standing outside, with enormous police-issue flashlights in their hands. I flung the door open with relief and they hurried in, pausing on the tiled section of the hallway to shake off what snow and ice they hadn't managed to get rid of out on the porch. Normally I'd have offered to take their coats, but given how cold the house was already, I decided to put on my own coat instead.

"You okay, Meg?" Vern asked. "I'd wish you a Merry Christmas, but I guess you're probably not feeling much holiday spirit at the moment."

"Hey, Meg," Horace said. "Is Watson okay?" He was carrying the bulky case that held his forensic kit.

"Merry Christmas," I said. "Very glad to see you both. Watson's fine—in fact, it was thanks to his barking that I spotted the reckless driver making his escape."

"He's very alert." Horace beamed with pride. I decided not to mention that Watson had slept through the finding of the body.

"And it must have been shortly after the reckless driver left that you found Castlemayne," Vern said. "Only about half an hour between your two calls to nine-one-one, and I'm betting you didn't sit around very long either time, agonizing about whether to pick up the phone. Was there some particular reason you went down to the library in the middle of the night?"

I explained about the sunroom door. And about finding the French doors in the library open.

"And I went over and shut them," I said to Horace. "And locked the sunroom door, too. I hope I didn't mess up your crime scene too much—I used the hem of my shirt to avoid leaving fingerprints—but I figured it was a good idea to keep cold air out of the house and intruders out of your crime scene."

"Yeah." He nodded. "I'll manage."

"And it'll keep the jays inside, at least the ones that didn't already escape."

"Oh, damn," Horace said. "The jays are loose?"

I nodded.

"Why don't you go down and start securing the scene?" Vern said. "Meg can go along in case you have questions, and I'll stay here to let in the chief and Dr. Langslow and whoever else will be showing up."

"Sounds like a plan." Horace hefted his heavy bag. "And can you get someone to bring out those big battery-powered floodlights we use for outdoor crime scenes?"

"On it," Vern said, taking out his phone.

"I know on TV the CSIs are always creeping around peering at fingerprints and blood spatter with a flashlight," Horace said as we headed for the hallway that led to the library. "But in real life we forensic folk like a lot more light on the subject."

"Meg? Is something wrong?" We all looked up to see Caroline standing at the top of the stairs, holding up a camping lantern. "Of course something's wrong," she went on as she started down. "Why else would two uniformed deputies be making a house call at three-thirty in the morning?"

"Someone killed Castlemayne," I said.

"Oh, dear," she murmured.

"Any chance you could get a couple more camping lanterns and bring them to the library?" I went on. "They should be in the basement—thank goodness that's wombat free now."

"The lanterns aren't in the basement," she said. "Rose Noire and I brought them all up to the kitchen last night. The lanterns and the camping stoves. We figured if the power went out it would be nice to keep people from having to stumble down the basement stairs in the dark. I'll go fetch a couple."

"Good thinking," I said as she dashed away.

I followed Horace down the hallway to the library. He stopped about six feet from the door.

"Stay back," he said. "I could use the light from your flashlight, but let me open the door."

"I'll give you the key," I began teasing it off my keyring. "And you can hang on to it. I expect you and the chief will want to secure the crime scene."

"Yes." He took the key when I handed it over, but instead of unlocking the door he tucked it into his pocket and began to study the door, with particular attention to the knob and the frame, his eyes and flashlight only inches away. "This was locked when you got here?"

"It was. And while that isn't the only key, we do try to limit the number floating around in the world."

He nodded and continued to scrutinize the door.

"Of course, the killer could have come through the sunroom door," he said. "You said you closed it just now—did you lock it up last night?"

"I didn't," I said. "Caroline and Rose Noire said they'd make my usual locking-up rounds, to spare my ankle, but I don't know if they were able to get in here to lock the sunroom."

"We can ask them."

"And oddly enough, Castlemayne must have turned in around eleven or eleven-thirty," I said. "I happened to be looking out the kitchen window around that time. I saw that the sunroom door was closed, and while I was looking the light went out in the library. He usually stays up a lot later, working on his painting."

"I thought painters were big on natural light." Horace was now down on his hands and knees, peering at the floor outside the library door and taking the occasional picture.

"Not this one," I said. "I don't think he was big on natural anything."

"Yeah, I noticed that," he said over his shoulder. "From those paintings of his."

I puzzled over this for a few moments while Horace continued to examine every square inch of the threshold.

"What do you mean about his paintings?" I asked finally.

"They don't really look alive, do they?" he said. "I mean, they're really accurate and everything. But I don't think he paints them from live birds. I figure he uses photographs. Or taxidermied birds. Or just dead birds, period. It's something about the eyes."

I pondered that a while, then nodded.

"Yeah, I can see that," I said. "It would explain why he was so clueless about taking the mockingbirds out of the cages. If he normally paints only dead birds, maybe he wouldn't be expecting them to fly away."

"Yup." Horace stood up and reached into his pocket for the key. "Probably just as well if we don't mention that part to your grandfather. He'll want to kill the poor creep all over again."

"Only if Castlemayne deliberately killed birds for the sole purpose of painting them," I said. "If he just picked up roadkill, Grandfather wouldn't care."

Although I had to wonder if any avid bird lovers had made the same deduction Horace had and suspected Castlemayne of slaughtering birds for his art. Might that give them grounds for murder? I should probably mention it to the chief.

"Mum's the word," Horace said.

A light appeared at the far end of the hallway

"And here's Caroline." I nodded toward where she was approaching, lighting her way with one of the camping lanterns and carrying four more.

"Yeah, her too," Horace murmured. Meaning, I supposed, that we should not speculate about Castlemayne's painting methods in front of her—since, like Grandfather she would take a dim view of Castlemayne using dead birds for his painting. Especially if she had any suspicion that he was the birds' cause of death.

I went down the hallway to help her. We set down the lanterns just outside the library door.

"I'll go see if Vern needs anything," she said. "And then I'll fire up one of the camping stoves and make coffee. Unless Rose Noire has started that already. I tried to sneak out without waking her, but she's even more of a light sleeper than I am. Coffee, and maybe some breakfast. I have a feeling we'll be needing it." She turned and headed back down the hall.

"Good," Horace said. I wondered if he was talking about the coffee or if he'd heard how much Caroline disliked Castlemayne and, like me, was relieved to know she was probably well alibied by Rose Noire. "So once I open the door, you hand in the lanterns. Then you can stay outside and talk to me through the doorway."

"What about the jays?" I asked. "We don't want them escaping to the rest of the house. And it's not as if I haven't already trampled all over your crime scene."

"Damn, that's right," he said. "Well, let's each take in a pair of lanterns. But once we get in, you close the door and stand just inside."

"Can do," I said.

We grabbed our lanterns and stepped into the library. No jays flew out, and I hastily pulled the door closed while Horace scanned our surroundings with his flashlight.

"Reeks of tobacco in here," Horace said, wrinkling his nose. "Castlemayne, I assume."

"Yeah," I said. "That's one of the reasons Michael and I decided to get rid of him. As in making him go back to the zoo," I added hastily. "And I figured he'd put up a fuss, so I'd already enlisted Mother and Caroline to help me do that today."

"Someone saved you the trouble." Horace bent down

and switched on two of the lanterns. Then he picked one up and began carefully making his way to the sunroom end of the library, sticking close to the shelves at the right-hand side of the room to avoid going too near the body just yet. He'd wait until Dad arrived and formally pronounced before doing that. But already he was snapping pictures like crazy, with the flash going off so often I could almost imagine he was a paparazzi stalking a celebrity. I turned on the other two lanterns and dragged the nearest wooden chair over so I could sit down. No sense aggravating my ankle.

Horace had reached the French doors and was photographing them and the doorsill beneath them. And taking samples of something. He had started humming tunelessly—always a sign that he was contentedly immersed in his work.

I stifled a yawn. Watching Horace work was nothing like watching forensics in TV shows or movies. On screen, one of the crime scene experts would already have exclaimed "aha!" and held up a fiber or a chunk of dirt or some other tiny object that would crack the entire case open. I knew from past experience that Horace was in for hours of close, meticulous work with no guarantee of any case-cracking aha moments.

"You didn't go outside, did you?" he called out. He had disappeared into the sunroom. "Out into the snow? Like maybe to grab the loose door so you could close it?"

"No." I shook my head, and then felt silly, since he couldn't see me. "I noticed someone had tracked in some snow, but I was only wearing my slippers, so I made sure not to step in it. And I didn't have to go outside to grab the door."

I glanced down at my slippers. Maybe I should have put on shoes and socks. I felt suddenly chilled in spite of my coat.

"Figured as much." The repeated flashes and clicks

showed he was still busily snapping pictures. "Someone came in this way. Tracked in snow. Most of it melted now."

"You're thinking the killer came from outside?" I asked.

"Seems likely. I can see where someone made a path through the snow, though it's getting covered up now by newer snow." He strolled back inside and rummaged in his bag. "Of course, it would have to be someone who knew Castlemayne was back here in the library."

"By now most of the people who have been showing up to badger him probably knew that," I said. "Madeleine, the ex-wife who trashed our library, not only knew but already got in that way. I caught Justin, the *Star-Tribune* reporter sneaking around in our backyard. And as for the rest of them, just because I didn't catch them skulking around in the backyard doesn't mean they didn't try it."

"But would he open the door for any of them?" He was putting a fresh battery in his camera.

"Maybe," I said. "Like if he got ticked off enough, he might open the door to give them a piece of his mind. I never got the impression he was physically afraid of any of them—just annoyed and trying to avoid them. And he was careless about locking the door. He could have gone outside for a cigarette and not bothered to lock the door when he came back in."

"So it could be any of them. Damn." He picked up something—a tape measure—and headed back toward the sunroom. "The chief always hates it when there's a million suspects. At least we know the killer came from outside the house."

"Do we?" I took a few steps farther into the room—just enough that I could see what he was doing. "If I wanted to kill him and steer suspicion away from those of us in the house, I think I'd try to make it look as if the killer came in through the sunroom."

"How?" Horace appeared to be measuring something—the distance between the little puddles of icy water on the sunroom floor. "I mean, I can think of smarter ways to muddy the waters if I were the killer."

"But you're a professional," I said. "How would I, the excited first-time murderer, try to cover my tracks if I were in the house? Well, when I finished killing him, I could walk outside through the sunroom door and make a path all the way to the street and back. Unless someone came along almost immediately, it would be impossible to tell that the tracks were made by someone who came from and returned to the house. And as long as I dried off my shoes before leaving the library, it would look as if someone came in from outside."

"Very possible," came a new voice.

Chapter 16

Horace and I both started, and I turned to see the chief standing in the doorway, lifting up his camping lantern so he could get a better view.

"Of course, a killer from inside the house would also need to have a key to lock up the library door when they left," the chief said. "How many people have them, aside from you?"

"Come in and shut the door so the jays don't escape." I pointed up at the balcony railing, where a pair of the jays was now perched, looking wide awake and ready for trouble. "Michael and Rose Noire have them," I said once the chief had closed the door. "And Castlemayne has one. Had one. Although it's been mostly Harris, his assistant, bothering to use it. I've been meaning to have a spare made for Harris, but so far he's just been sharing the one we gave his boss."

The chief nodded.

"Is this it?" Horace was pointing his flashlight at something lying on the floor near Castlemayne's left hand. A key on a ring attached to a vintage-styled black plastic motel key tag.

"If the plastic tag says 'Bates Motel,' then yeah," I said.

"Bates Motel?" the chief murmured "As in—"

"As in *Psycho*, yes," I said. "Gag gift from Rob. Neither Castlemayne nor Harris seemed to get the gag, though. They probably just think Michael and I are petty thieves."

Horace chuckled at that.

"I don't want to discount the possibility that the killer came from inside," the chief said. "But if it's someone who's actually staying here, they'd either have to have a spare key to the library door or they'd have had to go out through the sunroom, circle around to the front of the house, and come back in the front door. Vern's done a quick reconnoiter, and he didn't see any tracks in the snow to any other doors—or to any of the windows. And going around to the front door would be lot more trouble, not to mention a much greater chance of being detected. Seems less likely than someone coming from outside. Horace, is it possible that the tracks outside in the snow might be of any forensic use? Because if so, we should start taking pictures of them before the snow covers them up completely."

"A slim possibility, but yeah, we should photograph them." Horace suddenly looked slightly overwhelmed, and I remembered that he'd have been near the end of his shift when my call had come in to 911.

"I'll get Vern to take some photos." The chief turned to me. "If you could come along—I want to interview you about this, but I'll need to watch the door while Vern's outside. You have a key to the library door with you?"

"I have it, Chief." Horace tossed the key over and the chief caught it with a deft ease that suddenly reminded me of summers, when he and Michael would spend long hours in our backyard, playing baseball with Josh, Jamie, and Adam—helping them improve their batting, pitching, and fielding. Or just playing catch. Happier times, I thought, as I followed the chief down the hall to the front door, where Vern stood guard.

In fact, Vern was just opening the door.

"Sorry it took me so long!" Dad bustled in, carrying a big flashlight and the old-fashioned black bag that actually contained a fairly modern medical kit, complete with whatever extra items he needed for his role as medical examiner. "Body in the library, I gather?"

"Horace is there." The chief stepped aside and Dad trotted down the hall.

Mother followed him in. She was bundled up in a very elegant new down coat—a Christmas present from Dad that he'd probably insisted she open early when she decided to come along tonight. Well, technically this morning. She looked a lot more awake than I felt.

"Good morning, Chief." She leaned over to plant a quick kiss on my cheek. "Are you all right, dear?"

"I'm fine," I said.

"What can I do to be useful?" Her glance took in both the chief and me.

"Can you watch the door while Vern goes out to take some pictures?" the chief asked. "Let in any of my officers who show up, and turn away everyone else. Unless they're any of the people who showed up over the last few days to badger Castlemayne. I want to talk to them."

"Because they'd be suspects." Mother nodded her understanding. "Of course."

"We're going to keep the manner of death confidential for now," he added, looking at me.

"Got it," I said. "And trust me, you'd rather not know," I added to Mother.

"Of course not," she said. "I assume I can take those presents and put them under the tree so we have a little more room in here?"

The chief nodded, so she grabbed a stack of presents and carried them into the living room. I took a seat on the chair she'd just cleared off. My ankle wasn't hurting—not yet, anyway—but I felt a sudden wave of tiredness.

And guilt. Because now that the shock of finding a dead body was starting to wear off, I realized what I felt was relief. All of the problems Castlemayne had been causing were about to go away. Of course, my relief was complicated by the knowledge that his murder created a whole new set of problems—but for the most part they were the chief's problems, not mine. What I had to cope with was mostly logistics.

My mind was already focusing on things to do, and my fingers itched to make entries in my notebook. First thing would be to pack up Castlemayne's stuff at the Inn and vacate the room—no sense in Grandfather continuing to pay for a room whose occupant would absolutely never return. If it took a while to figure out where to send the stuff, we could haul it all out to the zoo—he'd probably left stuff there, too. I hoped Harris had some idea of how to get in touch with Castlemayne's family. Or his attorney. Someone we could send his stuff to so we wouldn't be stuck with it indefinitely. And then there was recapturing the jays along with the remaining mockingbird, and cleaning the carpet in the library and—

Was it heartless of me to be already planning how to wrap up our late guest's exit from our lives? Or admirable, that I could so quickly focus on getting my family's life back to normal? Not to mention back to having a happy holiday season?

Maybe it was just how I dealt with stress.

Just then Rose Noire entered from the kitchen. She was better prepared for the power outage than any of us, with a little LED headlamp strapped to her forehead. She had a steaming cup in each hand and four Pomeranians at her heels. One dog raced over to the chief to be petted— presumably Willie Mays, the chief's grandpuppy. Rose Noire handed a mug to each of us, and I was touched that she'd remembered my lack of enthusiasm for coffee and gone to the trouble of making hot chocolate.

"Let's talk in your dining room," the chief said, nodding to me.

He picked up a camping lantern and headed for the dining room. I followed him in. I played the beam of my flashlight around the room and was impressed to find that Mother and her minions had not only cleared away all the food and done all the dishes before leaving last night, they'd even restored the room to its original over-the-top holiday perfection. As usual it was decorated with a food theme. The evergreen swags and garlands festooning the crown molding were ornamented with gilded fake fruit—apples, pears, and bunches of cherries. More fruit ornaments, this time in blown glass, hung on the narrow four-foot Christmas tree on the sideboard. Flanking the tree were quite a lot of silver dishes and plates and etageres—all borrowed—that held still more vegetation and fake fruit. And the table was set as if we were about to host a ten-course dinner for twelve.

"Let's make a space for you to work." I began clearing off the near end of the table, picking up the plates, glasses, flatware, and napkins and stacking them on a chair that stood against the wall.

"You seem to be all ready for a very nice dinner," the chief said. "I don't want you to mess that up on my account."

"It's just Mother's idea of decoration," I said. "We don't have any fancy dinners scheduled until tomorrow at the earliest—and even if we did, with no power we'd be rethinking our plans."

"If you're sure." He still sounded hesitant.

"Mother will enjoy redoing it." Actually, Mother wouldn't lift a finger to redo it, but she'd enjoy recruiting half a dozen visiting relatives to restore the table settings, supervising their work, and experimenting with half a dozen possible alternate arrangements—but I didn't need to bother him with that.

I took him through being awakened to find the power out, hearing Watson's barking, spotting the fleeing car, and finding the body, although there wasn't much I could think of that I hadn't already told Debbie Ann. He already had a fairly complete list of the various people who'd showed up at the house wanting to talk to Castlemayne.

I'd reported even the polite ones, on the theory that it was only a matter of time before they, too, escalated to rudeness, threats, or trespassing. I gave him the names of all the friends and relatives currently staying at the house—only a dozen of them at the moment, thank goodness—along with the names of everyone who'd visited the previous day—Mother, Dad, Grandfather, Clarence Rutledge, Delaney, her mother, Manoj, several more zoo staff who'd come to help Manoj with the wombats, assorted local friends, and the various relatives who'd been staying either with Mother and Dad or elsewhere in town and had joined us for dinner. It made for a long list.

"And just so you know, Delaney and Rob don't know her mother is here," I added. "She came early so she and Mother could plot how to talk their kids into having a big, over-the-top wedding. Obviously catching the killer is more important than keeping Rob and Delaney in the dark, but—"

"Don't worry." He sounded amused. "I was already sworn to secrecy about Mrs. McKenna's presence when she and your mother called Minerva yesterday. They're thinking of hiring the choir and wanted to check on dates when they'd be available."

I closed my eyes and took a deep breath. The New Life Baptist Choir, which Minerva Burke directed, was justly famous. But they were only slightly smaller than the Mormon Tabernacle Choir. Mother and Mrs. McKenna were definitely going overboard.

Not my problem. Not today, at least.

"Not that I expect most of them will have any useful information on a crime that probably happened hours after they left," the chief was saying.

"But maybe one of yesterday's visitors came back and committed the crime," I said.

"Exactly. We'll be checking alibis. So the assistant is staying here."

"Yes," I said. "Grandfather balked at paying for two rooms at the Inn—he said if Castlemayne couldn't manage without an assistant, he could pay for the fellow's room. Castlemayne was going to put him up at the Clay County Motor Lodge, so I said we'd find a room for him here."

"That was kind of you." The chief nodded in approval.

"More like self-defense," I replied. "The Clay County Motor Lodge is notorious for bedbugs and cockroaches. We didn't want to take the chance of any nasties hitching a ride on his clothes or briefcase. We gave him the smallest room in the house—it was going to be empty anyway, since all the relatives complain when we put them in it."

"Can you show me where he is?" the chief said. "It's a bit early still, but we need to find out if he knows how to contact the next of kin. And frankly, I'd like to see his initial reaction when he hears the news."

"Hears the news?" I echoed. "I notice you didn't say 'when I tell him the news.' Let me guess—you want me to break the news so you can focus on watching him."

"There's also the fact that if I tell him I'll have to identify myself, and that would give him a heads up that something's amiss. But if you'd rather not—"

"No," I said. "I'm fine with breaking the news to him as long as you're there to help deal with any hysterics. Follow me."

I stuffed my flashlight in my jeans pocket and picked up the camping lantern he'd set on the dining room table. I led the way up the two flights of stairs and down the hall to the tiny bedroom Harris was occupying. The chief stood back while I knocked on the door.

"Harris?" I called softly. "Are you awake?"

I knocked and called several times until I heard a thud, accompanied by a sleepy exclamation of "ow!" The ceiling over the bed was rather low. Harris wasn't the room's first occupant to bang his head upon getting up too quickly.

Soft footsteps approached the door, which opened a few inches. I could see the glow of the phone screen Harris seemed to have used to navigate his way to the door.

"What time is it?" He sounded both anxious and groggy. "It's not even light. Is something wrong?"

"I'm afraid so." I held up the camping lantern so the chief could see Harris's face better. "It's Mr. Castlemayne. I—"

"Oh, dear, what now? Can you tell him I'll be down as soon as possible?" He let go of the door, which drifted open as he stumbled toward the bed. He made a gesture as if to put the phone in his pants pocket and then, finding no pocket in his pajamas, lurched toward the tiny curtained corner that served as the room's closet. "I should get dressed—if I go down like this, I might never get a chance to come up again. What—"

"There's no rush," I said. "I'm afraid something's happened to him."

Harris turned and stared at me.

"Something . . . what?"

"I'm afraid he's dead," I said.

"Oh, dear." He paused in the middle of the room and shut his eyes. "It was his heart, wasn't it? I've been nagging him to get it checked out. I should have tried harder. He claims it's only indigestion but—"

"It wasn't his heart," I said. "Someone killed him."

"Killed him?" Harris's mouth fell open in astonishment. Then his eyes rolled up and he crumpled to the floor, still clutching his phone, and striking his head on the bedframe on the way down. Blood spurted everywhere.

Chapter 17

"Well, that was dramatic." I stepped aside to let the chief dash in—he'd had EMT training—and took out my cell phone. "Staying out of your way unless there's something you want me to do."

"That cut on his head doesn't look good." He knelt by Harris's side and whipped a handkerchief out of his pocket. "I'll apply pressure. Can you call—"

"Calling Dad, to be followed by nine-one-one." I pulled out my phone, banging my funny bone on one of the walls in the process. I choked back a few swear words and stepped out into the hall before dialing.

"Meg? What's up?" Dad sounded distracted.

"Can you come up to the third floor?" I strolled over to the linen closet as I spoke.

"I'm in the middle of examining the body," Dad said. "Is it important?"

"Well, we don't have a second corpse for you yet," I said. "But it could be only a matter of time. Harris fainted and hit his head and is bleeding like a stuck pig, so—"

"On my way."

I pulled a couple of towels out of the linen closet—dog towels, as we called the worn towels we kept for drying off wet dogs and other grungy jobs—and handed them in to the chief, to supplement his handkerchief. Then I stayed out in the hall, partly so I could show Dad where we were and partly because there really wasn't enough space for me in the tiny room.

"How's he doing?" I asked, peering in the doorway as my fingers dialed 911.

"Still out for the count," the chief said. "I'm wondering if we should get an ambulance."

"Already calling. Do you—"

"Nine-one-one—what's your emergency, Meg?"

"We could use an ambulance," I said. "Harris, Castle-mayne's assistant, fainted when we broke the news about his employer's death, and cut his head open. The chief's with him and Dad's on the way up, but I figure there's a high probability they'll want to send him to the hospital for stitches and an X-ray."

"Roger," Debbie Ann said. "Stay on the line when your dad gets there and we can relay the patient's vital stats to the EMTs."

Just then Dad came barreling down the hall with a flashlight in his outstretched right hand and his medical bag tucked under his left arm, looking like an improbably round quarterback going for a touchdown. I waved, pointed at the door of Harris's room, and stood back out of his way.

"Ambulance is on the way, and Debbie Ann's standing by in case there's anything you want to tell them before they get here," I said as he dashed by me.

Dad nodded. I watched and relayed his comments as he worked over Harris—deftly assisted by the chief, who must have aced his EMT class. I was always amazed when I saw Dad at work in an emergency—suddenly you could see he was all business and impressively competent.

"Meg?" Debbie Ann said. "Is the chief still there?"

"Yes," I said. "Helping Dad."

"Vern found another injured person," she said. "White male in his twenties. Hit over the head with a blunt object and left out in the snow. He's unconscious, possibly hypothermic. I'm alerting the ambulance. It would help if your dad could check him out. If the patient he's with now is stable, of course."

I relayed this to the chief, who frowned, and Dad, who nodded almost absently.

"We definitely need to get this poor man in for stitches and an X-ray." Dad was applying butterfly bandages to a dramatic gash on Harris's forehead. "But I'll be down in a minute. Go down and see what's happening."

"Roger." While I wasn't as squeamish about blood as Rob, I wasn't sorry to miss the rest of Harris's treatment. And as I turned to go, I remembered something. "Caroline's a retired nurse, remember? And she's awake. I can send her up to help the chief while you check on the hypothermia victim."

"Perfect!"

I handed off the lantern to the chief, pulled out my flashlight, and raced downstairs as fast as my ankle would allow. By the time I reached the front hall, Vern and Sammy Wendell, another of the deputies, were carrying someone inside—a limp figure, well dusted with snow. Presumably the hypothermia patient. They set him down in the hallway, closed the door, and began clearing off the snow. Caroline was hovering over him and Mother was standing by with several thick blankets. I noticed with approval that they'd hung a camping lantern from the overhead light fixture and set another on the end of the bannister, greatly improving visibility in the hallway.

"His clothing's only a little damp," Vern said. "'Course it will be a lot damp if we get him warm enough for all the snow to melt."

"Take him in by the fire," Caroline said. "Get his clothes off and wrap him up well. Meg, where's your father?"

"Upstairs patching up Harris, who fainted when he heard about the murder and cracked his head open," I said. "If you could go up and take over there—"

Caroline was already dashing up the stairs.

"Do you have any idea who he is?" Mother asked.

"No, ma'am," Sammy said. "Once we get him settled, we'll check his ID."

Just then I got close enough to see the victim's face.

"His name is Justin Vreeland," I said. "He's a reporter for the *Washington Star-Tribune*."

"The one who's been so . . . persistent about wanting to talk to poor Mr. Castlemayne?" Mother asked.

"That's him." I had to fight down a smile at the thought that only being murdered could possibly have turned "that wretched man" into "poor Mr. Castlemayne."

Mother had picked up another lantern and was standing by to light Vern and Sammy's way into the living room.

"Careful of his head." Vern was picking up Justin's feet. "Looks like someone whacked him pretty hard."

"Probably with this." Sammy reached into his pocket and pulled out an eighteen-inch-long flashlight with a gleaming metallic blue shaft. He set it down by the hat-and-coat stand before squatting down to grab Justin's shoulders. "Found it in the snow near where he fell. Should we bag it now or wait until Horace has checked it for fingerprints?"

"Even a yeti would be wearing gloves in this cold," Vern said as they shuffled into the living room.

"The owner might have handled it before putting on their gloves," I pointed out. "And Horace will probably want to check for fibers."

"Good point. I'll bag it for protection once we get Mr. Vreeland settled, and we can take it to Horace. But first we need to get him out of those damp clothes and into the blankets."

Mother moved enough of the presents to clear a space by the fire and Sammy and Vern carried Justin in and set him down. The dogs woke and looked on curiously. The several young cousins who'd been sleeping there also woke up and began asking questions, until Mother rounded them up and shooed them into the kitchen to make themselves useful where they wouldn't be underfoot.

I took over Mother's job of holding up the lantern and watched as they worked over Justin. Curious, finding him so close to the scene of the murder. Could he be the killer? Maybe, if Castlemayne had hit him over the head with the flashlight just as Justin stabbed him. And if Justin had then managed to stagger outside before passing out from the blow.

Or maybe the murderer had coshed Justin on his way out. That made more sense, since as far as I knew Justin wanted to interview Castlemayne, not kill him.

"Let's get an evidence bag for the clothes," Vern said in a low tone. "There's traces of what looks like blood on the gloves and the jacket. And he doesn't seem to be bleeding anywhere."

"I'll take them in to Horace when we get them off him," Sammy replied.

Dad came dashing down the stairs, bag in hand, and we waved him into the living room. Vern and Sammy were undressing Justin, pulling the clothes off when they could, slicing them open with Vern's pocketknife when tugging didn't immediately work. Mother came running in with another lantern and several clean bath towels. Sammy gathered Justin's clothes and disappeared with them in the direction of the library.

Everything seemed to be under control. I went back to my seat by the door, where I could hear it if anyone knocked. The EMTs would be here any time now. The rest of the chief's officers would be arriving. With luck, some of the people who'd been prowling around yesterday would show up, and I could lure them in and turn them over to the chief for interrogation.

But I felt a curious lack of enthusiasm for any of it. I pulled out my phone to check the time. Five-thirty-two a.m. Not a time I saw very often. And I'd been up since around three. But it wasn't just tiredness making me out of sorts. I was missing Michael and the boys. I wanted to tell Michael what was happening. Have him reassure me that I wasn't a bad person for feeling relief that the problems Castlemayne had caused would be going away. That feeling both sorrow and relief was not only possible but completely normal.

Heck, just hearing him answer the phone would cheer me up. But five-thirty was much too early to call just because I wanted to hear his voice.

I probably had a couple of voicemails from him on my phone. If the gloomy feeling persisted, I could always sneak off to someplace quiet and listen to one or two of them.

Or maybe he'd call me in a couple of hours. In theory, he and the boys were going to check out of the ski lodge this morning, pack the car, and hit the slopes for a few last runs before hitting the road early enough to be home for dinner.

Of course, that was assuming the snow didn't complicate their trip home. That possibility depressed me much more than seemed reasonable.

If I had it to do over again, I'd have gone on the ski trip anyway. I could have had meals with Michael and the boys and spent the rest of the day reading in the ski lodge. It would have been a much more festive way to spend the holiday. Also a lot more restful than staying here and playing gatekeeper for Castlemayne.

And someone else could have found his body.

I saw the flashing lights that signaled the arrival of the ambulance—no sirens, which was a relief. I was hoping most of our houseguests would sleep through as much of the morning's excitement as possible. I heaved myself up and opened the door for them.

"Hey, Meg," the lead EMT said as he dashed in. "Hear you got a twofer tonight. Where are they?"

"Hypothermia and concussion in the living room, scalp laceration and concussion on the third floor," I said.

"And dead body in the library, I hear," he said. "But we'll have to come back for him later. Hey, doc! Where do you want me?"

"Upstairs!" Dad shouted back. "Third floor, far end of the hall. The chief is with him."

The second EMT raced in, pushing the wheeled stretcher, and joined Dad in the living room. Much dashing upstairs and downstairs, as Dad and the EMTs conferred with one another and with the doctors back at the hospital. Eventually they decided that Justin, who was in worse shape, would ride on the stretcher, while Harris, who was groggy but conscious, would be strapped into a wheelchair for the ride. Dad was torn between riding along with his two patients and staying to participate in the murder investigation. Eventually, Caroline volunteered to help out in the ambulance and keep him posted, leaving Dad free to rejoin Horace in the library.

I'd donned my boots and was out by the side of the road, watching the ambulance pull away—and taking a closer look at the hole in our hedge—when my friend Aida pulled up in her cruiser.

"Hey there." She stepped out and turned on her flashlight. "You okay?"

"It's been a trying morning."

"Tell me about it." She rolled her eyes. "This was supposed to be my day off. Why is Vern out there taking pictures of the snow?" She gestured toward the side yard where Vern was hard at work with one of Horace's cameras. "It's not like he's never seen snow before."

"Documenting the route the killer probably took to get to and from our library," I said. "Not that anyone will be able to tell anything by now, apart from the fact that yeah, someone came and went that way. How much longer is it supposed to keep snowing?"

"Dunno." We both looked up as if we could figure out the answer from studying the flakes that were still drifting down. And then we both shivered and headed for the house.

As I walked, I pulled out my phone.

"Supposed to taper off by noon," I said after glancing at my weather app.

"Well, at least we might have a white Christmas," Aida said.

"Almost certainly," I said. "It's not supposed to get above thirty for the next week. Not to mention the possibility of a second storm on the heels of this one."

"Brrr." She shivered, in spite of her heavy coat. "Let's get inside and see what the chief wants me to do."

Rose Noire had taken over door duty, so after greeting her we headed for the library. Not that Aida needed to be shown the way, but I was curious to see what Horace, Dad, and the chief were up to.

The department's bright battery-powered lights were on in the library, and Horace was still methodically searching for clues. The chief was standing beside him, holding an extra-large umbrella over his head and Horace's.

"The jays don't seem to like us," the chief said when he saw my puzzled expression.

"They keep dive-bombing me," Horace added. "And trying to eat the corpse."

"I think they're just curious," the chief said, in a soothing tone. "I'm sure blue jays aren't carnivorous."

"I'm not," Horace muttered.

A quick glance revealed that a sheet of bright blue plastic had been thrown over the body and the surrounding area, though I could still see a few bloodstains that weren't hidden by the plastic. Dad, bundled up in his coat and a thick woolen scarf, was drinking coffee and ruminating aloud on the time of death.

"It's complicated," he said. "Because the extreme cold

hastens the cooling of the body while retarding rigor mortis."

The chief nodded.

"Aida, I'll be heading out shortly," he said. "Can you stay here and take over keeping the jays away from Horace?"

He didn't add "and guarding his back," but he didn't have to. Horace tended to tune out the rest of the world when he was working a crime scene, which meant if the killer returned, the way they always did in Dad's beloved mystery books, Horace would be a sitting duck. Aida nodded and took possession of the umbrella.

"Meg, I've called Maudie down at the funeral home, and she's going to send their hearse pretty soon to take Mr. Castlemayne down to the morgue," the chief added. "I'm sure you'll be relieved to have the body out of the house. But don't start cleaning up until Horace is finished and I give you the go-ahead."

"Roger." I nodded.

"Sorry," he said. "I know you could use the space, with all these relatives here for the holidays."

"We weren't counting on having access to it anyway," I said. "With Castlemayne in residence. Although I was hoping to get rid of him today—by which I mean sending him back to work at the zoo."

Dad was frowning over his phone. From the way he was tapping on it, I deduced that he was using the calculator app.

"I might be able to pin it down a little closer if we knew how long the doors had been open," he said. "I can probably estimate when they were left open by comparing the various temperatures I took when I first got here—outside, here in the library, and in the rest of the house. But it would only be an estimate, and I'm hoping we can get more specific information from our hypothermia victim when he wakes up. Assuming he remembers the events leading up to his injury. There's no guarantee—retrograde amnesia's quite common with head injuries."

"What about the stomach contents?" I asked. "He had a plate of food from the buffet last night. Harris took it to him around seven. And supposedly he was picky about having dinner at seven on the dot—though you'll have to ask Harris if he wolfed it down right away or dawdled over it."

"Yes, that could be very useful," Dad said.

"But it's possible that none of this will get us a smaller window than we have now," the chief said. "Between midnight and three a.m."

Dad nodded.

"Yikes," I said. "You mean I might have come that close to running into the killer?"

Chapter 18

"I'm sure the killer would have tried to avoid you," Dad said.

"I'm not," I said. "But don't worry—you don't need to reassure me."

"Most likely the car that woke you up was the killer fleeing the scene," the chief said. "That would mean you were never in danger of meeting them."

"Yeah, except the car wasn't what woke me up," I said. "Something else did. I assumed that it was the silence—either I woke up when the power went off and the house suddenly got quiet, or maybe when I drifted up to a lighter level of sleep I gradually became aware that everything had gone quiet and that woke me up. I was trying to go back to sleep when Watson started barking and I heard the car plow into our hedge."

"Interesting," the chief said. "I wonder if some noise coming from the library might have awakened you. I'll try to find out when your power would have gone out." He scribbled in his notebook.

"Kevin would know," I said. "He's got all his computers and other electronic gadgets programmed so they shut themselves down in case of a power outage—and attached to universal power supplies so they've got enough time to do so. He'd know to the second when the power went off and his UPS kicked in."

"Good to know." The chief nodded with satisfaction. "How early does he wake up? I have something else I wanted to ask him to do."

"No telling with Kevin," I said. "Some days he's up at dawn and others he sleeps till sundown like some kind of vampire. I usually text him if I want to ask him anything. He's got a useful Pavlovian response to the ding of an arriving text, and even if it wakes him up, he never seems bothered."

"My fingers are still chilled," the chief said. "Can you text him about the time of the power outage? And also ask him if he can do an online search. Blast—I suppose he can't do that until the power comes back."

"I think he's still got his satellite phone," I said. "He can probably manage to work on that. For all I know he's even got our router and his computers on a backup power supply. And they've got a backup generator down at Mutant Wizards. So as long as he can get into town, he can do your search."

"If his car can't handle the roads, I'll get him a ride," the chief said.

"Good," I said. "Because even if you didn't want him to do anything, he'd want to go down there. He gets antsy when life takes away his electronics. What should I tell him to look for?"

"Any articles Mr. Vreeland has written about Mr. Castlemayne. And for that matter, any articles he can find that contain information about his divorces, or lawsuits against him, or quarrels he may have had."

"Anything that could suggest a motive for his murder." I nodded, and started texting.

"I'll schedule the autopsy as soon as possible," Dad said. "Meanwhile, Meg, do you know where your mother is? I should go and get a list from her of the items on the buffet, so I'll know what to look for when I open the stomach. I think—"

"No, you should not ask Mother about the buffet," I said. "You can get a perfectly accurate list from Rose Noire."

"But—"

"Do you really want to upset Mother by spoiling her memory of an elegant holiday buffet with the knowledge that you're going to be looking for traces of it in a murder victim's gastrointestinal tract?"

"Oh, dear." Dad looked stricken. "I hadn't thought of it that way."

No, he wouldn't have.

"And, Chief," I went on. "I'm fine with the library being a crime scene for now—in fact, even once you're ready to release it, can you keep it off limits until I can get someone in here to clean up the worst of the blood?"

"Of course," he nodded. "Speaking of that—Dr. Langslow, the blood seems rather concentrated."

It didn't look that concentrated to me. But then, this wasn't the chief's library.

"Yes," Dad said. "He was probably stabbed pretty much where we found him, and he'd have bled out quickly."

"But not immediately." The chief looked at something on his phone. Probably a photo of the body—I didn't try to see. "It looks as if he did have time to clutch the knife and try to pull it out."

"Maybe." Dad frowned. "He could have done it as an almost involuntary reaction. But there's something off about the hand position. I think it was placed there."

"There were no fingerprints on the handle of the knife," Horace said over his shoulder. "Only some smear marks that would be consistent with someone wiping it clean. I'm thinking the killer wiped the handle to make sure he hadn't left any fingerprints. But then the knife handle looked a little too clean, so he lifted the hand and tried to position it as if Castlemayne had grabbed the knife."

"That would be consistent with the hand position." Dad nodded.

"Lovely," the chief muttered. "That reminds me—Meg, do you have some tarps we could use? Three should do it."

"Pretty sure we do," I refrained from glancing over at

the blue plastic covering the body. Did he want something to hide the rest of the blood? That wouldn't take three tarps. "What for?" I asked. "Not that I'm trying to pry, but it would help to know what size you need, and whether you can use well-worn ones or if I should try to find something new and waterproof."

"I don't care how worn or waterproof they are as long as they're large enough to conceal a police cruiser," he said. "I want to talk to all those unwanted visitors of yours, but none of them seem to be local and we don't even know some of their names."

"But as long as the word doesn't get out that he's dead, they'll all start dropping by any time now." I nodded my comprehension.

"And the word of his death won't get out until we figure out who's Castlemayne's next of kin and notify them," he said. "I'll think of something noncommittal to say if the news media come sniffing around."

"Justin Vreeland was the only reporter sniffing around before this," I said. "And if any new faces show, you're investigating a death that took place during the snow emergency."

"I like that," he said. "But meanwhile, if anyone notices the police presence out here—"

"Three tarps coming up," I said. "We keep them in the toolshed—I'll run out there now."

I went back to the front hall and laced on my snow boots—which gave surprisingly good support for my ankle. I'd need that if I was going to wade through what was getting close to half a foot of snow.

I passed through the kitchen, brightly lit with half a dozen lanterns, where Rose Noire was supervising the dozen or so relatives slicing up fruit and cooking bacon, eggs, and toast over the camp stoves.

When I stepped outside and scanned the backyard with my flashlight, I could see that the snow was unbroken, apart from the trail that appeared from the side of the house and led to the sunroom door. I grabbed the old broom we kept by the back door, used it to clear a path across the stoop and down the steps, then began plodding toward the toolshed.

The toolshed was actually a former animal shed of some kind, almost a junior barn, which meant it was large enough to contain not only tools but also things like the riding mower, the mini-tractor, and the growing collection of carts, spare parts, attachments, and accessories that Michael seemed to think they needed. The front wall of the shed was formed by a pair of repurposed sliding barn doors cut down to size. The other three walls were lined with sturdy wooden shelves and floor-to-ceiling pegboards, making it easy for me to keep the place organized.

Given how expensive some of the tools and equipment were, we were careful to keep the shed locked up tight. So I was surprised and not a little displeased to find the padlock hanging loose. Still through the hasp, so the door wouldn't blow open, but unlocked, so anyone who happened by could get in.

I slid the door open, stepped inside, and took a quick inventory. The mower and the tractor were there. I saw no vacant places on the pegboards that held all the garden tools. No unexpected vacant spots on the shelves. Nothing at all out of place except a folding chair, one of a dozen we used for extra seating during picnics. When the weather had turned cold in the fall, we had dragged all the folding chairs into the shed and stowed them overhead, on a rack that hung from the ceiling. Now one was leaning against the end of a wooden shelf, folded, seemingly harmless, but completely out of place.

I returned to the open door and looked out. I had a perfect view of the entire back of the house—including the sunroom door.

I pulled out my cell phone and called the chief.

Chapter 19

"Someone's been in our toolshed," I reported. "I noticed it when I came out here to get the tarps. It may not have anything to do with the murder, because it must have happened before the snow—I waded through what seemed like completely unbroken snow to get to the shed. But someone's definitely been out here in the last couple of days." I explained about the padlock and the folding chair.

"When was the last time you were there?"

"Saturday night," I said. "The eighteenth. You remember Michael and the boys were taking off for their ski trip Sunday morning. And the weather forecast showed the possibility of snow, so we came out and put the plow blade on the tractor so it would be ready to go. It takes four hands, and we're the only ones who really know how to do it properly."

"And you're sure you locked the shed afterward?"

"Yes. What's more, before I left, I tidied up a bit—made sure nothing was lying around out of place. I'm sure all the folding chairs were all on the rack." I glanced up at it. "Kind of a tall rack that hangs from the ceiling," I added. "Michael and I have no trouble reaching it. Neither do the boys nowadays. But someone short would have had to stand on something to get a chair down."

"And maybe thought you wouldn't notice if they didn't bother to put it back up? I'll have Horace check out the shed when he finishes with what he's already doing. Lock up when you leave."

"Roger."

When we signed off, I went over to the shelf where we stored tarps. I found two big enough to cover a car, and another two that would do the job if combined, for the third cruiser. Then I locked the shed, tested the padlock to make sure it had clicked, and went back to the house.

Vern and I moved his cruiser, Horace's, and Aida's into the driveway and covered them up. Evidently Sammy had gone off on an errand. Locals would spot the chief's blue sedan and instantly know he was on the premises, but the stalkers, not being from around here, would have no idea. By the time we'd finished the sun had come up and the day was about as bright as it was going to get while the snow was still falling.

Inside, Rose Noire was mopping up the melted snow in the front hall—a job that would have to be repeated endlessly all day, no matter how well we all tried to shake the snow off our boots and wraps while we were still on the porch.

"Buffet breakfast in the dining room starting in a few minutes," she said, glancing up. "And that means you, too, Vern."

"Thank you, ma'am," he said. "I need to see Horace first—I'll let him know."

In the dining room, the elaborate Christmas decorations had vanished, a couple of camping lanterns had banished the worst of the dark, the covered chafing dishes we had used for last night's buffet were back, and the young cousins who had been sleeping in the living room were dashing to and fro with breakfast goodies. The chief was munching on a slice of buttered toast and staring disconsolately at his phone.

"Bad news?" I asked as I grabbed a plate.

"No, just feeling irritated about how blasted uncooperative the Clay County folks are going to be if I have to call them."

"Why would you have to?" Since he was in a talkative

mood—and presumably taking a brief breakfast break—I set down my plate and took the chair I'd occupied when I was giving my statement.

"Because I have the feeling that at least one of the people I need to talk to is staying at the Clay County Motor Lodge," he said. "And fat chance getting a straight answer out of them or Sheriff Dingell."

"Which suspect?" I asked.

"The redheaded woman who was staking out the zoo," he said. "The one we figure is the other ex-wife. When we didn't connect with her at the zoo, I had Aida check around with nearly every one of the local bed-and-breakfast owners, using that photo you took, and none of them recognized her. Most of the others I have a handle on. I know Mrs. McKenna is at the Inn. I've asked Ekaterina to keep an eye out for her—we'll catch up with her eventually. Not exactly a prime suspect, since she didn't know Castlemayne, but she could have noticed something that might help us out."

"Like if she spotted one of the stalkers using our shed to spy on the house," I said. "It's got a perfect view of the sunroom door."

"Exactly." He took another bite of toast and chewed thoughtfully while glancing down at his notebook. "And the ex-wife we arrested gave the Cheerful Gnome as her local address." He grimaced, and I understood why. The local bed-and-breakfast establishments were invariably overpriced, but most were charming and comfortable. The Cheerful Gnome was neither. It took its name from its owner's impressive collection of lawn ornaments—at last count, one hundred and thirty-seven gnomes, seventeen birdbaths, six rock cairns, twelve religious statues, four fountains, and more wind chimes than anyone had ever managed to count. I happened to know the numbers from the *Clarion*'s recent article on the town's ongoing effort to enforce its zoning laws. I hadn't seen the interior decoration, but I'd heard it made the yard look restrained and tasteful.

"I've asked Sammy to go over there at nine to round her up," the chief said. "And Caroline's going to let me know when Vreeland and Harris are well enough for questioning. But I don't have a clue about the other ex-wife, and even if we find her that leaves two of your unwanted callers unaccounted for."

"One was claiming to be a bill collector and the other supposedly an autograph hound," I said.

"Both suspect." The chief frowned at his toast as if he blamed it for something.

"Yeah," I said. "I have a hard time believing anyone would have been that crazy for Castlemayne's autograph— for all we know the avid fan could actually be a fanatic with a grudge against him. And I'm trying to imagine how big his unpaid bills would have to be for it to be worth someone coming all the way from Pennsylvania to collect them. That's where he lives, you know."

"His creditors could have hired local talent," the chief said. "Or the alleged bill collector could be using that as a cover."

"A cover for something even less welcome than a bill collector?" I asked. "Such as?"

"Good point." He shrugged. "Maybe a process server? I gather he was having some legal woes."

"If I wanted to serve a subpoena on him, I wouldn't pretend to be a bill collector," I said. "I'd repurpose an Omaha Steak delivery box, throw in a bit of dry ice for verisimilitude, and show up claiming I needed his signature to hand it over."

"I think you might have a real future in the process-service business," he said with a chuckle.

Just then his phone dinged to signal an arriving message— which had happened occasionally during our conversation, but this message galvanized him to attention.

"Out-of-town car headed this way," he said. "Could be one of your callers."

"Could be." I glanced at my phone. "Although if they think seven-thirty a.m. is a suitable time to call, they're deluded."

"Would you mind standing ready to answer the door if they're headed here?"

"No problem."

I walked down the hall—more walking than limping, I noticed, with satisfaction—and perched on one of the side chairs. The chief followed me into the hall and peered through the peephole.

"It's stopped in front of your house," he said. "Red-headed woman, about five four, a hundred and twenty pounds, late forties or early fifties. She's pushing your doorbell button—maybe she didn't hear about the power outage. Want to take a look?"

I took his place at the peephole.

"Yes," I said. "That's the woman who tried to get in without really explaining herself yesterday, and then showed up at the zoo."

"Who may be the other ex-wife." The chief had the eager look of a cat getting ready to pounce.

"I assume you'd like to talk to her," I said. "Let me see if I can lure her inside so no one has to chase her down the icy road."

I opened the door rather abruptly, catching her in the act of leaning on the doorbell button. I feigned the same annoyance I'd felt when she showed up yesterday.

"In case you hadn't noticed, there's a countywide power outage," I said. "So there's no use ringing our doorbell."

"And it's about eighteen degrees out here," she said, with what she no doubt intended as an ingratiating smile. "Why don't we talk inside where it's little warmer?"

She pushed on the door, and I pretended to lose my grip on it. She brushed past me, strode into the hallway—

And came to a dead stop when she saw the chief in his neatly pressed uniform, standing at the foot of the stairs, arms folded over his chest.

She turned as if to retreat, but by that time I'd slammed and locked the door.

"This is the woman who came asking for Castlemayne yesterday," I said to the chief. "And then lay in wait for him out at the zoo."

"Look, I just need to see Mr. Castlemayne," the woman said.

"Why?" the chief asked.

"That's my business, actually," she said.

"May I see some ID?" he held out his hand.

The woman reached into her pocket with visible reluctance and took out something—one of those gadgets that serves as a combination cell phone case and wallet. Was it just me, or was this a little odd? In her place, I'd have been asking what right he had to be demanding my ID. Was her willingness to comply a sign of innocence or a guilty conscience?

She pulled out a plastic card—I recognized it as a Virginia driver's license—and handed it to the chief. He studied it for a few seconds then lifted his eyes again.

"Ms. Bridget Westmoreland of Mechanicsville, Virginia." He was looking at her, but since I was directly behind her, he could easily see me as well. I shook my head slightly to signal that I'd never heard of her.

He handed back her license.

"I'll just get out of your hair now." She turned to find me leaning against the door, arms crossed, in a deliberate echo of the pose the chief had used.

"A minute ago you practically knocked me down to get in, and now you're suddenly all in a hurry to leave," I said.

"Look, I don't know what's going on here." She turned back to the chief. "Maybe you should explain—"

"Ms. Westmoreland." The chief's voice was soft and

calm, but it grabbed her attention. "I am here investigating the murder of Mr. Roderick Castlemayne."

"Murder? Are you—" Her mouth fell open for a few seconds. "Oh, my God. You're serious."

"So I'd appreciate hearing your reasons for showing up here and demanding to see him."

"Oh God." She scrubbed her face with her hands as if trying to wake from a bad dream. "And I bet you think I'm a suspect. Believe me, I wouldn't have come here today if I'd known he was murdered."

"How did you know Mr. Castlemayne?" the chief asked.

"I didn't know him." She took a deep breath. Then she pulled out her phone case again, extracted another plastic card, and handed it to the chief. "I'm a private investigator. Among other things, I do process service. I was hired by Hayes Saunders and Associates—they're a Richmond law firm—to serve a subpoena on Mr. Castlemayne."

Chapter 20

"A private investigator," the chief echoed. He studied the second card—probably her private investigator's credentials. Then he looked back up at her.

"I'll need to talk to someone at Hayes Saunders to confirm this," he said.

"I figured as much." She was still holding her phone case. Now she took out two business cards and handed them over. "Top one's the lawyer who's handling the case. I'd suggest starting with her admin—that's the other card."

The chief nodded, pocketed the two business cards, and handed her back her PI credentials.

"There won't be anyone there this early," he said. "But I'll go leave a voicemail message for them to get in touch with me as soon as possible. Stay here."

He disappeared into our dining room, closing the door behind him.

Ms. Westmoreland's lips moved. I wondered if she was praying or swearing. Her expression could go with either.

"Have a seat if you like." I nodded toward the hall chairs.

"Since I won't be going anywhere anytime soon, you mean?" She laughed mirthlessly and sat down in the nearest chair, which happened to be on the side of the hat-and-coat stand that was farthest from the front door. That was nice—it meant I could sit on the chair nearest to the door and still leap up to intercept her if she made a break for it.

Of course, if she did make a break for it, she wouldn't

get far. Whoever had warned the chief she was approaching would have the make, model, and license number of her car by now.

While we waited, I studied her. Could she have killed Castlemayne? She seemed to have a perfectly legitimate reason for wanting to see him—and no motive to kill him. But she'd been lurking around. She could have figured out that the sunroom door didn't shut properly. What if she'd come back late at night to surprise Castlemayne and serve her subpoena? And what if he'd reacted violently and she'd had to defend herself?

"I wish I'd known you were coming to serve a subpoena on the old villain," I said finally, just for something to say. "I'd have led you to him."

"Seriously?" She blinked and gave a brief short of laughter. "That's kind of unusual in my business, you know. Most people try to protect their guests."

"He wasn't exactly a welcome guest," I said.

Her wry smile suggested that under other circumstances she'd find my comment hilarious.

The chief returned from the dining room.

"So you came to here to serve a subpoena," he said. "I'll let the attorney tell me about the subpoena itself when she calls back. I assume they hired you because you were closer than a Richmond agency."

"Yeah," she said. "Saves them on mileage."

"I'd appreciate it if you could fill me in on your movements yesterday," the chief said, opening his notebook.

"Right." She reached into her left-hand pocket, took out a notebook that was almost a twin of his, and flipped it open. "Hayes Saunders contacted me yesterday morning with the assignment. My online research suggested that my subject might be staying at this address."

"Caerphilly Confidential strikes again," I muttered.

"I got here around nine a.m. yesterday and did a little reconnaissance," she went on. "Knocked on the door, and the person who answered told me Castlemayne was working at the zoo and staying at the Caerphilly Inn. Which didn't turn out to be true, but there's no law against lying to a process server."

"The person you talked to was me," I said. "And I didn't lie—I said he was *supposed* to be staying at the Inn and working at the zoo. Letting him come here was a big mistake, and we'd have been sending him back today."

"So I staked out the zoo," she continued. "And around one p.m. Dr. Montgomery Blake, for whom my subject was allegedly working, left the zoo in a large truck, along with several of his staff. I decided to follow the truck, and arrived back here."

So that explained why she had disappeared from the zoo by the time Aida had gone out there to check her out.

"I took advantage of the fact that Dr. Blake and the occupants of the house were distracted," she went on. "They seemed to be removing two odd-looking bear cubs from the basement and loading them onto a zoo truck."

"Bear cubs?" The chief glanced at me with a puzzled expression.

"She means the wombats," I explained. He nodded. Ms. Westmoreland gave me a strange look, but forged ahead.

"So I undertook surveillance from a vantage point that gave me a good view of the door into the library, where I surmised my subject was located."

"She picked the lock and hid in our toolshed," I interpreted.

"I observed a blond woman entering the sunroom at around two-thirty p.m." The chief probably noticed that she hadn't bothered to deny picking the lock. "Shortly after that I saw several Caerphilly police vehicles arrive, and a deputy entered the sunroom with his service weapon drawn, and both my subject and the blonde were driven away in police custody. Since I had no idea when or even if they'd be returning, I decided I should call it a day. I drove back to Mechanicsville, picked up a pizza for dinner, and by six p.m. the husband and I had our feet up on the coffee table, binging on pepperoni thin crust and *Breaking Bad*."

"Were you planning to use the Waterstons' toolshed again for your surveillance?" the chief asked.

"Was I going to repeat my trespassing offense?" She chuckled. "That kind of depended on the snow. And whether anyone in the house had made a path out to the shed yet. Surveillance is a lot harder in the snow."

"I'd appreciate if you'd come down to the station to make a formal statement," he said. "Once that's done and signed, you'll be free to go for now."

"Roger." She shook her head. "Man. Never had this happen before—having someone bumped off before I could complete service. Hope it doesn't turn into an uphill battle to get paid for it. Can I drive down to the station myself? I'd rather not have to come all the way out here to get my car when we're finished."

"I'll meet you at the station," the chief said.

She nodded and stood to go. I opened the door for her, then closed it and made sure it was locked behind her.

"I'm hoping by the time I'm finished with her I'll be able to talk to Mr. Harris and Mr. Vreeland," the chief said. "I'm leaving Horace here to finish the forensics, and Aida to keep an eye on things. Let me know if you think of anything else that would be helpful."

"Can do."

"Oh, and in case you were worried, Curly's been found," he said. "I told your mother already, and my wife, but if you see any other members of the Ladies Interfaith Council, please share the news so they'll all stop calling and emailing me."

"Good to hear it," I said. "And I'll do what I can to spread the word." I let him out and locked up again.

I headed back for the dining room. The way today was

going, I should probably have a good breakfast. Who knew what interruptions would happen before the end of the day?

I filled a plate with all my favorite breakfast fare and took the place where the chief had been sitting. I pulled out my phone to check the time. Five minutes to eight. Okay, at eight I could call Michael. Even if they were all four sleeping in after a strenuous day on the slopes, he'd probably need to get up by eight if he wanted to get them all packed up, checked out, and fed in time to hit the slopes. I'd call at eight sharp.

I was chewing the last bite of a perfectly cooked slice of bacon and planning to reach for my phone as soon as I'd finished—when the phone rang. Michael.

"Morning, angel," Michael said in his best Bogie imitation. "I didn't wake you, did I?"

"No," I said. "I've been up for hours. Literally."

"Sorry," he said. "And here I was hoping you'd get a chance to sleep in with us gone. Apart from that, how's everything going?"

"It's been interesting," I said. "You want the good news or the bad news first?"

"Let's start with the good news," he said. "Always eat dessert first."

"The good news is that Roderick Castlemayne is no longer living in our library."

"Huzzah!" he said. "That was quick work. Did your mother and Caroline help?"

"No, they didn't have to," I said. "The bad news is that he's no longer here because someone murdered him last night."

A short silence.

"Damn," he said. "I'm sorry. Wish I'd been there to help you cope."

"It's okay—lots of relatives here to help. And I had Watson with me."

"Watson?"

"Horace's puppy. Rose Noire thought I needed some nighttime company in your absence."

"Should I be insulted by the fact that she tried to replace me with an adolescent Pomeranian?"

"It's okay," I said. "Watson actually woke me up to witness what may have been the killer's getaway. And in the process may have saved the life of that annoying *Star-Tribune* reporter."

With that I launched into a description of everything that had happened in the last few hours. Well, everything but a description of exactly how Castlemayne had been killed. Not that I wanted to keep it a secret from him, but people kept strolling in to fill their plates, and even when there was no one in sight I couldn't be positive no one was close enough to overhear.

"Be careful," he said. "I know you're not alone, and the chief will probably catch the killer any time now, but I still wish I was there already."

"When will you be?" I asked. "Not that I'm impatient or anything—wait, scratch that. I am impatient—I miss you guys."

"Well, do you want the good news or the bad news?"

"Me, I like to get the bad news over with first, like ripping off the bandage."

"Probably not till sometime this evening," he said. "We're going to make a detour."

"Damn," I said. "But still today. And the good news?"

"The good news is that the reason for the detour is to pick up your grandmother."

"Cordelia's coming after all? Yay!"

"Yes—she found someone who can housesit and feed all her animals, and also someone with a snowmobile to bring her down off the mountain, so we're going to pick her up at the police station. And the boys and I can have a nice visit with her on the way back here."

"That's *almost* worth the delay," I said. "Incidentally, the storm took the power out, so the temperature inside is steadily dropping. Tell Cordelia to pack her warmest clothes."

"Yikes," he said. "Of course, our local utility workers usually get the power back on pretty quickly."

"Yes," I grumbled. "Since they've had so much practice."

"I should go," he said. "Unless I want to be responsible for the death by starvation of three very much improved skiers."

"Give my love to the boys," I said. "And take a lot of pictures."

"Will do. Love you."

Our call had significantly improved my mood. I refilled my plate—not a full refill, just filling in the corners, as the hobbits would say—and settled down to relax by communing with my notebook.

My phone rang. I stifled a sigh. Even if the news of the murder hadn't hit the media, the local grapevine would have begun to spread it by now. I glanced down to see who was calling and was relieved to see it was Caroline.

"How's it going down there?" I asked. I knew better than to ask how the patients were, because being back in a hospital setting might have reminded her of the existence of HIPAA rules, and I didn't want a lecture about patient privacy.

"Everyone's doing pretty well, all things considered," she said. "But I have a question for you. We're trying to sort out what to do about Justin Vreeland."

Chapter 21

"What to do about Justin?" That sounded ominous. "Is that a euphemistic way of asking if I know where to ship his body?"

"Good heavens, no." Her chuckle was reassuring. "He's not awake yet, and not quite out of the woods, but your father's optimistic. Meanwhile, how much do you know about him?"

"Precious little," I said. "Apart from the fact that he's a particularly persistent and annoying example of the genus reporter. Which in no way justifies anyone hitting him over the head and leaving him to die in the snow."

"Certainly not," she said. "He's lucky Vern found him when he did. Of course, the fact that he doesn't seem to have any emergency contact or insurance information did complicate things a bit when he got here. He's lucky this isn't one of those heartless places that would turn him away. The Caerphilly Cares Fund will handle it if worse comes to worst."

"He must have health insurance," I said. "He works for the *Washington Star-Tribune.* Surely they provide health insurance for their employees."

"Well, there was no insurance card in his wallet," she said. "I suppose he could be one of those feckless young people who don't bother to carry it because they think they're invulnerable. Or maybe he's part-time—that's one of the sneaky things companies do to keep costs down, you know. If someone's part-time, they're not legally required to give them the same benefits."

"More likely he's a stringer," I said. "Which would mean he gets paid by the article, and has no benefits whatsoever."

"That would also explain why he doesn't have anything in his wallet to identify him as a *Star-Trib* reporter," she said. "We wouldn't have known he was a reporter if you hadn't mentioned it. The hospital billing department is going to call the paper's personnel office as soon as it's open, in the hope of finding out that he has insurance through them. I haven't heard back about that, though."

I nodded. My mind was racing. So Justin probably wasn't a *Star-Tribune* staff reporter. A stringer or freelancer. Then again—was he any kind of reporter? Maybe not. He certainly hadn't behaved like a reputable one. But if you had some reason for trying to see someone or ask nosy questions about them, what better cover than pretending to be a reporter?

But if he wasn't a reporter, who or what was he? Perhaps a private investigator, trying to find out information for someone who was suing Castlemayne. Or planning to. But didn't private investigators have their own rules or ethics? Certainly the better ones probably did—the kind that would be hired by the Audubon Society or the American Birdwatchers Association or whatever nature organization was suing him. But maybe one of the ex-wives had hired him. Yeah, I could see that. A divorced woman whose feckless ex never paid the alimony probably couldn't afford to hire a classy PI.

Or maybe he was someone with a grudge against Castlemayne, and thought pretending to be a reporter would get him inside the door.

"Meg?"

"Sorry," I said. "I was thinking. Takes longer this time of the morning. Let the chief know if you find out anything about Justin. He's probably just a clueless freelancer. But if he's not any kind of reporter, what was he doing hanging around our house trying to talk to Castlemayne?"

"He's a suspect, then?"

"You'd have to ask the chief," I said. "But for my money, yeah. After all, he was found near the murder scene. He was sure as hell involved in *something* last night."

"He draws his trusty Swiss Army knife and stabs Castlemayne just as Castlemayne tries to bludgeon him with a giant flashlight?" She sounded skeptical.

"Stranger things have happened."

"But Justin was outside and Castlemayne inside." She sounded puzzled. "How do you figure it could possibly have happened? Castlemayne chases him outside, whacks him with the flashlight, gets stabbed, and staggers back inside to die? Seems far-fetched—I don't think he could have survived long with that wound, much less travel more than a few feet."

"If Justin is the killer, it's more likely the encounter happened inside," I suggested. "Castlemayne brings the flashlight down on Justin's head just as Justin is stabbing him. Justin wrests the flashlight away and staggers outside before collapsing."

"That's a lot more plausible. Head trauma's unpredictable. But I think it's much more likely that there was a third party there."

"To do the stabbing or the bludgeoning?"

"Either. Both. How should I know? I don't envy the chief on this one."

"Neither do I. Look, the chief has Kevin trying to find out more info on Justin. If he comes up with anything that would be useful to the hospital, I'll let you know. Or he will directly."

"Perfect."

"While we're talking insurance—what about Harris?" I asked. "Please tell me he has some. Because if it's up to Castlemayne to arrange that—"

"He has insurance," she said. "One of those terrible plans that costs the moon and doesn't cover nearly as much as it should, so Caerphilly Cares might need to help him out, too. But at least he has something. Got to run—talk to you later."

Kevin had texted me a couple of times during my conversation with Caroline. The first text said "I have some questions about this Justin person." The others all said either "Are you there?" or just "???"

Suddenly everyone was curious about Justin.

I fortified myself with another slice of bacon and braced for a barrage of texting with Kevin. And then decided I wasn't up to it. So instead I texted "Huge buffet breakfast in dining room" and settled back to commune with my notebook. Rob had recently said having Kevin around was like having a giant friendly roach in the basement. Michael had protested, saying it was more like having an infallible food detector on-site. But he hadn't disputed Rob's premise: set out food and Kevin would show up.

Sure enough, he appeared within minutes, looking warm and toasty in his down jacket.

"What's Rob chasing?" he asked as he stepped into the dining room and pulled off his gloves.

"Chasing?" I echoed.

Just then Rob dashed by outside the dining room door, heading toward the living room. He did, indeed, seem to be chasing something. Kevin stuck his head out into the hall again.

"I thought it was mockingbirds we had loose in the house," he said.

"It was," I said. "Only one left now."

"That's not a mockingbird." Kevin stepped inside and pointed at the door. A blue jay fluttered by, followed by Rob, returning from the living room.

I closed my eyes and took one of the yoga breaths Rose Noire was always recommending. It worked about as well as it usually did, which was not much.

"Yes, now we have blue jays loose in the house," I said. "Well, at least it makes for a change."

"Cool beans."

I glanced at him, frowning, then realized he was only expressing his approval of the breakfast buffet.

Rob ran by the door again, this time followed by Delaney. I shifted to another chair—one where I'd have my back to the door and didn't have to watch the blue jay hunt.

"Are we celebrating being rid of the old sourpuss?" Kevin asked, as he piled his plate high.

"That would be pretty cold," I said. "We're doing our best to make sure the visiting family have a nice holiday in spite of the murder. And showing our support for our men and women in blue."

"Caerphilly County uniforms are khaki," he said through a mouthful of scrambled eggs.

"Figure of speech." I stole a slice of bacon off of the heaping plate he set on the table. "What questions did you have about Justin?"

"Are you sure Justin Vreeland is his name?"

"Reasonably sure," I said. "When he introduced himself, he said 'That's Vreeland, like Diana, the fashion editor.' And then he spelled it, just in case. I suppose it might be a pen name—we could call down to the hospital to ask what's on his ID."

"If it's his pen name, he hasn't been penning very much with it," Kevin said. "No articles with his byline in the *Star-Tribune*. So I widened my search, and there are no articles with his byline in any newspaper that I can find."

"Maybe they're behind a paywall?"

"I can look behind paywalls." He rolled his eyes, as if to say "what kind of idiot to you think I am?"

"Hang on a sec." I pulled out my phone and texted Caroline, saying "Are we sure Justin Vreeland's name really is Justin Vreeland? And where does he live?"

I was setting my phone down on the table when she texted back.

"Yes—Justin Andrew Vreeland. Newport News, Virginia. Why?"

"Working on finding out more about him," I texted back. Then I showed her answer to Kevin.

"Mephort Moos," he said through a mouthful of pineapple. "Yeah, that fits."

"Fits with what? So you did find out *something* about him?"

"He did one year here at the college. Didn't come back as a sophomore—no idea why; his grades were okay. Money, maybe—two years later he went back and got a bachelors in communications from Christopher Newport University—which is in Newport News. Good school, and not exactly cheap, but not as pricey as Caerphilly. And maybe he could live at home—he's from around there."

"So am I, you know," I said. "I know where Christopher Newport is."

"Right." Kevin gulped his cranberry juice. "From what I can tell, the only journalism experience he's had outside of college newspapers was doing gossip articles for a defunct website called the Tidewater Tattler."

"The Tidewater Tattler?" The name strongly reminded me of Caerphilly Confidential. "A pity it's defunct."

"Why a pity?" He cocked his head in curiosity. "It's defunct because whoever was running it got slapped with a bunch of lawsuits for defamation and for doxing people, which is—"

"Revealing people's addresses and phone numbers and social security numbers and other confidential information," I said, eager to prove I wasn't a complete cyber dummy.

"Yeah. But then they published some information that spoiled a big multicounty drug bust and ticked off everyone from the Newport News Police Department to the DEA, so they folded the site and slunk away."

"Good riddance, then," I said. "I only said it was a pity because I'd love to see what it looks like."

"Ask and ye shall receive." Kevin tapped on his phone. "Remember, nothing ever really disappears on the web. Here we go." He held out his phone so I could see the screen.

The Tidewater Tattler site was the evil twin of Caerphilly Confidential. Same almost unreadably tiny white type on a black background. Same gaudy red and yellow accent colors. Even the same schlocky typeface and corny motto on the masthead.

"Oh, my goodness," I murmured.

Kevin had his mouth full, but he cocked his head questioningly again.

I picked up my phone and did a search for the Caerphilly Confidential site. It took me a little longer than it took Kevin, but half a minute later I held up my phone to show Kevin.

He frowned, then looked more closely and laughed.

"Whoa—I'd kind of blotted out how ugly that site is. For a sec I thought you were just showing me you know how to find the Tidewater Tattler in the Wayback Machine— that's the main tool for finding old websites, you know. Yeah, they're clones. Probably done by the same person. A person with a pretty lousy eye for design."

"Do you think you could find out who's behind this Caerphilly Confidential website?" I asked.

"Probably," he said. "Unless they're smarter than usual. And from the looks of that thing, I bet they aren't. Damn, this makes my eyes ache." He grimaced and put his phone facedown on the table. "You think this could have something to do with the murder?"

"I have no idea," I said. "Until we find out it doesn't, I bet the chief is going to want to know as much as possible about it. But from what you said about this Tidewater Tattler website—do you want something like that setting up shop here?"

"Freedom of the press, you know," Kevin said.

"Yes, but also accountability," I said. "If they're going to start doxing people and printing false or libelous information, wouldn't it be nice to know who they are?"

"Point taken." He took a large bite of a blueberry muffin and chewed more slowly than usual. "Yeah, I'll work on figuring out who's behind the site," he said, once he'd finally swallowed. "And whether this Justin dude is connected to it. Shouldn't be hard. I'll go get started. Might need to go into town to do it. We've got a generator down at the office."

"If you go to the office, take a carload of relatives with you," I suggested. "They can hang out in the employee lounge until our heat comes back on."

He nodded absently. He picked up his plate, did another pass along the line of chafing dishes, and strolled out with that distracted air that showed he was already pondering ways and means.

I helped myself to a few more slices of bacon and opened my notebook again.

"Meg! There you are!" Dad bounced into the dining room, waving his flashlight about wildly.

I braced myself. Like Mother's "Meg, dear," Dad's "There you are!" usually signaled that I was about to be recruited for a project.

Chapter 22

"Have some breakfast." I pointed to the chafing dishes, in case Dad had overlooked them. "I have a feeling it's going to be a long day."

"Good idea." He pulled off his gloves and picked up a plate. "But I'll just grab a quick bite—I need to get down to the hospital to check on my patients."

Probably no use mentioning that Caerphilly Hospital, though small, had an excellent staff, including several emergency medicine specialists who probably considered Justin and Harris *their* patients.

"Can you take me there?" he asked.

"Didn't you drive over here?" I responded.

"Yes, but your mother will be needing the car later," he said. "She has some shopping to do and some kind of meeting down at Trinity."

More probably she had a rendezvous with Holly Mc-Kenna, although she might not have mentioned it to Dad. Given his notorious tendency to spill secrets, she was probably still keeping him in the dark about her plotting with Delaney's mother. And the Inn, where Mrs. McKenna was staying, had an impressive bank of generators—enough to keep its pampered guests from being inconvenienced by the outage. In fact, most of them probably wouldn't even notice that the outage had happened until they left the Inn. It made sense that Mother would find a reason to spend the day someplace that still had heat, light, and ready access to perfectly brewed Earl Grey tea.

And it occurred to me that the hospital also had a full

complement of emergency generators. I'd probably have to hang around until Dad was ready to come home, but it would be nice to take off my coat for a while and recharge my phone. And driving Dad around would ensure that I knew all the medical details he'd observed.

Just then a posse of relatives in coats or parkas dashed by, evidently in hot pursuit of the fugitive blue jays. One of them actually had a butterfly net.

"I'd be happy to take you to town," I said. "As soon as you finish breakfast."

While Dad fueled up for the day, I packed my phone charger and made sure Rose Noire knew I was leaving her in charge.

"And keep an eye on the houseguests," I said.

"So far they all seem to be enjoying themselves," she said.

"Yeah, but so far the inside temperature's only down in the fifties," I said. "If the thrill of roughing it starts to wear off, they can always go down to the Inn for a leisurely lunch."

"Or I can send them down to the zoo and let your grandfather amuse them for a while," she suggested. "Especially the ones who are complaining that they didn't get a chance to see the wombats while they were here."

"Perfect," I said.

Just then I heard a commotion coming from the living room, so I went over to the archway to get a view inside. Evidently some of the blue jays had taken refuge in our Christmas tree. At least seven of them were perching on it—and instead of clumping together in a flock they'd scattered themselves up and down its length. If they'd been cardinals, they'd have blended in so perfectly with the tree's red-and-gold color scheme that we'd never have noticed them.

And half a dozen relatives carrying towels and table-cloths were sneaking up on the tree.

"No," I said, so loudly that one of the jays took flight. "That tree is absolutely covered with fragile glass ornaments. Just chase the jays away. If you try pouncing while they're sitting there, you'll break things."

They didn't seem to notice.

"And Mother will *not* be pleased," I added.

That stopped them in their tracks. A couple of them gently waved the corners of their towels or tablecloths, and all the jays took flight.

"Open the front door," I called to Rose Noire.

The jays circled the living room a few times, then escaped into the front hall. For one glorious moment I thought they'd actually fly out through the open door, but at the last minute they banked, wheeled, and headed for the kitchen.

"Oh, dear." Rose Noire shut the door and ran after them.

"That was exciting." Dad popped out of the dining room, still munching on half a slice of toast. "Did you know that a group of blue jays is called a scold?"

"We should be going," I said. "Rose Noire can take care of the scold."

It was a little past nine when we set out. On the way down, Dad filled me in on Castlemayne's body temperature, and fretted over how the effects of having the sunroom door open to the outside elements complicated his calculation of the time of death. And mentioned how the angle of the wound made suicide almost impossible.

"Is the chief actually considering suicide a possibility?" I asked. "Because I can tell you flat out, if you ever find me stabbed in the throat with a Swiss Army knife, you can be damned sure it wasn't suicide."

"Well, no," Dad said. "It's not a very plausible method of suicide—but that wouldn't stop some overeager defense attorney from trying to claim that's what happened, so it's just as well we can easily refute it."

Dad babbled on happily for a while about cases in which

only solid forensic analysis had prevented murders from being mistaken for suicides, while I tried to think of twelve citizens of Caerphilly who would be gullible enough to buy the suicide-by-Swiss-Army-knife scenario. I was still far short of a full jury's worth when we pulled into the hospital parking lot.

I let Dad off at the front entrance and went to find a nearby parking spot. Thank goodness Osgood and Beau Shiffley had been at work here with their plows.

I strolled into the lobby and breathed a sigh of contentment. It wasn't as brightly lit as usual, but the warmth was heavenly. I shed my coat and looked around. Dad was nowhere to be seen. The receptionist and an RN were hanging glitter-trimmed paper angels on the Christmas tree in the lobby—each angel representing a donation to Caerphilly Cares. I was pleased to see that they were having a hard time finding space for the latest batch of angels. They looked up from their task and greeted me with delight.

"What in the world happened at your house?" the receptionist asked. "Your dad wouldn't tell us a thing."

"Well, he said he'd tell us after he checked on his patients," the RN said, shaking his shiny, freshly shaved head. "But you know how he is. He'll be fussing over them for hours."

"He's probably trying to follow the chief's orders literally," I said. "And not say anything until the chief gives his permission."

"A death, then." The receptionist nodded knowingly. "They wouldn't want the news to get out until they've notified the next of kin."

"And maybe a murder, if the chief's involved," the RN said. "Is it—I mean, it's not—"

"No one local," I said. I could see them visibly relax. "You can probably get more out of the chief when he comes here to question them."

"He already went up," the RN said. "I'm not sure all three of them are awake yet."

"All three?" I echoed. "We only sent you two customers."

The faces of the RN and the receptionist took on the smug look of people who know something you don't know and have a cast-iron reason for not telling you.

"I know, you can't tell me—HIPAA regulations," I said. "When I see the chief, I'll ask if I can give you the inside story on my way out. Meanwhile, do you have any idea where Dad went? I assume he's checking on either Justin Vreeland or A. H. Harris, and I need to see if he wants me to hang around and take him home." And wherever Dad was would probably also be where the chief had gone.

"Vreeland, room 212," the receptionist said. "And Harris, room 216." She printed my name on a stick-on visitor badge and handed it to me. I obediently donned it and wished them a Merry Christmas.

Probably a good sign that they were on the second floor I thought as I strolled toward the elevator. The emergency room was on the first floor. If Justin and Harris were up on the second, they were probably out of immediate danger.

I stepped out of the elevator onto a relatively peaceful floor. Not a big surprise—with Christmas only a few days away, people would be putting off any elective hospital stays. Glancing down the hall I spotted the nurses' station, decorated with one of my favorite oddball Christmas decorations: a tree made of partially inflated white surgical gloves and festooned with a garland of silver tinsel. Nearly hidden behind the tree was Caroline, talking to the floor nurse. I went over to join them.

"He's awake, and Dr. Langslow thinks he'll be fine," Caroline was saying.

"Are we talking about Harris or Justin?" I asked.

"Neither," the nurse said. "Another of your father's patients."

"Who came in with a nasty bleeding head wound, like Harris, and hypothermia, like Justin," Caroline said. "A curious coincidence. But no concussion, thank goodness. Speaking of Harris—he's awake and not exactly happy that your dad wants to keep him a while for observation. I've told him we'll find someone to bring him anything he needs—could I enlist you to do that?"

"No problem," I said. "I'm also on tap to chauffeur Dad home eventually—and you, too, if you need a ride, since I don't imagine the EMTs will take you back. Shall I go in and talk to Harris? See what he wants me to bring him?"

"Perfect," she said. "And I don't suppose you've had time to find out anything else about Justin Vreeland."

"Actually, yes," I said.

Caroline and the nurse both looked eager.

"He doesn't work for the *Star-Tribune*," I began.

"Well, we know that," Caroline said. "The hospital's billing office already called the *Star-Tribune*'s personnel office."

"It's possible that he's freelancing—trying to get a story he can sell to the *Star-Trib*," I said. "Or build up a résumé in the hope of getting hired by them. But I suspect it will turn out he's working for Caerphilly Confidential."

"That horrible gossip website?" the nurse exclaimed. "We'd better not let that get around the hospital. Last week they published a list of Dr. Khan's facelift patients—the hospital ethics committee's on the warpath."

"Let's keep it to ourselves, then," Caroline said.

"I doubt if he's the one who's actually running the site," I said. "So let's do what we can to keep him alive so the hospital ethics committee can interrogate him about who is."

"Oh, yes." The nurse smiled and dashed off.

"Actually, for all I know he could be running the site," I confessed to Caroline. "But we don't need for that to get out just yet."

"Understood. Look, you are going to check in on Harris, right?"

"If it's allowed," I said.

"It would be helpful if you did." She yawned and stretched. "And stay there till I get back. I want to go down to grab breakfast in the cafeteria—breakfast and a jumbo-sized coffee. Your dad's in there now, but he's got other patients to see and the autopsy to schedule. He wants us to keep checking on Harris frequently—having someone stay with him for a while would be optimal. Just until we're sure he's not showing any danger signs of concussion—you want to watch for—"

"Headache, nausea or vomiting, confusion, vision disturbances, dizziness, memory problems—"

"You've got the picture. I'll be back shortly."

She nodded toward room 212 and strode off down the hall.

The door to room 212 was open, but the privacy curtain was drawn. So I rapped on the doorframe.

"Who's there?" Harris's voice sounded a little weak and more than a little cranky,

"Meg Langslow. May I come in?"

"Might as well."

"Yes!" Dad exclaimed. "Just the person we need!"

Evidently Dad had more work for me, I thought, as I slipped through the opening in the curtain.

Chapter 23

The head of Harris's hospital bed had been raised to a forty-five-degree angle, and he lay back, staring up at the ceiling. Dad was at his side, bending over to peer into his left ear with an otoscope. Harris wore the peeved look of someone who's tired of having his orifices peered into.

"Well, that looks fine." Dad removed the otoscope and beamed at his patient. "And no ringing or changes to your hearing?"

"No." Harris looked as if he were consciously refraining from shaking his head, though.

"Splendid." Dad patted him gently on the shoulder. He glanced up at me. "What a stressful day! We don't often get three emergencies in one night."

"Much less three such interesting emergencies," I agreed. "It's like your own little medical experiment. I understand you've got one hypothermia with possible concussion, one possible concussion with a bleeding head wound, and one bleeding head wound with hypothermia. Covers all the bases."

Harris looked slightly alarmed at that, but Dad's face lit up.

"I never thought of that," he exclaimed. "Of course, it's too small a sample to really be an experiment. But it could serve as the basis for a nice little article on some of the factors to be considered when treating patients with comorbid conditions." He stood nodding slightly for a few seconds, then snapped back to the present. "But no lollygagging—I'm going to go organize getting the CT scan for that head of yours." He dashed out of the room.

Harris looked after him with a mournful expression on his face and uttered an almost inaudible sigh.

"I know," I said. "It's annoying, being poked and prodded and wheeled down to Radiology when all you really want to do is rest. But won't it be reassuring to know you're going to be fine?"

"At the moment, I don't really care," he said. "I just want to be left alone. I feel awful."

Actually, he looked awful. But I didn't think it would be helpful to say so.

"You'll feel better once the pain meds kick in," I said. "And now that they've got all the blood cleaned up, you're looking pretty good."

He looked up at me with a lugubrious expression. I got the feeling he wanted to say something like "Pretty good? Are you kidding?" but was too polite.

"Okay, how about 'a lot better than the last time I saw you'—how are you doing otherwise?" I asked.

"It's been quite a shock." His voice was almost inaudible.

"I'm sure it has," I said. "And I'm sorry for your loss."

"I'm not sure I can claim it's my loss," Harris said. "Unless you mean my job, which I have most definitely lost, but that would be a rather petty reaction wouldn't it?"

"Not petty at all," I said. "Losing your job's . . . well, a pretty formidable challenge, isn't it?"

"Challenge," he repeated. "If you're using that as a euphemism for 'catastrophe,' yeah. But I'm still alive. And Mr. Castlemayne . . ." His voice trailed off and he frowned slightly, as if struggling to find the words he wanted. "I won't try to pretend that I liked him," he said finally. "Or that we had an easy relationship. But he was a great man. A great artist. And he gave me a job when I really needed one. I'm grateful, truly. But I keep thinking I should be feeling more. I'm shaken, but not as much as I'd have expected."

"Maybe it hasn't really sunk in yet," I suggested.

"That's it," he said, eagerly, as if I'd made an important point. "I think it's partly because they haven't told me exactly what happened to him—just that he's dead, and it's almost certainly murder. I keep thinking he'll come dashing in, knocking things over and asking why the hell I haven't mixed up his colors yet. His death doesn't seem real."

I thought of saying that he could take it from me, Castlemayne's death was very, very real. The image of the Swiss Army knife sticking out of his throat rose unbidden to my mind. Probably kinder to spare Harris the details like that.

"And also it's sort of sad," he went on. "The chief's going to ask me again who his next of kin was. Maybe he thinks I was too stunned to think when he asked me before, but I really don't know. If he has any family left, I've never met them. He's never even mentioned them in the three years I've been with him. I suggested the chief talk to the ex-wives. Surely one of them would know."

"And no current wife, I assume," I said. "Any prospects?"

"Prospects?" Harris looked puzzled.

"Any potential future ex-wives?" I said.

"Good heavens, no." Harris sounded slightly amused. "Frankly I have no idea how he managed to convince one woman to marry him, much less two. I rather think they must have been under the impression that he was a great deal more affluent than he actually was."

"And they divorced him when they figured out the truth?" Clearly Harris had a jaundiced view of the ex-wives, but then he'd seen a lot more of them than I had. "So however annoying his failure to pay alimony must have been, it couldn't have been a big surprise. Were either of them ever violent?"

"He and Madeleine got into a fistfight once, if you can believe it." Harris looked as if he couldn't quite believe it himself. "Iris was more . . . sneaky and destructive. She threw rocks through his windows at least twice. And slashed his tires. But then, Madeleine's been dealing with him a lot longer. She's had a lot more time to get frustrated."

"Do you think either of them is capable of killing him?"

"Yes." He didn't hesitate. "Capable, yes. I think either of them would in a heartbeat if she thought she could get away with it. They're that angry with him. But I think they're too smart to do it. I mean, they'd have to know they'd get caught. Besides, if they kill him, what chance do they have of ever getting their back alimony?"

"Maybe one of them decided she had a much better chance of getting her back alimony from his estate than she ever would from him," I suggested. "I mean, he could go on ignoring court orders indefinitely, but whoever handles his estate will probably just pay up, won't they?"

"If there's any money to pay them with, yes," Harris said glumly.

Now that raised interesting possibilities. What if Castlemayne had finally admitted to one of the ex-wives that he didn't have the money to pay her alimony? Didn't have it and might never have it. Admitted it, or finally gotten her to believe what he'd been telling her all along. Might one of them have reacted violently and stabbed him?

"Well, whatever the motive, they've got to be at the top of the chief's suspect list, don't you think?" I asked.

"Oh dear." He looked agitated. "I'm not trying to accuse one of them—really, I'm not. I have nothing specific against either of them. I don't really know them that well."

"Better than anyone else in town," I said. "Although I gather your interactions with them haven't exactly been under the best of circumstances."

"I'm not trying to point the finger at them." He sounded

suddenly defensive. "Shouldn't I be telling all this to the police?"

"Absolutely," I said. "I thought you'd already talked to the chief."

"He tried to question me while they were stitching me up." He sounded sulky. "I'm afraid I wasn't that coherent at the time. And he said he'd be back later to go over my story in more detail. Which I'm not looking forward to, because I already told him all the details I could remember. I really don't want to be interrogated."

"Sorry," I said. "I'm not trying to interrogate you—just still baffled and in shock over what happened. And feeling a little guilty that—well, do you think there's anything I could have done to prevent what happened?"

I tried to look anxious and troubled, hoping that he wouldn't notice that actually I was still trying to interrogate him.

"I don't think there's anything you could have done." He shook his head. "You warned us every time the ex-wives showed up. Or any of the other unwanted visitors. And I warned him to be careful of letting anyone in. Not that I thought anything like this would happen, of course. But all these interruptions—they interfered with the work. And we were already so far behind schedule." He laughed. "Well, *he* was behind schedule—but he'd act as if it was my fault. If I didn't have something done the second he wanted it—like stretching a new canvas or mixing his colors or cleaning his brushes—he'd act as if it was my malingering that was making us fall behind, instead of the hours he spent smoking and thinking and trying to get himself in the mood. He certainly was a character." He smiled as if his boss's behavior were endearing instead of massively annoying.

Someone knocked on the door. The privacy curtain was still drawn, which meant that all anyone standing in the doorway could see were my feet and ankles.

"It's Chief Burke. May I come in?"

Chapter 24

I glanced at Harris, who nodded, a look of resignation on his face.

"Come in," I said.

The chief slipped around the end of the curtain.

"Sorry to bother you, Mr. Harris," he said. And then he glanced over at me.

"I can leave if you want to talk to Mr. Harris alone," I said. "I was only keeping him company till Dad comes back to drag him off to his CT scan."

"Not really sure I need company," Harris said.

"Actually, I'm also watching for signs of concussion," I said. "It's either me or a nurse who will take your vitals every five minutes and badger you with questions."

"Now that you put it that way, you can stay."

"Unless the chief wants me to step out." I glanced at the chief.

"No need," the chief said. "I won't keep him long—I know he's probably not feeling too great. I just need to ask a few quick questions, and then I'll be out of your hair."

I got the definite impression that the chief not only didn't mind my presence but actually wanted me to stay. Possibly because having me around would make his questioning seem less official. Less threatening—and perhaps lead Harris to be more forthcoming?

"Mr. Harris," he began. "When did you last see Mr. Castle-mayne?"

Harris thought briefly.

"I think it was about ten," he said. "I could tell you more precisely if I had my phone."

"If you brought it with you it will be in the little bag they put all your possessions in." I suspected it was here, remembering how tightly Harris had been clutching it when he keeled over. The bag was hung over the back of the chair I was sitting in, so I rummaged in it, found the phone, and handed it to him.

"Thank you." He turned on the phone and tapped the screen a few times. "As we were wrapping up for the evening, he told me he was running low on Prussian blue. That's a color he expected to use a lot of to paint the blue jays, so it was important not to run out. Here it is. At ten eleven I sent myself an email as a reminder to go to the art supply store tomorrow. And right after that I wished him good night and went up to my room."

"And he was alone in the library."

"Yes." I could see Harris start to nod and check himself.

"How late were you awake?" The chief had his little notebook out, but seemed to be taking very minimal notes. Probably to avoid spooking Harris.

"I brushed my teeth, put on my pajamas, and went right to bed," he said. "It had been a very exhausting day."

"Did you wake up at all in the night?"

"No." Harris shook his head. "Not until Meg came up to break the news about . . ." His voice trailed off.

"Did he have any enemies that you knew about?" The chief appeared to be looking down at his notebook, but I could tell he was actually watching Harris rather closely.

"Oh, dear." Harris sighed and closed his eyes for a few seconds. "Yes, he did. He went through life making enemies. But if you'd asked me yesterday if I thought any of them wanted to kill him—were capable of killing him— I'd have said no. Of course not. None of them. People don't do things like that. But obviously one of them did, so I'd have been wrong." He frowned for a few seconds.

"I suppose if I had to point to anyone, I'd have to say the ex-wives. They hated him the most. And, as Meg just suggested, they might have imagined they could sue his estate for back alimony."

"Imagined?" the chief echoed.

"I think he was broke," Harris said. "I don't know for sure—it could be that he was just having a temporary cashflow problem. He was lucky this job came along when it did, because his landlord had locked him out for non-payment of rent. Mr. Castlemayne claims—claimed— the landlord had been dragging his feet on doing some necessary repairs and he was withholding the rent until that was done—but he might have been just saying that to save face. He always paid my salary, but the last five or six months it was always a day or two late."

The chief nodded.

"Is there anything else you can think of to tell me?" he asked.

"No." Harris shook his head almost imperceptibly— was he doing it so tentatively because movement hurt his head or just because he was afraid it would? "I did want to ask—do you have any idea how long you'll want me to stay in town? I need to start looking for a new job pretty quickly, and I rather doubt there's anything in my line around here."

"I understand," the chief said. "In the short term, having you around will be incredibly helpful—we know so little about your late employer, and you're probably the most reliable source of information on him. More reliable than the ex-wives, at any rate. The one I met seems a little . . . unbalanced."

"They both really hate him," Harris said. "Of course, he and I didn't exactly get along, either. He was difficult."

"But you managed to work with him," the chief said. "For now, you just focus on getting well. Try not to worry— but if you happen to think of anything that might help us find his killer, I'd like to hear it. The nurses all know how to reach me."

"And when the hospital releases you, you can come back to our house and rest for a while," I said. "Unless you have family that you were planning to see for Christmas."

"No," Harris spoke quickly, as if anxious to shut down the topic. "No family. At least none I keep in touch with."

"Then I'll find you a room where you won't have to worry about hitting your head every time you sit up—we don't want to aggravate that concussion. And you're welcome to join all our holiday celebrations, but if you don't feel like socializing, I'll tell everyone Dad has ordered you to stay in bed with no visitors to interfere with your recovery. Your call."

"Thanks," he said. "I'd appreciate that."

"Good news!" Dad bounced into the room, followed by a uniformed hospital technician. "Time for your CT scan! Chief, mind if I whisk Harris away for a bit?"

"He's all yours," the chief said. "I've asked him all the questions I can think of for the moment. Mr. Harris, I hope you feel better soon."

Harris smiled wanly. I wasn't a mind reader, but I didn't think I had to be to tell that he wasn't expecting the CT scan to be an improvement over the interrogation. I followed the chief out of Harris's room.

We found Caroline waiting in the hallway.

"Vreeland's still not conscious," she said when she saw the chief. "But he's improving. I'm going to stay here at the hospital and make myself useful. I'll let you know when he regains consciousness."

"I'd appreciate it," the chief said. "I'm going to head back and see how Horace is doing with the forensics. Merry Christmas to both of you."

We wished him a Merry Christmas in return and he headed for the elevator at a brisk pace.

"Gang way!" Dad shouted, emerging from Harris's room.

We stood aside and watched until the bed, wheeled by the technician, with Dad in the lead to run interference, disappeared around a corner at the far end of the hallway. Harris, clearly unhappy with the whole adventure, was clutching the siderails with a death grip.

"The CT scan's just a precaution," Caroline said. "I think poor Harris is more shook up about the murder than anything else. Oh, by the way, your mother called just now."

"And I bet she has something she wants me to do." I repressed a sigh and reminded myself that I'd gotten off rather easy lately, thanks to the ankle. "Should I brace myself?"

"Nothing onerous." She chuckled. "She wants you to help her track down Mrs. McKenna, who hasn't been answering her phone calls, and she wants you to check on Curly. I offered to do that myself, but she said he knows you and he'd be more likely to talk to you."

"I can try," I said. "Finding him's going to be the tricky part."

"Not today," she said. "He's here. Room 220."

Chapter 25

"Curly's here in the hospital? What happened to him?" I asked.

"Well, I assume you already heard about how that over-eager young attorney managed to get him released from jail in spite of the chief's best efforts. Come on." She headed down the hall, and I fell into step beside her. "And then the wretch hovered around to thwart everyone's efforts to get Curly safely inside again. Leaving the poor man to roam the streets in the middle of a blizzard."

"Don't tell me," I said. "He's the mysterious third patient—the one with hypothermia and a bleeding head wound?"

"Yes," she said. "Here he is."

I followed her into a room where Curly lay tucked up in a hospital bed, watching *Miracle on 34th Street* on TV with the sound off. I'd never seen him cleaned up before, and I was surprised—I'd always assumed he was in his fifties or sixties, but he was probably more of a weather-beaten thirty-something. And he looked quite serene and contented in spite of the bandages—a fat one that enveloped his entire right hand and another one like a skullcap covering most of his head. The unruly gray-brown curls that had given him his name had probably ended up in a trash can in the ER. He waved his unbandaged hand when he saw us.

"Merry Christmas, Meg," he said.

"Merry Christmas to you," I said. "What happened?"

"It's all that young lawyer's fault." He sounded sad and

disappointed rather than angry. "I know he means well, but he sure as heck messed up my holiday."

"What's wrong with your hand?" Mother would want specifics. "Frostbite?"

"Oh, no," he said. "Some of my toes were getting a little numb but they tell me they'll be fine. And I had my hands in my pockets."

"He put his fist through a plate-glass window," Caroline said, impatient—as always—to cut to the chase.

"I tried jaywalking and littering and then loitering in front of a couple of stores where I know the owners are fussy about me alarming the tourists," Curly said. "But that darned young lawyer kept coming over and scaring off the cops before they could arrest me. I had to do something. So I figured I'd break one of the front windows of the ice cream shop. The one that's had that big crack for months now—I figured their insurance would pay for a nice new window and I'd be in jail for destruction of property."

"Unfortunately, he managed to cut his hand very badly on the glass," Caroline said. "And several pieces of falling glass landed on his head. You're lucky you didn't lose an eye."

Curly dipped his head as if graciously conceding a point.

"Next time, use a brick," she went on. "If you throw it from a safe distance—"

"No, next time, call someone to help you," I said, with a stern glance at Caroline. "If you had called me, for example, I could have come downtown and filed a trespassing charge against you. Heck, I could probably even have found a broken window you could take credit for."

"But I haven't been anywhere near your house." Curly sounded puzzled.

"Yes, and the chief's investigation would prove that, and I'd realize I was mistaken and apologize," I said. "But that would take a few days."

"Ah." Curly smiled. "I'll keep that in mind."

Which didn't mean he'd do it. I was puzzled. I knew next to nothing about Curly—no one did. He seemed well spoken and completely sane, apart from his stubborn refusal to cooperate with anything he considered charity.

"And besides," he said. "It was the middle of the night when I finally realized I needed to do something. I wouldn't have wanted to wake you up."

"You're a lucky son of a gun," Caroline said. "All of the deputies on duty at that hour were off at the far ends of the county dealing with fender benders and fallen trees blocking the road and things like that. You might have died if Osgood Shiffley hadn't come along just then in his snowplow."

"Yeah," Curly said. "'Specially since I managed to stagger away from the window into the alley and fall down right beside the dumpster. Not sure how Osgood spotted me. Maybe he stopped to throw something in the dumpster."

"Maybe he was looking for you," Caroline said. "Everyone was worried about you. You'd think that lawyer could find something better to do than spend his day trying to make sure you froze to death. I bet he didn't offer to feed you or find you a place out of the cold, now did he."

"I wouldn't have taken them from him." Curly's mild-mannered face took on just a hint of stubbornness.

"But he didn't offer, did he?" Caroline asked.

Curly shook his head.

"I rest my case."

"Mother asked me to check on you," I said. "Make sure you had everything you need."

"Can't complain," he said. "It's pretty comfortable here. And the food's not bad. Not bad at all."

"Surprisingly good for hospital food," Caroline agreed. "And I don't think they'll need to keep you much longer."

Was it my imagination, or did those last words dampen Curly's mood—just a little.

"But no matter how eager you are to get out, don't hesitate to tell the staff about any symptoms you might be feeling," I said. "Especially any that might suggest you could be experiencing concussion on top of the cuts and hypothermia."

"Concussion?" Curly asked. "Not sure I know what the symptoms of that would be."

"Headache, nausea or vomiting, confusion, vision disturbances, dizziness, memory problems." I glanced at Caroline as I listed them. "Anything like that."

"Right." He nodded slowly, as if committing my list to memory. "Got it."

Caroline was fighting back laughter. I resolutely ignored her.

"We should let you get some rest now," I said. "But just press the call button if you need anything."

He picked it up to show he understood, then closed his eyes and relaxed. We returned to the hallway.

"Honestly," she said. "Telling him how to fake a concussion. I should report you to . . . to . . . to your father."

"Dad's pretty good at spotting hardcore malingerers," I said. "And don't you think after what Curly went through last night he probably needs a little recovery time?"

"True," she said. "I just wish we could figure out some way to get him off the streets for good. But let's worry about that later. I'm going to go in and check on Justin."

She didn't protest when I tagged along. She knocked gently on the doorframe before pushing through the privacy curtains. I followed.

She walked quietly over to the bed and began checking on things—Justin's pulse, his IV drip, the oximeter on his fingertip, the placement of the cuff that took his blood pressure at regular intervals, and all the incomprehensible numbers flashing across all the screens attached to him. I just stared at his face.

Justin looked awful. His head was swathed in bandages,

like Harris and Curly. His face was pale and drawn as if in pain. But what really unnerved me was a sense of . . . blankness. Was that typical of concussion sufferers who hadn't yet awakened? Or was it a bad sign—a sign that maybe this particular concussion patient wouldn't be waking up?

And he looked so young. I'd been building up a fairly strong feeling of resentment and dislike toward him since finding out that on top of badgering me he was running the sly, nasty Caerphilly Confidential site. The resentment didn't evaporate while I was looking at him, but I had something else to balance against it. He was young and naïve. He was just trying to make his way in the world. And maybe what he thought was his ticket to fame and fortune—or at least getting a few articles placed in a reputable publication—had backfired on him. He'd tried to get a big scoop, and it had gotten him gravely injured—maybe even killed.

Of course, my sympathy would be misplaced if he turned out to be the killer. But, in the meantime, I made a mental note to try to stop thinking of him as Justin the Weasel. Not that he hadn't earned it, but right now I felt guilty about calling him that.

Caroline finally stopped doing nurse things and stood for a minute or so looking down at him.

"Your vitals are looking better all the time." Her voice was low but clear. "You just rest as much as you need to. Wake up when you're good and ready."

Then she turned and led the way out of the room.

"Are his vitals really looking that good?" I asked when we were back in the hallway.

"Yes," she said. "A lot better than when we brought him in. And they were able to relieve the swelling, so that's a plus. He's not out of the woods, but I think he'll make it."

"Just make it?" I said. "Or come back as good as new?"

"There's still a good chance of that," she said. "Just not a guarantee. Head injuries are tricky."

I nodded. It occurred to me that Caerphilly Cares would

probably end up covering most if not all of the expenses for all three of Dad's patients—and in Justin's case, the bill might not be trivial. I opened up my notebook and scribbled a reminder that we should start planning some more fundraising projects for our beloved local charity.

My phone rang.

"It's Grandfather," I said, glancing at it.

"If he's calling to ask if you've seen me, tell him I'm heading over to pick him up as soon as I'm sure there's nothing useful I can do here," she said. "We're going to work on trapping the blue jays."

"Awesome," I said. "Afternoon, Grandfather. What's up?"

"I need your help."

That was Grandfather's more straightforward equivalent of Mother's "Meg, dear," and Dad's "There you are!" I was three for three today.

"Help with what?" I asked.

Chapter 26

"We need to get Castlemayne's junk out of the Inn before they charge us for another night," he said. "Can you go over there and take care of it?"

I decided not to point out that it was already past noon, the Inn's checkout time. I could talk Ekaterina into extending the checkout time—in fact, she might suggest it herself if she thought she could fill the room. Which was likely—this time of year there were always plenty of tourists who came to see Christmas in Caerphilly as a day trip, fell in love with the whole experience, and wanted to stay over and spend more time—and money—here.

"I assume the police have cleared doing this," I asked.

"Yes, the chief examined everything already, and Horace did his forensic routine," Grandfather said. "Which didn't take long, since obviously none of that stuff was anywhere near the murder. You can take it all out to the zoo and put it in that room we set up for him to use as a studio. Horace has cleared that, too. Of course, if you can find that wretched assistant of his, you might tell him to do it."

"I don't think he can," I began.

"Nonsense!" Grandfather exclaimed. "Of course he can! He's perfectly able-bodied, and he's got the card keys with the right access to let him into the zoo and the all-staff area where we set up the studio. Doing things like this is the reason I gave him the access in the first place. If that wretch says—"

"Harris is in the hospital," I said. "Getting a few dozen stitches for a cranial laceration and a CT scan to rule out concussion."

A slight pause.

"Blast," he said finally. "Did the killer try to off him, too? Is he going to be of some use as a witness, then?" Grandfather's tone implied that Harris being of use would be a novelty.

"No, his injury happened later and was accidental." No need to expose Harris to Grandfather's scorn by telling how the accident had come about.

"Probably tripped over his own feet. Well, he's out, then. So can you get over there and deal with it? I need to go over to your house and help Caroline recapture those blue jays that wretch set loose."

"Can do," I said. "And thanks in advance for your blue jay removal services. I'll fill you in later."

As I hung up, I found myself pondering. I could just call Ekaterina and ask her to have someone pack up Castlemayne's stuff and put it in storage for the moment. But asking her to extend the checkout time would go over better if I showed up myself, ready and willing to do the packing work. The Inn was only a mile or so away. Like the hospital, it had generators, so I could visit it in comfort. Dealing with Castlemayne's belongings would probably be less work than anything I'd get roped into doing if I went back to the house. And to top it all off, while I'd been visiting Harris, Justin, and Curly, Mother had texted to say that she hadn't seen or heard from Holly McKenna all day and did I have any idea where she was. Which was Mother's way of ordering me—or maybe imploring me—to find Delaney's mother. Since Mrs. McKenna was staying at the Inn, it would make sense to start looking for her there.

So I let the head duty nurse know where I'd be if Dad needed a ride and headed downstairs.

On the way out I ran into the receptionist. Her face

lit up, reminding me that I'd half promised to give her a scoop on my way out.

Actually, giving her a little information might not be a bad idea.

"If the chief comes and tells you this, pretend it's news," I said. "And don't tell anyone."

She nodded eagerly. I'd already seen that the lobby was empty, but just for effect I glanced around as if making sure no one was within earshot.

"One or both of those patients who came in here unconscious could be a witness to the murder," I said, barely above a whisper. "So if anyone comes asking for them, notify the police and stall them."

"Right." She actually did whisper.

"And you didn't hear this from me."

She nodded solemnly.

I strolled back out to my car feeling pleased. I'd made her day. She'd be happily keeping watch for suspicious persons all afternoon. And if someone did show up with evil intentions toward Justin or Harris, they wouldn't get past her.

I got in my car and made a point to tune in my radio to the college radio station, which had the best carols. The local commercial radio station had a collection of exactly twenty-three carols—I'd counted—and much as I admired, say, Bing Crosby's version of "White Christmas" or Whitney Houston's "Do You Hear What I Hear?" I didn't want to hear them every hour or two. The college radio station could draw on the much deeper resources of both the Music Department and the music enthusiasts who served as DJs. When you tuned in, you never knew whether you were going to get carols from Aretha Franklin, Pentatonix, the London Symphony Orchestra, Ludacris, or our own local New Life Baptist Choir, but you could be sure it wasn't going to be something you'd already heard ten times that week.

And it was always nice to have an excuse to visit the Inn at Christmastime. Ekaterina had been working with Mother to do the Inn's decorations for the past few years, and the results were sumptuous. One big reason for this was that they were working from what I jokingly called their long-range plan for Total Christmas Decoration Dominance. Every year Ekaterina would extract as large a holiday decoration budget as she could from the owners, pleading the ever-increasing cost of the fresh greenery that was such an important component of the Inn's aesthetic. Then she'd dispatch a party of bellhops with axes to the nearby woods to gather the greenery on the cheap while she and Mother figured out how they could use the savings to execute as much of the long-range plan as possible—adding to, rather than replacing, the previous year's magnificence.

The decorations started with evergreen garlands and weatherproof red bows all along the whitewashed fence that enclosed the Inn's grounds. The front gates were bedecked with wreaths, bows, and a few tasteful lights. In year one, they had started planting dwarf evergreen trees at intervals on both sides of the mile-long drive from the front gate to the Inn itself, and now they were all decorated with tiny battery-powered LED lights that could be programmed to show different colors. The last time I'd visited, the lights had been multicolored and flashed on and off in complex patterns. Today they were all blue and twinkled steadily.

More evergreen, red bows, and tiny blue lights decorated the edges of the parking lot, and two giant bows festooned the double front doors. The doorman, wearing a special uniform jacket with red piping and a red rose in his lapel, wished me a joyous holiday season and bowed low as he held one massive door open.

Inside the carols were muted and mostly classical and the air was scented with evergreen, cloves, and cinnamon.

The Christmas tree might have looked modest, since it only went halfway to the soaring forty-foot lobby ceiling, but there was nothing modest or restrained about its glittering red-and-gold theme. And the lobby was so toasty warm as soon as you stepped in you forgot about both the snow and the power outage.

And I had a good excuse to stay for a while, since I planned to kill two birds with one stone while I was here—taking care of Castlemayne's baggage and easing Mother's worries by checking on Mrs. McKenna.

I strolled over to the front desk, where a staffer I knew was humming along with "Joy to the World."

"Merry Christmas, Meg," he called out. "And welcome to the Caerphilly Inn."

"Merry Christmas to you," I said. "Say, Enrique, maybe you can help me. Mother's been trying to get in touch with Mrs. McKenna, who hasn't been answering her calls."

"She has not been responding to our calls, either," Enrique said. "Nor does she answer when we knock on her door. We are growing concerned."

I didn't like the sound of this.

"Has housekeeping seen anything unusual in her room?" Technically this wasn't any of my business, but I spent so much time at the Inn, visiting my friend Ekaterina, that the staff sometimes forgot that I wasn't one of them.

"Housekeeping hasn't been in her room—she hung up the Do Not Disturb sign right after she arrived and hasn't taken it down." He picked up the desk phone. "Let me tell Ms. Vorobyaninova that you are here—I think she would like to consult you on this matter."

I had to admire the ease with which the syllables of Ekaterina's last name rolled off his tongue—even after so many years, I usually had to take a breath before launching into it. And she appeared almost before he'd hung up the receiver.

"Meg, welcome." Ekaterina gave me a quick hug and nodded to the left. We moved away from the desk and thus out of Enrique's hearing. "You are seeking Mrs. McKenna."

"Mother is," I said. "She hasn't heard from her all day and is getting worried."

"I know." She frowned. "Your mother has already called several times with messages for Mrs. McKenna, which we had to slip under her door, since she is not answering the phone or the door. Chief Burke also wishes to interview her. And then your mother called not long ago, asking if we could check on her. I do not like invading the privacy of a guest—"

"Which is probably why Mother asked me to check on her." I had to chuckle. "To help ease your conscience about doing so."

"Well, your mother seems to think Mrs. McKenna is under a great deal of stress and there could be cause for concern. What if she has . . . harmed herself? We had that happen once before. It was very distressing for the entire staff."

I was about to open my mouth to say that however upset Mrs. McKenna was over Delaney and Rob's refusal to have a big wedding, I didn't think it would drive her to suicide. But she was behaving oddly—so eager one day to strategize with Mother and shutting out the world the next.

"Maybe we should go and check on her," I said. "After all—she was out at our house most of the day yesterday. Maybe it freaked her out, knowing she'd been someplace only hours before a murder happened there." Of course, she hadn't been anywhere near the library as far as I knew, but still. "Or worse—what if the killer spotted her and thought she knew something. Or saw something." None of these seemed to me like very plausible reasons for invading Mrs. McKenna's room, but Ekaterina seized on them eagerly.

"We will check on her safety immediately." She appeared

to draw herself upright, which was a neat trick, since her posture had been perfect to begin with. "Come with me, if you please. If she is unhappy at being disturbed, perhaps a familiar face will placate her."

Since Mrs. McKenna had been closeted with Mother almost the entire time she'd spent out at our house, I wasn't sure she'd find my face familiar enough to have a calming effect. But I didn't think mentioning this would be useful, so I followed Ekaterina to the guest elevator.

"Very timely that you came out to check on Mrs. McKenna," she said as we waited impatiently for the elevator door to open.

"Actually, I didn't," I said. "But I knew Mother was fretting, so I figured as long as I was here, I might as well ask. I was actually coming to see you about Castlemayne's room."

"Your cousin Horace came out and inspected everything." The elevator dinged, and she tapped one foot impatiently as the door slowly opened. "And told me not to let housekeeping in until the chief gives us permission," she added, stepping inside and punching a button.

"Chief Burke told me that it was fine to collect whatever luggage is left here and take it all out to the zoo," I said as I joined her. "You can check with him if you like. We can't get rid of the stuff he took to our house, since the library's still a crime scene, but there's no reason to keep cluttering up one of your rooms with whatever he left behind. We're going to keep it all out at the zoo until the chief gets in touch with Castlemayne's next of kin or figures out who else they should go to."

"Excellent." The elevator came to a halt at the second floor, and she dashed out before the door had opened more than halfway. "If you like, I could have one of our staff pack Mr. Castlemayne's possessions for you. I do not anticipate any difficulty filling the room—this time of year we always have to turn away so many tourists who want to stay over an extra day. And I'm sure your grandfather will be relieved to stop paying for the room." From the touch of asperity in her tone I deduced that Grandfather had browbeat her into giving him a particularly good rate. "I will extend the checkout time, of course. It is not your fault that the police took so long to inspect his room. Here we are."

She stopped in front of Room 215, took a moment to put on the professional yet friendly face she was careful to use with difficult guests, and knocked briskly on the door.

"Mrs. McKenna?"

No answer. Seconds passed. We exchanged a glance. I stepped forward.

"Mrs. McKenna?" I projected my voice as much as possible—you pick up useful skills being married to an actor. "It's Meg Langslow. Mother asked me to come by and check on you. Are you all right?"

No answer. No sound at all, except for a faint thudding noise. Possibly a repairman fixing something elsewhere in the hotel.

"Mrs. McKenna?" Ekaterina called.

Nothing but thudding.

"Should I open the door?" Ekaterina asked.

Wait a second. There was a pattern to the thudding. Thud! Thud! Thud! Thud-thud-thud! Thud! Thud! Thud!

"Yes, open it—quick," I said. "She's pounding out an SOS."

Chapter 27

Ekaterina whipped out her keys and unlocked the door. Luckily the inner security latch wasn't on. We dashed in, over the half-dozen pink WHILE YOU WERE OUT slips lying just inside the door, to find that the room was empty. The bed was unmade, and three suitcases stood in a clump in the middle of the floor, but apart from that I saw no signs that it was occupied.

The thudding appeared to be coming from the closet.

I raced over and slid open the closet door. A woman lay on the floor. She was bound hand and foot and had a gag in her mouth. She looked overjoyed to see me.

It wasn't Holly McKenna. It was another woman entirely—although, like Mrs. McKenna, she had red hair.

"Mrs. McKenna!" Ekaterina cried. "Are you all right?"

"She can't answer you through that gag." I was fumbling with it. Whoever the woman was, we couldn't leave her bound and gagged in the closet. "And she's not Mrs. McKenna."

"She's the Mrs. McKenna who checked in," Ekaterina said. "Do you mean she's an imposter?"

"She's not the Mrs. McKenna who spent yesterday at our house." I managed to untie the gag and pulled it off. "Here we go."

"I *am* Holly McKenna," the woman said. "Do you mean that on top of knocking the breath out of me, tying me up, and locking me in the closet that horrible woman has been impersonating me? I want to report her to the police."

"I'll finish untying her," I said to Ekaterina. "You call nine-one-one."

"Please hurry," Mrs. McKenna said. "You have no idea how badly I need to pee."

"Here." Ekaterina handed me a pocketknife. "I would suggest cutting her restraints. It will be faster—and don't the police always find valuable clues in the kind of knots a criminal ties?"

"They do in mystery books," I said. "I have no idea if that's true in real life. I hate to mention it, but this looks like the kind of cord you'd use to draw a curtain."

Ekaterina dashed over to the window and uttered several words in Russian—or one really long word. From her tone, I deduced it was probably not a word she would care to translate in polite company. Then she pulled out her phone and tapped on it to dial 911.

I managed to sever the cords without slicing Mrs. McKenna, and she dashed into the bathroom.

"She will want some privacy," Ekaterina said, striding toward the door to the hall. "Yes, Debbie Ann? I need a police presence. One of my guests has been unlawfully restrained. Held prisoner in a closet. Tied up and—"

The door closed behind her, cutting off the rest of her explanation.

After Mrs. McKenna had peed at length and washed up, she came back out, looking shaken but determined.

"Ekaterina's calling nine-one-one," I said.

"Good. You're Meg Langslow, aren't you?" She held out a slightly trembling hand. "Delaney's showed me pictures of you. Of your whole family."

"Unfortunately she's never showed us any pictures of you," I said as we shook hands. "Or the imposter wouldn't have been able to fool us."

"I always think I take an awful picture," she said. "I'm constantly making her delete them. From now on, I won't do that, even if they show both of my chins."

"What happened?"

She sat down—collapsed, really—into the room's armchair and took a deep breath.

"I gave that horrible woman a ride from the Richmond airport," she said. "I was in line behind her to pick up my rental car, and it was taking forever because she hadn't made a reservation and they had no more cars available—the holiday rush, of course. And she kept arguing with them, and it was four in the morning and all I wanted to do was to hit the road and get the last leg of the trip over with. Then at one point she said that she had to get to Caerphilly, and I felt sorry for her. I offered to give her a ride—after all, I was going there, too. And it finally made her stop badgering the clerk so I could have my turn. But apart from being really stubborn, she seemed harmless. In fact, she seemed rather nice once she stopped trying to browbeat the car rental folks. Is there a glass in here? I need some water. My mouth is so dry."

"I'll get it." I grabbed one of the glasses from the little table with the coffeemaker, flipped off the cardboard top, and brought her a glass of cold water from the bathroom sink.

"Nectar of the gods," she said, after gulping down nearly half the water. "Anyway, we talked a mile a minute on the way from the airport—at least I did. I didn't realize it until afterward—I had a lot of time to think while I was in that closet—but she didn't say much about herself. And I told her all about why I was coming to here."

"That explains how she managed to impersonate you," I said. "She knew so much about Delaney."

"That'll teach me not to be such a blabbermouth." She closed her eyes and shook her head slightly. "Anyway, when we got to the outskirts of town, I asked where she was staying so I could drop her off, and she said in a bed-and-breakfast, but her room wouldn't be ready until the afternoon, so I could just drop her off near a restaurant. And I said nonsense—it wasn't even six a.m. yet and she couldn't sit all day in a restaurant, even if we found one that was open. I told her she could come with me to the Inn, and we could have a nice breakfast here and I could drop her off at her bed-and-breakfast in the afternoon. I felt lucky, you see, because I'd originally planned to come the night before, but when that flight was canceled, I called the Inn to hold the room, because even though I wouldn't be there till early morning I was definitely going to need to crash and nap. Red-eye flights do me in."

She broke off and took several more gulps of water. I heard two brisk knocks on the door, and then Ekaterina returned.

"Vern will be here soon," she said. "Deputy Shiffley," she added, for Mrs. McKenna's benefit. "And the chief of police is coming himself."

"Thanks." Mrs. McKenna set the glass down carefully before continuing. "Anyway, come to think of it, she did behave a little oddly when we checked in. She said she was not dressed up enough for such a fancy place, and she'd hurry through the lobby and wait for me by the elevator. And I said fine, we can just drop my luggage in the room, freshen up, and come down for breakfast. But as soon as we got into the room, she punched me in the stomach, and before I could get my breath back, she tied me up and gagged me and started going through my things."

"Meg, she has been attacked," Ekaterina said. "We should summon your father to check her out. Shall I make the call?"

"Thanks," Mrs. McKenna said again. "But do you know what I really want first? Food. I haven't eaten since that little package of pretzels on the plane."

"She didn't even feed you!" Ekaterina exclaimed. "Barbarous! I will have a complimentary meal delivered as soon as possible." She rushed over to snatch the menu from the top of the desk, and for several minutes Mrs. McKenna's storytelling took a backseat to their joint discussion of the meal, followed by Ekaterina's phone call to the kitchen.

While waiting for them to finish—and for that matter, for Vern and the chief to arrive—I studied the room. The bed had obviously been slept in, but apart from that the room looked almost exactly as it would have when they arrived. A carry-on bag and two suitcases stood together in the middle of the floor, right in front of the desk. The navy-blue carry-on bag matched one of the suitcases—the nicer one. The other was a scuffed off-white hard-sided suitcase, so old-fashioned it didn't even have wheels.

The menu discussion ended. Mrs. McKenna had decided to start with a modified and enormous version of the breakfast she'd been about to eat when the imposter struck her, and Ekaterina hurried off to expedite its delivery.

"Quick question," I said. "Are all three of those yours?" I pointed at the suitcases.

"The blue ones are mine," Mrs. McKenna said. "The white one is hers. My purse seems to be missing, so I guess she took it in case she needed it to impersonate me."

"Curious that she left her suitcase behind," I said.

"I think she's planning to come back for it," Mrs. McKenna said. "She left me here all day yesterday, then came back here to sleep. But before she took off this morning she packed up everything and left it like that—as if she might be in a hurry when she came back for it."

When she came back for it?

I pulled out my phone and called 911.

Chapter 28

"The chief and Horace are on their way," Debbie Ann said, instead of hello.

"Tell them to come without sirens," I said. "And try to be discreet. The imposter might not know we've found the real Mrs. McKenna. She might be coming back."

"Giving us the opportunity to apprehend her," Debbie Ann said. "Excellent. Done."

We hung up.

"If that woman's coming back, I want to get out of here," Mrs. McKenna said.

"If we hear anyone coming, you can hide in the bathroom," I said. "And I'll deal with her."

Mrs. McKenna studied me for a few seconds, then nodded and leaned back in her chair as if reassured, and sipped at her water.

"And Ekaterina knows she's an imposter," I added. "She will have briefed the desk clerk."

I sent Ekaterina a quick text to make sure. Then I sat down on the edge of the bed and did my best to look fierce and vigilant. But my eyes kept returning to the battered white suitcase.

"I think we should check her suitcase," I said. "Just in case."

If Mrs. McKenna had asked "just in case of what?" I wouldn't have had a good answer. She only nodded and shifted slightly so she could get a better view of that I was doing.

Luckily the suitcase wasn't locked—if it had been, I'd

have had a hard time resisting the temptation to break it open. Inside was a tangled mess of clothes, a lot of them in the sort of bright greens and blues redheads often favored. Cosmetics and lingerie were mixed in with the slacks and blouses, as if she'd packed in a frantic hurry. Halfway down I found a fat manilla file folder with the words "Divorce stuff" scrawled in a careless hand on the tab.

I flipped the folder open. The top paper was a letter from a law firm to Mrs. Iris Hazlitt Castlemayne, enclosing a bill and giving a rather discouraging progress report on their efforts to extract alimony from her ex-husband. I'd have called it a no-progress report.

"She's Castlemayne's other ex-wife," I said nodding. It occurred to me that Mrs. McKenna had no idea who I was talking about. "That's the guy who was murdered in our library last night."

"Oh, my goodness!" She almost dropped her water. "You had a murder at your house? And she did it?"

"It's possible," I said. "She was probably coming to town to badger her ex about unpaid alimony."

"Her ex—that would be the crazy artist who took over your library? Your mother told me about that. He was the one who got killed?"

"Yes," I said. "And hearing you talk, this woman figured out you were invited to visit the very house she wanted to get into. She knew he'd have done anything possible to avoid her."

"With good reason, if she killed him."

"Well, we don't know that for sure," I said. "Although she certainly looks like a damned good suspect to me. So should I let the chief know, or should I just close the suitcase up and pretend I wasn't snooping?"

Mrs. McKenna chuckled softly at that.

I was about to tuck the file folder back inside and shut the suitcase—leaving until later the decision on whether to confess my nosiness—when I spotted the corner of something wrapped in a rather faded polyester slip. Just out of curiosity I unwrapped it. It was an olive-green plastic case, about a foot long, eight or nine inches wide, and several inches deep. A padlock hung from the handle and imprinted on the lid was the maker's name and the words "Fine Firearms." I opened it up. It was a handgun case with a molded foam liner. A half-empty box of .22 caliber cartridges filled a rectangular cutout in the foam. The gun-shaped cutout and two cutouts that looked as if they would hold ammunition magazines were empty.

I grabbed my phone and dialed 911 again.

"Yes, Meg?" Debbie Ann sounded brisk and business-like. If she was tired of hearing from me, she wasn't showing it.

"The fake Mrs. McKenna may be armed," I said. "Her name is Iris Hazlitt Castlemayne, and when I checked her luggage just now I found what I gather is a travel case for a handgun. The gun itself is missing and there's a half-empty ammo box."

At Debbie Ann's suggestion I texted her pictures of the plastic case and the letter from the divorce attorney.

"Sit tight," she said. "Deputies are almost there."

I heard a knock on the door.

"Someone's trying to get in," Mrs. McKenna whispered. She got up and headed for the bathroom. I looked around for something I could use as a weapon.

I heard the clicking noise of the door unlocking.

"Room service!" Two bellhops began to wheel in a heavily laden service trolly. Ekaterina followed them in.

She looked at me oddly when I drew aside the spotless white linen that covered the trolly to make sure no one was hiding underneath.

"The imposter may be armed," I explained. "And Mrs. McKenna is understandably nervous." While the waiters set out a veritable breakfast feast on the room's small table, I briefed Ekaterina on my finds.

The arrival of the food lured Mrs. McKenna out of hiding. She sat down and dug into a plate of ham and eggs. Ekaterina dismissed the bellhops and stood at Mrs. McKenna's elbow, beaming at her guest's obvious delight in the meal and hurrying to fill her plate whenever it grew even half empty.

Since I couldn't exactly go anywhere until the imposter had been caught and Mrs. McKenna felt safe, I decided now was a good time to bring Mother up to speed. I had to confess, I was almost enjoying the idea of telling her how thoroughly we—and mostly she—had been hoodwinked. I settled back more comfortably on the end of the bed and called her cell phone.

"Hello, dear," Mother said.

"I have good news about Holly McKenna," I said. "She—"

"Yes, I know, dear," Mother said. "She told me all about it—and of course, since I'm a martyr to headaches myself, I completely understand."

I glanced over at where the real Holly McKenna was inhaling her scrambled eggs and ham. She certainly hadn't been in any position to talk to Mother lately, and I was fairly sure she was the real McKenna . . .

"You've heard from her?" I asked.

"I ran into her filling up her rental car at the gas station," Mother said. "And she explained about her migraine. And also that she didn't want to come back to the house right away—she said she needed time to process the whole awful reality of the murder. I could certainly understand that. So we're having tea at the Frilled Pheasant. Their special Christmas high tea with the gingerbread."

Great. Mother might be on her way to have tea with a murderer.

Chapter 29

"So you're heading for the teashop now?" I asked. "To meet Mrs. McKenna?"

"We're already here. And I must say, I think you and Michael are absolutely right to resist having a generator—of course it's convenient for a business, but the racket those things make—"

"She's there with you?"

"Well, not at the moment, dear." Someone who didn't know Mother would probably have missed the tiny hint of irritation in her voice. "She went to the bathroom."

"Great," I said. "If she comes back from the bathroom—"

"People usually do, dear."

"Mother, how good an actress are you?"

"Meg, dear, is there something wrong?"

"Yes," I said. "The woman you ran into at the gas station isn't Holly McKenna. She's an imposter."

"But dear—"

"The real Holly McKenna gave her a ride from the Richmond airport, and when they got to the Caerphilly Inn, the woman you're having tea with knocked her breath out, bound and gagged her, and stuffed her into the closet—all so she could come over to our house and pretend to be Delaney's mother. And she could be armed. I found an empty gun case and a box of ammo in her suitcase."

Mother didn't say anything for a few moments.

"I understand." Something was different about her voice. "Could you check your calendar and get back to me with the dates when the garden *would* be available for a wedding?"

"I gather she's back," I said.

"That's correct." She sounded amazingly calm. Pretty much her normal self.

"Are there plenty of other people around?"

"Of course." And then in a slightly muffled voice, as if she were looking away from the phone. "I'm so sorry—it's the Tudor Place. They can be so hard to get on the phone that I didn't want to lose the chance to talk to them. This will only take a minute and then we can order."

"Do you think you can keep her there until I can get the police there?"

"Of course, d—don't worry." I had to smile at how she'd covered up starting to say "dear."

"Don't do anything rash," I said. "Don't make her suspicious of you."

"That's understood," she said. "And—I'm so sorry, but I didn't get your name. Who am I talking to again?"

"Her name is Iris Hazlitt Castlemayne," I said. "I think she's the other ex-wife. Which means she might be the killer."

"I understand," she said. "Thank you. I think we're on the same wavelength now, and I look forward to what you'll be sending me."

I hung up and dialed 911.

"Yes, Meg?" Debbie Ann sounded uncharacteristically anxious. Were my frequent calls beginning to stress her out?

"Send anyone you can find to the Frilled Pheasant ASAP," I said. "Mother's there having tea with the fake Mrs. McKenna."

"Right." I could hear her keyboard in the background. "Is your mother aware of the situation?" Thank goodness for whatever they called the system that let her continue talking to me while sending out an SOS by computer to all the deputies.

"Yes," I said. "And knows she's probably armed. Mother's going to try to keep her there until someone comes to arrest her."

"Horace is on his way. And Aida. And Vern's even closer. And Clarence Rutledge. He'll probably even beat Vern there—he's only two doors down in the hardware store."

Clarence Rutledge wasn't technically a deputy, but due to his size—he was as tall as the average Shiffley and three times as wide—his mere appearance tended to have a calming effect on many minor offenders, so the chief had given him a police radio and appointed him a special deputy. I tried to imagine how the denizens of the Frilled Pheasant would react when Clarence suddenly appeared in the midst of its cluttered Victorian elegance, all bone china, silk flowers, and antimacassars. I hoped he'd be wearing his biker's leathers instead of the more sedate white coat he wore for his veterinary practice.

"And the chief will get there as soon as possible," she said. "He was heading out to the Inn to talk to Mrs. McKenna, but capturing the imposter takes priority. Can you stay there and keep an eye on Mrs. McKenna for the time being?"

"Absolutely," I said. "Can you have someone let me know when Mother's out of danger."

"Can do."

With that we hung up.

I glanced over to where Mrs. McKenna was polishing off the last of her scrambled eggs. Ekaterina was looking on approvingly and refilling her teacup or her juice glass as needed. Luckily neither of them seemed to have paid much attention to my conversations with Mother and Debbie Ann.

"Good news." I smiled at Mrs. McKenna and made my tone deliberately cheerful. "They've located the woman who was pretending to be you. Mother is keeping her distracted while the entire Caerphilly police force converges to arrest her."

"Well, that was quick," Mrs. McKenna said.

"I am not surprised," Ekaterina said. "Our police force is highly efficient. Yet also forward-thinking and progressive," she added.

"You know, with all this going on, we're probably going to have to tell Delaney and Rob that I'm here," Mrs. McKenna said.

"Wait until they find out," I suggested. "Then you can do the 'oh, but I didn't want to worry you, dear' routine and make sure they know that it was because of their stubbornness that you fell into the hands of a dangerous kidnapper. With any luck, you can guilt-trip them into letting you and Mother plan that big wedding you want."

"What a clever idea," Mrs. McKenna said. "That just might work."

Yes, I thought it had a good chance of working. I wouldn't have mentioned it if I hadn't been positive that Mother would come up with the same strategy on her own.

Meanwhile I was impatiently waiting for word that Mrs. Castlemayne had been arrested and Mother was safe. Mrs. McKenna and Ekaterina were focused on the meal, but I was pacing up and down the room.

"Do have a seat," Mrs. McKenna said after a while. "Would you like some breakfast? There's plenty."

"I'm fine," I said. "I just wish they'd—"

My phone rang. It was Vern Shiffley.

"Debbie Ann said to let you know that we've apprehended the suspect," he said. "And your mother's fine—she said you'd be worried."

"Good," Mrs. McKenna said when I'd relayed the news. "I do hope they manage to keep her in jail."

"I heard that," Vern said. "And while I can't speak for what the court will do—kidnapping's a felony. Up to ten years in prison. Assault charges on top of that, and then you've got the fact that being from out of town she's a flight risk. I can't imagine any judge in town letting her out on bail, even if she wasn't a suspect for the murder. No, I think we can rest easy on that score."

"Good," I said. "Talk to you later." When we hung up, I relayed Vern's thoughts on the unlikelihood of the imposter getting bail, to Mrs. McKenna's great relief.

"And we will move you to another room," Ekaterina announced. "I'm sure you would rather not remain in the same room where you endured your terrible captivity. And in the unlikely event that your captor regains her freedom, she will come here—not to your new room. I will instruct the staff to say that you are no longer a guest. And I will leave your new room registered to Dr. Blake."

"If it's the room I suspect you're thinking of, you can leave it on Grandfather's tab, too," I said. "If he complains, tell him it's payback for the wombats."

"Wombats?" Ekaterina sounded puzzled. "I do not understand."

I pulled out my phone, opened up the text Kevin had sent me, and clicked on the link to his Wombat Cam. I held it up so Ekaterina could see.

"These are wombats?" she said. "Unprepossessing creatures. They appear to be sleeping."

"They would be," I said. "They're nocturnal."

"And they are out at your grandfather's zoo." She still sounded puzzled.

"They are now," I said. "They spent the last few days in our basement, which now needs the sort of deep cleaning you'd expect it to need after two fifty-pound herbivores have been living in it for several days. Grandfather owes me."

"Ah." She nodded her comprehension. "Yes, your grandfather has much to answer for. As I said, I can have our housekeeping staff pack up Mr. Castlemayne's belongings immediately. And then they can clean the room for Mrs. McKenna's use."

"I can help them with the packing," I said. "Or—"

My phone rang again. The caller ID showed that it was Chief Burke.

"What's up, Chief?" I said.

"Thank you for your very level-headed handling of a difficult situation," he said. "It's largely due to you that we have Mrs. McKenna's assailant in custody."

"And possibly also Castlemayne's killer?" I asked.

"Too soon to tell on that," he said. "One step at a time. Is there any chance you could bring Mrs. McKenna down to the station? I need to get her to formally identify the woman who attacked and imprisoned her. And I want to do it by the book, with a proper lineup, so no young whippersnapper of a defense attorney can try to shake it, so it needs to be here at the station."

"Sure," I said. "When?"

"Now, if that suits the two of you. We don't quite have the lineup in place yet—takes a while to round up half a dozen forty-something redheads in the middle of a snow emergency. But if she gets here early for the lineup, I can start taking her statement."

I muted the phone and turned to Mrs. McKenna, who had been watching me with a faint frown of anxious concentration.

"The chief wants to know if you'd be willing to go down to the station to pick the woman who's been impersonating you out of a lineup," I said. "He thinks—"

"Absolutely. Can we go now?" Mrs. McKenna stood up.

"Perfect," Ekaterina said. "While you are assisting the police, we can ready your new room and move your luggage into it."

I unmuted the phone again.

"We'll be right down."

The chief and I signed off. Ekaterina bustled out. Mrs. McKenna was looking around with a bemused expression.

"I know perfectly well that that horrible woman has my purse, but here I am, looking for it. You think there's any chance the police will give it back to me?"

"If they try to keep it, we'll organize a protest," I said. "I bet every woman in town will join in. Even the three women deputies. Is there anything in it that you need right now?"

"No, it's just the lifelong habit of never going anywhere without it." She walked into the bathroom, plucked a couple of tissues from the dispenser, and tucked them into her pocket as she came out. "I'm as ready as I'll ever be."

Chapter 30

As Mrs. McKenna and I got into my car, I began the mental calculations all locals had learned to do this time of year—how could I get from the Inn on one side of town to the police station on the other without getting caught up in the tourist traffic that clogged most of downtown? Christmas in Caerphilly was one of Mayor Randall Shiffley's most successful tourism projects, packing the town with enthusiastic—and affluent—tourists all through December and well into the new year. It had proven such a boon to the town's economy that we locals tried not to complain as we devised ingenious new routes to avoid the traffic.

But Mrs. McKenna hadn't seen Christmas in Caerphilly before. She'd have arrived before dawn, when the town was still dark and deserted, and driven straight to the Inn. Maybe she could use a little Christmas right now.

In earlier years I'd have taken her on the long, slow drive around the town square to see the town Christmas tree—reputed to be approximately the same height as the National Christmas Tree and, in local opinion, much more elegantly decorated. Mother and the Ladies Interfaith Council, who had taken charge of planning the decorations, had outdone themselves this year, and it was truly a sight to behold. But this year we'd actually turned the streets surrounding the town square into a pedestrian mall for the duration, so the best I could do would be to take her to the end of one of the blocked-off streets for a quick glimpse of the tree. And come to think of it, the lights wouldn't be on until the power came back. Well, doubtless Mother would arrange a full tour later.

But I could manage to take her by one of the corners where a band of singers and musicians in Dickensian costume were serenading the tourists with old-fashioned Christmas carols. We might be stalled long enough for me to call out a request—would she prefer "Deck the Halls with Boughs of Holly" or "The Holly and the Ivy"? Or did being named Holly mean she got sick of hearing those particular carols? I could ask if the occasion arose.

And then past the field where all the entries in the Christmas Chainsaw Carving Contest were displayed—a half acre of rough wooden Santas, reindeer, snowmen, angels, nativity scenes, stars, wreaths and stocking-laden chimneys. This year's contest was considered a rousing success, not only because of the number and quality of the entries, but also because the competition had produced only half a dozen injuries, and none of them so major that they couldn't be easily handled at Dad's first aid station.

Or maybe I should just wend my way through the crowded streets close to the town square, where nearly every house was decorated for the holiday and most were vying for ribbons in one of the many categories of the Best Seasonal Decorations Contest. We should definitely do the block where both the winner and the first runner up in the Best Christmas Display (Secular) category were across the street from both the Best Hanukkah Display winner and two finalists in the Best Christmas Display (Religious) race.

And the block that held my personal favorite for the Most Unusual Decoration ribbon—a house whose owner was so fond of Halloween that he filled his entire yard with gravestones, zombies, ghosts, witches, bats, skeletons, and every other imaginable thing that went bump in the night. Promptly on November 1 he put pilgrim hats on most of the figures, and on Black Friday he added enough Santa hats and holly to claim it was now a Christmas tableau. This year he'd added a truly awesome skeleton nativity— for my money, that alone should have gotten him the grand prize instead of merely first runner-up .

Yes, there was a lot worth seeing this time of year. So if the chief was still assembling the lineup, why not take Mrs. McKenna for a little sightseeing on our way to the station?

We wound our way slowly through the snow-covered streets, oohing and ahhing all the way. Mrs. McKenna kept up a running stream-of-consciousness commentary on the decorations and past Christmas experiences they reminded her of, interspersed with tidbits about her life and her daughter's. I learned more about Delaney's childhood in that half-hour drive than I had in the whole time she'd been dating Rob. Mrs. McKenna's talk, though nonstop, was curiously restful, like turning on an audiobook so you could just relax and listen. And I could well see how the imposter could easily have used the drive of more than an hour from the Richmond airport to learn enough to put on a reasonably well-grounded impersonation. But one thing I could already tell about Mrs. McKenna. She might talk a blue streak, with better breath control than an opera singer, but I had yet to hear her say anything the least bit petty or mean-spirited. Listening to her monologue had much the same mellowing effect as listening to Christmas carols.

And as we traveled, every so often I'd feel a surge of joy and relief that Iris Castlemayne was in custody and would probably turn out to be the killer. Yes, the chief had said it was too early to tell. But it made sense. We knew she was a kidnapper. I had no doubt that she'd pretended to be Mrs. McKenna to figure out how to get in to see Castlemayne. For all I knew, Mother might have given her a spare key to our house, to make their plotting easier—we'd planned to do that for Mrs. McKenna, so she'd feel more at home. She had motive, means, and opportunity.

I reminded myself not to jump to conclusions. Once Mrs. McKenna had identified Iris as the kidnapper, the chief could keep her locked up while he built his case against her for Castlemayne's murder.

Still, the chief might well solve the murder in less than twenty-four hours. He'd be proud. And the rest of us would be relieved that we could get back to enjoying the holiday season without a cloud hanging over it.

Mrs. McKenna was definitely in a much more cheerful mood by the time we arrived at the police station, and her mood only dampened slightly when we parked at the far end of the station's parking lot. Why was there such a crowd here?

As we crossed the parking lot, Mother came dashing out.

"Holly? At last!" She swept the real Mrs. McKenna into a dramatic embrace. "I cannot tell you how relieved I am! The whole time that horrible woman was impersonating you, I was positively cringing at the thought of poor Delaney having a mother like that. I should have known it wasn't you from the start."

Actually, I hadn't noticed that Mother had showed any lack of enthusiasm for the fake Holly, probably because the imposter had been clever enough to keep her mouth shut as much as possible, opening it only to express firm agreement with Mother's opinions and extravagant praise for her ideas.

I relaxed and let Mother take over. She was in full hostess mode as she led Mrs. McKenna into the station. I followed more slowly, not wanting to overdo it on my ankle.

Inside, Mother and Mrs. McKenna stopped briefly to admire the Christmas decorations—the small tree on the front desk, festooned with tiny gold guns, handcuffs, and badges, and the garlands made of evergreen boughs and red and yellow crime scene tape. The chief appeared and led them back into the interior of the station.

The reception area wasn't as brightly lit as usual. Unlike the hospital and the Inn, the police station only had enough generator power for the basics, like emergency lights and the phone system. But I was relieved that they'd decided heat was a basic. I stayed by the front desk, where a young man with a briefcase was arguing with George, the civilian employee who ran the desk during business hours.

"You must have him here," the young man was saying. "I demand that you take me to him immediately."

"I already told you." George's tone was admirably calm and neutral. "We turned him loose yesterday afternoon, like you insisted. He hasn't been back."

"You're lying to me!" The young man pounded on the desk so hard it startled me. George didn't look startled, but I could tell he was getting annoyed. So was Vern, who was standing by as if waiting for something.

"If you're talking about Curly, he's down at the hospital," I said. "Suffering from frostbite, hypothermia, and severe lacerations on his hands and face."

"Oh, no," George said. "Is he going to be all right?"

"As if you care," the young man exclaimed.

George gave him a venomous look but said nothing. Vern narrowed his eyes.

"Dad's optimistic," I said to George.

"I'll go down and make sure he's being properly treated," the young man said.

Oh, brother. Maybe I shouldn't have butted in. This was almost certainly the lawyer responsible for Curly being kicked out of jail.

"You're welcome to try, counselor," I said. "But I'm not sure the deputies who are guarding him will let you in."

"Deputies guarding him?" The lawyer looked puzzled. So did Vern and George, who knew full well that none of their colleagues were guarding Curly. Luckily they decided to wait and see what I was up to.

"He may be a witness, you know," I said. "To the murderer's escape. They're keeping him under twenty-four-hour guard until the killer has been apprehended. I don't think they're letting anyone in to see him other than his doctors."

"But I'm his lawyer," the young man protested. "They have to let me in."

"About that. Do you have a business card? One with your cell phone on it?"

The lawyer reached into his pocket, pulled out a monogrammed silver business card case, and held it up in a way that made sure we could all get a good look at it while he slowly extracted a card and handed it to me. The card announced, in impressively hard-to-decipher blackletter, that he was J. Eustace Monkton, Esquire, Attorney at Law. I reached into my tote, pulled out my wallet, and stowed the card there.

"Now if you'll excuse me," Monkton said. "I need to go confer with my client."

"Your ex-client," I said. "He has secured new representation."

"He what?" Monkton began spluttering. "This is unacceptable. Interfering with my relationship with my client. I want to know—"

Since I still had my wallet in my hand, I pulled out a business card that I'd taken to carrying around, one belonging to my lawyer cousin Festus. I handed it to Monkton and was gratified that when he saw it, his jaw fell open and he turned pale. Festus Hollingsworth had an enviable reputation with his fellow attorneys as a highly skilled and impeccably ethical crusader for justice—and also as someone you didn't want for an opponent. Counselor Monkton might be young, but evidently he wasn't entirely unfamiliar with the doings of the Virginia legal community.

"I'm sure that given your deep concern for Curly's well-being you'll be delighted to brief Mr. Hollingsworth if he wants background on how the case has been handled so far," I said.

Monkton didn't reply, but he gave me a look of sulky and baffled resentment that reminded me of how the Pomeranians reacted when I had to snatch them away from eating or playing with something that would kill them. Monkton pulled himself up to his full height, squared his shoulders, and marched out of the police station.

"Maybe we should have told him to stick around," George said. "In case we get an arrestee who might actually need an attorney."

"The kidnapper already has one," Vern said. "And even if she didn't, I think the chief would rather have one of our regular local defense attorneys. They may be annoying, but at least they aren't idiots."

Since I still had my phone out, I called Festus. These days he split his time between his farm on the other side of Caerphilly County and wherever he was trying his latest case—and he was planning to join us for most of the family holiday gatherings.

"Don't worry," he said instead of hello. "I couldn't get away until this morning, but I'm back in town now and planning to show up for tonight's dinner. And I brought surprise goodies."

"Great," I said. "But actually I didn't call to nag. I just got you a brand-new pro bono client—rescued from the clutches of an unscrupulous young colleague. Can you drop by the hospital as soon as possible to meet him?"

"No problem," he said. "What's his name?"

"Curly. If he has any other names, I don't know them." I turned to George. "Do you know—" I began.

"No." George shook his head. "And even if I did, he wouldn't answer to them anyway."

I relayed this to Festus, who declared himself intrigued and reported that he was already in his car and heading for the hospital.

I had just finished texting Caroline, asking her to brief Curly and fend off Monkton if necessary, when the station's front door opened.

"Hey, Maudie," George exclaimed.

I turned to see Maudie Morton, manager of the local funeral home, coming through the door.

"Boy, is it ever cold out there!" She stomped in the entryway to get as much snow off her boots as she could, then stepped closer to the desk. "I'm here for the lineup!" she exclaimed, pulling off her knitted cap to reveal her hair, its elegant upswept do only slightly mussed by the hat and its bright copper-red color gleaming brightly.

"Welcome," Vern said. "If you could step into the chief's office with the rest of the redheads, I think we're going to start in a few minutes. We don't have one of those fancy rooms with the one-way glass like you see on TV, so we're just going to sit our witness out here and have y'all parade by holding numbers."

"This is exciting," Maudie said. "I've never been in a lineup before."

She followed Vern out of the waiting room. I heard a door open, and then a chorus of excited female voices.

"Maudie!"

"Look who's here!"

"This is so much fun!"

The door shut again, cutting off the voices.

"Can I stay and watch the lineup?" I said. "After all, I'll probably need to hang around anyway, to take Mrs. McKenna back to the hotel afterward—"

"I can't imagine anyone would mind as long as you don't interrupt or anything," George said. "I'm looking forward to it myself. And besides, aren't you one of the folks who can testify that she was impersonating Mrs. McKenna yesterday? You should be looking at the lineup, too."

Vern began arranging the waiting room, moving aside the plastic chairs, which were either bright orange or intense purple and looked as if they ought to glow in the dark. Perhaps I should get Kevin and Grandfather to test them while they were working on the wombats. Vern set two purple chairs at the far end of the room and began to stack up the rest. I snagged one and sat down beside George's desk, which looked as if it would be the best place for kibbitzing on the lineup.

A door opened, and a few seconds later the chief strode out into the reception area.

"Is everyone here?" he asked George.

Chapter 31

"Almost," George said. "We're still waiting for—Never mind, here she comes."

I leaned forward so I could see past the desk. Muriel, the owner of the local diner, came dashing in. She was carrying a large plaid picnic cooler, which she set down beside the front desk.

"Sorry!" she said. "And I know, I know—the nearest one is always the last to arrive." She pulled off a scarf to reveal her magnificent head of red hair.

"You're just in time," the chief said. He turned to George. "Can you have Aida bring the other ladies out? I want to brief them before we get started."

George spoke into the intercom, and a minute later the reception area began to fill up with redheads. In addition to Muriel and Maudie, I recognized Angel and Ruth, owners of the Caerphilly Beauty Salon; a woman professor from the Music Department; the proprietor of a downtown antique store; and Bridget Westmoreland, the private investigator who'd showed up at our house this morning.

"Not on your way back to Mechanicsville?" I asked when she passed by the desk.

"Well, it took a while to get my statement typed up and signed," she said. "And then suddenly everyone ran out in a big hurry. I'm nosy; I'll admit it—occupational hazard. I stuck around to see what was happening, and then the chief asked me if I'd mind sticking around a little while longer so he could have as many redheads as possible in his lineup. I never heard of a redheaded lineup before. Is that why y'all were so gung-ho to check me out? Telltale strand of red hair found at the scene of the murder?"

"Not that I know of," I said. "But the victim did have an ex-wife who's a redhead. And the suspect he's doing the lineup on is someone who knocked out another redhead, tied her up, stuck her in a closet, and took advantage of the color of her hair to impersonate her."

"Must be a dye job," Ms. Westmoreland said. "A real redhead wouldn't have done that to another member of the sisterhood."

The assembled redheads did seem to have bonded and were having a great time. Angel and Ruth were fussing with everyone's hair, making sure it was pulled back in a casual ponytail, the way the fake Mrs. McKenna wore hers. And then I reminded myself that she had a name now. Iris Castlemayne. Unless she'd gone back to using Hazlitt. But until and unless I found out different, I was going to work on thinking of her as the second Mrs. Castlemayne.

Muriel joined the group, and after Angel and Ruth had spent a couple of minutes rearranging her hair slightly, they pronounced her ready. The chief, who had been observing the scene carefully, nodded with approval.

"Thank you, ladies," he said. "I think we're ready to get started." After a minute or so of hushing each other, the group quieted down and stood shoulder to shoulder, beaming back at him. It was astonishing. Their hair colors ranged from carroty orange to a deep red with overtones of maroon, but they were all redheads, all about the same age as Iris Castlemayne, and all within an inch or two of her height. And they were all wearing knit pantsuits in redhead-friendly colors, none identical to the one the imposter had been wearing, but none all that different.

"The Redheaded League," I said under my breath. I opened up the camera app on my phone to document the occasion.

"We could never have done it without your mother,"

George said softly. "She knew exactly who to call and told them what to wear and how to fix their hair."

"Excellent," the chief pronounced. "Now, ladies, I'm going to ask you to go back to my office while I bring in Mrs. McKenna. Aida will give you your numbers, Vern will bring in our suspect, and then they'll lead you all out here. Now remember—most of you know each other, or at least have had a chance to take a good look at each other. If you feel the need to study the suspect to get an idea of her facial expressions and body language, get it out of your system before you come out here. It's important not to stare at her during the lineup"

"Understood," Maudie said.

"Don't worry," Muriel said. "We're all experts at giving the old side-eye."

They filed back out, and the chief and Vern followed them.

The chief returned a minute later, escorting Mother and the real Mrs. McKenna. Trailing along behind them was a man I recognized as one of the more competent of the town's defense attorneys. Over the years I'd referred more than one wayward friend or family member to him. We exchanged friendly nods, and then he grabbed a chair from the stack and dragged it to the far end of the room so he could sit near, but not directly beside, Mother and Mrs. McKenna.

"We're ready," the chief said.

George spoke into the intercom and within seconds the assembled redheads began filing into the waiting room. It was amazing. They all wore the same slightly surly expression on their faces. They all slouched and dragged their feet ever so slightly. They all cast one piercing glance at Mother and Mrs. McKenna before deliberately focusing their eyes somewhere—anywhere—else.

Had Mother recruited the members of the Redheaded

League not only for their appearance but also for their acting ability?

Mrs. McKenna didn't appear to react. She just studied each member of the lineup in turn. Then she glanced up at the chief.

"Can I speak now?" she asked.

"Of course," the chief answered.

"Number three." She pointed at her choice and held the pose dramatically.

She'd chosen Iris Castlemayne.

"Maybe you could have them turn sideways?" the defense attorney suggested. "Just in case—"

"I don't need to see them sideways," Mrs. McKenna said. "I'd know that face anywhere. Last night I begged her to let me go to the bathroom. She wouldn't let me. She would only let me pee in the coffeepot—and stared at me just like that the whole time. I may never drink coffee again!"

The other seven members of the lineup stepped away from Iris as if fleeing some kind of contagion.

"I should have known it was too good to be true," Iris said.

"Mrs. Castlemayne," the defense attorney began.

"I just needed to figure out how I could get in to confront Roddy," Iris went on. "The jerk was really good at getting people to run interference for him. And then this opportunity falls into my lap—not only is she going to the same house he's staying in and anxious about meeting a bunch of people who have never seen her before—she's a redhead like me. How could I resist?"

The defense attorney almost managed to stifle a sigh.

"Thank you, ladies," the chief said. "Vern, Aida."

The two deputies escorted Iris down the corridor that led back to the interrogation rooms—and eventually the jail. The chief and the dispirited defense attorney followed them.

But the Redheaded League wasn't in the mood to disband just yet. Muriel scurried back to her picnic cooler and pulled out giant thermoses of coffee and boxes of doughnuts, bear claws, and croissants. The ladies dug in, and a hum of happy conversation arose.

George didn't seem to object, possibly because Muriel had poured him the first cup of coffee and parked a box of bear claws right beside him.

I helped myself to a croissant and sat back to nibble it in peace. Mrs. McKenna's assailant was safely in custody. And was quite probably Castlemayne's killer. Now that they had her, they could start building their case against her, and—

My phone rang. I glanced down to see who was calling. Dad.

"Meg! Are you here at the hospital?"

"No, but I'm not far away," I said. "Do you need a ride?"

"Not yet. But is there any chance you could do an errand for me? I'm trying to talk Harris into staying overnight—he won't admit it, but I suspect he's having headaches and dizziness, and I really want to keep him under observation a little longer. He seems determined to go home—but if he had some of his own things—some clean pajamas, his toothbrush, and so on—maybe he'd be readier to settle down."

"Makes sense." I felt a twinge of guilt. Caroline had asked the same thing earlier. Of course, I had been rather busy since leaving the hospital. "So I should go home and pack an overnight bag for him?"

"If you can. Including some clothes for him to go home in eventually, of course. And the sooner the better."

"I can take off now," I said. "See you back at the hospital."

I grabbed another croissant for the road and wished George a Merry Christmas. When she saw me putting on my coat, Muriel dashed back to her picnic cooler and came over to hand me something—a smaller thermos and a cardboard cup with a travel top.

"Hot chocolate," she said. "Since I know you're not big on coffee. Merry Christmas!"

"You know me too well," I said.

She gave me a hug and hurried back to rejoin the rest of the redheads.

When I got to my car I poured myself a cup of hot chocolate and took a sip. Delicious—unlike most places, Muriel's Diner didn't over-sweeten the hot chocolate, so the dominant taste was the rich, strong, flavor of semisweet chocolate instead of the sticky sweetness of sugar. I took a few swallows and then hit the road.

About halfway home I realized how very tired I was. After all, I'd only gotten about three hours' sleep, and I'd been on the go all day. Maybe after I delivered Harris's overnight bag I could come home and take a nap. Better yet, maybe I could find someone else to deliver the bag.

I was contentedly sipping my hot chocolate and humming along with "We Three Kings of Orient Are" when I rounded the corner and saw Deacon Washington's driveway. His farm was the next one over from Seth Early, our across-the-way neighbor. Whenever I spotted the deacon's mailbox, I knew I was almost home.

And as I drew near, I could see Osgood Shiffley's snowplow parked in the driveway—facing out, which meant that as usual he'd given our elderly neighbor's long driveway a free plowing. He was eating a sandwich. He waved, and on impulse I parked along the side of the road. I still had a lot of hot chocolate. He might welcome a hot beverage. And maybe I could satisfy my curiosity about how he'd happened to find Curly. So I grabbed the thermos, hopped out, and strolled over.

Chapter 32

"Merry Christmas, Meg," Osgood called.

"Same to you." I held up the thermos. "Want some of this? It's hot chocolate from Muriel's."

"Anything hot would go down easy right now—and I never say no to Muriel's hot chocolate." He rummaged around in the cab, unearthed an empty travel mug, and held it out. I filled it to the brim.

"I was just over at the hospital," I said. "Seeing the results of your good deed. Lucky you found Curly before he froze to death."

"Wasn't really me who found him," Osgood said after swallowing a big gulp of hot chocolate. "It was some woman. Her car was pulled over by the side of the road, right in front of the ice cream shop, and at first I was annoyed because I thought I'd have to plow around it, which would be a real pain if someone had decided to abandon it there for the whole night. But then she came running out into the road to flag me down. I guess she'd spotted him there by the dumpster and pulled over to help him. I'd never have seen him way back there. She probably saved him from bleeding to death, too—she'd found an old rag and put pressure on the gash. And tried to call nine-one-one, but her cell phone wasn't getting a signal."

"A good thing yours did." Even in town, cell phone reception was notoriously bad during storms.

"I carry a satellite phone on account of times like these," he said. "But when I called, Debbie Ann told me the ambulance was out at your house, so I told her I could run him over to the hospital."

Wait—if the ambulance was out at my house . . .

"What time was this?" I asked.

"'Bout three a.m. Maybe three-thirty. You could ask over at the hospital—they'd have logged exactly when I brought him in. Me, I just zone out and keep plowing. Long as there's still snow, time doesn't matter much."

"What happened to the woman?" I asked.

"She helped me get Curly into the cab of the plow and then she took off like a bat out of hell. Tourist, I figure, on account of the rental car. Maybe from someplace where they don't get so much snow. She seemed really spooked by it."

Spooked by the snow? Or by something she'd seen—or done—earlier in the evening.

"And she wasn't anyone you knew?" I asked. "A pity not to let her know how much we appreciate her good deed. What did she look like?"

"Short," he said. "A good bit shorter than you. And yeah, I know you're not short, but most women look short to me." Osgood, at six foot seven, was even taller than most Shiffleys. "And kind of round, but I think that was mostly 'cause she had on a puffy down coat."

"What about her face?"

"Red cheeks from being out in the wind," he said. "Red ponytail. And red hands, too, 'cause she wasn't wearing gloves, which was pretty feckless in weather like we had last night."

A redhead. Maybe the same one Mrs. McKenna had just identified in the lineup? I pulled out my phone, opened up the photos I'd taken of the redheaded lineup, and picked a good closeup shot of Iris Castlemayne.

"Could this be her?" I held up my phone.

Osgood peered at it and nodded.

"Yeah, that's her. Someone you know?"

Would telling him the whole story complicate things for the chief?

"Sort of," I said. "Long story. You might want to tell the chief what happened. Anyone out that time of night could be a witness to something connected with the murder."

He nodded and chewed a bite of his sandwich thoughtfully. Then he swallowed.

"A witness or a suspect?" he asked. "Because if the ambulance had time to get from the hospital to your house, she had time to get from your house to the town square."

"Yeah." I nodded. And shivered—time to get back in the car. Or was I reacting to more than the cold?

Osgood was still looking at me. I decided it wouldn't do any harm if I filled him in about Iris.

"Apparently she's one of Castlemayne's exes," I said. "And it's just possible she might be the one who killed him. So I think the chief would really like to hear anything anyone knows about her."

"So it's that way." He frowned. "I'll go tell him. And I may have some evidence for him." He turned suddenly and rummaged again in his cab. Then he held up something—a cloth that had started out white, but was now more than half stained with drying blood. But on the end that was still white I could see colors. Bits of yellow and green. And a very large smear of blue—the same bright Prussian blue you'd use if you were painting a blue jay.

"She didn't wrap this around the big cut—she was just holding it down," he said. "I think she was a little squeamish about the blood. I wrapped his hand up good and tight with my wool scarf and tossed this in my trash bag. But maybe I should take it over to the chief."

"Definitely." I held up the thermos. "Want me to top your cup off?"

"I don't want to deprive you," he said.

"I'm headed home. I can make plenty more there."

"Then I thank you."

He held up the cup and I emptied my thermos into it. Then we said goodbye. I scurried back to my car and started the engine. Osgood's snowplow rumbled into life. He pulled out of the driveway and turned back toward town, waving as he passed me.

I took out my phone and called the chief.

"What's up, Meg?"

"Did you talk to Curly while you were at the hospital?"

"Not yet." He sighed in exasperation. "I heard about his crazy stunt with the plate-glass window. Been kind of busy with the murder case, but I figure I'll talk to him later this afternoon. Darned lucky Osgood found him."

"Talk to him ASAP," I said. "And send someone over to search the dumpster by the ice cream shop. Osgood didn't find Curly—a redheaded woman driving a rental car found him and flagged down Osgood. Iris Castlemayne—I showed Osgood her picture and he recognized her. And it's a good thing she stopped—Osgood said Curly wasn't easily visible from the street. He'd stumbled over into the alley by the dumpster."

"I wouldn't have pegged her as a good Samaritan, but people will surprise you sometimes," the chief said. "But what are you expecting us to find in the dumpster?"

"I have no idea," I said. "But I don't think she stopped because she spotted Curly. I bet she wanted to throw something in the dumpster."

"Like what?" the chief said. "Whoever killed Castlemayne left the murder weapon behind."

"No idea," I said. "In fact, maybe whatever she wanted to get rid of didn't even make it to the dumpster. Osgood's bringing you a piece of cloth she used to stop Curly's bleeding. Looks like a painter's rag to me. The sort of thing you might grab to wipe your fingerprints off something."

"Like a Swiss Army knife," he said. "Or a doorknob. Or

an enormous flashlight. Got it. You said Osgood's bringing it—where from?"

"He was taking a lunch break in Deacon Washington's driveway," I said. "Took off a few minutes ago. Should be there in ten minutes."

"Thanks. I'll wait here at the station for him. And send someone to check the dumpster, just in case. Good work."

I tucked my phone back in the holder and started up the car again. I still needed to pack that overnight bag for Harris.

Chapter 33

Back at the house I could tell that the visiting relatives had been busy in my absence. The front walk was cleared, along with a path up and down both sides of the road as far as there were parked cars. All the cars had been cleared off, though it didn't look as if many of them had gone anywhere. Neat paths crisscrossed the yard, leading from the back door to the toolshed, the llama shed, the chicken coop, and the barn. And in a wide shoveled space between the back door and the barn, half a dozen bundled-up relatives were cooking things on our fleet of grills.

They'd even kept my usual parking space open, bless their hearts. I waved to the grilling crew and made my way to the front door, humming under my breath.

But when I stepped inside, I found Rob, Delaney, and Rose Noire in the front hallway, all looking agitated.

"Here's Meg," Rob said. "She'll know what to do."

"What to do about what?" I asked, as I traded my damp outdoor jacket for a slightly lighter one and donned my favorite straw hat.

"Mom isn't answering her phone." Delaney took her phone away from her ear and glared at it, as if the problem were the phone's fault. She was wearing an odd bit of headgear—a vintage-style leather flying helmet, the sort of thing you'd see in photographs of Amelia Earhart.

"She's been calling and calling for more than twenty-four hours." Rob had untied the earflaps of his Sherlock Holmes–style deerstalker hat and was pulling down on them as if afraid his head was about to launch itself into orbit. He looked even more distraught than Delaney.

"I only called twice yesterday," Delaney said. "I wasn't too worried, because sometimes she forgets and leaves her phone at home or forgets that she has turned it off in a movie or something. But when I didn't get a call back this morning, I got worried. And I must have called a dozen times today."

I glanced at Rose Noire, who was wringing her hands.

"Didn't you tell them?" I asked.

"No," she said. "Because she should still be answering her phone."

"Tell us what?" Delaney demanded.

I realized that perhaps no one had told Rose Noire yet about the real Mrs. McKenna's kidnapping and all the other dramatic events of the past couple of hours.

"Your mother's fine," I began.

"Meg!" Rose Noire shrieked.

"How do you know?" Rob asked.

"Because I just saw her half an hour ago down at the police station," I said.

"Here in Caerphilly?" Rob asked. "What's she doing here? She's not due till the twenty-third."

"And what the devil is she doing at the police station?" Delaney demanded. "What is going on?"

"Delaney, your mom—" I began.

"Meg!" Rose Noire exclaimed. "You promised!"

"I didn't promise to lie to them." I frowned at her. She wilted and nodded. I turned back to Delaney. "Your mom changed her flight. She came in yesterday morning on a red-eye flight so she and Mother could plot together and figure out a way to talk the two of you into letting them organize that humongous wedding they have their hearts set on."

"Oh, brother," Delaney muttered. "Even so, couldn't she just answer her phone and lie to me about where she was?"

"She was probably planning to," I said. "But unfortunately she ran into Castlemayne's other ex-wife and gave her a ride from the Richmond airport. And the ex-wife knocked her wind out, tied her up, locked her in a closet at the Inn, came over here, and pretended to be your mother all day yesterday."

Rose Noire gasped and covered her mouth with her hands. Rob's jaw dropped.

"Pretended to be Mom?" Delaney said. "But why?"

"Probably so she could scout our house out and figure out a way to get in to accost her ex," I said. "And it's looking as if she succeeded in getting in to see him—in fact, she might even be his killer. But Ekaterina and I found your mom, Mother helped the police capture the imposter, and she's now safely locked up in the jail. The imposter, that is. I think your mom is heading back to the Inn."

"Oh, my God," Delaney murmured. "But she's all right?"

"She's fine," I said. "Ekaterina and her staff are probably spoiling her rotten. And she's probably got her phone back by now—the imposter was using it and may have let the battery run down, but she'll have it up and running soon. You should be able to call her."

"Of course, now that you know she's in town, does she need to stay at the Inn?" Rose Noire asked. "Her room here is all ready, and I bet she'd like to see her daughter."

For my part, I'd have been tempted to suggest that we swear secrecy and pretend not to know what Mother and Delaney's mom were up to. But Rose Noire was probably right. The fun had probably gone out of their little plot by now. It had almost certainly gone out a long time ago for Mrs. McKenna.

"Why don't you call Mother?" I suggested to Rob. "Tell her how worried you've been about Delaney's mom. If they're still in the mood to keep their secret, she'll probably say something like 'Oh, I just talked to her—she's fine, but she's been having the most awful problems with her phone.' More likely she'll say, 'Don't worry—she's right here,' and hand her the phone."

Delaney and Rob exchanged a look and a small smile. The sort of conspiratorial smile that contained an entire conversation's worth of communication. The sort of smile I might exchange with Michael if he were here. It made me glance at my watch and wonder how much longer till Michael and the boys and Grandmother Cordelia arrived.

"Yeah," Rob said. "Let's call Mother. Fun to have one up on them for a change."

"But let's start heading downtown while we call." Delaney stuck her phone in her pocket.

They threw on another layer of wraps and hurried out of the house.

"So the woman who was here yesterday was an imposter," Rose Noire said. "I'm so relieved. I was having a hard time warming to her. And while I'm sure she would never have said anything, I think your mother was feeling the same way."

"That's good," I said. "Nice to know that neither of you bonded with someone who might be going on trial for murder."

"Yes, but exactly what all has been happening this afternoon?"

"Long story." I suddenly felt tired at the idea of trying to explain it all. "Can I fill you in later? Dad wants to keep Harris in the hospital overnight, and he thinks he'll have better luck talking him into it if I show up pretty soon with an overnight bag."

"Good idea," she said. "I could pack it if you like. The kitchen volunteers are starting to prep for dinner—we're going to serve it in the living room and just put all the kerosene space heaters in there. I need to tell them a few things first and—"

"Go worry about dinner," I said. "I'll take care of Harris."

I took it slow going up the stairs. My ankle was feeling fine, and I wanted to keep it that way.

On my way from the second floor to the third, I passed a Pomeranian going down. He—or possibly she; I couldn't tell which dog it was—looked up when passing me and greeted me with a short bark and a quick wag of his fluffy tail before continuing on downstairs. I paused and leaned over the railing until I saw him reach the front hall and scamper off in the direction of the kitchen.

Where was he coming from? And what had he been doing there? I might never know. I had a sudden daunting feeling that our house was full of several dozen parallel worlds that only accidentally overlapped with what I thought of as my own world. Kevin's cyber world in the basement. Rose Noire's herbal, New Age world in her sunny second-floor bedroom and her combination greenhouse and herbal workroom in the backyard. The computer game and travel-oriented world of Rob and Delaney, who would probably remain in residence until they found a house they liked. Not that they seemed to be looking very hard—I could easily see them staying on indefinitely and adding nieces and nephews to the household in the years to come. The strange and hard-to-imagine world of the various dogs. The llamas. The poultry. Add in the temporary residents: the visiting relatives, the captive birds—although no subterranean wombats any longer, thank goodness. The house suddenly seemed a strange and not altogether familiar place.

"You'll feel better when Michael and the boys get back," I told myself. And then I focused on the task at hand.

I continued down to the far end of the hall and unlocked Harris's room. I braced myself before opening the door—hadn't there been rather a lot of blood here, just as there had been in the library?

But when I opened the door and swept my flashlight beam over the interior, I realized I'd been worried unnecessarily. After all, this wasn't a crime scene like the library. No one had coshed poor Harris over the head—he'd managed that himself. So there was no reason to keep the bloodstains intact, and in my absence Mother and Rose Noire had made sure they were gone. The twin bed was neatly made. The old-fashioned white chenille bedspread was spotless—either someone had washed the bloodstains out of it or they'd brought in a fresh one from the supply we kept in the linen closet. The rag rug that had been beside the bed was gone—either it was still in the wash or they'd decided it needed to be sent out for special cleaning. The polished oak floor was spotless and gleaming. The room smelled faintly of lavender.

The space was back to being a serene and inviting if curiously small guest room.

I looked under the bed—the only place where one could possibly stow luggage—and found a modest-sized suitcase and an unmatching carry-on bag. The carry-on bag should be large enough. I pulled it out and began filling it.

Harris's shirts, pants, and jackets were arranged with military precision in the tiny curtained-off corner that served as a closet. I grabbed a blue shirt and a pair of jeans and stowed them in the carry-on bag.

No books on the bedside table, only the charging cord for his phone. I added that to the bag.

His toiletries were all stashed in a blue canvas zip bag placed on top of the bureau. Placed smack dab in the center. Did he normally keep them organized in this way or had whoever tidied the room done it? Probably Harris himself—Rose Noire's sense of order ran more to gracefully balanced asymmetry.

The top drawer of the small bureau contained socks and briefs, all folded with uncanny neatness. I'd seen pictures on Pinterest from Marie Kondo followers that weren't this well-organized. After studying that drawer, I pulled the shirt and jeans out of the carry-on, folded them as neatly as I could manage, and placed them back carefully before adding socks and underwear. I snagged a sweater and

Harris's spare pair of pajamas from the second drawer, along with the slippers that were placed so precisely under the edge of the bed.

I probably had everything he would need—well, except for his coat and gloves, which were downstairs—but I opened the bottom drawer of the bureau, just in case. There I found the first really individual notes in a room that was otherwise almost monkish in its minimalism.

A sketchbook. A few loose sketches. A wooden watercolor box. A mesh pencil case crammed with pencils, pens, and erasers. A second mesh case containing pastels. Several bottles of ink. Everything was neatly arranged— the sketches in a tidy stack, the edges of the mesh cases aligned with the edges of the drawer. But the sheer number of art supplies—especially in contrast to the spare order of the rest of the room—gave the feeling of abundance. Almost excess.

I glanced at the loose sketches. Two of them bore Roderick Castlemayne's large, bold signature—one of a cardinal and the other of a blue jay—and were in his sweeping, freewheeling style. The other four, along with the two dozen or so pages that had been drawn on in the sketchbook, were almost certainly Harris's work, although there was no signature—not even a small self-effacing H in one of the bottom corners. His style was very different. Precise, methodical, painstakingly accurate.

Curiously, his birds looked rather wan and spiritless. Castlemayne's, by contrast, seemed to leap off the page— but I didn't like them any better. He wasn't showing you the bird, he was showing you how well he could draw a bird—and getting half the details wrong. No wonder he and Grandfather had had shouting matches over the two paintings he'd completed so far. Grandfather was a stickler for accuracy. By contrast, Harris captured the details perfectly, but somehow didn't really inspire you to look at his birds. If Harris could learn a little of his boss's boldness, he'd probably be a much more successful artist. Too late for Castlemayne to learn any of Harris's precision.

Then I remembered something—when I'd been talking to Harris about his work, I'd gotten the definite impression that he looked down on representational work. All these sketches were about as representational as they could be. Curious.

I flipped through the sketchbook again, and something fell out. Three four by five–inch photos of . . . something. Possibly a child's paintings—they looked rather like some of the brightly colored daubs the boys had brought home from grade school. Then I took a closer look and realized these were photos of canvases. The colors were bright and clashing; the vague shapes jagged and curiously menacing. I was indifferent to most abstract art. These paintings . . . I wouldn't want them around.

And then I spotted something in the lower right-hand corner—a tiny, jagged H, slashed onto the canvas with bold strokes.

Was this Harris's work? It was certainly nonrepresentational. And not something I could easily see him selling. If I ran into it in a museum, I'd avert my eyes and move on to another painting. Clearly we had very different ideas about art.

But none of this was any of my business. I tucked the photos back into the sketchbook. I arranged the sketches as I'd found them, in a neat stack, edges all aligned with one another and with the edges of the sketchbook. And I tucked them all back into the bottom drawer.

It occurred to me that maybe if Mrs. McKenna decided to come here to the house, we could give Harris her room at the Inn. I had the feeling that even if we arranged things here to give him a bigger room, he'd much prefer the Inn. Not because it was more luxurious but because no matter how hard Ekaterina tried to achieve warmth and hospitality, it was still a hotel room. Still just a little impersonal. I suspected that, to Harris, impersonal would feel more like privacy. And safety.

I found myself hoping Dad talked him into staying in the hospital, at least overnight. We had enough going on at the house without having to take care of a depressed and traumatized Harris.

But I could worry about that later. Once I dropped his bag off at the hospital, I'd be finished with my chores. Well, actually my notebook had plenty of chores remaining in it. But none that had to be done today. So as soon as I finished this trip, I could relax and start enjoying the holiday.

Unless I'd just jinxed myself.

I turned to leave, noticing that even with a flashlight in my hand I had to resist the instinct to switch off the light on my way out. Then I heard it: a soft "chuck-chuck-chuck." One of the noises blue jays made.

It was coming from inside the room.

I shut the door again.

There weren't that many places a bird could hide in this small a room—how had I missed it? I swept my flashlight beam around again. And then another time, aiming upward. Aha! A solitary blue jay was perched atop the curtain rod.

"I should probably just tell Rose Noire you're here," I told the jay. "She'd chuck-chuck back at you and convince you to walk into the bird cage all by yourself."

The bird flicked its tail dismissively.

I set my flashlight on the bureau and pulled the chenille cover off the bed. The bird took flight, but I lucked out and guessed which way it would go. Within seconds I had it bundled up in the soft chenille bedspread.

"Gotcha!" I said.

I slung Harris's overnight bag over one shoulder, then picked up my flashlight again and headed downstairs with a bundle that occasionally emitted muffled jeering noises.

Chapter 34

Downstairs I ran into Rose Noire.

"Do we have a birdcage?" I asked. "I nabbed one of the jays."

"Wonderful!" she said. "I'll take care of it—we still have a least one cage in the library."

I handed over the bundle and was completely unsurprised to hear her making soothing chuck-chuck sounds at it as she headed down the hall toward the library.

I could hear voices in the living room, so I stuck my head in to see who was still here at the house. A surprising number of people, and they were all remarkably cheerful in spite of having to wear hats, coats, and gloves inside. I had to turn down half a dozen invitations from relatives who were organizing festivities and expeditions—most of them either outdoors or elsewhere, in places that had generators. Thanks to my ankle, it was a no-brainer to pass on both the cross-country skiing crew and the party setting out to shovel sidewalks for the elderly. The ankle also let me weasel out of Grandfather's birdwatching party. I hoped everyone who signed on for that was aware that any J. Montgomery Blake–sponsored nature expedition would be more like a triathlon than a gentle country walk. The family cinema buffs, instead of sulking, were going downtown to the Mutant Wizards office where, thanks to the generator, they could begin their annual Christmas movie marathon. I convinced them to start with a few of the movies I was just as happy to miss, like *Santa and the Ice Cream Bunny* and *Jack Frost 2: Revenge of the Mutant Killer Snow-*

man. And, given my limited sewing skills, I was relieved to skip the Christmas quilting bee out at the Inn. But the caroling party was tempting—they planned to hit the assisted living and the hospital, ending up in the town square to serenade the tourists.

"I have to head down to the hospital," I told them. "I'll keep my eyes open—maybe I can join you there."

Or maybe after I'd delivered Harris's bag I'd just come home and join the crew that was camped around the fireplace and clearly had no intention of leaving the house if they could help it. The living room was actually pretty comfortable, thanks to a roaring fire and a couple of the kerosene space heaters, so they were only wearing sweaters or light jackets. And they were toasting marshmallows in the fireplace, drinking hot chocolate or mulled wine, and playing board games like Settlers of Catan or Monopoly— all of which corresponded precisely with my idea of the proper way to spend a snowy afternoon. I decided I'd hurry through my errand so I could come back and join these kindred spirits.

I did wander down to the basement to have a word with Kevin. I found him leaning back in his well-padded desk chair with a blanket wrapped around him and Widget asleep in his lap, staring at a computer monitor. For a moment I felt a surge of excitement—had the power just come back on? Then I realized that the monitor, his computer, the Internet router, and a couple of other pieces of essential hardware were all hooked up to his banks of batteries.

The monitor showed a view of the two wombats, glowing gently as they rummaged around their habitat.

The habitat—at least the part currently visible in the camera—had blank white walls. Curious. Grandfather's staff included several talented amateur artists who could be called on to decorate any habitat to match whatever kind of landscape its occupants would want around them in nature. Then again, the wombats were relatively new arrivals at the zoo, so perhaps the staff hadn't yet had time to plan and execute the necessary murals.

Ian and Bruce didn't seem to mind the stark walls. One of them seemed to be contentedly scratching his back against a brush that was attached to one of the several large trees surrounding their burrow. The other was snuffling along the floor of the habitat, occasionally finding and chomping on small clumps of hay.

"Is that all they get to eat?" I asked. "Hay?"

Kevin started slightly, and then tried to pretend he hadn't, because that would mean I'd been able to sneak up on him.

"Great says you have to be careful about overfeeding them, because they have a tendency to become obese in captivity," he said. "He keeps them on a low-energy, low-protein diet of hay and grass, which is pretty much what they eat in the wild. And makes them forage for it, so they get some exercise."

The one wombat who had been scratching his back was now climbing on top of the rocky feature that covered their burrow. The other one had foraged his way off camera. Kevin touched a couple of keys and the camera tracked right until the foraging wombat appeared on-screen again. Eventually it disappeared into the farther reaches of the habitat. Kevin focused the camera back on the other wombat, who was now standing atop the rocks as if playing King of the Mountain.

Kevin spun his desk chair around to face me.

"By the way, I looked into the Caerphilly Confidential website," he said. "Vreeland's definitely the owner—of that and the Tidewater Tattler. And I'm pretty sure he's also the whole staff. Site hasn't been updated since sometime last night, and you know it would have something about the murder if there was anyone to post it."

"Good work," I said. "When he regains consciousness,

I'll have a discussion with him about the site's future direction."

Assuming he ever regained consciousness.

Kevin nodded and spun his chair around again. I left him sitting there, feet on the desk, with no light other than what came from the monitor, petting Widget and watching the wombats.

I felt more cheerful once I tossed Harris's carry-on bag in my car and headed for town. The boys had started texting me pictures. Of my grandmother, once they collected her in Riverton. Of each other making silly faces. Of the town limit signs they passed, each one a little closer to home.

They'd be back well before bedtime. Maybe in time for the end of dinner.

That did more than anything else to restore my Christmas spirit. Still, I decided I'd OD'd on carols for the moment, so I turned the radio off and focused on enjoying the snow.

And eyeing the gray sky, which suggested that maybe we weren't finished with snow for the week. I finally turned on the radio when the digital dashboard clock clicked over from four fifty-nine to five, to catch the college radio's top-of-the-hour news and weather report.

Yes, the threatened second storm was barreling down on us. But at least it should hold off long enough for Michael and the boys to get home. After that—let it snow. The boys would love it.

The hospital parking lot was mostly empty when I pulled in. I waved at the receptionist before heading up to the second floor—after all, I still had on my visitor's badge.

I knocked on the doorframe of Harris's room.

"What now?" came the slightly cranky answer. "More blood? Another cheek swab?"

Cheek swab? Evidently Horace—or someone—had been in to get a DNA sample.

"It's Meg," I said. "I have no designs on any of your bodily substances."

"That's a relief. Come in."

I stepped through the privacy curtain. Harris was lying in bed, arms crossed, looking as cranky as he'd sounded. And he certainly didn't look like someone who should be leaving the hospital.

"They took my DNA." He sounded aggrieved, as if he only had so much of it and was in danger of not having enough left for his own use.

"Mine, too," I said. "For elimination purposes. I'm sure they'll be swabbing everyone who spent time in the library over the last few days. But especially you and me, since we spent the most time there."

Actually, Horace hadn't had to get a sample from me, since he already had my DNA, and that of an ever-increasing number of our relatives. Studying our family DNA had become his and Grandfather's newest hobby. But I suspected it would be more likely to mollify Harris if he thought I'd also been recently swabbed.

"But will they understand that our DNA could be there for perfectly innocent reasons?" Harris was obviously in the mood to fret. "After all, how many murders can the police chief possibly see in a . . . tiny little town like this?"

I suspected he'd only just barely stopped himself from saying "a hick town like this?"

"Not nearly as many as he saw during his decade or two as a Baltimore City homicide detective," I said. "Don't worry. He's a very experienced and capable investigator."

Harris didn't look reassured.

"And if it makes you feel any better, he's got a suspect in custody."

"Who?" He looked dubious.

"Iris, the other ex."

"Why her instead of Maddie?" he asked. "Maddie was

the one who showed up at the house and tried to throttle him yesterday."

"Yes, but Iris was the one who was lurking around the house in the middle of last night," I said. "And who drove off at around three in the morning, stopping along the way at a dumpster to discard a bloodstained paint rag."

His mouth fell open in astonishment and he just stared at me for several seconds.

"That's amazing," he said. "And I always thought she was the nice one. But are they positive?"

"I'm sure they still have a million things to do to rule out all the other suspects, you and me included," I said. "And to get as much evidence as possible against her. But the police have her dead to rights for another crime. My brother's fiancée's mother was coming to visit, and we'd never seen her before. Iris tied her up, locked her in a closet at the Inn, and came out to the house to impersonate her."

"When? Yesterday? I didn't see her."

"I suspect that was deliberate," I said. "She'd have known you were there, and since I assume you knew what she looked like, she'd have been very careful to avoid you."

"Oh, yes." He winced slightly—in fact, it was almost a flinch. "I've had to cope with her more than once. I just never knew—" He broke off and closed his eyes as if daunted by the thought that he'd dealt with someone who turned out to be a murderer. "So, I suppose they're thinking she came to reconnoiter. Scout out the house so she would know how to get in and could kill him."

"I have no idea what the police think," I said. "I think she just wanted to see him, and knew he'd do everything he could to avoid her. But once she got in, presumably tempers flared and she stabbed him. It didn't exactly look like a premeditated crime. More like something done in the heat of a quarrel. Maybe even self-defense."

"Yes." He nodded slightly. "I see." He stared down at his own chest and frowned for a little bit. Then he glanced up. "Thanks for coming to fill me in."

"Actually, I came to bring you this." I set the carry-on bag on the side of the bed. "Pajamas and toiletries, in case you decide to stay here. Clothes, for whenever you go back to the house."

"Right." He stared at the carry-on with a rather morose expression on his face, as if he didn't exactly welcome its sudden arrival. Perhaps he didn't. Perhaps it represented the need to make a decision about whether to follow Dad's advice and stay at the hospital or check himself out against doctor's order and return to . . . what? His job was gone. He didn't really seem in good enough shape to start looking for a new one. He needed rest and recuperation.

And surely he was smart enough to have figured out the advantages of being here in the hospital if it turned out that he wasn't as completely recovered as he thought he was. Concussion was tricky, as Dad was so fond of remarking. Wasn't it better to be here, within easy reach of medical assistance, until he was definitely out of the woods? Could I say anything that would encourage him to stay?

"Frankly, if I were you, I'd stay here," I began. "If they think you might have a concussion, peace and quiet is the main thing you need to recover. And that's a little hard to come by around the house right now, what with the library still being blocked off as a crime scene and the police coming and going."

Actually, the main destroyer of peace and quiet was the increasing crowd of visiting relatives. Having the library still barricaded with crime scene tape did mean that the board and role-playing games that would normally have been happening there ended up in the living room, which was already crowded with caroling and conversation. But that added only slightly to the normal holiday chaos. I found I was looking forward to rejoining that familiar chaos—but I suspected it would be a form of torture for Harris.

"You'll probably see less of the police here," I said. "And less of all the relatives who are dying of curiosity about the murder. They'll badger you to tell them everything you know, and then they won't believe you when you say you have no idea who killed him."

"Why not?" He looked alarmed. I'd gone too far. "What could I possibly know that I haven't already told the police. And—"

"Of course." I made my tone reassuring. "But you know how people are. They'll think since you met his ex-wives of course you'll know whether either of them could be the culprit. They'll demand that you tell them about who his enemies were and whether you think they could be responsible. You'll get more peace and quiet here."

He glanced around as if to suggest that peace and quiet wasn't exactly a feature of hospital life, either.

"And besides, we can use it for the sympathy factor," I went on. "For finding you work. Michael knows a lot of people in the college Art Department. Unless you have an objection, I was thinking I could get him to ask around. See if anyone knows of any jobs, either at the college or elsewhere in the field. Brag about your qualifications. Rhode Island School of Design is pretty impressive. And they're bound to be impressed by your working with Castlemayne."

"Actually, they probably wouldn't," Harris said. "They don't take him very seriously in academic circles."

"No, but the fact that you managed to hang on to a job with an egomaniac like him for three years is impressive," I said. "The more I got to know him, the more impressed I was by that."

He gave a quick smile at that.

"Look, there's no guarantee that it will come to anything," I said. "But why not give it a try, okay?"

He nodded.

"And don't discount the sympathy factor," I said. "Plenty of people get hauled off to the ER, but kept for an overnight stay, even if it's only for observation—that'll get sympathy. We can use that."

"I'll keep that in mind." He was frowning slightly, and his expression suggested he was trying to work up to saying something. I waited patiently.

"What's going to happen with the project Mr. Castlemayne was doing for your grandfather?" he asked finally.

"I have no idea." I realized, somewhat to my own surprise, that I hadn't even thought about it. "Obviously he's not going to scrap the whole thing—the text for the book is nearly finished, and I think he's seen signs of interest in it from several publishers." Actually, I knew very well that his literary agent was sorting through competing offers from three different publishers—I even knew which publishers and how much they were offering. But bragging about that would be indiscreet, so I'd leave it to Grandfather. "I suppose he'll have to find another artist to do the rest of the illustrations." Or maybe all of the illustrations, since only the first painting, the one of the cardinals, had been both finished and accepted. Castlemayne hadn't yet made the technical corrections Grandfather had requested on the mockingbird painting and had barely begun working on the blue jays.

"Do you think there's any chance he would consider letting me take a stab at finishing the project?" Harris asked.

Chapter 35

Hire Harris to finish the paintings? I tried not to show how surprised I was at the question. After all, I knew he was an artist. He'd worked with Castlemayne for three years. Should I be surprised that he would suggest taking over for his late employer?

I pondered the idea. Were the publishers interested primarily in Grandfather's text or had Castlemayne's involvement added substantially to their enthusiasm about the project? I wasn't the right person to ask—I hadn't even heard of the man before he'd come to Caerphilly—but perhaps his was a name to conjure with among the avid birders at whom Grandfather's book was aimed.

"I have no idea," I said. "Remember, when it comes to art, I'm a Philistine. But I say it doesn't hurt to ask."

"There's bound to be greater interest in his work now," Harris said. "What with all the notoriety from the murder. And—well, your grandfather could advertise the series as begun by Roderick Castlemayne and completed by his longtime assistant. Obviously my name wouldn't mean much, but I'm sure the publicity could be worded in a way that suggested that my contribution was relatively minimal."

Whereas in reality his contribution would consist of more than three-fourths of the total—nine out of twelve pictures. And that was assuming you included what Castlemayne had already done on the blue jay painting. But unless he'd made miraculous progress in the last few hours before he'd been murdered, it still consisted mostly of a few Prussian blue blobs on a pale green background. Curiously, although I'd spent a nontrivial amount of time in the library after his body was found, I couldn't remember even glancing at the unfinished painting.

"And it wouldn't be the first time I'd helped out," Harris said. "You know how unhappy your Grandfather was with the cardinal painting when he first saw it? Because the shape of the black face mask on the male was completely wrong, and he'd left out the subtle reddish tints on the female's crest and tail feathers."

"I remember they had words about it." In fact, they'd had several long, bitter arguments before Castlemayne had finally agreed to make the necessary corrections. I didn't remember exactly what the issue had been, but it sounded as if Harris did.

"I fixed that." Harris looked anxious, as if not sure he should be revealing the part he'd played—or maybe not sure I'd believe him. "And that wasn't the first time. He was wonderful at the composition and color palette, and the whole mood of a piece. But he hated details. And really hated having to correct things. So once he figured out that I could do it in a way that kept intact the integrity of his work, he trusted me to make minor technical corrections."

Translation: Once Castlemayne was sure Harris had learned to imitate his style, he let him work on his paintings. Do the parts that bored him.

"I could . . . I could do this." Harris was doing his best to sound confident and assertive, and not succeeding all that well. "It would mean working outside my own style, but I can do that. It's one of the things we do as art students, you know. It's one way of learning different techniques. Jarring us out of our own habits and comfort zones."

I thought of pointing out that it was also how clever art forgers operated and decided not to. But I had a feeling Grandfather would react as I had—that it was one thing for Harris to make technical corrections to his employer's paintings and quite another to pass off eight or nine Harris paintings as genuine Castlemaynes. But more than anything, Harris needed encouragement right now.

"I have no idea how any of this works, so don't ask me," I said. "But I know Grandfather is certainly going to be seriously worried about his book project. So why not ask him? But this is a big thing. Don't just dash off and ask. Get your strength back. Practice doing your pitch to him. Rehearse it with Caroline—she knows a lot about how he thinks. You need to give it your best shot. And—getting back to the subject of your immediate plans—I think you should stay here, at least tonight. Get some peace and quiet and rest. I know it probably seems like the hospital routine is designed to interfere with rest, but believe me, it would be even worse back at the house. Everyone would be so kind, and so eager to make you feel better, and so completely clueless about how tiring it is to be fussed over."

"And Rose Noire would make me drink that ghastly herbal tea of hers."

"Ah, so you've had her herbal tea," I said.

He shuddered slightly and closed his eyes as if in pain.

"So you get it," I said. "And you can stay here and rest up so you're ready to endure all the pampering. And meanwhile I'll ponder the best way to approach Grandfather about whether he'd consider letting you finish the project."

"I could audition, you know." His face lit up with an eager expression. "You know, finish the blue jay picture, and then he could see if it works for him."

"That might get his attention," I said. "And hey—this could be the start of a whole new career for you."

His face fell again.

"Yeah. Of course, it's not the kind of painting I really want to be doing. Representational art is so . . . twentieth century. But my work—well, anything really new and original tends to be hard to sell. I think—"

Dad bustled in.

"Meg! You brought his things? Excellent." He turned to Harris. "Although I hope you're going to stick around. I'd feel a lot happier if—"

"Don't worry," Harris said. "Meg's convinced me that I'll probably get a lot more rest here."

"Excellent!" Dad beamed at us both. "Now let's just do a few quick tests to see how you're progressing."

"I'll leave you to it." I stood and headed for the door.

"Now follow my fingers, but without moving your head," Dad was saying as I exited.

Out in the hall I glanced up and down. No nurses in sight. I could go in search of one and ask how Curly and Justin were doing.

Of course, with Curly, I could just stick my head in the door and ask him himself.

He was two doors down from Harris, in 220.

"It's Meg Langslow," I called as I knocked on the doorframe.

"Come in."

I slipped through the privacy curtain and took one of the two visitor chairs. Curly was working on a late-afternoon snack—or was it a light dinner? A plate of cookies, a glass of milk, and half a dozen small cups of lime Jell-O. Standard hospital fare? Or had someone from the Ladies Interfaith Council arrived with room service?

"I like Jell-O," he said when he saw me eyeing little plastic cup in his hand.

"And lime's the best," I said. "How are you feeling?"

He paused as if checking out all systems before answering.

"Not too bad," he said. "The cuts ache a little, but they give me something for that every few hours. And your dad says he's optimistic."

Optimistic? I'd have thought that of last night's three casualties, Curly was the one whose case was relatively straightforward. Were there some complications I hadn't heard of that could give rise to pessimism in someone less determined than Dad?

"He wants me to stay in for observation, though." Curly's smile showed that, unlike Harris, he was delighted at the prospect of an extended stay. "Since they'll probably need to take me over to the jail when I'm released. He wants to make sure I've built my strength up before that."

"Good thinking," I smiled and nodded at him, and he smiled and nodded back. The thought that at least for the immediate future he was in good hands and cooperating with his care raised my spirits enormously.

Someone else knocked on the doorframe, and a second later Osgood Shiffley stuck his head in through the privacy curtains.

"Hey, Meg. Hey, Curly," he said. "Mind if I come in?"

"Sure thing," Curly said. "I guess I need to thank you. Meg says it's mainly because of you that I'm still around."

"Well, me and that woman who stopped and kept you from bleeding out." Osgood ambled in and perched on the other chair. "Which was kind of weird when you come to think of it," he went on, turning toward me. "Didn't she turn out to be the one who killed that painter guy?"

"We don't know for sure yet," I said. "She claims it wasn't her."

"Well, she'd have to, wouldn't she?" Osgood said. "On account of not wanting to incriminate herself. But even if it turns out she did it, maybe she should get a break. She could have just kept on running, but she stopped to help Curly. Maybe even saved his life. They should take that into account when they sentence her."

"Yeah," Curly said. "I owe her one."

"And you owe me, too, buddy." Osgood looked stern. "Had to miss my break to bring you over here, and you bled all over the cab of my snowplow. Going to be a big job, cleaning it all up."

"I'm really sorry." Curly looked more than a little upset. I didn't blame him—why was Osgood laying into him like this? It wasn't like him at all.

"It's okay," Osgood said. "I figured out a way you can repay me."

"Um . . . okay." Curly had his head cocked, like a dog hearing an odd sound.

"I need a night watchman," Osgood said. "Over at the filling station. All you gotta do is stay in the back room from midnight when we close to six a.m. when we open. You call the cops if someone tries to break in, and you call me if there's anything else weird. My uncle Vermeer used to do it, but since his rheumatism has gotten worse, he doesn't find the cot very comfortable, and he's gotten so deaf it would take a damned careless burglar to wake him up. Been needing to find someone to replace him. So if you want to pay me back for saving your life, you can take his place for a while."

Curly looked startled at first, then he smiled.

"It's a deal." He held out his hand—the left one, rather than the bandaged right—and they shook solemnly.

"And now I'll leave you to get some rest." Osgood rose to go.

"I should go, too," I said as I stood up. "Let me know if there's anything you need."

"Can't think of anything right now." Curly glanced around, eyeing his surroundings with as much satisfaction as if he were in a luxury suite at the Inn.

"Work on it," I said. "You know how the Ladies Interfaith Council is. They cause a lot less trouble if you give them something to do."

He smiled.

"I'll work on it."

I followed Osgood out into the hall.

"Well, that went pretty well so far," he said as we strolled toward the elevator. "I think he feels guilty enough that he'll show up when he gets out of here. And with luck, after a few months, he'll be so used to dossing down in my back room that he'll just keep showing up. He's a creature of habit, Curly. Or I could try to hire him for the job."

"You're doing a good thing," I said.

"Just trying to do what needs doing," he said. "If we don't look after each other, who else will? Besides—I really could use a watchman. And I figure if he's hanging around the station, maybe the ladies from the Interfaith Council will start showing up occasionally with food for him. Only they'll know he won't take it if they think it's just for him, so they'll have to try to feed me, too. Yessir, I figure I'll be eating a mite better once I've got Curly settled in at the service station."

"Brilliant," I said. "If the Ladies Interfaith Council doesn't think of it, I'll drop them a hint."

The elevator arrived and he stepped in.

"I'd appreciate it." He stepped in and stabbed the hold button with one long, calloused finger. "You coming?"

"Not just yet," I said. "I'm going to look in on one more patient."

"That's nice. You have a Merry Christmas, now." He released the hold button and the elevator doors swooshed closed.

I strolled back up the hallway. I saw Dad ducking back into Harris's room with a nurse in tow. Probably just as well that I'd finished my errand to Harris. I continued on to Justin Vreeland's room.

Chapter 36

Justin's privacy curtains were closed, but I could see a light inside. I knocked and waited. After a bit, when there was no answer, I peeked through the slit in the curtains.

Justin's eyes were closed, but he appeared to be sleeping restlessly—maybe because someone had left a light on over his bed and it was shining down into his eyes. As I watched, his eyelids fluttered, he winced, and lifted his right arm an inch or two off the bed. I got the impression he wanted to shield his eyes with his hand but didn't have the strength to lift his arm that far.

I slipped in and walked over to the bed. As I was reaching to turn off the light, Justin's eyes opened and he flinched slightly, as if afraid of me.

"It's okay," I said. "I was just going to turn off this light so it doesn't shine in your eyes."

"Okay." His voice was hoarse. "That's good. But turn on some other light. Don't want it dark."

The bedside table held a small adjustable gooseneck lamp. I angled it so it wouldn't shine into his eyes, turned it on, and turned off the glaring overhead lights.

"Better?" I asked.

"Yeah." He moved his lips slightly. They looked dry.

"Water?" I asked. There was a glass with a straw on the bedside table. He nodded, so I picked it up, guided the straw to his lips, and held it while he sipped.

"Thanks," he said finally. "Hospital, right?"

"Caerphilly Hospital." I set down the water and took

one of the visitor chairs. "Do you remember what happened to you?"

He scrunched up his face as if thinking was an effort. A sudden look of panic crossed his face and he began to breathe heavily. Then panic was replaced with pleading.

"Keep her away from me," he said. "Don't let her hit me again."

"She's gone," I said. "You're safe. You're in the hospital."

His eyes roamed around the room, taking in all the medical paraphernalia. I wouldn't have found all that very reassuring, but he seemed to. His breathing began to slow.

I wanted to push the call button, but it was on the other side of his bed. To push it, I'd have to reach across his chest, and I didn't think that would play very well. I could always walk around the foot of the bed, but I got the definite impression that I should keep still to avoid upsetting him. So I took out my phone and texted "Justin's awake" to Dad, and then to Caroline.

"She tried to kill me." He sounded surprised and indignant. Also, I was relieved to hear, stronger and more coherent.

"Who?"

"That woman."

I was torn. Should I be interrogating him or encouraging him to rest and calm down? I didn't want to wear him out with questions before the chief had a chance. But—grim thought—what if this was a brief moment of alertness before he sank back down into unconsciousness—or worse?

"What woman?" I asked.

"I don't know," he said. "The one who was there earlier. I followed her around the back of the house. She—" He stopped and frowned. "I think she hit me. She must have hit me. And she had blood on her. I think she killed him."

"Castlemayne?"

He nodded. His hand stirred slightly, as if he wanted to touch his head but wasn't strong enough.

"I guess she knocked you out," I said. "Can you remember anything after that?"

He frowned. Then he shook his head and winced slightly.

"Not until I woke up just now." He blinked. "My head really hurts. Can you get me something for my head?"

"We can call the nurse," I said. "The call button is over there."

He looked at it, then back up at me, and closed his eyes. I went around the foot of the bed to his left side and pressed the call button.

I heard a knock on the door and Caroline stuck her head through the curtains.

"He's awake," I said. "And says his head really hurts."

She nodded and vanished.

As far as I could tell, Justin was conscious, but clearly not in the mood to talk. I returned to the side of the bed where the visitor chairs were and sat down again. I figured someone should keep an eye on Justin until help arrived.

A minute later, Dad burst into the room and raced to Justin's side.

"He's awake," I said. "And he can talk. But his head really hurts."

"Got it." Dad was glancing back and forth between Justin and the various readouts and information screens surrounding him. He didn't look as happy as I'd have expected him to be about having his patient regain consciousness. "Mr. Vreeland?"

A nurse dashed in, followed by Caroline. I decided they wouldn't want me underfoot, so I slipped out into the hall.

But I decided to stay around until I could hear an update from Dad on how Justin was doing. There was a bench a little way down the hallway. I plodded over to it and sat down. I noticed an outlet near the bench, so I fished my phone-charging cord out and plugged it in.

I was toying with the idea of stretching out on the bench for a nap when I spotted a familiar figure exiting the elevator—Chief Burke. He looked around, then headed in my direction.

"That was quick," I said when he drew near my bench.

"What was quick?" He looked puzzled.

"I assume you came over to see Justin Vreeland," I said.

"No, I came over to see Curly." He glanced down the hall toward the door to Justin's room and frowned. "No one told me Mr. Vreeland was out of his coma."

"I think you have to be out for longer than a few hours for it to count as a coma," I said. "And he only came to about five minutes ago. Dad and one of the nurses are in there now checking him out."

Just then a white-coated doctor raced down the hall and disappeared into Justin's room. Hard on her heels was the shaven-headed RN, pushing a cart with some piece of equipment on it.

"I should probably wait until they're finished with . . . whatever they're doing." The chief sounded uneasy.

I nodded. I thought of pointing out that just because the medical team was hurrying didn't mean anything bad was happening. They might be merely excited that Justin was conscious and eager to do whatever tests or treatments were advisable for someone just waking up from a pro-longed unconsciousness. But the chief probably already knew that, and he still looked worried.

"Did he say anything?" he asked. "Anything coherent?"

"Wasn't all that coherent," I said. "But he did say something. I pushed the call button as soon as I could, but he seemed to want to talk."

"Fill me in." He pulled out his notebook and sat down beside me—but angling his body so he could more easily keep his eyes on the doorway to room 212.

I related everything Justin had said or done—it wasn't all that much. And how he looked—how frightened he had been when he first woke up. How quickly he seemed to tire. When I finished, the chief sat for several minutes looking down at his notes.

"It's not a lot," I said. "Sorry."

"More than I expected, really," he said.

"But you don't look thrilled," I said. "You don't even look mildly pleased. Is it because you're worried that Justin won't survive to testify about what little he remembers? Or just that a sharp defense attorney could use the severity of his head wound to cast doubt on his testimony?"

To my surprise, he chuckled.

Chapter 37

"I hadn't gotten that far yet," he said. "I was still comparing what you're telling me with the statement I got about an hour ago from Mrs. Iris Castlemayne."

"I gather they don't match."

"You gather correctly." He nodded. "She claims she saw Mr. Vreeland stab Mr. Castlemayne."

"Seriously?"

"Yes. She says she walked in just in time to see it. She gasped in shock, he saw her, and he chased her outside. They tussled, she struck him over the head in self-defense, and fled in terror, not realizing that she'd knocked him out." He blew out a breath in exasperation.

"Wow," I said. "A perfect he said, she said."

He nodded.

"Always possible that he's lying," he said.

"Doesn't seem very likely, though," I said. "He was still pretty woozy. I don't think he's sharp enough yet to come up with a plausible lie. But ask Dad—he knows more about that kind of thing."

"I will," he said. "But it's going to be blasted hard to figure out which one is telling the truth. And even when we do, there's always the danger that a capable defense attorney could use the conflicting stories to show reasonable doubt."

"So feel free to tell me it's none of my business," I said. "But did you find anything in the dumpster by the ice cream store?"

"Yes." He smiled. "A fence post, a tangle of barbed wire,

and a whole lot of boxwood twigs." The smile faded. "Plus a pair of women's black leather gloves that will probably turn out to have slight bloodstains on them."

"Slight?"

"Yes." He shook his head absently. "The stains are almost certainly too slight to have been acquired during the commission of the murder. Unfortunately, the same is true of the slight bloodstains we found on Mr. Vreeland's gloves and coat."

"So one of them killed Castlemayne, cleaned off most of the blood—possibly with the rag Iris later used to stop Curly's bleeding—and then transferred blood to the other in the tussle outside."

"Looks that way." The chief nodded. "The rag is in the latest batch of evidence on its way down to Richmond—they'll be testing it to see if it contains only Curly's blood or a combination of his and Castlemayne's. And to see if there's any DNA on it to prove that Mrs. Castlemayne had touched it. No matter how the tests come out, I'm not sure it will prove anything. The fact that Iris Castlemayne ended up with it doesn't mean she was the one who carried it out of the library. Mr. Vreeland could have done that and lost it to her in the struggle. What a mess!"

I nodded. I wondered if Horace had taken samples for himself before the evidence had gone off to Richmond. He often did, if it was possible without compromising the evidence, and used his own lab skills to get a sneak preview of what the state lab would ultimately report. Horace's efforts were especially useful now that Grandfather let him use the rapid DNA sequencing system he'd acquired for the zoo's scientific labs. And while the chief would need the state lab results to convict the killer, Horace's more timely tests could help steer the course of his investigation.

Assuming they showed anything to prove which of the two was lying.

I thought about it for a while.

"What's Justin's motive?" I asked. "Easy to come up with possible motives for an ex-wife. But what possible reason could Justin have for knocking off Castlemayne? As far as I can tell he was hoping to get some kind of big scoop and use it to get a foot in the door at the *Star-Tribune*. Wouldn't that give him a motive to keep the wretched man alive?"

"So you'd think," the chief said. "I talked to several editors at the *Star-Tribune*. Mr. Vreeland has frequently submitted stories to them on spec, but so far they haven't taken any of them. I got the definite notion that they weren't very impressed with his journalistic skills."

"Which might give him a motive to bump off an editor or two, but why Castlemayne? Why kill the goose you hope will lay you a golden egg?"

"It seems to be a crime of impulse," the chief said. "Perhaps Mr. Vreeland took advantage of an unlocked door to enter the library and Mr. Castlemayne resented the intrusion. I can easily imagine him becoming belligerent. Perhaps even violent."

"And Justin stabs him in self-defense?"

"It's a plausible scenario. In self-defense, or perhaps in a moment of anger and frustration when Castlemayne refused to talk to him. Of course, the same scenario would work for Iris Castlemayne. She barges into the library to confront him over his failure to make his alimony payments. He becomes belligerent."

"And she stabs him in self-defense?" I asked. "Or in sheer exasperation when he shows no signs of turning over a new leaf and paying what he owes?"

"Either is plausible," he said. "But none of it's provable."

We sat there for a few minutes, both staring at the door of Justin's room and lost in our own thoughts.

"We've got Mrs. Iris Castlemayne locked up," the chief said. "Judge Shiffley denied bail. And we'll be keeping Mr. Vreeland under guard until he's well enough to join her."

He glanced at his watch. "Sammy should be over here any minute."

"That's going to be a pain, isn't it?" I said. "You'll be down one deputy."

"Can't be helped. By the way, I know you're probably hoping to get your library back soon, but I'd like to keep it sealed for a little while longer. Give Horace a chance to look around again and see if he can find anything that proves or disproves either of their stories."

"I figured as much," I said. "Any objection if I ask Horace to take a couple of good shots of the canvas Castlemayne was working on? Grandfather's going to need to figure out what to do about the paintings he needs for his book."

"No problem," he said.

"Thanks. And what about the stuff Castlemayne left at the Inn? Still okay to take that out to the zoo to hold until we figure out where to send it?"

"No problem with that," he said. "Apparently neither he nor his assistant had been back to the Inn for a day or two, so Horace's initial examination should be more than adequate."

"Thanks," I said. "I'll probably collect his stuff and drop it off at the zoo before I head home."

"Good." He nodded and stood up. "I'm going to stick my head in and see how Mr. Vreeland is doing. Talk to you later."

He strode off down the hall. I retrieved my phone and charger cord and took the elevator downstairs. One more errand—taking Castlemayne's stuff to the zoo—and I could stand down.

My phone dinged as I was getting into the car. I answered it and heard a loud and mostly on-key rendition of "I'll Be Home for Christmas." Michael, the three boys, and Cordelia. I leaned back in the car seat and listened. They finished with lovely three-part harmony on "if only in my dreams," and I applauded as loudly as I could with one hand holding the phone.

"Bravo," I said. "And I applaud the sentiment."

"Actually," Michael said. "We should be home in an hour—maybe an hour and a half if we make another pit stop."

"Awesome," I said. "And I have good news."

"You're going to let the wombats come back?" Jamie asked.

"I can't believe you got rid of the wombats before we got a chance to meet them," Josh added.

"The boys have been watching Kevin's Wombat Cam," Michael explained. "And turning the black light on and off. We may have to take them out to the zoo pretty soon to commune with the wombats."

"I wouldn't mind seeing them myself," Cordelia put in. "But they belong at the zoo, not at your house. What was Monty thinking?"

"Aw, Gran-gran," Josh began.

"We could invite them back," Jamie suggested.

"The wombats are happier at the zoo," I said. "Believe me. No, the good news is that Chief Burke may have caught the person who killed Mr. Castlemayne."

"Awesome!" Adam Burke exclaimed. "I knew Grandpa would do it."

"So who is it?" Michael asked.

"Either his second ex-wife, or the guy who showed up and claimed to be a reporter from the *Washington Star-Tribune*. Each claims to have seen the other one do the deed, so it could take a while before the chief figures out which one is guilty."

"Can't Uncle Horace help?" Jamie asked.

"He's working on it," I said. "And since one suspect is under guard at the hospital and the other is locked up in jail for kidnapping Delaney's mother, I think we can all feel a lot safer."

"Wait!" Michael exclaimed. "Kidnapping Delaney's mother? When did that happen?"

So I leaned back and told them a reasonably full version of my day. They made a highly satisfactory audience, oohing and ahhing at the exciting bits and laughing at my occasional joke. They particularly enjoyed hearing about how cool Mother had been when facing down an armed kidnapper, and were suitably worried about Curly, Mrs. McKenna, and even Harris.

"He's kind of a drip," Josh pronounced. "But he's not nasty like Mr. Castlemayne."

"Now, Josh," Cordelia said.

"Do you know when we're going to get the library back?" Michael asked.

"Could take a while," I said. "Poor Horace is going to spend some more time in there, trying to find some evidence to show which of our two suspects actually did it."

"Bummer," Josh remarked.

"Hey, maybe Horace will let us watch him," Jamie suggested.

"We should let you get back to whatever you're doing," Michael said. "Don't let the horde of relatives eat up everything before we get there."

"If you see Grandpa, tell him I have a surprise for him and Grandma," Adam requested.

"Give Spike a treat," Jamie ordered.

"And don't let the Pomeranians bother him too much," Josh added.

"Tell your mother 'well done' for me," Cordelia added.

With that they signed off.

I started the car and reached automatically for the radio. Well, why not? My conversation with the family had cheered me up. A sneak preview of the happy reunion to come. A first taste of what would be, after all, a merry holiday season. Castlemayne's death had cast a pall over things—less from sorrow about him than from the stress of knowing a murderer was loose in town. And while it could take the chief some time to figure out which of his two suspects was the guilty one, at least neither of them was still roaming free. We could feel safe. I was back in the mood for carols again.

So I turned up the volume and found myself singing along even to carols that weren't among my favorites. "Jolly Old St. Nicholas," for example, which normally struck me as overly cute and quaint.

No one was parked by the Inn's front entrance, so I left my car there. The doorman gave me his lowest bow as he swept the door open. Inside, Enrique was still at the desk.

"Ah," he said. "Here to retrieve the luggage. Where is your car?"

"Right in front," I said. "I thought that would be easier, especially if he had a lot of stuff."

"Alas." Enrique sounded sad. "Merely two suitcases. And not very large ones at that. Not much to leave behind, is it? Go back to your car—I will bring them out. It would be bad luck to let you do it."

I wasn't sure I understood why it would be unlucky for me to carry the suitcases, but I didn't want to put too much stress on my ankle, so I was happy to let him do it. After all, I'd be doing my bit of luggage toting when I got to the zoo. I went outside and popped the trunk. Enrique appeared almost immediately with the two suitcases. Rather nice suitcases, made of soft leather in an old-fashioned style, and so well-worn that they had obviously made many journeys.

Enrique refused to let me tip him for carrying the suitcases.

"No, no," he said. "That would also be bad luck—like taking money from a dead man."

Was this a hotel superstition, a Catholic superstition, or just an Enrique superstition? I could ask Ekaterina later—and by doing so let her know Enrique had earned my gratitude. For now, I thanked him profusely, then climbed into the car and drove off.

As I was pulling out of the Inn's driveway, I noticed that it had started snowing again.

Chapter 38

I felt a momentary twinge of—what? Not panic. I could deal with snowstorms. I actually enjoyed them, as long as I could stay home and observe them from indoors. Why this sudden negative reaction to the sight of the snow?

Maybe it was just tiredness. It had been a long day. I wanted to be home already. And not just home, but reunited with Michael and the boys and finally getting to relax and enjoy the holiday.

Maybe it wasn't bad luck, hauling around a dead man's luggage, but it was kind of a downer. Under other circumstances, I might have tried to cheer myself up by visiting some of my favorite animals. Like the little blue penguins, who would be delirious with joy at having snow to play in. Or the meerkats. Hard to think of a time when I was so down in the dumps that watching Grandfather's meerkats didn't make me smile. And while normally he reserved his most intense interest for predators, I suspected he also had a sneaking fondness for meerkats, given the several large habitats he'd devoted to them and the amount of time he spent studying their behavior.

Maybe I'd swing by the meerkats if they weren't too far out of my path to the Aviary, where Grandfather had given Castlemayne a space to work in. I parked just outside the zoo's staff entrance, hauled the suitcases out of the trunk, and let myself in with my VIP-access card key. I didn't see anyone around. No tourists, of course. The weather forecast had inspired Grandfather to close the zoo to the public. I knew he did this less out of concern for the safety of the tourists than to ensure that any staff who could make it through the snow—or were willing to stay on the premises for the duration—could focus on the well-being of the animals. And given the bitter cold, any staff on site were bound to be hunkered down in the warmest sections of the various buildings, keeping watch over their charges. A good thing the security system was on the generator I thought, as I swiped my card and let myself in.

Someone had plowed paths from the cluster of administrative buildings near the entrance to every building that contained animals in need of food, water, and shelter—paths wide enough for the little electric carts the staff used to zip around the park and to haul things. Off in the distance I could hear the sound of the plow—along with the humming of the distant generators—but I saw no one as I plodded along the path with its patchwork of asphalt and ice. Thank goodness every other light or so was hooked to the generators. The day had been overcast to begin with, and now the sun was setting.

The Aviary, of course, was one of the farthest buildings from the gates. A good thing the suitcases weren't all that large, although they did feel a lot heavier now than they had when I'd taken them out of the car. I decided to take a shortcut. I used my card key to let myself into the Small Mammal Building and paused for a moment to appreciate how nice and toasty the interior was. Grandfather was definitely not neglecting his small mammals' comfort. Then I set out by the most direct course possible for the other end of the building.

Out of consideration for the animals, the Small Mammal Building went into night mode at sunset, so it would have been dimly lit under any circumstances. The emergency lighting was so dim I considered pulling out my flashlight, but after a few moments my eyes adjusted. I paused for a few minutes beside the meerkat exhibit. Just long enough to put down the suitcases and rest my arms.

The meerkats, being diurnal, were doing a little last bit of scurrying around their habitat before disappearing into their burrow for the night. The two sentinels standing back-to-back by the mouth of the burrow kept a close watch on me.

I took a seat on the meerkat-watching bench, as I called it, and settled in for a few minutes of enjoyment. After all, I still had quite a distance to haul the suitcases. And the meerkats would be asleep by the time I came back this way.

But after a few minutes even the sentries disappeared—after giving me one last suspicious glance. I stood, picked up the suitcases, and continued.

At the far end of the building, instead of going out into the cold again, I swiped my card through the reader by a staff-only door and let myself into what I thought of as backstage at the zoo. I went past windows looking out into the various habitats, most now curtained to give the animals greater privacy. I passed staff workrooms and storage rooms for food and cleaning supplies. A small but very well-equipped veterinary clinic—empty, I was glad to see, except for a cage containing a weasel with a bandage on one of his tiny back feet and a cone of shame around his neck. Finally I arrived at a door marked KINGDOM OF THE NIGHT: BACK ENTRANCE.

The original Kingdom of the Night—Grandfather's special habitat for nocturnal animals—had been directly under the dome containing the desert habitat. But it had proven so popular with the tourists—not to mention so amusing for Grandfather—that he'd expanded it substantially. The new addition occupied most of the space underground between the Desert Dome and the Small Mammal Building, with the new Pollinator Garden on top of it.

I went down the long stairs, resisting the temptation to bump the suitcases along behind me, and used my card on yet another reader to enter the Kingdom of the Night.

And there were the wombats.

They were in an enormous glass-fronted habitat to the right of the door. The habitat was much larger than it had looked on camera. Grandfather was doing the wombats proud. Someone—either Kevin or Michael and the boys—must have turned on the black lights, because both wombats glowed gently. They appeared to be half asleep in the tree-shaded mouth of what I assumed was an artificial wombat burrow. Wasn't it a little early for them to be so fast asleep? Before an animal was introduced into the Kingdom of the Night, the zookeepers gradually shifted its sleep cycle until it was twelve hours off the rest of the world. At night, glaring lights in the Kingdom produced the illusion of daytime, so the animals would take to their burrows and sleep. Then, when dawn broke out in the real world, the underground lights dimmed to a soft level that approximated moonlight, and the nocturnal animals would come out to feed and play—and entertain the visitors. Most of the animals here would be just settling down for the what would look like daylight to them, but the wombats looked out for the count already.

Perhaps their sojourn in our basement had reset their schedule. And while this part of the underground building was more brightly lit than the small mammal house upstairs, it wasn't nearly as glaring as usual. In fact, it was nowhere near full daylight—more like the way the light looks just before a heavy rain breaks. Probably a special power-saving mode for when the whole zoo was running on the generator.

I studied the wombats briefly—and their habitat. I could see Kevin's Wombat Cam overhead, with a little red light slowly blinking—probably an indicator that it was on. Yes, I saw it move slightly to focus more directly on the mouth of the burrow, where Bruce and Ian were napping.

One of the wombats made a soft grunting noise and wiggled slightly, causing a rustling sound as it settled more comfortably into the hay and straw that covered the floor of the burrow.

Then they both stopped glowing. Kevin must have turned off the blacklight.

I picked up the suitcases and moved on. My ankle was doing pretty well, probably because it had the extra support that my snow boots provided. Maybe when I got home I should let them dry off and then wear them indoors for the next few days.

I kept up a brisk pace through the bat cave. It wasn't quite as creepy in the dim twilight of the power-saving daylight mode as it would have been in the near darkness that prevailed when the zoo was open. I knew the bats weren't vampire bats—Grandfather had a separate habitat for those near the building's main entrance. The bat cave harbored the unimaginatively named little brown bats, which would have absolutely no sinister designs on my person—in fact, they consumed enough mosquitos and other bugs to be classified as highly beneficial to humans.

It was still creepy, being in the tunnel that ran through their cave-like habitat—the more so since the sides of the tunnel were made of a fine wire mesh. It kept the bats out of the tunnel—and for that matter, nosy visitors away from the bats—but it was no barrier to sound or smell. The cave was filled with the fluttering and whooshing noises of the bats' flight, their high-pitched squeaking, and the strong ammonia smell of the guano that covered the floor of the habitat.

I breathed a sigh of relief when I exited the bat cave— and then took another deep breath for pure enjoyment. I'd entered the Lower Eucalyptus Forest, home of Grandfather's growing collection of nocturnal Australian animals. I passed the habitats of the ring-tailed possums, the greater gliders, and the platypuses. I actually stopped to gawk when I caught a glimpse of a platypus basking at the edge of the pond that filled most of its habitat. Grandfather was very up front about being more concerned for the welfare of his animals than the wishes of the zoo's visitors. All of his charges received large habitats with plenty of cover for when they weren't in the mood to be stared at. If the tourists complained, too bad. And the platypuses took greater advantage of this than most other animals.

Eventually the platypus got up and waddled into the tangle of roots that concealed the mouth of its burrow, and I moved on.

Invigorated by the rest, I hoisted the suitcases and strode briskly through the African section, past the crocodiles, the aardvarks, the bush babies, and the springhaas. Soon I found myself just inside the entrance to the Kingdom, with vampire bats to my left and naked mole rats to my right. The boys could happily spend hours here, but it was my least favorite part of the exhibit. I hurried past, and, bracing myself, went out into the snow again.

I felt as if someone had lifted a weight off my back. I realized that the whole of the time I'd been traveling through the Kingdom of the Night I'd been—well, not exactly looking over my shoulder. But hunching my shoulders ever so slightly, as if expecting someone—or something—to leap out of the shadows at me. There were certainly plenty of shadows in the dim emergency lighting.

I reminded myself that both Iris Castlemayne and Justin Vreeland were under guard and deliberately untensed my shoulders.

I could see the Aviary now, just past what Grandfather grandly called the Reptile Pavilion. Behind his back we'd taken to calling it Slitherin' House. Another of the boys' favorites.

As I drew near the Aviary, I could see the little blue penguins at play in the outdoor part of their habitat, to the right of the entrance. They were diving into the stream, swimming around, hopping back on land, and eventually running through the flap to go inside. And then dashing out again to repeat the whole process. Evidently it was cold enough that even penguins were happy to spend part of the day indoors. And at least it wasn't their mating season, thank goodness, since the little blue penguins seemed to celebrate that event with an unabashed enthusiasm that caused even some zookeepers to blush.

I swiped my card through the reader and entered the Aviary.

I was getting tired of hauling the suitcases, so I strode briskly down the middle of the dimly lit main chamber, catching only occasional glimpses of the birds I was passing. The bald eagles, who had perfected the art of gazing nobly into the distance, as if it were beneath their dignity to notice the arrival of a mere human. The buzzards and vultures, who always seemed to watch passersby with disconcertingly hopeful expressions. The enormous tropical bird habitat—Springtime in Parrots, as the staff called it—containing several dozen species of parrots, macaws, caiques, Amazons, lorikeets, conures, finches, and cockatoos, all busy squawking and trilling and fluttering and preening in what would be, by daylight, a blaze of color and sound. Even now, as its inhabitants gradually settled down for the night, the main hall of the Aviary was alive with birdcalls and the fluttering of wings.

At the far end of the corridor I let myself into another staff-only door and was suddenly surprised at how quiet it was without all the various bird sounds. Quiet and dark. Here in the part of the building designated mostly for humans, only a few emergency lights illuminated the long corridor ahead of me—a mix of the old fluorescent fixtures and the new LEDs that the maintenance staff were gradually installing as the last few fluorescent bulbs burned out.

I followed the corridor until it dead-ended at the door of a storage room. Smaller, even more badly lit corridors led left and right. I took the right turn and eventually found myself at the door of a room that was normally used both as a staff breakroom and as an isolation area for newly arrived birds who needed to stay in quarantine until the veterinary staff were sure they didn't have any contagious diseases to spread to the Aviary's other residents.

But now the door bore a new temporary sign that declared it to be MR. CASTLEMAYNE'S STUDIO.

A pity he hadn't stayed here. We'd have had a much more peaceful time the last few days. And maybe he'd still be alive. Grandfather's security here at the zoo was pretty impressive. Not that he'd have been all that worried about Castlemayne, since he'd have had no way of knowing that someone had homicidal plans for him. But Grandfather cared deeply about his animals, and Castlemayne would have been a lot safer here, ensconced in the midst of Grandfather's furry and feathered charges, with the zoo's trained security staff to fend off intruders.

I swiped my card and opened the door, reaching for the light switch by habit. Nothing happened, of course. I sighed, pulled out my phone, and turned on the flashlight app before stepping into the room.

Chapter 39

Two steps in and I must have tripped a motion detector—two rather dim fluorescent emergency lights gradually fluttered into life. I pulled the suitcases in, let the door close behind me, and pocketed my phone.

Not a bad room, I thought, as I looked around for the best place to stow the suitcases. Not as nice as our library, but I wouldn't have minded working here. Especially if I were someone who'd been locked out of my apartment and studio for nonpayment of rent. A shabby but comfortable couch, two mismatched armchairs, and a coffee table with a well-scarred top made a conversation area to my left. To my right were a kitchenette and a small bathroom, complete with shower. An enormous empty birdcage occupied the far-right corner of the room. The far-left corner contained three easels, seven cardboard boxes, and a card table used to hold art supplies. The easels were lined up in a precise row, like soldiers on parade. The boxes were arranged in size order against the far wall. The art supplies were as carefully arranged as the implements on a surgeon's tray. I had to chuckle at that. Proof positive that Castlemayne hadn't been out here in days—only Harris, who had been making one or two trips a day to fetch things that had been left behind. Highly inefficient, which wasn't like Harris. But whenever I was tempted to suggest that he just pack up everything and bring it over, I reminded myself that we didn't really want Castlemayne getting too comfortable in our library. And by the second day I'd figured out that fetching things was Harris's only way of escaping his employer's oppressive presence, even temporarily.

And the whole room was as neat and tidy as I'd ever seen it. Not that Grandfather's staff were total slobs, but normally the room had the kind of disheveled comfort you find in a shared space that's cared for but not fussed over. Now it was "wipe your feet so you don't track in invisible dirt" tidy. Maybe even "the photographers from *Architectural Digest* will be here any second" tidy.

I set down the suitcases beside the boxes, being careful to line them up neatly. After all, with any luck it might be Harris rather than me who ended up taking care of packing everything and arranging to have it all returned to whoever now owned it. No sense adding to his stress by disturbing the precision of his arrangements. And then I went over to look at the easels.

The first one held the painting of the cardinals—the one Castlemayne and Grandfather had had so many arguments over. The one Harris claimed he'd finally corrected. I had to admit, it was nice. Bold, colorful, yet—thanks to Harris's efforts—detailed and I assumed accurate at last, since Grandfather had finally signed off on it.

The second held the mockingbird painting. Grandfather had said it was almost as bad as the cardinal one, but since I lacked his expert knowledge of the fine details of mockingbirds' plumage and anatomy, I had no idea what was wrong with it.

The third easel surprised me—it held a partially finished picture of the blue jays. Partially finished, but still a lot further along than the painting I'd seen in our library. And taped to the pointy top part of the easel was a color photograph of some blue jays. A photograph that was definitely taken in our library—I could see books in the background, out of focus behind the protective plastic, but still recognizable. Several other photos were neatly stacked on the card table with the art supplies.

I remained staring at the unfinished picture for so long that the motion-sensitive lights went out. I did a few jumping jacks to remind them I was still here—lopsided jumping jacks, to avoid putting pressure on my ankle—and they grudgingly fluttered into life. Then I took out my phone and called Horace.

"What now?" he said, rather than hello.

"Oh, no," I said. "I didn't wake you, did I?"

"Wish you had," he said. "I'm in your library again, checking something out before I go home to hit the hay."

"Is the blue jay picture still there? The one Castlemayne was working on before he was killed."

"Yeah."

"You're sure?"

"I'm looking at it. Why?"

"There's another one here. At the zoo, in the studio he turned up his nose at."

"Yeah, I saw that. Maybe he wasn't happy with it and started over when he got here."

"I doubt it." I explained about the photos of the jays—though I didn't mention the possibility that Harris could have been the painter.

"Beats me, then," he said. "You think it's important? By which I guess I mean do you think it has anything to do with the murder?"

"Beats me," I echoed. "I'll let you get back to whatever you were doing. Get some rest soon."

"Roger."

I went back to stare at the painting again. The painting and the photos. I took pictures of the jay painting. Then I set my phone down on the card table, leaned it against a brush holder so it shed a little more light on the surface, and shuffled through the photos. I realized that it wasn't just the fact that they were taken after Castlemayne had moved to our library that bothered me. He had made such a big deal about never stooping to paint from a photo—always from life. And yet here were half a dozen photos of the blue jays, obviously being used as models. I'd bet anything it was Harris doing this painting—not Castlemayne.

Maybe Harris had come up with the idea of auditioning to replace his boss earlier than he was admitting. Castlemayne had made almost no progress with the mockingbirds while he and Grandfather had been arguing about the shortcomings of the cardinal painting. And the blue jay painting had seemed to stall while they argued over the fixes needed to the mockingbirds. Maybe Castlemayne hadn't been worried about Grandfather's growing frustration over how the project was going. Maybe he hadn't even noticed. But Harris had. I couldn't count the number of times he'd apologized to me for the slow progress, and asked me to tell Grandfather about various things that might excuse it.

What if Harris had been worried that his boss would stall and argue until Grandfather got fed up and fired him? That would certainly torpedo not only the alimony payments the ex-wives were hoping for, but also Harris's salary. Since he'd already proven that he could touch up paintings without anyone knowing, maybe he'd decided to do one from scratch. And he could have it ready so when Grandfather finally lost patience, he could whip it out and save the day. Assuming Castlemayne's ego allowed him to take credit for a painting someone else had done. But would he? I didn't know him well enough to guess.

What if Harris had been playing a deeper game all along? He'd have seen the trouble his employer was having meeting Grandfather's expectations. What if he'd started working on this painting so he'd be prepared for the moment when Grandfather finally lost patience with Castlemayne? Maybe even before Castlemayne was killed, Harris had been planning to show it to Grandfather. "Here. I'm not as famous as he is, but I can paint just like him, I'm a lot more accurate, I'll charge a lot less, and I'll actually meet your schedule."

I could see that. In fact, I could even see Harris sabotaging Castlemayne's productivity in a deliberate attempt to engineer a situation where he could step in and take over the project. Maybe Castlemayne wasn't being fussy when he kept complaining that Harris never had anything ready when he needed it. Maybe it hadn't been an accident that Harris always seemed to be running an errand or in the bathroom when the harassers showed up at the library door.

Maybe he'd even set the mockingbirds free. Anything to sabotage the project.

And then still another possibility struck me. What if Harris had been doing all the painting all along? I realized that I'd never actually seen Castlemayne painting— only standing brush in hand, in a pose that was clearly meant to symbolize deep thought. What if he was having whatever you call the painter's equivalent of writer's block?

Or what if he was just bone lazy and did everything he could to avoid work? I could see that even more easily. Michael and I knew several professors at the college who operated that way, recruiting talented grad students to do their research and write the articles that would go out under the professors' names. Not, thank goodness, in the Drama Department, where both the dean and Michael, who as assistant dean was his designated successor, were diligent about quashing such practices. But it happened. And I was well aware that once upon a time, many painters had studios that worked much like factories, turning out a steady stream of paintings done under the master's eye, but not necessarily by his hand. Was Castlemayne doing this? Having Harris do the actual painting to his specifications, and then taking credit for it?

And if that was what Castlemayne had been doing . . . how would Harris feel about it? Was he grateful to have a job? Or resentful of what probably felt like involuntary servitude? If I'd spent the last three years painting in a style that wasn't my own—a style I actually despised—and didn't even get any credit for it, I think I'd be at least a little resentful. Maybe a lot resentful.

Resentful enough to do something about it?

I was suddenly glad that the chief was reasonably sure either Justin or Iris had committed the murder. Because if I hadn't known that, I could all too easily have started to imagine a scenario in which Harris committed the crime.

Just then the lights went out. I started doing my lopsided jumping jacks again. The lights began to sputter back on.

The door opened.

I turned in mid–jumping jack to see who it was.

Harris.

"What the hell are you doing?" He looked as if my calisthenics dismayed him rather than merely startled him.

"Motion-sensitive lights," I said. "Which means if you stop for too long—like to rest your injured ankle—suddenly you're in darkness."

I felt curiously reluctant to admit that I'd been staring at his blue jay painting.

"And while resting your ankle you were staring at the paintings," he said.

"Not much else to look at in here," I said. "I suppose that's one reason your late boss preferred our library. Not sure I'd have felt that way, though."

"You like this better than your library?" He sounded incredulous.

"No, I like our library a lot better," I said. "But if I were doing some kind of work I needed to focus on, I'd prefer this space to do it in."

"Yeah." He looked around and nodded. "It's not fancy. But it would be a workspace. Your own workspace."

"A pity Castlemayne didn't feel that way," I said. "Or maybe he'd still be alive. Zoo security is pretty good—I don't think either Justin or Iris could have gotten past them."

He nodded. He'd been standing in the doorway. Now he moved farther in and set down the carry-on—the one I'd packed.

But he was still between me and the door.

Why did that bother me so much?

"I have to say, since unlike Grandfather I have no idea what precise markings a mockingbird has, I'd have been perfectly satisfied with this." I waved at the middle painting. "And I can't tell where he left off and where you stepped in to the rescue on this one." I pointed to the cardinal painting, and then to the partial one of the jays. "Nor do I have any clue whether this is something he started before he moved to our library or something you were doing just in case."

"Just in case of what?" He crossed his arms and frowned. "Why would I do that?"

"Because you could see better than anyone how badly the project was going," I said. "I have no idea why. Was he going through some kind of creative block? Was he stalling because he liked the cushy setup he had at our house? Or was he desperate to hang on to a place to stay, since he was locked out of his apartment and his studio? I don't know, but I bet you did. And maybe you started this painting as an insurance policy in case things came to a head. Maybe you were planning to show it to Castlemayne and say 'here, we can give him this—he's no art critic; he won't be able to tell it's not yours.' Or maybe you were going to show it to Grandfather if Castlemayne got fired, so he'd let you take over the project."

Harris didn't look pleased, so it was probably just as well I didn't mention the third alternative—that he'd been planning to show the painting to Grandfather and suggest firing Castlemayne. Or a fourth alternative—that he was somehow involved in the murder. Even if Justin or Iris was the killer—what if Harris had deliberately let them in? Or what if—

"Let me show you something." He picked up the carry-on bag again and walked over to the line of boxes. He set it down at the opposite end from the leather suitcases. Then he studied the line of boxes for a second before going over to the second from the left.

I felt curiously relieved that I no longer had him between me and the door. I circled around a little closer to the door, flexing my ankle and wincing, as if I were moving mainly to ease it.

"I knew as soon as I did it that telling you was a mistake." He turned around again.

He was pointing a gun at me.

Chapter 40

I froze for a few seconds. I stared at the gun, wishing I'd listened to that gut feeling that had made me so anxious when Harris stepped into the room. His hand was shaking slightly, but I knew better than to assume that that meant he wouldn't shoot. In fact, I suspected that if he was nervous he'd be that much more likely to shoot, and at this distance I couldn't count on him missing. And what reason would he have for pulling a gun on me unless the chief had the wrong suspect—the wrong two suspects—and Harris had killed Castlemayne? I tried to keep my voice calm.

"This is overkill, you know," I said. "I can assure you that I have no intention of telling Grandfather you did the fixes to the cardinal painting. In fact, I wouldn't even tell him if I thought you'd been doing all the paintings. Which I suspect was the case. I never actually saw Castlemayne painting. I barely even saw him holding a brush. Which I assumed was because he didn't like people kibbitzing, but I guess it was more because you were actually doing it. Well, that doesn't have to come out, but I'm sure if you tell Grandfather and show him that, there's a good chance he'll hire you." I nodded at the jay painting.

"I'm not buying it, you know." He looked sad. In fact, downright depressed. "No use pretending you don't know. I have no idea how you figured it out, but if you can, your police chief will sooner or later. I guess my best chance is to disappear before he does."

"Why would Chief Burke care if you've been doing

Castlemayne's paintings for him?" I asked. "I suppose he might care if you were suspected of being an art forger, but even if you were, with him gone they'd have a hard time proving it. So if you are an art forger and either Justin Vreeland or Iris the ex did you a honking big favor, just don't tell me."

"He was exploiting me, you know." Harris's usually soft and colorless voice was suddenly more resonant and deeply angry. "He found out about something that could cause me big problems if it got out. He used it to squeeze me. Made me sign this contract that I had to work for him and couldn't tell anyone about it. And I was sick of it. Sick of being at his beck and call every minute of the day and night. Sick of him strutting around like a peacock when he did a show and people fawned over him, and he'd only let me come if he needed me to be his gofer. And sick of painting those damned birds."

"I thought you liked birds," I said.

"No, I've never liked birds," he said. "I know a lot about them, but that's because my parents were rabid bird-watchers. I spent most of my childhood getting dragged around so they could add to their life lists. My dad was only a few short of eight thousand birds when he died."

"Impressive," I said.

"Yeah, right." He snorted. "Can you imagine how much time that took? How much hiking in dark, dreary woods and wading through cold, muddy swamps? And even if I liked birds, that wouldn't mean I wanted to paint them— not in that boring, outdated representational style. I want to do work that's free! Visionary! Creative! Revolutionary!"

"I can understand that." Actually, I couldn't, but he seemed to be getting worked up, and I was afraid he'd accidentally squeeze the trigger in his excitement.

"I wasn't planning on doing it," he said. "I was there painting, and he was lounging around watching. I was going to squeeze some more Prussian blue on my palette and asked him to hand me the Swiss Army knife—it's got a little tool that's perfect for trimming the dried-up excess paint that can block the opening of the tubes. And he just laughed and said get it yourself. It was right at his elbow and a good ten feet away from me. And I just lost it. I went over and grabbed the knife, and he must have realized how furious I was, because he got up and started backing away, and I just flailed out at him."

"With the Swiss Army knife," I said.

He nodded.

"Involuntary manslaughter," I said. "And a good lawyer could use the fact that he was blackmailing you—because I'm pretty sure that's what they'd call it, if he was forcing you to work for him by threatening to reveal something that would cause you trouble. And if you add in the difference in your sizes, you could probably even make a plausible case for self-defense."

"I couldn't prove self-defense," he said.

"You wouldn't need to prove it," I said. "You'd only need to show reasonable doubt. A good lawyer could do that easily. And having Justin and Iris each claiming to have seen the other kill him wouldn't hurt, either."

"Maybe," he said. "I still think disappearing is my best option. It's not like I have any strong ties anywhere. Or a whole lot of worldly goods to slow me down. He carried a lot of cash, you know. It's not so much that he didn't trust banks—he knew anything that went into the bank he'd probably lose to his creditors or his ex-wives sooner or later. He thought he'd hidden it well enough that I wouldn't find it, but I knew it was there. Just like I knew this was there." He nodded at the gun. Which was trembling more visibly than before. It was a fairly big gun, and either he was getting progressively more nervous or it was heavy enough that his hand was tiring.

"So tie me up and hide me somewhere," I said. "The zoo's short-staffed. They probably won't find me till tomorrow, and you'll have plenty of time to make your escape. Just make sure it's a place with heat—you don't want another death on your hands. One of the janitor's closets would do nicely. They'll be feeding the animals regularly, so you wouldn't want to pick a feed room, but it will probably be a day or so before the cleaning staff can get here."

"But then you'd tell them." He shook his head. Then he reached sideways toward the card table and picked up something with his free hand.

My phone. Why had I set it down there instead of tucking it safely back into my pocket?

I tried not to show how dismayed I was.

"I'm sorry." He tucked the phone into his pocket. "I just don't see any other way."

He was working his way up to shooting me. A smarter or bolder man would have done it already. He was having a hard time doing it. Which was lucky for me, so far. But sooner or later, either he'd screw his courage to the sticking place—why had that line from this summer's production of *Macbeth* popped into my mind?—or something would startle him and he'd react by pulling the trigger. And high on the list of things that would startle him would be any attempt from me to distract him or make a break for the exit.

"Just tell me one thing," I said, and then racked my brain for something I wanted to know, because getting him talking would be an excellent delaying tactic—and surely a security guard would come by on his rounds sooner or later. "How did you manage to get out of the library?"

He frowned for a second, then a smug look crossed his face, and I quietly rejoiced that I'd probably postponed the moment when he'd shoot me.

"It was quick thinking on my part," he said. "I was still standing there, looking at him—at his dead body—when I heard someone coming in through the sunroom. My first thought was to run up the circular staircase to the balcony, but I realized I didn't have time, so I just ducked behind the nearest couch. And then Iris walked in, calling his name. I peeked around to see what she was up to. She was just looking around, puzzled—and then she spotted him. She yelped 'Roddy! Oh, no!'—as if she was sorry to see him dead."

Maybe she was, I thought. After all, she must have loved him once.

"And then she knelt down and I guess she thought she could save him by pulling the knife out," Harris went on. "Wasn't hard to see he was dead. Maybe it was a reflex, but anyway, she touched the knife. And then she shrieked and pulled her hand away. She picked up one of my painting rags and wiped the handle of the knife. And then the doorknob on her way out. And then I heard another shriek outside, and I stayed behind the sofa for what seemed like forever. I kept thinking someone was going to come in. Then I heard her car start up outside, and I decided maybe it was safe to come out. I locked the library door, took the key off my key ring, wiped it clean, and threw it near the body. Then I went out through the sunroom. There was quite a path through the snow by that time. I let myself in the front door, and as soon as I got in I heard you coming down the stairs. I had to hide in the coat closet until you went down the hall to the library, then I crept upstairs and went to bed."

"You did a good job of pretending to be surprised when I came to tell you about his death," I said. "And pretending to faint was a nice touch, although it backfired, didn't it?"

"I wasn't pretending to faint," he said. "I really did faint. When I saw the chief standing there behind you, I thought he'd figured it out already and was coming to arrest me. And afterward—"

Just then the lights went out. I'd been hoping we were still enough for this to happen, and had already decided what I'd do if it did. I made a dash for the door, which had the immediate benefit of taking me out of the path of the two bullets Harris fired at where I'd been standing. The lights began flickering on, which let me see well enough to fling the door open, run through it, and begin sprinting down the corridor as well as I could manage—thank goodness for adrenaline and the ankle support from my snow boots.

When I got to the intersection, I hung a quick left, and then scanned the nearby doors. To my relief, I spotted the door that led into the tropical bird habitat. Perfect—the habitat was large and full of lush jungle plants that I could hide behind. Its inhabitants should be fast asleep, and even if I woke them up, they were unlikely to do me much harm.

Ignoring all the many warning signs about washing your hands before entering and not startling the birds or letting them escape, I slid my staff key card through the slot, ducked in, and threw myself down behind a fake tropical log, startling two sleeping parrots into wakefulness.

"Help!" one squawked. "I'm being repressed!"

"She turned me into a newt," the other replied.

I made a mental note to warn Grandfather that the zookeepers had been teaching the parrots Monty Python quotes again. I knew he hated that.

From my hiding place in the darkened habitat, I could see when Harris burst out into the main body of the building—which, though dimly lit, was still brighter than where I was. He whirled around, looking everywhere. He dashed off into one of the two side rooms. I stayed put. He reappeared, seconds later, and dashed across to search the other side room.

"You will never find a more wretched hive of scum and villainy," a nearby parrot remarked sleepily. "We must be cautious."

Great. First Monty Python, and now *Star Wars*. Grandfather would be livid.

Harris emerged from the side room and ran in the direction of the front door. Now would be a good time to make a move. If I could make my way across the tropical bird habitat, there was another exit into another staff-only corridor that would lead me almost to the front door. I could exit there.

Was it safer to just stay here under cover and hope that Harris didn't find me?

No. Too uncertain.

Or should I sneak back into the area we'd just left and see if I could find a working phone? At the house our phones usually went out when the power did, but Grandfather might have done something to alleviate that here at the zoo. I knew he'd done something to ensure that the zoo's internet connection still worked, even when everything was on a generator—and Kevin's playing with the Wombat Cam proved that was working. If I could find a landline or an unlocked laptop, maybe I could try making contact with the outside world. Like calling 911.

But that would take time. And what good would it do if the police knew I was being stalked by the killer if he caught me while I was talking to them. No, my best option was probably to exit at the front of the building and make my way back closer to the front gate, where there would definitely be someone on guard.

So maybe I should make a break for—

No. Harris was back. I could see him peering into the habitat across the way. Probably a good thing I hadn't moved yet. I might have startled a few parrots into motion and that would have been suspicious.

He stopped staring into the habitat across the way and approached the enormous mesh screen that separated the tropical bird habitat from the main body of the building.

Staring straight at where I was hiding.

Chapter 41

Harris's approach startled a parakeet that was sleeping right next to the screen. The bird fluttered his wings and uttered a terse but obscene remark before settling down and tucking his head under his wing again.

"You rude thing," Harris muttered. Then he leaned against the screen, cupped his hands to the sides of his head to block out even the soft light behind him, and stared into the habitat.

Okay, so maybe he hadn't spotted me yet.

I narrowed my eyes to slits and tried to breath as quietly as possible. I didn't even flinch when something wet landed on my shoulder, courtesy of one of the birds sleeping on a branch above me.

After what seemed like an eternity, Harris backed away from the mesh and moved on, presumably to stare into another habitat. I waited a couple of minutes before starting to crawl as quietly as possible along the floor of the habitat. I made it to the shelter of a large log in the middle of the habitat and paused there. My breathing was getting a little noisy. It hadn't been that strenuous a crawl, so it was probably the stress getting to me. I concentrated on slowing my breath, all the while listening for any sounds from Harris.

"Where the hell *is* she?" he muttered, and it sounded as if he was at the far end of the building, so I decided it was safe to crawl the rest of the way to the other exit door.

I lurked in some tropical shrubbery for a couple of minutes, peering toward the front of the habitat and straining my ears. Finally, I decided I might as well risk it. I stood up, found the camouflaged card reader, and swiped my card. The click of the lock sounded overloud in the silence and a few of the nearby parrots stirred slightly.

"You backtrack the rabbit," one of them said. "I'll follow the girl."

I could ask the Aviary staff later what that quote came from. And also whether the birds had a Pavlovian response, associating the sound of the lock with food. Harris hadn't reappeared, though, so I eased the door open, peered up and down the empty staff-only corridor, then hurried out and gently closed the door behind me.

I made my way cautiously. After all, Harris also had a card key that would let him into staff areas. I wasn't sure he had as much access as I did. His was only intended to let him get into the zoo and then to and from the studio. Mine was designed to let me into any place Grandfather wanted to send me—or, for that matter, any place Grandfather might want me to let him into when he had misplaced his own access card again. Occasionally junior staff members would complain that it wasn't fair for me—and Michael, for that matter—to have more access than they did. Tonight I was profoundly grateful that Grandfather always ignored such complaints.

I reached the end of the corridor. To my left was the door that led back into the main hall of the Aviary. Ahead of me was the door that led out of the building. Logically, I should take that door. Dash over to the Desert Dome. From there I could retrace my steps through the Kingdom of the Night to the Small Mammal House, and then I'd be almost within sight of the front gate and the guard station.

But a few hundred yards of open space lay between me and the Desert Dome. What if Harris had given up on looking for me in the Aviary and gone outside? Either to look for me or to race back to his car to escape?

I glanced around until I spotted a cleaning supplies

closet. I swiped my card, eased the door open, and scanned its contents for potentially useful objects. Not that I expected to find anything really useful, like an invisibility cloak or maybe a Kevlar vest and matching riot duty helmet, but you never knew. I grabbed a floor mop that I could use as a cane if my ankle escalated from aching slightly to really bothering me and a spray bottle of ammonia-based glass cleaner. If I got close enough to Harris, I might be able to spray it at his face to incapacitate him, at least long enough to take away his gun.

Or maybe if he saw the mop and the spray bottle, he'd mistake me for an overly zealous zoo maintenance worker. At first, that idea made me giggle, but then I realized maybe it had some merit. The closet also contained three of the khaki overalls the zoo's cleaning staff wore. Two of them were way too small for me—was Grandfather employing child labor to mop the floors? But the third would fit me, provided I shed my bulky coat.

I'd be cold without the coat, but I would only be outside for a little while—and Harris knew what my coat looked like. He'd be looking for that, not khaki overalls. I shed my coat, pulled on the overalls, and returned to the door that led to the outside.

I opened the door and looked around. Only snow, either falling or lying around in heaps. I slung the mop over my left shoulder, grabbed the spray bottle in my right hand, and ambled out of the door in my best imitation of a weary maintenance worker heading for her next floor-mopping assignment.

Outside everything was quiet—the hushed kind of quiet you get when every sound is muffled both by the existing snow and the new snow falling. My footsteps sounded thunderously loud, and I had to work to keep my breathing steady. To keep my pace slow and relaxed. Nothing to see here. These aren't the droids you're looking for.

Clearly Jamie and Josh's habit of quoting *Star Wars* was rubbing off on me.

Thinking about the boys, and Michael, and my grandmother, who must all be nearly home by now, gave me a sudden rush of anger. Dammit, I was not going to let Harris—wretched little Harris—keep me from seeing my family again. I had to push down the anger and force myself to keep slouching along.

I was starting to feel the absence of my winter coat now, but I was nearing the door of the Desert Dome. Twenty more feet. Fifteen feet. Ten feet.

"Stop! I see you!"

I instinctively flung myself to the ground and heard a sharp noise. Something pinged against the stone side of the building. I heard running feet behind me.

I leaped up again, covered the last few feet between me and the door, swiped my card, and dashed in. And then I shoved my trusty mop through the handles of the double doors, so if he tried to pull on them, the mop would keep them from opening. He might manage to break the mop handle eventually, and he could always run around the corner to the other set of doors, but either of those options would slow him down.

I let myself into a staff-only door and stepped into a corridor. He wouldn't spot me the second he entered the building, but he'd probably guess where I'd gone. And could use his staff card to follow me. I needed to find a place to hide.

No, maybe I needed to get some help. I spotted one of the fire alarms. Bingo! I pulled the lever.

An earsplitting alarm began to sound. I scurried down the corridor until I was far enough away that the sound of the alarm didn't hurt my ears.

Good. Whatever staff were on the premises would be converging on the Desert Dome.

Wait—Harris was armed. What if a staff member accosted him and—

Too late to worry about that now. I opened another staff-only door, raced down the stairs that led me to the Kingdom of the Night, dashed in there, and stopped to catch my breath and think.

And to blink against the sudden brightness. Damn. It was too bright in here. Not as bright as usual, but still, there was light everywhere—including inside the habitats. Enough light to send all the nocturnal animals scurrying into their dens and burrows. Enough that Harris would spot me easily if I tried to hide in a habitat, as I had in the Aviary. Damn.

Okay, these were all the habitats of nocturnal animals. They all had dens, nests, or burrows of some kind to hide in during the artificial daylight hours. Could I think of an animal that was large enough that I could hide in its burrow, but mild-mannered enough that it wouldn't actually eat me or do me serious damage if I invaded its space?

I'd lost track of where I was. I was beside a habitat, but the curtain was pulled closed over the large glass window that gave the keepers a view inside when they wanted one. I pulled it slightly open and—

Teeth! More teeth than seemed reasonable for any normal small mammal to have. I realized I was looking into the face of a possum, hissing and baring its teeth at me. Grandfather's voice suddenly rang out in my mind.

"The Virginia opossum, like all members of the family *Didelphidae*, has fifty teeth—more than any other North American land mammal."

Only fifty? I could swear this possum had at least twice that many. Maybe it was a mutant possum. Just then it keeled over. I knew it was only playing dead, as they tended to do when they felt threatened, but I still felt guilty. I silently apologized to the possum and closed his privacy curtain. His habitat wasn't a good bet for hiding in. Whatever

burrow he had would be too small for me and besides—
all those teeth. What if it woke up and decided to fight
instead of faint?

I thought I heard footsteps approaching—though it was
hard to hear over the fire alarm. But with the fire alarm
going, Harris might not worry about being quiet.

I began moving again, as fast as I could, but keeping my
footsteps soft.

Where to hide? I could probably conceal myself in the
bat cave—but no, I couldn't face hiding there in the midst
of all the guano. There was enough room in the African
swamp habitat, but since its main occupants were the crocodiles, not a healthy choice.

Wait—the wombats. Caroline had said they were vicious, but surely they couldn't be all that bad. I could
imagine Grandfather having a lapse of judgment and
bringing a few moderately fierce animals to live in our
basement, but I knew that if the wombats were really dangerous, Kevin wouldn't be keeping them anywhere near
his beloved Widget. And hadn't Caroline said they were
both juveniles, and thus more mild-mannered?

But even if the wombats weren't all that friendly—they
had a nice big habitat with several large faux trees I could
climb to get out of their way. And besides, they had the
Wombat Cam. What were the odds that Kevin wouldn't be
watching?

I didn't necessarily have to stay in the wombat habitat.
But if I could get in there, even briefly, and attract Kevin's
attention . . .

I was passing through a cluster of staff spaces—small,
shared offices. Storage rooms. A training room. The veterinary clinic.

I ducked into one of the offices and rummaged through
the desk until I found a thick-nibbed black marker. And
a pair of heavy leather gloves. And—ooh. A gun of some
kind. It looked like some kind of futuristic weapon—it

had a long, thin barrel and a stubby grip with a CO_2 canister attached. A dart gun—I knew Grandfather's staff kept them around as a last-ditch method of tranquilizing animals when needed. Technically, this one should have been locked up, but maybe it was good luck for me that a staff member had been careless. The dart gun could be useful.

Or dangerous. If I zapped a wombat—or Harris—with a dose designed for one of the elephants, I could kill them. Then again, I knew the staff sometimes used dart guns to give vaccines or antibiotics to particularly difficult animals. It wouldn't do me much good if I tried to sedate a rampaging wombat or an armed killer and only ended up administering an unnecessary rabies shot.

I almost put the dart gun down, but then it occurred to me that maybe I should take it, in case Harris caught up with me. True, I had no idea if the dose was calculated for a seven-pound skunk or a seven-hundred-pound crocodile. It could have no effect on Harris, or it could kill him. And it wouldn't necessarily work quickly—most of the tranquilizers the zoo used took at least a minute or two to take effect. But it was better than nothing. And maybe just the look of the thing would scare him off.

So I grabbed a couple of spare darts and stuck them and the gun in one of the larger pockets of my coverall. Then I raced along the corridor until I was outside the access door to the wombat habitat.

I took a deep breath and considered just hiding in a janitor's closet until the fire department arrived. Then, over the squawking of the fire alarm, I heard running footsteps.

I swiped my card in the security lock and stepped into the wombat habitat.

The wombats appeared to be asleep in the mouth of their burrow—at least I assumed the fur-covered lump across the habitat was composed of Ian and Bruce.

I walked swiftly over to the wall behind them. That

blank white wall that Grandfather's staff hadn't yet transformed into the Australian bush or rainforest or whatever kind of terrain wombats favored. It was a blank canvas for me and my marker.

Keeping an eye open for any sign of life from the wombats, I printed in large letters:

HELP!
HARRIS KILLED CASTLEMAYNE
HE HAS A GUN
SEND HELP TO THE WOMBATS

I ran out of room to write "wombat habitat," but I figured Kevin would get the idea. I stuck the marker back in my pocket and looked around. Should I find someplace nearby to hide or—

Just then Harris appeared in the public corridor outside the habitat. I tried to duck behind the wombats' burrow, but he spotted me and took aim at the glass front of the habitat. But then he changed his mind. The glass fronts were supposed to be bulletproof, hurricane-proof, and engineered to withstand the impact of a charging rhino, so maybe he'd fired at one earlier in our chase and found out that the bullet would only ricochet off. But he glanced around, spotted the nearest staff-only door, and headed for it.

And it was nearby, which meant he'd be entering the staff-only corridor almost on top of the door to the wombat habitat. I leaped up and grabbed on the overhanging branch of the nearest tree. At least I hoped it was a real tree and not a paper mache prop. To my relief, it was solid, and I was able to hoist myself up and walk along the branch to the trunk. A eucalyptus tree. If worse came to worst, at least I'd die with clear sinuses. I was just nestling among its leaves when the habitat door burst open and Harris ran in. He looked around, puzzled. I froze, hoping he wouldn't think to look up. At first it looked as if it had worked—he ran back to the door and peered out into the corridor.

Then one of the wombats grunted and made rustling noises. Harris looked back . . . and up. Damn.

He smiled a rather nasty smile and lifted up his gun.

"I'd give it up," I said. "The fire department will be here soon. And zoo security. And probably the police, if they've read my message."

I pointed at the wall that was now decorated with my foot-high letters. He frowned. Then he glanced around and saw the camera. The smug expression vanished.

"Right now you could probably plead self-defense on the murder," I said. "But I doubt if you can talk your way out of killing me on camera. And—"

Someone was banging on the glass at the front of the habitat. Harris and I both started, and he accidentally pulled the trigger of his gun, sending a bullet into the side of the wombats' burrow. It didn't hit either of them, but either the bullet or the pounding woke them up, and they began making annoyed-sounding grunting noises.

I turned so I could see who was pounding on the glass—it was Josh, Jamie, and Adam. My grandmother Cordelia was standing behind them, aiming her phone at the habitat. She was filming us.

But where was Michael?

Probably coming to rescue me. He'd have his card key, one that had the same universal access as mine. What if he didn't know Harris had a gun? Or did know and came barging into the habitat anyway? Harris might try to shoot him. Or he might try to shoot at Cordelia and the boys—and what if the glass wasn't as bulletproof as it was supposed to be?

Harris looked frantic, like a trapped rat, glancing nervously between me and the wombats, who seemed to be waking up in exactly the sort of cranky mood anyone would be feeling if your alarm clock had been someone putting a bullet through your burrow. If Harris shot the wombats . . .

I had to do something. I pulled out the dart gun and fired at Harris. Good aim—the dart hit near the base of his neck and stayed there with its hot-pink feathered stabilizer quivering slightly.

"You . . . you bitch!" He reached up and felt where the dart had hit. "You shot me."

I reloaded the dart gun, just in case.

Harris seemed stunned—probably from the sheer audacity of my shot, since I knew whatever chemical it contained could hardly have taken effect so quickly. He reached up as if to pluck it out and then keeled over. From the dart? Or had he fainted again?

Just then the door to the corridor clicked open and Michael dashed in.

One of the wombats growled. They were looking at Harris with definite displeasure.

"Quick!" I shouted. "Drag Harris out before the wombats attack!"

"What about you?" Michael asked. Though he was already picking up Harris.

"I'll be fine up here until the wombat keepers come to deal with them," I said. "Take his gun away and call an ambulance—I have no idea what's in the dart I shot him with."

Michael managed to haul Harris through the door and close it just before one of the wombats hit it, squealed in rage, and then went galumphing around the habitat as if to work off his disappointment. The other wombat went over to the glass and stared out balefully at Cordelia and the boys. And the half dozen zoo staff and firefighters standing behind them. Michael appeared from the right and gave me a thumbs up sign, which I took to mean that Harris was no longer a threat to anyone.

I waved at the watching crowd and made myself comfortable on my tree branch. It would take a while before the wombats calmed down and the zoo staff could figure out how to rescue me. I was in no hurry. Michael and the boys were home safe, and Castlemayne's killer had been caught. All was right with the world.

Chapter 42

December 23

"Merry Christmas, Meg!"

I opened the door to let in another batch of party guests. Several out-of-town aunts, uncles, or cousins hugged me and shed their wraps.

"So lovely to have heat and light again," one of them said, glancing around with satisfaction.

"We heard about your adventures at the zoo last night," another said. "You must tell us all about it."

"I will," I said. "But later." After spending much of last night telling the chief about it and most of today briefing the relatives in residence I was, at least for the moment, tired of relating my adventures.

"We'll hold you to that!" one of them said. And then, to my relief they all marched off to the dining room to deliver their contributions to the potluck dinner. There they would probably encounter Mrs. McKenna, who still seemed to enjoy telling the story of her kidnapping to new audiences.

Right behind the relatives was Chief Burke.

"I feel guilty," he said. "I came empty-handed."

"It's okay," I said. "Minerva's already here, and she brought ham biscuits. Glad you could get away."

"I'll probably have to go back to the station later," he said as he shed his coat. His hand went to his hat and paused. "Should I still be keeping this on?"

"Only if your head's cold," I said. "We're down to a single escaped blue jay, and he's safely locked in the library."

"Good." He set his hat atop one of the overflow racks. "Yes, unfortunately I have more work to do later tonight. Iris Castlemayne didn't want any of our local defense attorneys. Spent all day trying to round up one from Richmond, and he only just got here. I figure it'll take him at least an hour to confer with his client, and I could surely use a break from talking to suspects and their lawyers. Probably a good thing we let the other ex out on bail, or we'd be short on cells for the usual Christmas drunks."

"You think you'll be keeping Iris over the holidays?"

"We'll be charging her with kidnapping and assault," he said. "And in addition to being from out of town, her DMV record shows that she moves around a lot. I don't see our courts being all that eager to let her out on bail."

"So you've got her and Harris and Justin Vreeland, then? Or is Justin still at the hospital?"

"No, we let Mr. Vreeland go." He shook his head. "Apart from the trespassing, which we'll definitely pursue if you want us to, we don't have anything to charge him with."

"Didn't he lie and say he saw Iris kill Castlemayne?"

"No, he said she must have killed him because she came running out of the library covered with blood. Unfortunately, jumping to conclusions isn't even a misdemeanor. And he admits that he got overexcited and exaggerated a bit—Iris Castlemayne was definitely not *covered* with blood. But if I tried to charge him with lying to me or obstructing my investigation, any attorney with half a brain could bring up his concussion and get him off. Even that eager beaver Monkton, who caused poor Curly such problems. So I read him the riot act about how he wouldn't be lying in a hospital bed with a concussion if he hadn't done a bunch of illegal, unethical, and downright stupid things. And then I let him go. I hear the hospital cleared him for release this afternoon"

"Just as well," I said. "And Harris—are you going to charge him with murder?"

"His attorney wants to cut a deal for voluntary manslaughter, but I'm not buying it." He shook his head and grimaced. "Of course, it's the county attorney's call, not mine, but I can't see her letting him off that lightly. And if it goes to trial, I predict they'll float temporary insanity or self-defense or maybe both. I don't see any of that, either. But even if I'm wrong and they let him off with manslaughter, we've got him dead to rights on attempting to murder you. Which carries a heavier penalty than voluntary manslaughter. I hope your grandfather isn't too upset—I gather Mr. Harris was hoping to step in and replace Castlemayne on his painting project."

"Grandfather may be upset," I said. "But I bet he's also relieved he didn't agree to let Harris continue the project. He was pretty ticked when he heard Harris had been running around the zoo taking pot shots at his wombats. And me, of course."

"Of course." He smiled. "By the way, I bet you're eager to get your library back. I'm hereby releasing the crime scene. Feel free to send anything Castlemayne left behind here over to the zoo with the rest of his stuff. I've got a line on a sister who will probably take it all off our hands eventually."

"Great," I said. "It'll make the holidays a lot easier, having the library for some of the relatives. By the way, it's none of my business, but Harris seemed to be implying that Castlemayne was blackmailing him—do we have any idea what that was about?"

"Well, it's not definite yet," the chief said. "But when Harris's arrest hit the news, I got a call from the Metropolitan Police in D.C. Seems they want to interview him in connection with an art theft that happened a couple of years ago at a gallery where Castlemayne was having a show. I'm not sure whether they think Harris was the thief or whether they think he was only his employer's accomplice, but I can definitely tell that Harris isn't looking forward to talking with them. I'll keep you posted."

"Thanks," I said. "Now go and hit the buffet—I bet you're famished."

"I am that." He nodded, and ambled off toward the dining room. I perched on the nearest chair and leaned back. The power was back, and with it heat, light, and Christmas carols from the speakers. And the doorbell, of course, which would ring again at any moment, so I figured I might as well play doorman for a while.

Just as I got comfortable the doorbell rang again. I looked out the peephole and saw a figure whose head was wrapped in a white bandage. Justin Vreeland. I thought of just ignoring him till he went away, but decided that would be a Scrooge-like thing to do, so I opened the door and tried to look welcoming. Okay, maybe just polite.

"Nice to see you're on your feet again," I said.

"Hey," he said. "You left me a voice mail? That you had some information that would be helpful to me?"

The tentative note in his voice was a nice change.

"I seem to recall suggesting that you call me," I said. "You could have saved yourself the trouble of coming all the way out here. Since you're still not a hundred percent." I tried to keep my voice neutral, but he could probably tell I wasn't exactly thrilled to see him show up on our doorstep.

"Sorry," he said. "I thought—never mind." He turned as if to go.

I relented.

"Since you're here anyway, come in for a sec," I said.

He stepped inside but didn't move to take off his coat—he only stood in the hallway, shoulders more hunched than usual, as if expecting a blow.

"Do you really want to be a journalist?" I asked. "A gainfully employed journalist, working for a reputable publication, earning a steady paycheck?"

"Not many jobs like that these days."

"No, there aren't," I agreed. "And those that do exist get snapped up by journalists with actual experience on their résumés. You need to build your résumé. Would you be willing to do it with an internship?"

"Would it pay?" he said. "I have to make ends meet."

"It would pay, but not much, and at least to start with it wouldn't be full time," I said. "You'd need a side hustle of some sort to get by. But you could build your résumé. Get a foot in the door."

"And where would this door be?" I could detect a note of interest, maybe even excitement, under the deliberately blasé tone.

"Here in Caerphilly. The owner of the *Clarion* could use a part-time reporter, website manager, and general dogsbody. Only part time, because it's only a small weekly paper. But he knows everyone in town and might be able to help you find another gig to fill in."

"So I'd be covering the church potlucks and the school board meetings and earth-shattering stuff like that."

"The school board meetings are pretty hot stuff for the *Clarion*, so you'd have to work your way up to that. And as for the church potlucks, you should be so lucky. You'd cover whatever you're assigned to cover, and you could learn a lot from the editor. He's a good journalist."

He stood there looking down at his boots for a bit.

"I shut down the Caerphilly Confidential website, you know," he said. "I realized it really wasn't where I wanted my career to be going."

I nodded. I happened to know that he'd actually shut down the website this morning after Kevin had threatened to out him as the owner of both Caerphilly Confidential and the Tidewater Tattler—and reveal his whereabouts to all the people who wanted to sue him or have him arrested. I suspected they'd all find him sooner or later, but for now, I was just happy to see Caerphilly Confidential gone.

"It might actually be kind of nice to have people like a story I wrote," he said. "So what do I have to do to apply for this glamorous and exciting new job?"

"Drop into the *Clarion*'s office as soon as you feel well enough," I said. "But don't go tomorrow—the paper comes out Fridays, so tomorrow will be the editor's busy day. Why not read Friday's issue and drop in Monday?"

"Okay." He nodded. "Thanks."

He actually looked penitent. And grateful. We'd see how long it lasted. Meanwhile, since he was, at least in theory, going to be a neighbor . . .

"There's a buffet if you're hungry," I said. "You can hang your coat there." I pointed to one of the overflow racks.

He looked up, surprised, and gave me a faint smile. Then he hurried to shed his coat and, after he hung it up, he followed me back to the dining room.

In the dining room Justin joined the end of the buffet line. I spotted Grandfather and Caroline inching their way around the table and stepped forward so I could offer to hold their plates. Both of them tended to forget they were holding anything—especially if they started arguing with each other—and the last thing we needed was to have them gesticulate with full plates and shower food all over the other guests.

"Thank you, Meg," Caroline said. "So what's happening with your book?" she said, turning to Grandfather. "Have you found another painter to do the rest of the illustrations?"

"No." Grandfather speared a melon ball as if delivering the coup de grâce to an enemy. "I've had it up to here with painters." He held his hand up to his chin. "In fact, up to here." He lifted the hand up above his head, where it accidentally got tangled up in one of the decorative garlands. Luckily Michael and Vern Shiffley were nearby—both of them were tall enough to reach the garlands and they managed to untangle Grandfather before he brought too many glass balls and fir needles down on the buffet.

"So what's the plan?" Caroline asked, when the untangling was complete. "Just use the three paintings you already have?"

"Only two-and-a-half paintings," Grandfather said, as he helped himself to a generous amount of country ham. "And apparently Castlemayne didn't even do those—it was that homicidal assistant of his. I'm not having his work in my book. No, I'm going to get Baptiste to do some photos."

Baptiste was Grandfather's longtime staff photographer. Months ago, when Grandfather had first started the difficult negotiations with Castlemayne, I'd suggested using Baptiste. I doubted he'd remember that.

"Excellent idea," Caroline said. I wondered if she had also suggested using Baptiste. "Odds are he already has beautiful photos of the birds you want to feature."

"And even if he doesn't, it'll be a damn sight quicker for him to take new photos than to wait for some fool painter to get around to doing his job." Grandfather scowled at Minerva Burke's famous ham biscuits as if they were responsible for his plight. "No more painters," he said, as he added a trio of the biscuits to his plate. "And what's happened to my blue jays? Baptiste might need the blue jays for his photos."

"We've captured all but one of them," Caroline said. "They're back in the Aviary. We caught the last mockingbird, too."

"What about the missing jay?"

"I suspect Baptiste can manage with only eleven jays," Caroline said.

"Blast it all, I'm not worried about Baptiste," Grandfather thundered, waving the spoon from the bowl of mashed potatoes in the air. "I'm worried about that jay. What if something has happened to him?"

"Nothing has happened to him." Caroline relieved him of the spoon and helped herself to potatoes. "He's as fat and sassy as—well, as the proverbial jay bird. He's been too clever to go into our traps so far, but we've got him cornered in the library, and sooner or later we'll catch him. Come on—Michael's saving a seat for us in the living room."

"I haven't gotten any desserts."

"You don't have room on your plate for desserts right now," she said. "And neither do I. We'll send the boys back to fetch desserts when we're ready."

Still wrangling they began pushing their way through the crowd. I followed them into the living room, where I spotted Festus Hollingsworth sitting in a corner with a Pomeranian on his lap. He was chewing on something with a look of ecstasy on his face and ignoring the puppy's begging face. He held his plate and fork high up, out of the Pomeranian's reach, and I saw that it contained a slice of *The* Pumpkin Pie, a family recipe so beloved that to host a holiday dinner without it would be considered ample grounds for shunning and disinheritance.

"Merry Christmas," I said. "And I see you're celebrating in style."

"Absolutely." He glanced down at the dog. "No, you can't have any, you silly mutt. It's got booze in it." He was right—the recipe called for half a cup of Amaretto. But clearly the Pom cuteness was having its effect on him. He reached over, stole a bit of roast beef from a nearby cousin's plate, and fed that to the dog instead.

"Thanks for being willing to take on Curly as a client," I said. "I hope it wasn't too much trouble."

"No problem," he said. "It should be fun, seeing what I can do for him."

"Do for him?" I echoed. "You mean, something beyond just chasing away J. Eustace Monkton, Esquire?"

"Definitely. Curly's very averse to charity—"

"Tell me about it," I said, with a sigh.

The Twelve Jays of Christmas

303

"But it turns out he's quite amenable to seeking any benefits to which he might be legally entitled. Especially if he thinks the bureaucracy will fight tooth and nail to deny him, so that claiming his due can only be achieved through the bold and persistent efforts of an exceptionally skilled attorney like me." Festus leaned back, hooked his thumbs into his vest, and beamed genially. The Pomeranian whined softly, and Festus raided the unsuspecting cousin's plate again.

"Sounds like fun for you," I said. "But just what benefits are we talking about?"

"We'll be looking into job training, subsidized housing, a nutritional program, some kind of medical coverage."

"Everything the Ladies Interfaith Council and the town social services department have been trying to offer him for years." I shook my head in disbelief.

"The challenge will be to convince some of the agencies involved that they need to put on at least a token show of red tape and bureaucratic foot dragging," Festus said. "He needs to believe we're working the system, if not beating it. But don't worry. I'm having fun. And I'm dealing with Counselor Monkton, too."

"Not too harshly, I hope," I said. "I think he genuinely believed he had Curly's best interests in mind. And it's not exactly his fault that he's an idiot."

"Well, I pondered pursuing sanctions and filing lawsuits against him on Curly's behalf," Festus said. "But in the end I decided to invite him to the next meeting of the Caerphilly County Trial Attorneys Association."

"I didn't know we had such an organization," I said.

"We do now," Festus said. "I got three, four other lawyers to go in on it with me. Our main official activity will be meeting for lunch at Muriel's Diner once every week or two and shooting the breeze about local goings on— including, but not limited to, ongoing court cases. Apparently young Monkton has been having a hard go of it down in New Kent County, where he grew up, so he decided to look for a smaller pond where he'd have a better chance of being a big fish. Caerphilly didn't quite turn out to be the legal backwater he was looking for."

"But he's staying on?"

"Jury's still out on that," he said. "But in case he does, better to have him in the tent peeing out. And if he does decide to stick around, the sooner he learns about how the community actually works, the better. And meanwhile, a couple of us can pat ourselves on the back for thinking of a way to combine having a bunch of tax-deductible meals at the diner with doing a good deed. What's not to like?"

Just then Josh dashed over.

"Mom! We have something to show you."

Chapter 43

Josh lifted the puppy off Festus's lap. "Mind if I borrow Teddy for a little while?"

"Be my guest." Festus looked relieved to be able to lower his pie plate to his lap.

"We have an early present for you," Josh said. I followed him as he threaded his way through the crowd to where Michael and Jamie were sitting on the hearth, right beside the Christmas tree. They each had a lap full of Pomeranians.

And the Pomeranians had an audience. The relatives at this side of the room had drawn back to make a rough half circle around the hearth and were pointing at the Pom pack and remarking how adorable they were.

I wasn't at all sure I wanted to see a present whose unveiling required the presence of a full quorum of Pomeranians. But after adding Teddy to the collection of puppies on Michael's lap, Josh reached over and handed me a large box wrapped in bright-red paper.

"It's something we thought you'd find really useful," Jamie said.

"Go ahead—open it!" Josh insisted.

In accordance with long-established family rituals, I hefted the package and shook it a couple of times before opening it. It was about the size and shape of a copier-paper box, and so light that I could almost have imagined it empty. The only sound it produced was a soft whooshing.

"No clue," I said. I untied the bow and slipped off the paper to reveal . . . a copier paper box with the familiar green and white colors of the recycled paper that was a household staple. I lifted the lid.

The box was full of brightly colored dog toys. I had a feeling there would turn out to be seven of them. I lifted the top one, a bright pink elephant.

"Okay," I said. "Is one of you going to throw it for me to fetch?"

"They're for the puppies to play with," Josh said. He refrained from rolling his eyes, but I could hear the impulse in his voice.

"They're squeak toys," Jamie said. "But the squeak is so high that only dogs can hear it. That's the part that's a present to you."

"Go ahead," Josh said. "Test it."

I squeezed the elephant's round plush belly a couple of times. I could tell there was something more than just stuffing inside, but they were right. I couldn't hear a thing.

But evidently dogs could. Suddenly, all seven Pomeranians were at my feet—whining, yipping, jostling each other for position, and pawing at my shins.

I squeezed the elephant vigorously a few more times, revving up the Poms' excitement into near hysteria, then tossed it over their heads into the middle of the open space. They all gave chase, but before they started tussling over it, I pulled out a lime-green gator, squeezed him a few times, and threw him in another direction. The boys pitched in, squeezing and tossing plush toys, until all seven toys were lying in different parts of the living room floor, each being chewed with great energy—but in complete silence—by a Pomeranian. Peace and quiet reigned. Well, except for the hum of conversation, as the relatives all gathered around to watch the puppies and tell each other all over again how cute they were.

"Okay, I have to admit it," I said. "This could turn out to be a really useful present."

Just then I spotted Spike. He was lurking behind the

Christmas tree—one of his favorite places for avoiding the puppies—but evidently he'd been drawn out by the ultrasonic squeak toys.

And there had only been seven toys in the box.

"Spike! There you are!" Josh exclaimed.

"We've been looking all over for you!" Jamie said.

Spike emerged from his hiding place. It wasn't like him to do anything undignified, like wagging his tail furiously, running around in circles, or whining with delight, but you could tell by the look on his face that he was glad to have the boys back. He allowed himself to be hoisted up and placed with his head in Josh's lap and his tail in Jamie's. Josh was rubbing him behind the ears while Jamie scratched a favorite spot just above his tail.

"Mom, can you hand me that present?" Josh asked.

"The purple one," Jamie added.

"It's for Spike," Josh explained.

"Maybe you could unwrap it for him?" Jamie asked. "He's pretty comfortable."

So I unwrapped the present—a bright-purple plush elephant. I squeezed it, and couldn't hear a thing—but Spike's ears perked up, and he wagged his tail slightly.

"All for you," Jamie cooed. I reached out carefully to hand Spike the elephant. He didn't even pretend to snap at me—just reached out and gently took the toy, with another slight wag of his tail. He didn't go wild like the puppies—he just sat there slowly chewing on it with his eyes closed and a look of utter contentment.

The boys didn't actually come right out and say "don't worry, we love you more than those silly Pomeranians." Then again, judging from the expression on Spike's face, maybe they had, in the language Spike understood best.

"Attention, please!" Mother had taken a place by the hearth, with Mrs. McKenna at her side. Curious how Mother didn't seem to be raising her voice and yet all over the ground floor, people either stopped talking of their own accord or were hushed into silence. Family members either picked up the various Pomeranians to keep them from being stepped on as people crowded into the living room or hustled them out into the hallway where they wouldn't be in the way.

Mother waited until everyone was quiet, and most of the people who couldn't fit into the living room were milling about in the hall, looking over each other's shoulders to see what was up.

"Rob and Delaney have an announcement." Mother graciously gestured to Rob, who stood up looking as if she'd caught him by surprise.

"Um . . . okay, you all know Delaney and I are engaged," he said. "Well, we decided to tie the knot."

Cheers greeted this announcement, although if Rob thought it was news to anyone, he underestimated the efficiency of both the Caerphilly County and Hollingsworth family grapevines.

"We were just going to get the Reverend Robyn to come out here for the big New Year's Eve party, and tie the knot at the stroke of twelve," Rob said when the cheers had died down. "But both our mothers were really upset that we weren't letting them organize a big wedding. And as you probably heard, Delaney's mom came all the way from California to help Mother talk us into letting them do the wedding and got kidnapped and locked in a closet at the Inn. I mean, she really went through a lot on account of this whole wedding thing. So we decided to let them do it. Plan a big wedding, that is. You're all invited. Save the date." He sat down looking relieved.

"So what is the date?" called out several people from various parts of the room.

"I don't know," Rob said, to much laughter. "The mothers are planning it. I guess they'll tell me when they figure it out."

More laughter.

"Saturday, May fourteenth," Mother said. "And don't worry—we'll make sure Rob shows up."

The crowd broke into cheers and applause, and then half a dozen of the cousins who had been helping out in the kitchen dashed in carrying trays full of champagne flutes, and the party flowed on, albeit with an amped-up noise level.

"Meg, dear." Mother appeared at my elbow, handing me a champagne flute. "Chief Burke says we can have the library back."

"I know." I sipped my champagne and closed my eyes to savor it. "I'll pack Castlemayne's things tomorrow and get Michael to take them out to the zoo, and then maybe we can get it cleaned and have it ready to use for the holidays."

"The cleaners are coming tomorrow," Mother said. "At seven. If you like, I can pack those things now."

"You keep the party going," I said. "I'll go and pack them."

"If you're too tired," she began.

"No, I'm fine," I said. "And I want to pack his stuff. Call it a closure thing. It won't take long at all."

"Good." Mother sounded relieved and I realized she wasn't all that keen to see the library while the bloodstains were still there. "I already found some boxes—I put them in the hall. Let me know if you need more."

"Will do."

I finished my champagne, grabbed another flute from a passing tray, and headed for the hallway that led to the library. At the far side of the front hall I could see a pile of four copier-paper boxes waiting for me. I picked up two with my free hand, figuring I could come back for the others if I needed them.

"Hey, Meg." Rob had followed me into the hall. He glanced around as if to make sure no one else was in earshot. "Can I ask you something?"

"Ask away—especially if you can do it on the way to the library. I'm going to pack up Castlemayne's stuff. Grab those boxes."

"Even better." He picked up the remaining boxes and fell into step beside me. "Do you think you and Michael could sneak away from the party, just for a little while? Maybe an hour?"

"We can probably manage it." I pulled out my key and opened the door to the library. "What's up?"

As I spoke I stepped inside, and Rob followed me. We both gazed around for a few seconds, and Rob shut the door.

"I guess you know that Delaney and I agreed to let the mothers throw us a big wedding," he said.

"I heard the announcement just now." I didn't tell him that I had mixed feelings about the news. Yes, it would make the mothers deliriously happy. But it wasn't the mothers' big day. It was theirs. Did they really want to let the mothers hijack it? None of my business, I reminded myself. I set one box down, took the other one over to the card table, and began packing the brushes and tubes of paint into it.

"I figure after that, anything we actually give them for Christmas is like an anticlimax." Rob took another box, glanced around, and began picking up trash, dirty dishes, and other bits of junk. "Which is a pity, because we got them some really nice stuff in Miami. They probably won't even notice."

I nodded. I was listening, but a little distracted by how with every brush, every tube of paint, every bit of painting gear that went into the box, the library felt more like home again. It still had a way to go, but this was helping. Maybe I'd take Rose Noire up on her offer to do a cleansing here in the library. A little sage to banish the lingering stench of tobacco.

"But it's not what we want for our wedding day." Rob went

on. "We figured we'd let them throw a wedding, but it won't be our real wedding. It'll be kind of like a renewal of our vows. We're going to meet Robyn at Trinity and get secretly hitched. With you and Michael as witnesses, if you can sneak away. Assuming you can keep the secret afterward."

Was he serious? I turned to see that he had a big grin on his face.

"I think we can manage that," I said. "Both the sneaking away and the part about keeping your secret. When are you meeting Robyn?"

"In about forty-five minutes."

"Cool," I said. "Let's finish packing up this stuff—it won't take more than another minute or two, and then Michael and I can use taking it out to the zoo as our excuse for sneaking out."

"Awesome. Let me just get another box for his dirty laundry." He straightened up and strolled over to the door. He picked up another copier-paper box and returned to where he'd been working. "And then—"

He froze. He was staring at the box in which he'd been packing the trash and dishes.

"What's wrong?" I asked.

"Ssh. Don't startle it." Moving like molasses, he reached over, picked up the lid of the copier-paper box, crept a little closer, and then slammed it down onto the box.

"Got it!" he exclaimed.

"Got what?" I hurried over. I could hear frantic scrabbling noises inside the box. "It's not a mouse, is it? Or a rat? Or—"

"Relax," he said. "It's only a blue jay."

"Seriously?"

He nodded.

"Then that's the last of them," I said. "The only one that was still on the lam."

"Then the twelve jays of Christmas are all safe and sound," he said. "Good deal!"

We exchanged an exuberant high five.

"Okay," he said. "I'll take this box to Caroline so she can take charge of the bird. And then I'll find Michael and send him here to help you with the rest of the boxes. Remember, mum's the word."

He ran off, whistling "The Twelve Days of Christmas."

I pulled out my phone to call Michael. No way I was letting Rob steal the fun of telling him this news.

"Guess what?" I said when he answered. "We're getting another early Christmas present."

Acknowledgments

Thanks once again to everyone at St. Martin's/Minotaur, including (but not limited to) Joe Brosnan, Lily Cronig, Hector DeJean, Nicola Ferguson, Meryl Gross, Paul Hochman, Kayla Janas, Andrew Martin, Sarah Melnyk, and especially my editor, Pete Wolverton. And thanks also to David Rotstein and the Art Department for yet another glorious cover.

More thanks to my agent, Ellen Geiger, and to Matt McGowan and the staff at the Frances Goldin Literary Agency—they take care of the practical stuff so I can focus on the writing.

Many thanks to the friends who brainstorm and critique with me, give me good ideas, or help keep me sane while I'm writing: Stuart, Aidan, and Liam Andrews; Deborah Blake; Chris Cowan; Ellen Crosby; Kathy Deligianis; Margery Flax; Suzanne Frisbee; John Gilstrap; Barb Goffman; Joni Langevoort; David Niemi; Alan Orloff; Art Taylor; Robin Templeton; and Dina Willner. And thanks to all the TeaBuds for two decades of friendship.

Above all, thanks to all the readers who make Meg's adventures possible.